THE LAST CONQUEST

Berwick Coates was educated at Kingston Grammar School, and read History at Christ's College, Cambridge. Since then he has been, at various times, an Army officer, writer, artist, lecturer, careers adviser, games coach, and teacher of History, English, Latin, General Studies, and Swahili.

He is the author of nine works of non-fiction and he works as a school archivist in the West Country.

The Last Conquest is his first novel.

THE LAST CONQUEST

BERWICK COATES

**SIMON &
SCHUSTER**

London · New York · Sydney · Toronto · New Delhi

A CBS COMPANY

First published in Great Britain by Simon & Schuster UK Ltd, 2013
A CBS COMPANY

This paperback edition first published by Simon & Schuster UK Ltd, 2013

1 3 5 7 9 10 8 6 4 2

Simon & Schuster UK Ltd
1st Floor
222 Gray's Inn Road
London WC1X 8HB

www.simonandschuster.co.uk
www.simonandschuster.com.au

Simon & Schuster Australia, Sydney
Simon & Schuster India, New Delhi

A CIP catalogue record for this book
is available from the British Library

Paperback ISBN 978-1-47111-196-9
Ebook ISBN 978-1-47111-197-6

Typeset by M Rules
Printed and bound by CPI Group (UK) Ltd, Croydon, CR0 4YY

To a lady whose name I cannot remember. In a remote country primary school, when I was seven, she gave me my first history lesson. I remember saying to myself, 'Here – there could be something in this.' And, as Fate would have it, the lesson was about William the Conqueror and the Battle of Hastings. She would be pleased, I hope, to know that that seed sown so long ago has at last borne some fruit.

Contents

Historical Note

The only real point of writing this historical note is to say that there isn't one.

A work of fiction is a work of fiction – anyone interested in finding out how a historical novelist gained his information, selected his facts, made his judgements, and produced his interpretations, can go and read the same sources and form his own opinions. Indeed, the novelist can count it as a bonus that he has stimulated his reader sufficiently to make him want to do so.

Nevertheless, a work of fiction can still have historical value. The historical novelist, like the historian, tries to arrange the evidence he collects into a pattern that coheres, that makes sense, and that persuades. He hopes to re-create, and he hopes to 'get it right'. He wishes, naturally, to entertain, to make the past interesting, but that does not necessarily imply a disdain of cold fact. Within his academic and literary capabilities, he aspires to bring the past into focus, and to create sympathy for the people who lived in it.

The wise historian, in his tireless search for hard evidence, appreciates the value of the occasional leap of informed imagination; the sensible novelist should not be so bewitched by the glitter of a good story that he consciously ignores the main body of accepted truth. Each, in his own way, if he works honestly, is serving the cause of history in general – and a very worthy cause that is too.

List of Characters

Norman

William II, Duke of Normandy – the Bastard, later the Conqueror, William I of England

Odo, Bishop of Bayeux, half-brother to the Bastard

Robert, Count of Mortain, half-brother to the Bastard

Sir William Fitzosbern, kinsman, companion and chief adviser to the Bastard

Sir Baldwin de Clair, kinsman, companion and quartermaster to the Bastard

Geoffrey de Montbrai, Bishop of Coutances, in charge of military training

Sir Roger of Montgomery, commander of the Norman right at Hastings

Sir Walter Giffard, commander of the Norman centre at Hastings

Count Alan of Brittany, commander of the Norman left at Hastings

Robert of Beaumont, a junior commander at Hastings

Eustace of Boulogne, standard-bearer at Hastings

Crispin of Bec, a monk, chief clerk to Baldwin de Clair

Ranulf of Dreux, chief military engineer to the Bastard

Fulk Bloodeye, captain of Flemish mercenaries

Matthew, a doctor, companion to Fulk

Florens of Arras, sergeant of Flemish mercenaries

Rainald of Delft, corporal of Flemish mercenaries
Dietrich, a Flemish soldier
Ralph of Gisors ⎤
Bruno of Aix ⎬ all three scouts in the Norman army
Gilbert of Avranches ⎦
Taillefer, a minstrel
Sandor the Magyar, chief horse-handler in the Norman
    invasion fleet
William Capra and
Ralph Pomeroy, soldiers of fortune in the Norman army
Brian, a Breton swordsman
Adele, wife of Gilbert of Avranches

The first eleven of the above people are specifically mentioned by name in the contemporary chronicles as having been present at Hastings. Taillefer's name figures in the later, more romantic accounts. There were also Bretons, Flemings, scouts, clerks, horse-handlers, engineers, and soldiers of fortune present. I have simply taken the liberty of giving names to some of them, and of providing one of them with a wife.

English

King Harold II, Harold Godwinsson, King of England
    (Jan.–Oct. 1066)
Gyrth, Earl of East Anglia, brother to Harold
Leofwine, Earl of Kent, brother to Harold
Edwin, dog-handler to the King
Gorm Haraldsson, a Sussex miller
Sweyn, Gorm's son
Rowena ⎤
Aud ⎬ Gorm's daughters
Edith ⎦
Godric, Gorm's foster-son

Wilfrid, a housecarl
A sheepman, one of the Berkshire levies who fought at
    Hastings
Owen, a Welsh archer who fought at Hastings

Of the English, only three have their presence at Hastings
vouched for by the documents – Harold and his two brothers –
all of whom died there. The remaining characters are fictitious,
but, I hope, not unlikely.

The Name of the Battle

It is a typical irony that the best-known battle in English history,
and arguably the most decisive, did not take place at Hastings;
it was fought on the ridge of a hill about seven miles away, on the
site now partly obscured by the modern town of Battle.

Some Normans later called it the Battle of Hastings, because
the town of Battle obviously did not exist then. The name
'Senlac' appears in a Norman chronicle of the twelfth century,
and was adopted by the great Victorian expert, E. A. Freeman.
It is suggested that the name may be a corruption of the sandy,
marshy area at the foot of the hill – 'Sandlake'; even that the
'Sen-' of Senlac comes from the French 'sang' – 'blood'.

The Saxon name for the area was 'Caldbec' – 'the cold stream'.
The Anglo-Saxon Chronicle says that the battle was fought 'at the
grey apple tree' – '*aet haran apuldran*'.

I have tried to incorporate most of these ideas into the nar-
rative, hoping that they add to the interest without blurring the
clarity of the picture. In general terms, I have made the English
refer to it as Caldbec Hill, and the Normans as Senlac.

'Far, far to a distant land'

A buzzard lifted itself from the grey branches of a dying apple tree and drifted away westwards from the scrubby hill. It soared and circled above spreading woods, scanty field-clumps, and shallow, south-flowing streams, scorning the element below, shunning the many beings who had so suddenly made it difficult to keep to regular habits.

One of those beings shielded his eyes against the afternoon sun as he squinted upwards at the curiously blunt silhouette.

'They are annoyed with us,' said Gilbert.

'Hardly surprising,' said Bruno, not bothering to look.

Ralph glanced up. 'If they are patient, they will have carrion enough to feed them for a year.'

Gilbert spat. 'Great Jesus, Ralph! Is that all you can think of?'

Ralph sighed inwardly, and looked sidelong at Bruno. Bruno let his eyebrows do the talking.

They rode on in silent file, their leggings scratched by fern and bramble, the hooves of their heavy horses thudding into soft soil. They scanned trail and landscape on either side, but there was little knowledge to be gained.

Then, after a while, they breasted a small rise and came in sight of a settlement. They reined in beneath the last trees, keeping their helmets out of the sunlight.

Not much down there either, thought Ralph. He looked at Bruno, who was already shaking his head and pulling down the corners of his mouth.

Ralph screwed up his eyes at the sun. Maybe three hours of daylight left. Time to go back. He and Bruno had been in the saddle since daybreak. There was nothing here that they had not already seen a dozen times.

When Ralph turned his horse's head, Gilbert looked surprised.

'Are we not going down?'

'Not worth it.'

'How do you know? You said yourself—'

'I said a lot of things,' said Ralph, his shoulders now aching all the more at the prospect of camp and rest ahead. 'Now I say it is not worth it.'

'I can go,' said Gilbert.

'Please yourself,' said Ralph over his shoulder.

Gilbert looked surprised. 'Do you mean that?'

Ralph paused.

Gilbert seized upon his hesitation. 'How can I improve unless I try my own judgement? You said yourself—'

'Yes, yes.'

Ralph looked at Bruno.

Buzzards and other birds hovered closely round the settlement. There was no sign of smoke.

Bruno nodded.

Ralph turned to Gilbert. 'Go then. But be careful. We shall not hurry back. You can catch us up. If you lose our trail, go back by the way we came. You remember the landmarks, I presume?'

Gilbert tilted his head scornfully. 'Of course.'

For the first time, Ralph grinned. 'All right. But take no

risks.' He began to turn away and suddenly remembered. 'Oh, and—'

'I know,' said Gilbert. 'Look after the hauberk.' He plucked at some of the shining links of mail that he never tired of polishing.

They both laughed.

Ralph watched him pick his way down towards the settlement. 'I can see no risk, can you?'

'No,' said Bruno. 'None whatever.'

Ralph looked sharply at him. 'Well?'

Bruno shrugged. 'If there is no risk, there is no test.'

'He thinks there is, so there is.'

'Will that make him a better scout?'

'In his own eyes, yes.'

'And in yours?'

Ralph avoided Bruno's gaze. 'I see clearly enough,' he muttered.

'No man sees clearly through a veil.'

Ralph glared. 'And what does Bruno the great prophet see so clearly?'

'I am no prophet.'

Ralph swore. 'Say it!'

Bruno shrugged again. 'Very well. The boy is a loser.'

'Damn you to hell.'

But Bruno was already on his way.

With another curse, and a final glance in Gilbert's direction, Ralph turned for camp.

Edwin put his head in the doorway without knocking. 'Anyone at home?'

'Come in, Edwin,' said Rowena, without looking round. She carried on with slicing some vegetables.

'And bring no mud with you,' said Aud.

Edwin grinned as he spoke to Rowena. 'That is a fine welcome from your sister.' He turned to Aud, who was frowning, and gave her an ironic bow. 'But I have brought a peace offering.'

He put a bundle of packages on the table.

'Well, what is it?' said Aud, still unwilling to look grateful.

Edwin gestured vaguely. 'Oh, this and that. From my lord's kitchen. Nobody will notice.'

Rowena pretended to look serious. 'You wait till my lord Harold catches up with you.'

Edwin laughed, and ruffled the fur round the neck of his dog. 'No danger. He is far too busy right now – no time for hunting. Eh, Berry?'

Rowena became really serious now. 'Is there any news?'

Edwin became serious too, and sat down without being invited. 'No. We know they have landed, but that is all.'

'What is the King doing about it?'

'The King is not here.'

'Where has he gone?' said Aud.

Edwin shook his head. 'No idea. But he has taken his body-guard – I do know that.'

'The housecarls.'

'Yes.'

'Where?'

Edwin shrugged and spread his hands.

For a few minutes nobody wanted to share doubts or worries. Nobody seemed to know where anybody was.

At last Edwin lifted his head. 'Where is Godric?'

'Working with Father in the mill,' said Rowena.

Aud sniffed. 'She means Godric is working and Father is sprawling somewhere.'

Edwin nodded. 'You mean . . . ?'

'He has pots hidden everywhere,' said Aud.

Edwin stood up. 'I must talk to Godric. Excuse me a moment.' He went out towards the mill. There may be no news, but there were rumours. Of burnings and wasting parties. Godric needed to know.

Gilbert paused on the edge of the settlement. There was no sign of life. Left behind were the neat stacks and bulging barns. Gilbert had seen them everywhere that he and Ralph and Bruno had been. Here was a fat land indeed. And nobody to look after it, much less defend it.

He expected peasants to flee, but where were the fighting men? He had not seen one. That would not do; Sir William Fitzosbern would want information.

'Never fear to tell the truth,' Ralph would say. 'If there is nothing there, you must say so. Fitz will be pleased to hear it. Remember, a scout is the only man in the army who is allowed to think. The only man who can speak the truth to his betters. Ours is the finest work in the world.'

Gilbert always felt a glow of pleasure when he heard Ralph talk like that.

Taking care to make little noise, Gilbert went forward to make sure. But there were only a few scavenging pigs. An overturned bucket by a door; gates left open; a pitchfork cast at random on the ground – hasty departure. Dried cowpats – gone several days.

Gilbert felt a sudden surge of patronising pity. Poor devils – what chance did they have? A life of constant toil, and it could all collapse at the mere whisper of danger.

How glad he was that he was a soldier. Soldiers made fortunes; peasants made do.

Ralph did not see it that way. 'The peasants always lose and the peasants always win.'

Gilbert could not understand why it annoyed him. He picked up a stone and hurled it aimlessly at an open door. It clanged against an iron pot.

But Ralph was right; there was nothing to be gained here. He would eat and move on.

He found some neglected, rather green apples in the orchard, pulled down a hunk of stale salt pork from a beam, fished out some hard cheese, and filled his flask from a leaf-strewn water-butt. He picked up the bucket and sloshed some water into the stone trough for his horse, then sat down to make the best meal he could.

Sir Baldwin de Clair counted bales of fresh hides as they were carried past.

'Fifty. As they said.'

Beside him a thin, blue-jowled monk scribbled uncomfortably, resting his lists on the lid of a barrel. A sea breeze flapped the edges of his habit.

Scowling troops staggered up the beach, their shoulders bowed with casks of nails, bundles of spears, huge sheaves of arrows. Captive Saxons slipped and stumbled among the pebbles, lugging between them great stretchers piled with sacks of tools and their ash handles, already fashioned for fitting.

Sir William Fitzosbern jumped ashore from another ship, which had just been dragged up on the shingle. Impatient to hear the news, he had had himself rowed out to it before it beached. He stumped across to Baldwin. Behind him the puffing crew made fast, and began at once to unload. From the far side, patient grooms tried to coax wary horses on to uncertain land. A few late recruits leaned on their hands, hung their heads, and thanked the God of journeys that their ordeal by water was over.

Fitzosbern stood beside Baldwin, put his hands on his hips, and watched the never-ending procession.

'If Ranulf says he can not build a castle with this lot, I shall tell William to send him back to Dreux.' He extended a hand towards a colossal pile of seasoned planks waiting to be taken inland to the chosen site. 'I wish some of my floors had timber like that, I can tell you.'

Baldwin did not fish for compliments. He and Fitz knew each other too well for that. All credit to the Duke for laying down supplies of sound timber, and at a time when the idea of an invasion of England seemed to many the height of lunacy. (It still did, but most of the doubters were now shivering round their timid hearths in Normandy.) But all credit to him too – Baldwin de Clair, quartermaster to his Grace Duke William II of Normandy – for concentrating those supplies, and for moving them so efficiently.

He knew that, and he knew that Fitz knew. So did the Duke. But they had long become so accustomed to the rarity of the Duke's praise that they had got out of the habit of bestowing it upon each other.

With the bond they all three shared, few words were necessary. Baldwin and Fitzosbern had each lost a father who had given his life as guardian to the young bastard Duke William. Bad times. Three thirteen-year-old orphans had sworn a tremulous oath of mutual loyalty. After so many years of survival, they understood each other perfectly.

'How is the lady Emma?' asked Baldwin.

Fitzosbern did not look at him. 'Mother is recovering. And the lady Sybil.'

'Good.'

Baldwin blinked and grimaced.

Why should it have been Agnes? Why take his sister and leave Fitz's mother and Geoffrey's old paramour? God's Teeth! They all lived in the same convent.

Fitzosbern continued to avoid his gaze. 'It was Geoffrey's man who brought the news.'

'Thierry?'

Fitzosbern shrugged. 'You know what I am like with names. He is the one who eats all the time.'

Baldwin pulled himself together. He indicated the ship – barely more than a barge – that Fitzosbern had just left. Some of the new arrivals were climbing out of it with great care.

'Great God!' said Baldwin. 'They look as if they are balancing eggs on their heads. Where did Thierry dig those up?'

'God knows. Vermin. William is scraping the barrel now.'

'If that is what we are reduced to,' said Baldwin, 'we are better off without them.'

'Expendable,' said Fitzosbern, 'I agree. But employable. Not like that total waste over there.' He waved towards the last ship in the small flotilla of new arrivals. 'Half full of hounds and personal tenting. Enough canvas to set up a fair.'

Baldwin growled. 'Only one young man would have the cheek for that. Treats an invasion as a glorified hunting trip.'

'Just so,' said Fitzosbern. 'His father ought to know better. When every inch of deck space is vital.' He pointed, again, at the new men. 'At least we can use this lot for wasting parties and any other dirty work. It saves the real troops.'

Baldwin growled once more, unconvinced. He gestured towards the horses, now being coaxed across the shingle by swearing owners. Behind them came small squads of grooms and servants lugging armfuls of equipment.

'You call them knights?'

'They have all the gear.'

'Geoffrey will not touch them with a scaling ladder. All those weeks he has spent with his training schedules and his trumpets and his straight lines? Half a dozen of these in a charge would reduce it to a rabble.'

Fitzosbern refused as usual to be drawn into argument. 'If Geoffrey can not use them, I can. In any case, the horses will still be valuable. You can never have too many mounts.'

'Wait till Geoffrey sees them,' said Baldwin. 'Just wait.'

Again, Fitzosbern declined the challenge. 'I shall accept Geoffrey's word on tactics, just as I shall accept Walter's word on the standard of the horses. Just as I accept your word on anything to do with stores and equipment.' He paused. 'Just as I expect my word to be followed on the overall allocation of our resources.'

Baldwin laughed. 'Why is it, Fitz, that nobody can ever have a row with you?'

'Takes two.'

'True, I tell you. I had it from my brother, and he had it from his best friend.'

'What does he know?'

'Courier. He rode a thousand miles in two days.'

'Oh, yes?'

'A mighty host – ten thousand ships. More numerous than the pebbles on the shore, so they say.'

'Amazing.'

'Something else too. He was seen.'

'Really?'

'The man himself. Seven feet tall. Now do you believe me?'

Gilbert munched at his pork and cheese, leaned on an elbow, and looked about him. Where on earth were the enemy? Over a week had passed since the landing at – where was it? – Pev – Pevoncy – something like that. And nobody had seen a single Saxon soldier.

It did not make sense. The English had known they were coming for months. Harold's fleet had been patrolling the Channel coast since May. Great Jesus! He had seen their sails for himself. The Duke had sent them on endless foraging expeditions – as far afield as Ponthieu and Flanders in the north, the Vexin in the south, and the Bessin and Cotentin towards the west. While they were doing that, he gathered an army and built a transport fleet.

Everybody snatched time, when they could, to make rushed visits to family whenever they came nearby. Fitzosbern would go to see his mother at the convent of St Amand. Geoffrey would go with him to see the lady Sybil. Baldwin would visit his sister's grave. Gilbert himself would rush to his father's tiny holding near Avranches. At first it was hugs and backslappings. His sister Mahaut would cry, but Mahaut always cried. His brother Robert said little. In the morning he would carry some buckets of water for his mother. But he was relieved when Ralph came to fetch him.

Off they would go again to locate supplies of fodder, requisition corn, arrange for round-ups of sheep and cattle; commission consignments of sacks, hides, ropes, casks, arrows, spearheads; conscript smiths, carpenters, fletchers, coopers, wheelwrights.

Now and then they would stop at Rouen, and the Duke would be visited by the lady Matilda. Gilbert would slip away to see Adele and the baby. After the first urgent passion of reunion was spent, he found that the unresolved shame of his knowledge lay like a great cold stone in the bed between them. What made it worse was that he really loved the boy. When he had first held him in his arms, he had loved with all the pride of a first-born's father. His heart had been given to Hugh, along with the dearest name he could think of bestowing upon him, and no amount of knowledge, guilt, or shame could get it back.

Back on patrol with Ralph and Bruno, he would gaze towards England and think of his quest. There! Somewhere over there lay Adele's ravisher. There too lay excitement, honour, fortune – and peace of some kind.

Gilbert of Avranches had never killed anyone in his life.

Well, now he was here . . .

He sat up with a start, threw away the apple core, and brushed the crumbs from his chest. What would Ralph say to see him daydreaming like this?

He packed and mounted, and gave a final look about him.

Ralph was right: there was nothing here. But the sun was not down yet. Suppose there was something further west. Suppose he found it. Suppose it was he, Gilbert of Avranches, who was the first scout to bring news of the approach of the Saxon army. Ralph would surely be impressed with that, and it would be one in the eye for Bruno. Ralph would tell Sir Baldwin, and Baldwin would tell Fitzosbern, and Fitzosbern ...

Robert of Beaumont swore at his sweating grooms.

'Tighter than that, you idiots. I do not want to be drowned in canvas with the first good blow.'

'But, sir—'

'Just do as you are told, and you may get paid. Then you can go and feed the hounds.'

'What with, sir?'

'Find something, damn you. The Flemings always do. Are you even more stupid than the Flemings?'

'Sir.'

'And I want my dinner within the hour.'

The buzzard showed itself again. Gilbert watched it float towards the summit of a bare, scrub-covered hill.

His scouting training, sharp though not yet refined into instinct, told him to view the countryside from any available high ground. It was up there that he would have to go.

On a ridge near the summit stood a solitary, and very old, apple tree. Grey lichen stippled its bark. Sickly patches of livid green showed. The foliage was thin, the fruit wrinkled and sparse. Even worse than the bitter fruit he had recently eaten. And that was not sitting comfortably on his stomach.

The ground sloped away steadily towards his right, to the south, and levelled out round a small swampy brook. Clumps of rushes grew out of pale sandy soil. Beyond that the ground rose again, to the woods of Telham Hill. Gilbert knew the name because he had already reconnoitred it with Ralph and Bruno. It was barely more than an hour's brisk ride from the Duke's new castle at Hastings.

To the west lay a maze of grassy humps and gorse-grown gullies.

Gilbert stood in the stirrups to get a better view, then settled back again.

'If I were Harold,' he thought, 'marching south, I should not like to have to cross that low ground, slosh through a sandy brook, and fight my way up Telham Hill. And if I were the Duke –' he happily identified himself for the moment with his commander '– I should fortify Telham, and clear some of the timber on the lower slopes. Use the wood for stakes and a palisade.'

A twinge in his stomach brought him back to reality, and jerked him from command strategy to humble scouting. His Grace the Duke, when he made his report to him, would not listen to immature judgements on fortification engineering; he would prefer a sensible report on the ground about him – all of it. That meant going to have a look at the northern and eastern sides of the hill as well.

The Duke's eyes scanned the neatly ordered piles of supplies, which his quartermaster had proudly persuaded him to come to see.

'Yes.'

Baldwin sighed. He should have known better.

William's restless pupils darted to left and right, as if he expected outlaws to spring out.

'This will do then – yes?'

Baldwin glanced towards the man at his side.

Ranulf of Dreux made a long face, which both Baldwin and the Duke ignored. Ranulf was always making long faces, but he was a good engineer.

'Hard to tell at this stage, my lord. Sir Baldwin keeps me short of labour, and Sir William Fitzosbern is not generous with funds.'

William made a sweeping gesture. 'Splendour of God, man. How much more do you want? As for labour, go and tell Fitz to get that riff-raff from the ships and put them to work. And you are not here to buy things; you take them.'

Ranulf made another face. 'I can do no more than my best, my lord.'

'You have enough flooring here for two castles. And I want no broken legs from flimsy steps and rungs. We leave nothing to chance. Nothing.'

Geoffrey de Montbrai, Bishop of Coutances, was in a foul mood.

The training had gone badly all day. There was still no room to deploy large numbers. The shingle beach was out of the question. The land between the beach and the new castle was a boiling sea of wagons, oxen, fatigue parties, ruts and holes. Despite the fiercest of orders from Baldwin and Fitzosbern, shanties and bivouacs continually sprang up in the most impossible places and clogged the channels of movement. If any area was levelled to make a space, more shanties sprang up like mushrooms in the night. Inland, around the castle, the trees had been cleared to provide timber for the rougher needs of exterior building and to remove all cover; but the stumps were still there – deathtraps for any detachment of knights over twenty or so in number.

The further Geoffrey went in search of suitable open ground, the more the knights distanced themselves from the security of the castle and the main camp, and the more they tired the horses.

There was a little scope for practice in small groups – reminding them of the standard rates of advance that Geoffrey had tried to instil into them; repeating the trumpet call codes, until even the stupidest could remember the full sequence; getting them to wheel and turn about in a limited space (the tree stumps were quite useful for that).

But there was no substitute for a full rehearsal – moving mounted knights in blocks of two hundred, three hundred. It mattered little; whatever Geoffrey organised, the men loathed it. They loathed all forms of joint practice. That was for common infantry or peasant archers, not for those who were knightly born. Were they not professionals? Did they not understand their business? If they did not know how to handle horse, shield, spear, sword and mace, they would not have disgraced their honour by being there.

In all his years of training fighting men, Geoffrey had found that the biggest obstacle to achieving his dream was not lack of strength, lack of talent, lack of experience, or lack of money; it was lack of will. They simply did not believe that what he was demanding of them was either possible or desirable.

But he hung on to his dream: a combined charge of heavy cavalry, by the hundred, which would keep the same pace and line, and which, if need be, could be recalled.

Nine knights out of ten thought he was crying for the moon. God's Bones – they had toiled under a summer sun in Normandy, and now this dreamer Coutances expected them to do it all over again in Sussex, when the weather was uncertain, when the castle was not finished, and when nobody knew where the enemy were. And look at the ground. Besides, they were as good as they were ever going to be. It was common knowledge that, man for man, the mounted Norman knight had no superior on any battlefield in Christendom.

That was the view of the core of the Norman knights. The attitude of the soldiers of fortune who had just arrived for the adventure bordered on the mutinous. They had been prepared for hardship, danger, boredom; that was the price one paid for glory, women, and loot. What they were not prepared for was the endless practice, practice, practice.

Not even the abuse of the Duke himself converted them. 'You ravening saddle-scum! What do you think this is – a Viking raid? Do you take me for a church looter? Do I look like some coast-crawling scavenger?'

He waved his arm about him. 'Have you the faintest idea of what we are up against? The full might of a kingdom. A kingdom! This is no summer-sun siege to pass the time of day. I offer you the greatest prize of your stupid lives, and all you can think about is your precious honour. Only an army will take England, and you will be no army until Lord Geoffrey tells me that you obey, and obey with your foul mouths shut.'

He paused, his eyes darting to right and left with their customary restlessness.

'I know what you say: "It is all very well for him; he gets a crown." True. A mighty prize. But I offer you shares in that crown beyond a man's wildest dreams of avarice. Think on it. And think on this: I lead no rabble to win my crown. If you covet your share of that prize, then by the Splendour of God you labour for it.'

They laboured, but with a bad grace. When Thierry arrived, Geoffrey was as relieved as they were to stop. They dismounted, flung helmets and spurs at wincing grooms, and stumped off. Sir Walter Giffard and Sir Roger of Montgomery, the two senior squadron commanders, sent servants scuttling for refreshment.

Geoffrey slid off his mail coif, and beckoned. Thierry hustled forward as quickly as his girth would permit, anxious to give the impression of haste and breathlessness. Geoffrey held out his hand.

Thierry kneeled and kissed the ring. 'My lord.'

'Well?'

'I came as soon as I could, my lord,' said Thierry, with enough hint of puffing to suggest urgency. 'His Grace the Duke questioned me in great detail.'

'No doubt,' said Geoffrey drily. 'And his Grace's cook then fed you in great detail.'

Giffard and Montgomery looked at each other and grinned. Thierry's reputation was well known. Glutton he might be, but there was no better gleaner of news.

'Of course, my lords,' he would say. 'If you want to know what is happening, ask the table servants or the grooms or the squires or the valets. Is it my fault that they sit in the kitchen?'

Thierry furtively wiped the last grease off his fingers on the backs of his leggings.

'Twelve hours at sea, Lord Geoffrey. And not a morsel. Stretched over the rail in agony.'

Geoffrey waved aside his familiar excuses.

'News, news!'

Thierry gulped in his eagerness to turn Geoffrey's mind away from his recent gorging.

'Excellent, my lord. The lady Sybil has made a complete recovery. She acted as reverend mother while the lady Emma regained her strength. Indeed, they say in the kitchens –' he checked himself '– it is said that she has proved to be as good a mother abbess as the lady Emma in her prime.'

Geoffrey could feel the eyes of both Giffard and Montgomery on the back of his neck. The Devil. What if they were looking? And listening? They knew all about him and Sybil. She was well again; that was what mattered. Thierry could tell him the rest later in private.

Thierry would also tell him about the building at Coutances. Goscelin should have most of the roof timbers up over the nave by this time. That would be one in the eye for Odo; the last he had heard of Odo's cathedral at Bayeux, Odo had been forced to disgorge half-a-dozen carpenters for the construction of his brother's invasion fleet. That could push him behind by several months by the time the campaign was over. It almost put Geoffrey in a good mood just to think of it.

'Anything else?'

Thierry understood. Move on to military intelligence. He cleared his throat importantly.

'Brittany is quiet, lord; no forays over the Couesnon. Ponthieu, in the north, behaves itself. No raids from Champagne in the south-east. And the King has not moved from Paris.'

The whole of France, it seemed, was still, rapt, hypnotised by the possible outcome of the great gamble of Normandy's Duke.

Sir Walter Giffard grunted. 'Waiting to see which way the cat will jump.'

'No news is good news,' said Montgomery.

'Maybe in France,' said Geoffrey. 'But not here. Holy Virgin! Where are the English?'

Thierry hovered respectfully, his ears ready to pick up any titbits that he could trade round hearth and campfire. Geoffrey dismissed him.

'Off! You might as well do it with permission now.'

They watched the portly figure disappear among the tents and wagons.

'The longer we wait, the more difficult this training becomes,' said Montgomery.

'I do not need to be told that,' said Geoffrey sourly.

'And it will not do the slightest good,' said Giffard. 'All it needs is a windy day, and your trumpets will be useless. Gabriel himself would not be heard. And as for this unison charge – great God, Geoffrey! Five hundred men.'

'You exaggerate,' said Geoffrey.

'Very well – four hundred. Three hundred. A hundred. You will never get them to strike at the same instant. And you will certainly never recall them. A knight is a knight. You are up against generations of habit and tradition; you will never change it.'

'Have you seen the fyrd?' Geoffrey said. 'Have you seen the

might of England in one place? How can we break that up with petty hit-and-run? And if they have a palisade, it will be worse.'

'Then we see to it that they do not,' said Giffard. 'God's Teeth, Geoffrey, we are the ones with the cavalry; we move the faster. It is up to us to choose the ground. We are the invaders; Harold must come to us. He has no choice.'

Geoffrey shook his fists in his urgency. 'Walter – think! Imagine! Two hundred knights moving as one mighty human hammer. What a blow could we strike! No army on earth could stand against it. Is that not an end worth striving for?'

Giffard shook his head. 'It is not possible, it is not natural, and it is not necessary. And it is not honourable,' he added.

Geoffrey turned in frustration to Montgomery.

Montgomery put up his hands in a sign of peace. 'I know, I know. I shall try to do what you say, if that is what the Duke wants. So will Walter; you know that. But permit us to have our doubts, Geoffrey. You only train them; Walter and I have to lead them.'

Gilbert turned his horse northwards, away from the ridge, away from the grey apple tree. The ground rose gently to the true summit. Here, Gilbert paused in wonder; he could see the countryside for miles around in all directions.

Great Jesus, what a position!

To the east, he could see the land fall away into a mess of small clefts and gullies. Nothing much worth noting there. That left only the north, where the hill sloped softly away from the summit towards the forest at its foot.

He winced as another pain nipped his stomach. He became aware that he might soon have to dismount. Out on the open hilltop he felt suddenly vulnerable and un-private. Almost as if he expected a hefty Saxon to spring out on him from nowhere.

Make for the trees! He dug in his heels. His stomach grumbled again at the greater movement.

The line of long grass and bramble that screened the entry to the forest looked almost welcoming.

Suddenly the ground disappeared. His horse tumbled. He heard earth and stones spilling. The breath was knocked out of him as he fell.

At once he began rolling uncontrollably. He heard his horse neighing in fear. He was careering down an almost precipitous slope, crashing through bracken and thorn, bringing cascades of earth and leaf mould after him. Visions flashed past his frightened eyes – his horse's staring face, sliding tree trunks, fern fronds in the sky, his own flailing arms. He was sure he heard voices.

Ambush!

He felt the snap of one of the straps holding his scabbard to the belt. The scabbard banged against the tree trunks. As he fell over some loose stones, the handle of his knife dug painfully into his hip. Something wrenched at his ankle.

Ambush!

His mind raced even faster than his body. He must be ready for them. What would Ralph say about his being caught like this? He grabbed wildly for the hilt of his sword. How would they kill him? Would it hurt? Would Adele weep for him?

With a tremendous thump, he hit level ground. By a huge effort, he stopped himself rolling into the water. He lay there a while, totally winded.

As his breath returned, he raised his head, slightly surprised to be still alive. Looking to either side, he was more surprised to find no boots or leggings there. He turned over and looked further. There was not a living creature in sight.

He was in a smallish ravine, partly wooded and very steep, with a tiny streamlet in the bottom. The far bank was even higher than the one he had slipped down. Holes were everywhere, and he could smell and see badger droppings. He gazed up to the top. Half one side of this cleft in the ground seemed to be made up of one huge badger sett. Clods of earth still trickled on to his shoulders. He moved to avoid them, and winced at a fresh pain in his ankle. He must have caught his foot in one of the holes.

He wriggled into a sitting position and examined himself for further damage. Apart from a dense coating of dirt, there did not seem to be much else wrong. As if to correct him, his stomach turned again, and he almost retched.

He leaned back on his hands and rested his head far back on his shoulders. He took some deep breaths, gazing around and upwards.

What a place for an ambush! Thank God he really was alone. Bruised, winded, and sick, he could have been finished off by a half-blind old crone with a skinning knife.

Suddenly his nerves were jarred by a loud rustling slightly further up the ravine. He wrenched himself about, almost whimpering with shock and fear, and tugged again at his sword. Worse, there was another, heavier noise. He scratched and scrambled his way to his feet, and succeeded at last in drawing the weapon.

His horse appeared, trailing its reins. Gilbert collapsed into a sitting position, and laughed hysterically.

When he regained composure and tried to stand up, his twisted ankle reminded him that he had another problem besides his stomach. He started to hobble towards his horse; every step was agony. His scabbard now hung awkwardly from its single strap, and threatened to trip him.

Puffing and grimacing, he reached his patient mount and prudently tied it to a tree. He cut an end off a saddlebag strap, and fashioned a makeshift leather thong to support his scabbard. Taking the water flask from the saddle horn, he unfastened the stopper. Bad water or no bad water, he needed a drink. It might have been the apples; it might have been the bad pork or the stale cheese. What did it matter? The damage was done.

And now he had to get out of the ravine. It was just as well that he had tethered his horse so firmly. The animal could never have stood still while he made so many attempts to get into the saddle. When he tried to put his left leg in the stirrup, his right ankle shrieked with the pain of taking all his weight, however briefly. When the horse moved and he had to hop on it in order to stay upright, he cried out loud. He went round to the other side and tried putting his bad foot in the stirrup first, but could not stand the twisting that it involved. For one desperate moment he contemplated climbing a tree and dropping into the saddle, as he had seen tumblers do at Rouen during the Easter Sunday celebrations. Then he thought of the large wooden pommel at the front of the saddle, and shuddered at the awful possibilities. In the end he pulled the horse towards himself, grabbed both ends of the saddle, and hoisted himself over it until he drooped down either side like a bag of onions. Puffing and cursing, with his face pressed against the creature's shoulder, he heaved and bounced until he fetched his injured leg over and down the other side. So ashamed did he feel that he instinctively turned to left and right to see if anyone was looking.

There was his water flask lying on the ground. He swore viciously, dismounted, collected it, and went through the whole painful business again.

It was then that he noticed that a spur was missing. Still cursing, he peered from the saddle at the mess of earth and stones where he had fallen. He could see nothing. He raised his eyes to the top of the ravine. A hopeless quest; it could have come off anywhere in the descent.

He could not go through the indignity of mounting like that a third time. He wrenched hard on the reins and dug in his one good foot. At last, at long last, he emerged on to the slope outside the rampart of grass and bracken through which he had fallen.

Now what?

He was hot, flushed, uncomfortable, in pain, and furious with everything. What on earth was he to do now? What did he have to report? That he had made all the wrong choices, botched everything? He remembered Ralph; he must think clearly.

What did Ralph say? 'There is always something you can do to improve things, however small.'

He was hot. His hauberk was unbearably oppressive. He was alone in a deserted countryside. Very well – it would come off. He kept sufficient presence of mind to stow it carefully in the bedroll behind the saddle. If he lost that Ralph would be furious beyond words.

Many months before, on the Duke's punitive campaign against Count Conan, Ralph had salvaged that hauberk from a casualty at the siege of Rennes. He had cut it carefully away from a disembowelled Breton. It had then taken many hours of patient work by a surly armourer, and some handsome payments, to get it into proper condition. Ralph polished it lovingly. When, without warning, Gilbert had it presented to him, he was so staggered, and so touched, that it was difficult to hold back the tears. Quite apart from the generosity of the gift, it meant that Ralph approved. Gilbert hugged him in his delight, and he did not care if Bruno did shake his head.

Feeling cooler and more in command, Gilbert thought about the best thing to do. He glanced up at the sun. Still some daylight left. He had noted the landmarks. He could find his way back. What was wrong with another search further westwards? What sort of scout was it who gave in to a twisted ankle and a grumbling stomach? He could see Bruno's eyebrows lifting yet again. Well, we would have no more of that. Even if he found nothing, he could look Ralph in the eye and say that he had used every scrap of daylight. But – suppose he found something! He – Gilbert of Avranches . . .

No – west it would be.

*

Bruno was seeing to the horses when Ralph came back. He asked a question simply by turning round.

'Fitzosbern,' said Ralph.

'What did he say?'

'About as much as you. You know Fitz.'

Bruno patted his horse's neck, then bent to examine its forelegs. 'No contact then?'

'None. Nobody has seen a thing. Fitz says to rest and then spread out further – bigger sweeps. In threes and fours – maybe more. In case.'

'Only a matter of time.'

Bruno moved to check the back legs, his hand gently running down, squeezing and massaging. He never gave the impression of being rushed off his feet, but at the same time he was never idle. At work or at rest, he was usually engaged in some humdrum chore or other. Normally, Ralph found it soothing. Now the patient, deliberate movements suddenly annoyed him.

'Does it not bother you?'

'No.'

Ralph ticked a tussock of grass. 'Well, it bothers me.'

Bruno stood up. He was a long, gangling man, and towered over Ralph. He wiped his hands on a piece of cloth waste. 'It is not the English that bother you.'

Ralph liked Bruno being there, just as he liked the sun being out. But the sun annoyed him sometimes with its heat; just so could Bruno sting him; he was not unkind, but he spared no truth.

'There is no danger, or you would not have let him go. He is probably simply lost.' He contrived to make it both a reassurance and a comment on Gilbert's lack of experience.

Ralph tore a piece from a blackened carcase hanging above the tiny spit, and chewed moodily. Bruno had a down on the boy. He gave him no credit. What about that time on the cliffs at Etretat? He belittled everything Gilbert had said.

It must have been about the second week in September. They had been watching the sea yet again, straining their eyes for the English fleet. It looked as if it had just been disbanded. Why? Where had it gone? Gilbert had jumped in as usual.

'Harold has taken his ships for repairs and fresh supplies. You wait – he will be out to sea again in a few days.'

Bruno hawked and spat. 'He *has* no supplies. He has sent his men home to get in the harvest. I should have thought a farmer's son would have known that.'

Gilbert blushed. Ralph tried to come to his rescue. After all, the boy had only been trying to gain their respect by his reasoning.

Ralph held out his short cloak. It flapped noisily.

'Harold knows the importance of the wind as well as the Duke. So long as it is in this quarter, no invasion fleet can depart from Normandy, and Harold knows this. Now is a good time to send his men home.'

Gilbert's face lit up with inspiration. 'But the wind that keeps the Duke in harbour will bring the Norwegians. It will release the longships.'

'Nobody knows what Norway is doing,' said Bruno.

Gilbert's eyes snapped in excitement. 'Perhaps Harold has gone north to find out.'

Bruno tilted his head in tolerant amusement. 'A strategist as well as an admiral.'

Gilbert fought back. 'Would it not be good for us if Harold did meet Norway? Whoever survives will be that much weaker. Our task will be that much easier. What matters, surely, is not who wins the first battle, but who wins the last.'

Bruno pursed his lips.

Ralph laughed. 'He has you there. Now find an answer for that.'

'My business is scouting,' said Bruno. 'I stick to what I understand. I know my place.'

It was Bruno's way of keeping the distance between Gilbert and himself. Privately, to Ralph, he was more explicit.

'Earth in his ears. He does not listen.'

'He does,' said Ralph. 'All the time. He hangs on my every word.'

Bruno sighed. 'Well, he may listen, but he does not hear. He is trying to catch distant bells of honour and glory, and does not hear the sounds around him.' Bruno tapped his ears. 'A scout needs these for his life.'

Ralph fell back on sarcasm. 'And Bruno of Aix hears all.'

Bruno was ready for him. 'More than Ralph of Gisors. Ralph listens to the words of Gilbert, but he hears the voice of his dead brother.'

It was the smoke which first caught Gilbert's notice. It took him almost by surprise as he emerged from a wood on the shoulder of a hill.

He backed hurriedly, dismounted – with great care – and tethered his horse to a young beech. He limped forward, his heart beating with excitement, and remembered just in time to take off his helmet in case the low sun caught it and gave him away.

This could be a Saxon encampment just ahead of him. Great Jesus – perhaps the whole army!

Leaving the shelter of the trees, he crawled to a vantage point behind a large clump of ferns. Ready to have his breath taken away by what he would see, he parted the ferns and looked down.

Nothing. A small valley, just as uninteresting as the others. Except that this one had a few people in it. No soldiers, true, but human beings at least. It made a change from the ghostly emptiness that they had seen earlier in the day.

Away to the left lay a cluster of peasant homes. One or two women were in a nearby field, gleaning. An ox-cart was creeping painfully along a path from the surrounding trees, straining under a huge load of firewood. The air was so clear that Gilbert could hear the creaking of the great wooden wheels. Two young girls were beating clothes on large stones by the stream that split the buildings into two rough halves. An old man was lifting vegetables from a garden patch. A boy was teasing pigs by throwing stones at them.

Gilbert's spirits fell. It was all so normal. The large load of wood was bigger than any individual peasant was entitled to. The local lord was clearly making his usual preparations for the winter as if nothing was impending.

Ralph's comment on the English came back to him.

'They never take notice of danger until it forces them to fight for dear life.' He had added, 'Then you had best be wary of them.'

The absence of excitement caused Gilbert's mind to take notice of his stomach again. Wincing in discomfort, he switched his attention to the opposite end of the valley, upstream.

There lay the mill. Rising from it was the smoke which had first attracted his attention. It was rising in the still air as straight as a shipbuilder's pine. It was set slightly back from the stream, but Gilbert's eye could follow the course of the mill leat which had been dug from the main watercourse higher up. It led to a well-filled pond behind and above the mill, whence a timber sluice gate and mill race fed the wheel itself. Gilbert's ear could easily pick out the regular grinding of the great iron-bound, oaken shaft and the slapping of the flanges.

A cart was drawn up at the main door. A huge peasant – the first fit man Gilbert had seen – was loading flour, humping the great sacks as if they were weightless. The elderly driver was involved in an altercation with the miller, a balding, overweight figure with hands whitened to the elbows. As the miller waved his ghostly arms about in annoyance, Gilbert smiled to himself; altercations with millers were clearly as commonplace in England as they were in Normandy.

A young woman came out of the mill house, and went towards the chicken coop. She was tall, and moved beautifully. Even at a distance, her full figure was obvious under the shapeless dress. Gilbert felt a stir of longing, and at once a stab of guilt.

A second woman, thinner and plainer, came to the doorway. Her voice was edgy and plaintive. Suddenly a third, more stocky figure rushed out past her, and took shelter beside the skirts of the first one.

Gilbert began to wonder what this small domestic drama was about, but was interrupted by another wrench from his stomach. A wave of nausea made him feel hot and cold.

Some of the pigs were running in his direction, and the boy was still throwing stones after them. He could raise his eyes at any moment.

Gilbert knew he would have to move. There was nothing here to report. The pigs were coming closer up the hill, and the wretched boy was still following. If the nausea continued, he knew he was going to be sick, and the boy could not fail to hear the noise of retching.

Cursing again at the impossible situation in which he found himself, Gilbert crawled and scrambled back to the shelter of the wood. Sweating with the effort, he now discovered that it was not his stomach that was going to let him down but his bowels.

Well, at least it was not going to make such a noise. He was crouched in anticipation when he heard a rippling snarl. He stood up hurriedly, just managing to stifle a cry of pain from his ankle, and pulled frantically at his leggings. He peered into the undergrowth all around him. There was another throaty snarl.

Suddenly another noise came up to him from the mill. A female voice. He peered cautiously between some leaves. It was the tall fair one out in the yard again. She was calling the boy back. Gilbert could not understand the short hard English words, but the strength and sureness in the voice were unmistakable.

The boy stopped, and tried to argue. But the young woman,

confident of her authority, had turned away. Tossing his head sulkily, the boy flung one last stone with extra spite, and trudged downhill.

Well, that was something. Now all Gilbert had to do was locate the dog. If it barked, the boy would still hear it.

'Always try what you are good at.'

He had not always paid proper attention to Ralph's comments, and was surprised at how many of them came back to him when he needed them.

He was good at dogs.

'It might benefit you one day,' his father had said. Which had turned out to be true. It had gained him his first employment, with his Grace Bishop Geoffrey of Coutances, in charge of the hounds.

Gilbert fished in a leather wallet at his waist, and brought out a biscuit. It was going to be a very unusual dog that was not hungry. He made soft chirping and clicking noises with his lips and tongue.

A rustle betrayed the animal's presence at last. Slowly, a muzzle emerged from the thicket, then a wild-looking but wiry body. Gilbert held out the biscuit. The dog edged forward, then, surprisingly, whimpered. It was limping. Gilbert felt sympathy at once; they had something in common.

He saw the twine tight round one of its forepaws. Then, following the twine with his eyes, he made out the remains of some animal trap or other, half hidden in the long grass. The poor creature had dragged the trap from its moorings in its efforts to free itself, but of course had tightened the twine round its paw, which was chafed almost raw, and bleeding. It had hidden itself when it heard Gilbert blundering about, and had growled in fear and pain, not anger. There was no anger in its eyes – only entreaty.

*

'The northern host is broken. Earls Edwin and Morcar in full flight.'

'Oh?'

'Hardrada has wasted York. Twelve more cities too. The whole of Northumbria is in flames. The Archbishop himself – hanged.'

'Really?'

'As I live and breathe.'

Gilbert could not do it. It was against all reason, but he could not do it. He was ill; he was tired; he was several miles from camp; and it was getting late. He had to bring back information, even if it was that there was no information. A dozen of Ralph's remarks about the needs of scouting came into his head, but he ignored all of them. Crouched in front of him, in this foreign land of empty farms and lonely furrows, was the first living thing that needed him. Besides, it was a dog. And it had not betrayed him. He was good at dogs. 'Do what you are good at.' Even Ralph had said so.

With the aid of the biscuit, and with more friendly noises, Gilbert soon insinuated some fingers behind the animal's ears. Safer, he put both hands about its head, coaxing all the time. He forgot his pain; authority took its place. The dog began to relax.

Gilbert offered another precious biscuit. Then, without letting go of the fur at the back of the dog's neck, he edged his other hand, slowly, very slowly, down the dog's injured leg. It whimpered again, and tried to lift it up. Working as gently as possible, Gilbert loosened the twine and eased it off. Tearing off several handfuls of soft green grass, he spat on them and washed the dirt out of the wound as best he could. What he needed now was water, and a bandage of some kind. They were both with his horse.

Still holding the dog's neck, he shuffled on his knees to where the horse was tethered. He opened a saddlebag, and pulled out a spare worsted shirt. With his knife he cut into its tail and tore off a strip. Making a pad of it in his hand, he soaked it with some water from his flask, and wiped the dog's paw again. Then he unrolled the pad, and used it to bandage the wound. He pulled out the leather lace at the neck of his shirt and twined it round to secure the bandage. It would not stay on long, but the coolness and softness would give the animal comfort for a while.

To his great joy, it whimpered again, this time clearly in gratitude.

Suddenly he doubled up with yet another spasm in his stomach, and was forced to see to himself, almost too late. When he at last fastened his half-soiled leggings, he noticed that the dog was still there.

Now the face of Ralph appeared before him in all its wrath. He packed everything as fast as he could, and made vigorous gestures to make the dog go away – which it ignored. Indeed, it wagged its tail.

He went through the charade of mounting yet again, and made off eastwards. The lowering sun cast long shadows before him.

He was swaying now in the saddle, his eyes half closed at times. Once he passed too close under the bough of a tree, and received a thump on the forehead that nearly knocked him to the ground. The dog was now following him.

Gilbert cursed trees and green apples and hidden ravines and scabbard straps and stale water and God and himself, and anything else he could think of. His bad ankle, constantly shaken by the movement of the stirrup, shrieked at him. He had to pause for a while.

He slid his feet out of the stirrups and stretched his legs. An early evening badger scurried across his path. The horse stirred. It was not a large movement, but Gilbert was totally unprepared. He slipped and fell, his ankle twisting under him yet again. As he lay on his back to recover, the nausea rose in his throat once more, and he knew he was going to be sick.

He struggled to a kneeling position, propped himself on his hands, and vomited copiously. All the strength seemed to go from his limbs. He could not move. He found himself gazing at the backs of his hands as if they did not belong to him. For a moment he panicked, but no matter how urgent his thoughts, his body would not respond. He – could – not – move.

Then he felt pins and needles in his arms and legs. He had heard stories from old soldiers about sickness and seizures and creeping death. There was no pain, they said; you just slipped quietly away.

His panic was replaced by a mixture of curiosity and surprise. So this was it. This was what it was like. He had often wondered. He had sometimes imagined that it might come suddenly, though he could have wished it had not come quite so early. Pity.

It struck him that it would be undignified to die, actually to pass away, on all fours like an animal. His limbs would not respond, but now he felt no worry or fear. It was simply a practical matter of how to get himself into a better position in which to end his life, a more becoming posture in which to be found.

He tried to lean so that extra weight was put on his left arm. Sure enough, it buckled, and he rolled over on to his side and then his back. The hilt of his sword dug into his hip, but it was not so painful now. There was no point in moving into a more comfortable position, because the end could not be far off. Blades of grass rustled round his ears and swayed over his eyes.

Would they steal his hauberk, as Ralph had cut it from the dead Breton soldier with the spear in his stomach?

He put his hand inside his jerkin and fumbled anxiously. He sighed in relief as his fingers closed over Adele's crucifix. Suddenly he wanted to gaze on it. Unable to reach the clasp, he tugged sharply. With his weakened arm it took two or three attempts before it finally came away.

He held it in both hands above his face, and took comfort

from what he saw. His arms could not hold the position, and he soon let them flop on to the ground.

He stared straight up. He thought of his father and mother, his gruff brother Robert, his sister Mahaut (who would of course cry). Baby Hugh smiled at him, and Adele held his hand . . .

The sky looked more sombre now. Or was it his eyes darkening? Those old soldiers talked of the eyes of dying men clouding over. He sighed quietly. He would shut his eyes for a moment. Just for a moment. Then he would open them when he felt the time coming. Men did that too, said the soldiers, immediately before the end.

Ralph peered blearily in the bad light. 'Does friendship mean nothing to you?'

Bruno sighed. 'Friendship is not the point. The point is professional skill. I told you when you were sober, and I tell you again now: if you want him to be a scout, he learns to take his chance. If you do not want him to be a scout, you nurse him – and next time you leave him behind.'

Ralph stretched his hand out into the night. 'If it were you out there, I should look for you.'

'I should do the same for you. I am your partner.'

Ralph glowered. 'And Gilbert is not, I suppose.'

'He is not mine.'

'Well, he is mine.'

Bruno continued sharpening his knife. 'He is not. He is not even a friend. He is a hope, a dream.'

Ralph swore.

Bruno pursued him. 'He is a liability. You are too soft with him. You give him too many chances.'

Ralph blustered. 'I am hard on him. He says so.'

'Which proves my point.'

'Sandor says so. Taillefer says so.'

'Taillefer is not a scout. I am. So are you. We are professionals.'

'And Gilbert is not?'

'No. And I do not think he ever will be. He will certainly not be if you have to chase across half Sussex looking for him in the dark. If you found him, he would not be grateful.'

'He would be alive.'

'You have no guarantee. We could both die looking for him. Where is the professional responsibility in that? Fitz wants every man out to the north as soon as possible. The Bastard wants to know where Harold is; what would he say if he found out that two of his best scouts were wasting their time looking for a lost dog-boy?'

Ralph's eyes twitched. 'You do not understand. Gilbert is—'

'Gilbert is not Michael. And Michael is dead.'

Ralph turned away, sighed, and hiccuped.

'Go on, boy! Find him! Find him!'

Quite what Edwin hoped his dog would find he had no clear idea, but he was so overjoyed at seeing it return that he was prepared to indulge almost any whim.

The dog paused and looked back, making sure that his delighted master was following.

'Go on, Berry. Seek! Seek!'

Perhaps it was fresh game caught in one of Sweyn's traps. Edwin had noticed at once the livid mark on Berry's leg, and knew what had caused it. While he bathed and bound it, he cursed Sweyn for setting his traps on this near edge of the forest. If he had told the fat little oaf once he had told him a score of times not to set traps across the line of his exercise runs with the hounds. There was enough woodland and waste in which to set a whole wilderness of traps; all the idle toad had to do was walk a few hundred paces further.

Sweyn was too lazy, too stupid and too spoiled. The more

Edwin scolded, the more he whined, until in the end he went running to his father. Gorm always took his son's side. It was useless to argue; Gorm was narrow-minded, bad-tempered and blind to his son's faults. He had sired him too late in life, after his suffering wife had presented him with three daughters.

Edwin gave up in disgust, and let his annoyance be overridden by his joy in finding the hound he had been worrying about nearly all day.

When it became clear that Berry wanted to show him something up on the hill, he was happy to follow. However, it was late, so he took Godric with him. He checked the knife blade, and made sure that the weapon slid easily in and out of the sheath. He picked up a spare axe handle, and nodded towards a pitchfork. Godric picked it up without a word.

Everyone knew that the Normans had landed. There had been a steady trickle of fugitives through the valley, each with his own garbled version of events. There was talk of fires and killings, of fighting patrols and foraging parties, of near misses and narrow escapes.

Edwin had kept his eyes open, but had so far seen no enemy. That was no proof, he knew, that nobody had ridden this far from Pevensey, though the indications were against it. All were agreed that the Bastard had landed at Pevensey, but he would make for London, and so would have little cause to be diverted so far westwards. Still, it would pay to be prudent.

Motioning to Godric to follow, Edwin set off after the eager hound.

Berry ranged restlessly up a narrow sheep track, and paused at the top near the edge of the trees.

Edwin was about to shout encouragement again when an earthy hand closed firmly over his mouth from behind. Another hand pinned his knife arm to his side. He felt an instant of panic, which vanished as quickly when he smelled Godric's familiar odour.

He relaxed, and nodded. Godric released his grip, put a hand on his shoulder and pointed with the other.

Edwin knew a Norman horse when he saw one. A riderless Norman horse could mean several things. He glanced at Godric, who nodded ahead towards the dog. It was circling something in the long grass behind a thicket of ferns. Without a word, they separated, spread out, and came towards the dog from opposite directions.

A young Norman soldier lay on his back. Edwin recognised the short, almost monkish haircut. Blood trickled past the soldier's ear from a dirty graze and bump on his forehead. He was moaning softly, and was shaking uncontrollably.

The thrill of fear that passed through Edwin was not caused entirely by the fact that the body was Norman. It looked as if there was some kind of hideous fever present. Edwin caught sight of dried vomit in the grass nearby. Its fetid smell was still offensive in the evening air. He hung back, uncertain.

Godric moved past him, stooped, and gently removed both sword and dagger. The soldier made no attempt to prevent him. Godric passed them back without looking behind him. Edwin took them. Not for the first time, he found himself obeying out of sheer respect for Godric's common sense.

Godric bent over the prostrate young man. He felt his forehead and under his sagging chin. He peered inside the top of his shirt and looked for any spots or blotches. He ran his hands over the whole body, sniffing all the while. He turned him over, looked at his back, and let him drop gently into his original position. Edwin kept the sword at the ready, feeling a little foolish with his own stick and Godric's pitchfork clutched awkwardly together in his other hand.

Godric went over to the horse, tethered it, and examined it. He looked carefully at saddle, bridle, reins, and stirrups. He unlaced and peered into each saddle bag. Reaching into one, he pulled out something that he kept in his hand while he undid the bedroll. The glittering hauberk flopped open. Without even glancing at Edwin, he folded it again, rolled it inside a travelling cloak, and strapped it back behind the saddle, keeping out only the dark woollen blanket.

He came back to the soldier, crouched, and began rolling him in the blanket as easily as if he were a baby.

'Well?' said Edwin impatiently.

Without interrupting what he was doing, Godric answered, 'He has no fever, and no bones are broken. There are no holes; he is not wounded.'

'What about his head?'

'That is no wound. It is not clean. It was made by no weapon. There are pieces of bark round it. Perhaps he struck his head on a branch.'

'A strong young Norman on horseback, and he does not look where he goes?'

'Young, yes. Strong, no. See, he is weak; he shivers. And he has fallen more than once. A strap has broken on his scabbard. He has mended it in haste. See the mud and leaf mould on his arms and back, on his leggings. There is only grass here. And he has lain a good half-hour; the dew has begun to soak into his clothes.'

It seemed so simple when Godric explained, and his voice was so mild that Edwin felt no annoyance.

'Smell,' said Godric. 'He is sick in the belly. He has soiled himself. Look at this cheese, this meat.' He tossed it away. 'If this is Norman camp diet, their bellies will beat them before the King does.'

He pointed downwards. Gilbert, his teeth chattering, put out a trembling hand, and, as if he were in bed, pulled the blanket up to his chin. Berry hovered in concern.

'What do we do now?' asked Edwin.

Godric kneeled beside Gilbert, put his arms underneath him, and lifted him with no apparent effort.

'We move him.'

It was not a request or a suggestion; it was a plain statement of fact. Godric did not wait for confirmation.

'But what do we do with him?' said Edwin.

Godric, who was already on his way back, stopped and turned. 'Do you wish to kill him?'

The question, though simple, was unnervingly direct.

'No!' said Edwin, shocked.

It was as well that Edwin could not see what an odd figure he looked, loaded with his own knife, two Norman weapons, and a couple of farm implements, each capable of killing a prostrate enemy. The faintest of smiles crossed Godric's swarthy face.

'Do you wish to leave him then? The dew and the night will kill him.'

'No ... No.'

He shrugged, and followed Godric. He could not bring himself to take a life like that, nor did he want it on his conscience to be the wilful cause of the man's death through neglect. Edwin had seen Normans before; they were invaders, and they were the enemy, but they were not devils in human shape. He had lived among them once for several months; he knew that they were ordinary like everyone else. This young man was about his own age too.

Conscience or no conscience, it would be foolish to leave a dead Norman lying about for an armed patrol to find. If they killed and buried him, it would not be difficult for a determined search party to find the grave, and that would be even worse. There were many stories already about Duke William and his wastings and burnings; they had floated across the Channel on breezes of gossip and rumour for nearly twenty years, and now they were swirling round Sussex like autumn leaves in a gale. It was stupid to provoke a situation in which they could find out how true these stories were.

Besides, even if they concealed both the killing and the body, there was the question of the horse.

Edwin stopped dead.

The horse!

He dashed back and untethered it. He stuffed the Norman's knife in his belt on one side, the sword on the other, grasped the club and the pitchfork in his left hand, and took the reins in his right. After a last nervous glance towards the woods, he turned once again to follow Godric, who was now well on his way towards the mill and Rowena.

Ralph reached out for the jug, looked into its depths, sniffed as if he had been crying, and lifted the rim to his lips.

'Spare a spot of that, lads, for two thirsty warriors?'

Ralph and Bruno looked up.

Two travel-stained, unkempt soldiers edged into the firelight. Behind them lurked the shadows of two horses and a groom. Leatherwork was blackened and frayed. Faces and hands were grey with dirt. Dried vomit clung to the front of their hauberks. They smelled to high Heaven.

Ralph burped. 'Who are you?'

'William Capra, knight of honour, fresh from our lovely Normandy. And whom have I the honour of addressing?'

The bow was a mixture of humour and insolence. The eyes had taken in the whole scene. The elaborate question was a way of throwing Ralph's drunkenness in his face.

Ralph's voice went quiet. 'Ralph of Gisors. This is Bruno of Aix.'

'Scouts,' said Bruno, as if the word had been forced out of him.

William Capra laughed and turned to his companion. 'You hear that, brother? The same name as yours.' He turned back. 'Then we are truly comrades in arms. May I present my brother

Ralph Pomeroy.' He bowed even lower. 'Two knights come to win a kingdom for the Bastard.'

Ralph's nose puckered. Dirty, sly, shifty, crude – the very worst type of riff-raff that was still drifting into the army at the last minute, hoping to snatch the profits without having had to work for them. No honour, no manners, no breeding – common as the dirt on their faces. And likely to run at the first onset. Fit only for wasting and pillage. Just right for Fulk and his Flemings.

Ralph pointed. 'Go down that way, then turn right at the end. Past a line of privies. You will see two or three large wagons. Report to Fulk the Angevin, or his sergeant, Florens.'

William Capra reacted at the name Florens. 'Flemings?'

'Yes.'

'They are infantry.'

'They are scum,' said Bruno, bent over his knife with a whetstone.

Capra glared, and his hand moved towards the hilt of his dagger. Bruno held up his knife and pretended to examine the point. Ralph laid down his jug.

Capra thought better of it, and drew himself up in a parody of dignity.

'Come, brother. We know when we are not wanted. Men of honour never stay uninvited.'

They slouched off.

Bruno resumed sharpening.

Ralph picked up the jug again, and brooded into it. 'You have a down on him. Yes, you do. A down. Go on; admit it.'

Rowena took charge.

'Lay him here. Aud, some water.'

Aud glared, pouted, and finally flounced out carrying a bucket.

Rowena looked at Edwin and sighed. Edwin shrugged.

'Edwin, go and get those fresh sheepskins from the loft. You will find them put to air by the stack. It is time they came down for the winter anyway.'

As Edwin climbed the splinter-shot wooden ladder, he heard Rowena's voice soften as she spoke to Edith.

'Here, Dith. Come here, my pet. See? He can not harm you.'

Edith crept from the corner where she was hiding. Rowena took her hand and pulled her gently forward.

'See? He is like a baby. He is sick, and you must help us to make him well. You would like to do that? Help Rowena?'

Edith nodded, wide-eyed.

Rowena eased her forward another pace. 'He is just like your baby, like Mimma.'

Edith's eyes strayed to the corner where a toy cradle was propped. 'Mimma?'

Rowena patted Edith's shoulder. 'Edith bring a clean cloth? We are going to wash our new baby.'

Edith clapped her hands. 'Yes. Edis help. Edis help.'

Rowena hoped she had concealed the tremble in her hand as it lay on her sister's shoulder. She had sent Aud for water partly as a means of keeping her mind occupied. Aud had been torn between terror and morbid curiosity. Sweyn, after one glance of wide-eyed horror, had fled – no doubt to find his father.

Rowena knew that it depended upon her to damp down the fear. She was too shocked to feel angry at this danger that was suddenly thrust upon them. The only hope of coming out of it was to do what they were doing. She agreed with Godric: they had no other choice.

Thank God it was a solitary scout; it could have been a fully-armed wasting party. Stories were flying. A fine irony it would have been – to have all the men away to save them from the threat in the north, and to be devoured by men from the south.

Godric built up the fire. While Rowena prepared an extra tallow lamp, he set up a trestle table, and covered it with Gilbert's blanket. He laid the young Norman gently on it, and began to undress him.

Edwin returned with the sheepskins, and made up a bed as close to the fire as safety allowed. Aud came in with the full bucket, and tottered forwards with rapid, bird-like steps to show everyone how awkward it was. As the soldier's clothes were removed, she glanced guiltily at the white flesh of his body, which contrasted so strongly with the deep tan of his face and neck.

Edwin sensed Rowena's nerves, but could detect none in Godric. He watched the two of them at work. There were hardly any words. Not for the first time, he found himself admiring the stillness between them. If ever God made two people for each other, it was these two.

Edwin sighed. Was it not typical of God in His wilful way to give a glimpse of the most wondrous chances, and at the same time to deny their fulfilment? He had done it to Edwin two years before, and Edwin still felt the pain. He was doing it now to these two good people, who had led godly lives and never hurt a single soul.

Gorm had depended upon Rowena ever since his wife had died. It was Rowena who ran the household and tended the garden. It was Rowena who dealt with irate neighbours when her father was too idle or too drunk to operate the mill machinery. It was Rowena who tried to knock sense into her brother, Sweyn, when he was not telling tales to his father. It was Rowena who acted as a second mother to Edith and who alone tolerated her unpredictable moods. It was Rowena who sought to soften Aud's constant bitterness about not getting a husband. It was Rowena who unceasingly strove to keep the peace between her father's drunken rages, and Sweyn's spiteful teasings, and Edith's tears and furies, and Aud's shrewish outbursts.

There was never any question that Gorm would let his eldest daughter go in marriage, certainly not until Sweyn was grown up. Probably not then either; she was far too useful.

Meantime, Godric served him loyally and uncomplainingly, on the land, in the mill, around the house, in whatever duty Gorm chose to lay upon him, and there were many. If Rowena's character managed everything, Godric's strength carried everything. Gorm was equally unpleasant to them both, in the usual way in which weak people dislike those to whom their debt is greatest.

Godric picked up the stranger, laid him on the fresh soft sheepskins, and placed two more over him. He was still shaking from head to foot, but he had ceased moaning. The fever in his mind seemed to have gone. As the flames of the fire warmed his face, and the thickness of the sheepskins began to take effect, the trembling slowly died away, and he fell into a deep sleep. Berry came and lay right beside him, and watched with his chin on his paws and the firelight reflected in his eyes.

Edwin came and stood over the invalid. What was going to happen when this young soldier recovered? What would he do?

'How is Sawin?'

'Still nursing his blisters. How is your Edward?'

'Well, at least he has stopped using his stick.'

'God, these men! Think they are still eighteen years old.'

'We can thank the saints, Fleda, that they never reached the battlefield. Fancy – joining the levy. Just because the King crooks his little finger. And who is this man Hardrada, anyway? Where does he come from? Is he a Dane or something?'

'No idea. The King's problem, not ours. And certainly not Sawin's, not at his age.'

'Nor Edward's. Besides, a king is only a king. Harold or Hardrada – what is the difference? Kings are all the same.'

'Yes. Remember Cnut? Foreign, but not too bad. So my father used to say.'

'What happened anyway?'

'What do you mean – what happened?'

'At the battle.'

'God knows.'

Gorm was furious.

'Why was I not told? If it were not for Sweyn—'

Sweyn smirked beside his father.

Gorm swore. 'How is he to be fed? Who will pay for it? Suppose we catch some foul disease?'

'He is not ill like that, Father.'

'All right – when he recovers. What then? Suppose he gets up in the night and cuts our throats.'

He constantly wiped his palms on the thighs of his rough sacking breeches. He spoke in hoarse whispers, with frequent glances over his shoulder at the sleeping invalid. As he leaned forward on his stool, his heavy jowls glistened in the firelight. Sweaty fear rose from him like fumes from a midden.

'Have you heard the stories? I have three daughters. Do I have to spell it out?'

Aud surprised herself at the twinge of excitement that she felt.

Edwin sat silent. He was not of this household. If he spoke, Gorm would be within his rights to order him out. Godric, confident in Rowena, left the room.

'We could do nothing else, Father,' said Rowena. 'If we had left him, he would have died.'

'Good riddance.'

'The Normans would have found him, and they would decide it was our doing.'

'What if he dies now? They will think we killed him. They will not believe us.'

'He will not die. He has only a sickness of the stomach. Godric says in a day or so he will be better.'

Gorm spat. 'Godric! That ox. What does he know?'

'He knows.'

Gorm knew that he knew. Godric always knew. It only worsened Gorm's temper because it inflamed his fear. For the thousandth time he cursed his own good nature in taking on a bastard orphan because he owed a kinsman a favour. Where had the boy learned what he knew? Certainly not on their endless travels on the rutted roads of Anglia. All those plants. Always gazing into the fire. Never answering back. Never complaining. His eyes saw things beyond Gorm's wit and comfort. Gorm had often struck in fear and bafflement as much as in anger.

And now look what he had done. Gorm stood up and looked about him.

'God – I need a drink.'

Ralph tried to sleep, but saw again Michael's pale face, drawn and racked in fever, the eyes wide and baffled, pleading for help that would never come.

Ralph opened his eyes, and searched the dark sky for answers. Why did it torment him when he could least cope with it? He turned over and groped for the jug. There were a few dregs in the bottom. He fell back and wiped his lips.

What if Gilbert did look a bit like Michael? Coincidence – pure coincidence. Gilbert had the makings of a good scout – he really did. Tall, strong, keen, anxious to learn. It was unnerving sometimes to notice how intently the boy listened. God's Breath! It was rare enough these days to find somebody who was prepared to listen at all. Far too many thought they could learn it in a couple of weeks. And how long did they last? You could be good, and still get killed – if the odds were against you.

Like Aimery – patient, long-suffering Aimery, who put up

with a companion's moods and tempers with a shrug and a gri-
mace – 'very well, if you will have it so'.

Ralph made up his mind. He would teach Gilbert everything
he knew.

And in the morning? In the morning, know-all Bruno could
come with him or he could not come. Devil take him. He could
please himself.

Rowena made sure the soldier was comfortable and put Edith to
sleep. Edwin fed Berry, re-bound his leg, and curled up by the fire.
Rowena asked him to stay the night. Having Edwin in the house
was an added reassurance. Edwin readily agreed; he was curious
to find out why his dog seemed so attached to this young Norman.

Godric stabled the man's horse, and carefully hid the precious
hauberk and the weapons.

Rowena lay back in her corner behind a woollen curtain. She
could hear her sister hissing rapid prayers of mindless habit. She
pushed a lock of hair from her face, and put her hands behind
her head. She saw in her mind's eye Godric climbing the wooden
ladder to the loft and stretching out his massive limbs on the
straw mattress beside the chimney stack.

In the mill house, Gorm groped behind some sacks, pulled
out a dusty pot, and took a long draught. He wiped his lips and
cursed his bad luck.

It was his good nature once again which had induced him to
stop on his travels and get the mill machinery working properly.
The silly old fool of a miller was never going to manage it. There
was not much that Gorm Haraldsson could not make or mend
when he put his mind to it. He had even married the old man's
wan daughter for him. And what had she done? Died giving him
Sweyn, and leaving him with three daughters – one an empress,
one a shrew, and one an idiot. He had nobody to talk to. It was
not fair.

He sighed and had another swig. It would be up to him in the morning to see to it all. Man to man. A drink or two. Perhaps offer a daughter by way of good relations. Might do Aud a favour; she was desperate enough to find out.

That was all it needed – common sense and a bit of worldly wisdom. But they would not be grateful, not one of them.

'Such wealth ... adorns your bloody swords'

Ralph grappled with the fallen horse. Its eyes stared; it whinnied in fear; its legs flailed in frantic effort. Ralph tugged on the reins, and shouted in urgent entreaty. Suddenly one hoof caught him under the ribs.

He opened his eyes. Bruno was standing over him.

Ralph glared. 'What did you do that for?'

'It is time.' Bruno turned away to murmur to his horse.

'For what?' said Ralph, and winced as iron spikes went through his head.

'To go and look for him.'

Ralph struggled to his feet and looked to right and left. 'So he did not come back?'

'Have your piss and go and get some breakfast. I have told Sandor to have something ready.'

Bruno turned back to his horse.

Ralph sniffed. 'You talk more to Sorrel than you do to me.'

'Hurry. Do you want Fitz to find out what we are doing on our rest day?'

*

Gilbert thought it was raining when he woke up. Then he smelled dog. It had just come in from its morning run, and had shaken off the dew. Gilbert saw the fresh scar on the foreleg.

He made a noise that spoke reproach but meant affection. He put out a hand from under the sheepskins and ruffled the hair behind the dog's ears. He could not help himself. He forgot where he was. His father had always said he was too soft with dogs...

'But it might do you some good one day.'

'No,' said Gilbert. 'I shall be a soldier.' He easily topped his elder brother, the stolid Robert. 'I want none of your ploughs and your middens.'

His father gave him a ringing box on the ears. 'You shall do what you can do, and you will show respect. Wait for your chance.'

It came sooner than he expected. One day, Bishop Geoffrey of Coutances stopped by on his way to see his brother bishop at Avranches. Lord Geoffrey's pack of hounds was his pride and joy. Gilbert's father seized the moment. Before he could turn round, Gilbert was saying goodbye to his father and embracing his mother. Robert said nothing, and his sister Mahaut cried – but Mahaut always cried.

Gilbert travelled all over Normandy with Bishop Geoffrey. He kept his ears and eyes open, and never forgot his desire to become a soldier. He called himself 'Gilbert of Avranches', though he had visited the town only once in his life. What a piece of luck it was that—

A noise from the doorway made him tense. A young Saxon stood there, blowing on his hands, and stamping off the worst of the dew, just like the dog. Each sensed the fear in the other, and each tried to hide his own. The Saxon put up both palms as he came forward. His cheeks were flushed with the freshness and good humour that came from sharp exercise with a favoured companion. Fair stubble stood out brightly on his cheeks.

'You are – you are feeling better?'

Gilbert was surprised to hear French – and Norman French at that.

'I think so – yes.' He moved his head to indicate the whole building. 'Where . . . ?'

'You were sick. We found you. You would have died, Godric says.'

Gilbert's mind raced. Apples, pain, cascades of earth and badger droppings, blows on the head, the smell of vomit, grass blowing above his eyes, Adele's crucifix.

He ran his hands over his body under the covers, half expecting to find himself stripped or bound. He was not.

Without thinking, he stretched his legs and flexed his toes. He winced at the pain in his right ankle. He put his right hand down again and felt a bandage. He put his left hand to his head and found another.

The Saxon watched him. 'I did say you were sick.'

Gilbert lay back, and found himself savouring the warmth and softness of the sheepskins. He could not remember having had such a good sleep since landing in England. He heaved a great breath of wellbeing in spite of himself.

The Saxon crouched and began to revive the fire.

There was an awkward silence. The Saxon fiddled unnecessarily with a small log on the edge of the flames. At last he gestured towards Gilbert's head bandage.

'The pain – it is going?'

Gilbert felt again.

'Yes,' he said. And added, 'Thank you.'

'And your leg?'

Gilbert grimaced, and put up both his hands. He drew them apart to indicate swelling.

The Saxon grinned. Then, as if he had offered too much, he turned away and poked the fire again.

Gilbert pointed towards the dog. 'He is yours?'

The Saxon nodded, and put an arm round its neck. 'Yes. He is called Berry. He is a fine hunter – eh, boy?'

'Berry.' Gilbert made a pretty fair attempt at the Saxon pronunciation.

It made the Saxon grin again. 'He knows you,' he said.

'Yes. I tried to bind his leg.'

The Saxon was instantly interested. 'How was that?'

Gilbert explained, but was careful to leave out everything else.

Edwin had guessed most of it, however. There was not much else a solitary Norman soldier could be doing this far from the main camp, and he knew from Godric's search of his equipment that he was not carrying a message. There was a handful of Norman clerks left in England who could read one.

It had been one of the first things he had thought of. There were still those in England who would welcome the Normans. The saintly King Edward had not been liked because of his Norman leanings. A Norman mother, a Norman education, a Norman exile – small wonder he arrived in England with a crowd of Norman friends, friends whom he proceeded to promote and reward. It had taken Harold's father, Earl Godwin, nearly ten years to get rid of them, and Edward never forgave him for it.

Edwin had heard the tale many times. Harold, with a drink or two inside him, was a fine storyteller and a splendid companion. No wonder most Saxons were pleased now to call him King.

No wonder too that those Normans who lost their estates when they were expelled would want to get them back. Many of their tenants and retainers would be pleased to see them too – men who had pledged themselves to foreigners for quick reward and who now, in the absence of their protectors, suffered the vengeful spleen of lesser Saxon rivals. Oh, yes, thought Edwin, there would be those in Sussex and Kent who would welcome the Normans.

As he listened to the story, Edwin wondered how much this young scout knew. Did he know that the King had gone north? Did he know that the Viking host could strike in the north at any moment? Perhaps Hardrada had already landed. Did this scout know the size of the King's army and where it was? Did he know that the King had had perforce to send many men home for the harvest? That the fleet had been broken up in the Channel and sent to London? That the King had had to perform miracles of leadership to keep any army together at all through the long summer of waiting – did he know that? Edwin hoped not.

Edwin did not want England to become a Norman land, and he loved his King Harold, but, as he listened to the soldier's story and watched his animation in referring to the dog, he found it difficult to dislike him. He could not be far from his own age either.

The young Norman had stopped talking and was looking at him.

There was another stiff silence.

Gilbert gestured towards Berry. 'I too like dogs.'

Edwin blushed. 'Yes. Yes. Berry is a fine hunter.'

Gilbert pointed to himself. 'I too have worked with dogs – hunters like your Berry.' He still hesitated over the name.

'I also care for hunting dogs,' said Edwin. 'My lord is – my lord is away now.'

The Norman did not press him. Instead, he said, 'My name is Gilbert . . .' He could not resist adding, '. . . of Avranches'.

'I am Edwin son of Edward.'

Gilbert began to take his hand out from under the sheepskins. He caught sight of Edwin watching the movement, and stopped. Edwin had also thought of putting out his hand, but, seeing the Norman's hesitation, could not bring himself to complete the gesture.

Gilbert felt his cheeks go warm. He swallowed. 'How do you know French?' he asked at last.

'Many Normans had lands here once,' said Edwin. 'I was born on one of their estates.' He shrugged. 'In the master's house you learn to take orders, in any language.'

Which was true enough. Edwin took care not to mention that his Norman lord had been exiled, and that his new master was none other than Earl Harold himself, as he then was. Nor did he think it wise to let slip where else he had learned even more French.

He dusted his hands self-consciously, and stood up.

'I shall see about some food,' he said. 'Then we shall look at your bandages.'

Berry followed him out.

'What about our money?'

Florens of Arras tipped up his mug to catch the last of the hot soup. He wiped his lips with his hand.

'Would you rather drink silver pieces for breakfast? Do you know what the others have to make do with?'

'The others can eat and drink what they like. Fulk made a contract with the Duke. One third a week after landing. The rest after the battle. That was what he said.'

Several other Flemings growled in surly agreement.

'It is now ten days,' said the spokesman. 'And no money. We want it.'

Florens tossed his mug towards the cook, who caught it expertly.

'Then it is Fulk you need to speak to, not me. It was not I who drew up the contract. I am not a writing man.'

The spokesman hesitated.

Florens sneered. 'Scared to speak to your own commanding officer?'

'No. It is just that—'

Florens poked him in the chest. 'A man who loads his pockets down with silver before the battle runs the risk of not surviving it. He can not move quickly enough. I for one prefer to wait.' He waved towards their cook's wagon. 'You are the best fed and the best equipped troops in the whole army. What more do you want?'

'What is ours.'

Florens threw his head to the sky in disgust.

'I can get that money, lads,' said a voice.

Florens turned round. The men parted in front of him to reveal the owner of the voice.

Recognition came. It was the newcomer of the previous evening. Florens looked him up and down, his expression one of deepening contempt.

'Oh, you can?'

The newcomer bowed elaborately. 'William Capra at your service, gentlemen.' He stood up again, and surveyed the curious faces round him. 'But there is, of course, a charge.'

He had everybody's attention now. Including his brother's.

He pointed at Florens. 'Your gallant sergeant told me last night that I could expect no payment until after the battle. Arrived too late, you see. Now, I happen to think that is very unfair. Here I am – and my brave brother – ready and willing to do our bit towards the army's effort. Was it our fault that storms held us up in Normandy, when we wanted nothing more than to come here and share your hardships?'

'Get to the point,' said the spokesman, trying to regain the initiative.

Capra flashed a challenging glance at him. 'Very well. Here it is. I can negotiate with your Fulk for you; he is an Angevin, I am a Norman. We have the bond of the French language – and of our knightly birth.'

He placed a grubby hand across his chest in a charade of nobility. Florens grunted.

'I wish to give no offence, gentlemen,' continued Capra smoothly, 'but perhaps there is a slight language problem here.

You know – the faintest shade of meaning lost in speaking a foreign tongue? With the best will in the world?'

'What is the deal?' said the spokesman.

Capra sprang the trap. 'I get your money. And you give me a full share of the first third payment.'

There was a buzz of furtive discussion.

The spokesman spoke too soon. 'I do not accept.'

'Well, we do,' said somebody else.

The spokesman cursed and stumped off.

Capra bowed again. 'And the same for my brother.'

The men hesitated. Florens smiled to himself; this scruffy newcomer had the cheek of the Devil.

'I should accept,' he said out loud. 'It will be worth it for the entertainment alone. And you will be no worse off.' He looked at Capra. 'You have your chance now. Here he comes.'

Two minutes later, William Capra was on his hands and knees, wiping away blood that was pouring from his nose. Nearly everybody was laughing at him.

Fulk pulled on his gloves. 'You want money, my beauties? I shall give you money today, and more. I have just come from my lord Fitzosbern. Do you know what he said to me? He said –' Fulk furrowed his brow in mimicry of Fitzosbern '– "Now, listen – er – I want you to go out as far as – er – and I want you to – er – and – er – as far as – er – and come back by way of – um" –' Fulk put on a veritable caricature of a struggle to recall.

The men roarcd with laughter.

Fulk waited until the moment was exactly right. 'But he did not tell me what we could not do. And you know what that means.'

He waited for the ribald comments to die down. 'So – today, my lads – we enjoy ourselves. No more camp fatigues. We draw horses from the reserve pool; no walking for my Flemings. If Fitz wants a lot of damage done, we must have time to do it. I told him that. And we must have energy for – er – I told him that too.'

More vulgar guffaws. Eyes met each other furtively; grins were exchanged. Fulk was a character; you had to give him that.

'And who knows?' continued Fulk. 'Perhaps a nice fat column of refugees on our way back. A bag of silver under a nun's habit? Which would you grab first, eh?'

Back came the regular answer: 'Either – they both get you into the habit.'

There were more hoots of delight. Florens, also timing the moment precisely, clapped his hands.

'Right then. Hup! Hup! Hup! Let us be moving. Draw your rations. Column of twos. Lively now.'

Fulk turned back to William Capra, who was about to lever himself to his feet. A huge kick sent him sprawling into the embers of the cook's fire.

As he lay there, spitting ashes, Fulk bent down beside him and put his scarred face close to an ear. 'You have just learned rule number one,' he said.

Capra tried to retrieve a scrap of dignity. 'And what is rule number two?'

'To remember that there is only one rule. Now get on your feet, and show me what you can do. Bring your scarecrow of a brother with you. I may need him to shoo away the birds from our handiwork today.'

As he stalked away, Fulk passed close to Florens. 'I take it you did not tell them?' he said quietly.

'Not a word. It is in the usual place.'

Fulk glanced in the direction of the cook, who nodded back.

Gilbert lay back and looked about him. This was no ordinary villein's hut; the presence of a stone chimney told him that. And the iron utensils; many households had to make do with wood. Nor was it a lord's house; the furniture was too rough. He heard the sound of running water, regular slapping noises, and the creak of machinery. Of course – the mill! Holy Blood! Was it only yesterday?

Suddenly he saw a tall, fair young woman framed in the doorway. How long had she been watching him?

She came forward and put a simple meal beside him. Gilbert felt a thrill of recognition; he would know that queenly walk anywhere. As she crouched, he was close enough to savour the scent of womanhood for the first time since leaving Adele. She made a gesture for him to eat, turned her eyes away, stood up, and went about her work.

One by one, the other members of the household came in – the stringy, whining woman, the idiot girl, and the boy. Then the swarthy giant. They went about their daily routine. Gilbert could not understand a word they said to each other, but he learned from the weary authority of the tall fair woman, the complaints of the thin one, the moon face of the youngest girl, the pouts of the boy, and the towering presence of the giant. A whole foreign world opened to him, like a morning flower in the summer sun.

Foreign it may have been, but not strange. As the household became absorbed in their work, they cast fewer glances at him, almost forgot him. To his amazement, he began to feel that he belonged.

That could be his father's scythe in the rack. Those baskets of apples and nets of onions hanging from the beams could have been put there by his mother. Saxon households, it seemed, also had one chicken more daring than the others, which ventured further from the doorway across the earthen floor in order to locate more choice scraps in the cleaner rushes. The scanty, rough furniture, the general clutter, even the smells, took him back ten years as if in a wizard's spell.

One of his father's neighbours had a spoilt son like this one. Another had an idiot daughter. The dark shrill young woman reminded him of an aunt who dragged out a tight, lonely spinster's life in the kitchen of his father's lord.

The big man and the fair woman filled the room with their mere presence, but Gilbert could not fathom their relationship. He was struck with the odd thought that if they were not man and wife, then they ought to be.

His comfortable musings were broken when Edwin returned.

'We will see your leg,' he said.

The big man came and crouched beside him

'This is Godric,' said Edwin. 'He will see your ankle.'

Godric gave Gilbert the slightest of nods. Gilbert was surprised. He had naturally thought that the fair one had tended to him. He felt almost disappointed. When Godric touched him, he received another surprise; he had no idea that such strong hands could be so gentle. He watched, fascinated, as if the leg did not belong to him.

When Godric had finished, he looked up and nodded in question towards Gilbert's forehead.

Gilbert touched the bandage 'No, no. It is well. Tell him it is all right,' he said to Edwin.

A few words of English passed. Edwin turned back to Gilbert.

'He thinks you should rest longer. Your ankle is still –' he spread his hands apart as Gilbert had done earlier '– big, and your stomach is still weak.'

Conscience returned in a rush.

'I must return. I have—' He checked himself, and there was a guilty silence.

Godric whispered to Edwin. Edwin turned to Gilbert.

'Godric says you must rest or you will be sick again. He says if you leave after midday you can still reach your camp by sunset.'

This was terrible. Gilbert struggled to a sitting position. 'I am recovering,' he said. 'Look.'

He held up the half-empty wooden plate, and, as if to prove his claim, picked up some dark bread and crammed a large lump into his mouth. Still with his **mouth** full, he clambered to his feet. The sudden effort made him sway; he moved quickly to adjust his balance, and winced at the pain in the ankle. By the time Godric had caught him and eased him down again, he felt sick once more. He made no resistance as they covered him, made up the fire, and took away the rest of the meal.

'It looks as if he went up there.'

Ralph reined in his horse beside a sandy little brook and pointed up the hill. Open scrubland stretched all the way to the top, where they could just make out the silhouette of a solitary stunted tree.

For most of the morning they had followed their own trail of the previous afternoon, and then Gilbert's trail when he left them. That had taken them to the settlement they had first seen. Pursuing it after that, they had now found themselves at the foot of this gently-sloping hill.

Ralph was in a savage mood. His head was still aching. He was annoyed that they had to be out at all, when he knew that they should be resting before their long sweep of the next day – the one that Fitzosbern wanted them to make. He hated being unprofessional. He knew too exactly what Bruno was thinking.

He was even more annoyed with Gilbert. Why had the boy continued beyond that settlement? He was only supposed to have a quick look, then come back. What had made him change his mind? The chance of heroics? Pray God not.

Damn Gilbert! And damn all English beer! If Bruno dared to open his mouth . . .

Ralph looked up the slope. He could be up there. The tree on its ridge was gaunt, twisted . . .

'Well?' said Bruno, nodding uphill.

Ralph pointed to the western end, where it sloped down towards a grassy knoll at the foot. 'Let us look round there first.'

'Why?'

'Because I say so!'

He spurred his horse forward, without waiting to see if Bruno was following.

When he reached where he was going, he circled several times, gazing at the ground. After a few minutes he came upon a fresh set of hoofprints. They came down from the top of the hill, and went away north-westwards, in the opposite direction from camp. It was unquestionably Gilbert's horse; the smith at Rouen had his own unmistakable mark on the shoes.

Ralph was incredulous. 'Why do that?'

Bruno shrugged. 'You are the expert on novice scouts, not me.'

Ralph could have hit him.

'At least he is alive,' said Bruno, reading his mind.

Ralph cast one more glance at the top of the hill, and pulled his horse's head round to face west again. 'Come then.' Once again, he did not wait for Bruno to agree.

The trail was clearer now, and Ralph was so absorbed that he neglected to take regular precautions. It was Bruno who called a warning.

They burst out of the side track on to the main one, and nearly ran into a small column of refugees, who stood rooted to the ground in terror.

A carter was poised with his whip in mid-air; a monk trembled beside the oxen, both his chins sagging loose. Women clutched the heads of their children to their stomachs. Two or three old men rested on their staffs, glad of any rest, whatever the cause. After a moment, a sweating priest tottered forward, fumbling at his waist for his crucifix on its chain. He fell on his knees, and held up the cross in dumb, hopeless entreaty, his head bowed, his eyes tight shut at the impending blow.

*

Carpenters and their boys paused on the scaffolding to watch Ranulf of Dreux limping round the stacks of freshly piled timber. Any excuse to take a break from the work; the Bastard wanted the impossible – a castle up in days, not weeks.

Ranulf put out a hand and touched a plank as if it were leprous. His mouth was turned down at the corners.

'Is this the best you can do?'

Baldwin threw up his hands. 'God's Eyes, man! What more do you want? Some of this stuff has been seasoning for months. What do you think you are building – St Peter's?'

Ranulf looked bleakly at him, and coughed wheezily. 'I am about to construct a hall for my lord the Duke of Normandy. I am used to working with the best materials.' He waved a hand to the timber behind him. 'I suppose you realise I shall have to reject some of this; I am not sure there will be enough left.'

Baldwin looked at Sir Walter Giffard and raised his eyes Heavenward. He turned back to Ranulf. 'You miserable cripple, there are three full shiploads there. If you were to burn half of it, you would still have enough left for two halls.'

'There are always more walls and palisades; the Duke is never satisfied.'

'And neither are you, you gloomy fraud.' Baldwin waved an arm to indicate the country about them. 'You have enough forest out there to build a whole town. I have had fatigue parties lopping trees for a week. You could build walls and palisades from here to London. To London.'

Ranulf shook his head. 'Ah. Well . . . That may be . . . All that planing . . . insufficient tools . . . and the Duke is in such a hurry.'

Baldwin prodded him in the chest. 'Now you just get on with what I have brought you – at great trouble and expense, may I say. Let us have a hall to be proud of. Proud of.'

Ranulf of Dreux made a great show of easing his bad leg into a more comfortable stance. Sir Walter Giffard smiled to himself; it had never occurred to Ranulf, in years of service, that his

masters and his colleagues had long since seen through his sub-
terfuges.

'My lord Baldwin, I have enough trouble attending to my own
duties; I do not presume to advise you on the allocation of your
accumulated food supplies. I should be grateful if you would
accord me the same courtesy.'

Coming from any other person, it would have provoked an
outburst of rage. Coming from Ranulf, it usually produced little
more than silent amusement. If the Duke was prepared to tolerate it, so was everybody else.

Baldwin pretended to lose patience. 'Come, Walter. Let us
leave this prophet of doom to his private catastrophes.'

They left Ranulf to his long face.

Giffard grunted in disgust. 'Ranulf thinks *he* is hard done by.
Come and see what the ships have brought *me*.'

They threaded their way past the Angevin contingent's tents
and the archers' lines, past smiths and armourers, to the central
pool of spare horses, where unwilling carpenters were knocking
together hasty stalls to accommodate the new arrivals.

Baldwin had no more than a sound working knowledge of
horses, but he could appreciate that they were of poor stock.

'I see what you mean,' he said.

Giffard spat. 'Offal. Four-legged offal. Fit only for wasting parties and light haulage. I let some of them out to the Flemings
today; they are too ignorant to know any better. Just look at
them, Baldwin! It is a wonder they survived the crossing. They
are no use for any kind of action at all. Show them a fully armed
knight, and they would break in the middle.'

'What about the fresh knights who came in yesterday?'

Giffard spat again. 'Human offal! And their mounts are not
much better. I tell you, Baldwin, this battle had better be over
quickly, or I shall never be able to provide enough spare mounts
to last.'

Baldwin grinned. 'Losing your profits, Walter?'

He knew, and Giffard knew, that every respectable knight in the army provided himself with at least two, sometimes three battle destriers, to say nothing of spare mounts for the approach march and the withdrawal to camp afterwards. What was annoying Sir Walter Giffard was that he might not have enough mounts of suitable quality to sell to knights who had accidents or casualties among their stables.

Giffard growled. 'I am expecting some proper mounts from Longueville. The very last I can manage.'

Sir Walter Giffard made a habit of protesting that the horses he trained and offered were always the last, the very last, that he would be able to provide without impoverishing himself, or exhausting his breeding stock. Buyers made a similar habit of reminding him that the prices he charged should help him to avoid total ruin.

Giffard nodded in the direction of the shore. 'I have sent the little Magyar down to meet the next tide.' He made a noise of annoyance in his throat. 'Another know-all like your precious engineer.'

'Not my fault. William hired him. All the way from Sicily. From Sicily.'

'Well,' said Giffard, 'he does know his business. I give him that.'

'So does Ranulf. William would not keep either of them a minute if they did not.'

Baldwin was one of the very few men in the army who referred to the Duke, not as 'the Bastard', but as 'William'. Giffard had never got right to the bottom of the story, but he knew it had something to do with some oath or other that the three of them had sworn as boys – William, Fitzosbern and Baldwin – after the murder of Baldwin's and Fitz's fathers. Three orphans – all about twelve or thirteen years old – in a hostile world – it was scarcely surprising. What was surprising was that they had all three survived and prospered. Fitz was the Bastard's right hand, his other self; it was uncanny they way they reflected each other's thoughts in their speech. Baldwin's skills lay in another direction. He was dull and stuffy, but he was also deliberate, and thorough. The perfect quartermaster.

Oddly, too, there was a bond between Baldwin and the lady Matilda, and Giffard had not really got to the bottom of that either. It was common knowledge that, after the murder, Baldwin had taken refuge in Flanders, at the court of Count Baldwin (a lucky coincidence of names perhaps), and Matilda was the Count's daughter. They were young then – Matilda was barely out of the nursery.

But they had become genuine friends. She teased him – 'Baldwin, why are you so old?' – but it was obvious that she liked him, and he clearly enjoyed her company.

Giffard shrugged. It was none of his business. The Bastard did not seem to mind, so there was nothing in it. Heaven help the man he so much as suspected of making advances to my lady Matilda.

They were walking back towards their tents now. Baldwin blew on his hands.

'I shall be glad to stand by a fire for a while. Will you come in and take something?'

Giffard grinned. Baldwin's perpetual complaints about the cold were a camp joke, but he was free with his hospitality, and the fire could be relied upon to be a big one. Moreover, as quartermaster, he usually had good fare to offer.

'Thank you. I will.'

They stood for a while, holding out their hands to the blaze. Then they went inside. Baldwin poured the drinks.

'Where do you think they are?' said Baldwin after a while.

Giffard looked up. 'The English? Search me. They have to be on their way somewhere. Not to know we are here – it is inconceivable.'

'They could have been drawn the other way.'

'Norway, you mean?'

'Yes.'

'Then surely we should have heard something by now. News like that would travel on the wind. Hardrada and the northern host move, and nobody knows? Impossible.'

Baldwin tossed away the dregs of his drink. 'At least it gives us more time.'

'We do not need time,' said Giffard. 'We need action.'

'You need an enemy for that. An enemy.'

Giffard pointed to the north. 'I tell you, Baldwin, if we do not soon find an enemy out there, we shall start finding enemies for ourselves, among our own number. How long do you think the Bastard can hold them? We only keep those damned Flemings out of trouble by sending them out to cause trouble elsewhere. If it were up to me, I should not have any infantry here at all.'

'They are a vital part of William's plan,' said Baldwin. 'And their commanders have a good reputation.'

Giffard made a face. 'Fulk has a good record, I grant you, but who trusts mercenaries?'

'Alan of Brittany, then.'

'A mountain man. And who trusts them? They are all the same – Auvergnais, Swiss, Pyreneans. I have been in Spain too, in the sierras. I have seen them in action. Wild, undisciplined. One against one, in a tavern brawl, they are unmatchable. Shoulder to shoulder, in line of battle, they will be like kindling in that fire of yours – loud and brittle, and soon gone.' Giffard leaned forward to stress his point. 'These are the troops that the Bastard plans to use in his first assault. The first, vital assault. If they run, it could panic the whole army.'

'Fitz seems to think it is a good idea.'

Giffard leaned back again. 'Fitz plans everything like a game of chess. Too clever by half. You can plan too much.'

'Geoffrey approves too.'

Giffard waved the cup in the air. 'Ah! Geoffrey and his precious straight lines. Waste of time.'

Baldwin laughed. 'So it always comes down to this: Sir Walter Giffard is right and everybody else is wrong.'

Giffard rose to the challenge. 'No! Experience and tradition are right – not me. Common sense. Realism. The verdict of the last fifty years. Baldwin, there is no substitute for the heavily armed, properly trained, professional knight. Throw enough of those at the enemy and no line can stand against them. Least of all infantry – which is all the English have.'

'Suppose we do not succeed at the first assault?'

'Then we regroup and try again.'

'That is all Geoffrey is trying to perfect.'

Giffard snorted. 'Geoffrey wants us to do it to order, to trumpets. In perfect lines. Great God, Baldwin! This is a battlefield, not a dancing floor. What is everyone afraid of? That they will chase us – on foot? And where does it leave a man's honour? What use does it make of individual talent?'

Baldwin shrugged. 'It is what William wants. What he wants.'

Giffard handed the cup to a servant, one of many who were creeping closer to snatch valuable pieces of military gossip.

'It may be what he wants, but it will not be what he gets. Oh, yes – Roger and I, and Montfort, and young Beaumont, and all the rest – we shall try, but it will not work. You wait. Once the first proper charge is loosed, it will be up to the likes of Roger and me, and the knights we lead. It will be up to our strength and our judgement. Geoffrey's trumpets might as well be on the moon.'

Gilbert fumed at his own weakness.

He had to return, but it would be no use starting in this condition; the important thing was to reach camp, not merely to set out. If he fell off his horse again, he could not count on another Berry to find him or another Godric to minister to him.

As he fretted, the nausea grew worse, and he knew he was going to bring up his morning meal. He got up and crawled on his hands and knees to the door. He was barely two paces beyond the threshold before he vomited. Helpless and miserable, he wiped his dripping chin, and suddenly jumped.

Not ten paces away stood a fat man well struck in years. From his still, watchful stance, he too had only just caught sight of Gilbert. He had paused in the act of wiping some grease off his hands. His eyes seemed to go small. Fear covered and froze him like hoar frost.

Without moving, the fat man called Godric and Edwin. The voice was loud and harsh, but there was no confidence in it. When they appeared, he simply pointed.

Godric practically carried Gilbert back indoors, and put him under the covers again. Edwin placed a large wooden bowl beside him. Gilbert waved it away. He did not expect to be sick again; he felt too weak and empty. Godric nodded to Edwin, who left it anyway.

'That was Gorm,' said Edwin, in answer to the question in Gilbert's eyes when Gorm was gone. 'He is the miller. This is his house. Godric is his man.'

'And you?'

'I am not of this house.'

Gilbert lay back; he did not have the strength to pursue his questions. He had to rest. Perhaps later in the day.

When he woke, he felt better. He sat up and waited for the sickness to return. It did not. He crawled warily to a stool and sat on it. Still no sickness.

When Edwin and Godric returned, he told them he had to return. Godric demurred and Gilbert insisted. At last he agreed to wait until the afternoon sun dropped low.

'Your horse will be ready,' said Edwin.

The horse! Gilbert realised he owed them another debt.

While he waited he sat and talked to Edwin. Now that a term had been set to his waiting, the time passed more quickly. Now that each knew that the awkwardness would soon come to an end, each felt a twinge of regret; each tried to pack in as many words as possible.

The talk was of dogs, and great chases, and dangerous moments. Many times they found themselves laughing together. While they talked, Gilbert had idly picked up a small, knotted piece of wood. With a kitchen knife, he began carving a crude head and face. When the blade proved too blunt, Edwin lent him his own.

'Your weapons will be ready too,' he said.

Gilbert blushed as he nodded. A third debt.

When the moment arrived, they all came into the house – all except Gorm, who was nowhere to be seen. Gilbert tightened his leggings and pulled on his boots. The swelling was much less. Godric brought his sword and dagger. He used the scabbard as a prop to get him to the door.

The others fell silent. They had not seen him standing upright before. The sick stranger had become a Norman soldier again.

Gilbert felt more sure of himself, but sad that a curtain had come between them.

The fat boy hovered in the background. Of the three girls, only one met his eye. Again he thought her bearing was royal.

He bowed slightly to her and said, 'I am obliged to you.' It seemed ridiculously inadequate.

She nodded.

Gilbert turned to Edwin. 'Tell her what I said.'

'She knows,' said Edwin.

Gilbert turned to Edith. He pulled the piece of wood from his belt; he had fashioned it into a rough doll's head and body. He stooped and held it out to her. She cowered back behind Rowena's skirt and looked at him wide-eyed. Gilbert offered it again. She still stared at him.

Gilbert was about to withdraw, when he heard Godric say something. Slowly, Edith's hand came out and closed over the doll. She clasped it to her chest without taking her eyes off him.

Satisfied, Gilbert stood up and looked at Godric. He could read little in the still, dark face. Before he could think of anything to say, Godric turned and walked away.

Gilbert held out his hand to Edwin. Edwin took it firmly. Once again, Gilbert felt sad that no words came. Edwin shifted awkwardly.

'I will get your horse,' he said. Gilbert followed him out of the house.

When he brought it, Gilbert could see that it had been thoroughly groomed.

'That was for Berry,' said Edwin.

The rest had followed outside. They stood around as if they were expecting him to say something. Gilbert looked from one to another and swallowed. Red with embarrassment, he turned to his horse.

'One more thing.'

Godric had returned, and was carrying a bundle.

Dear God! The hauberk! Gilbert felt almost sick again with the shock. To forget his own bedroll was bad enough. But the hauberk! The greatest gift Ralph had given him. And Ralph or no Ralph, for a soldier to forget his hauberk ... If he had been told that around the campfire, he would have laughed like anybody else.

And what had he been doing? Trying to think of something to say by way of farewell to a family of Saxon peasants.

Sweating with shame, he pulled the hauberk over his head, and readjusted his belt and weapons. He fixed the helmet and bedroll behind the saddle.

His cheeks still burned as he struggled to mount with his bad ankle.

Suddenly he heard a gate being opened and slammed. Then hurrying footsteps.

'Listen! Listen! Something has happened. Something big, I swear. In the north.'

Gorm came round the corner, and stopped abruptly.

He gaped at Gilbert, his eyes dwindling in fear again. Sweat burst out on his face.

The silence became loud.

'What does he say?' said Gilbert.

There was another pause.

'Nothing,' said Edwin.

'He has news,' said Gilbert.

'It is nothing,' repeated Edwin. 'He is drunk again, that is all. He has been drinking and gossiping.'

He looked Gilbert in the eye.

Gilbert stared at Edwin, then at Gorm, then at the others, who moved more closely together. Gorm rubbed his palms down his sides.

Gilbert swallowed. 'He did not sound drunk.'

Edwin spoke flatly again. 'Nevertheless, he is drunk. He is often drunk. Ask Rowena.'

At the sound of her name, Rowena tilted her head back an inch, but enough to make it a challenge.

In the stillness, Gilbert could hear the rasping of Gorm's breath. He saw that Godric had picked up a pitchfork, and was leaning on it with his hands cupped over the top of the handle.

Think of something. Think of something! One of Ralph's remarks came to his rescue. 'When you have gathered important information, your duty is to get back with it quickly.' This was his escape.

After another undignified scramble with his bad ankle, he mounted and rode away without another word.

As he rode, he began to gather some lost confidence.

Very well – so he had made a bad start. So he had allowed himself to fall ill. So he had been distracted by a lame dog. So he had consorted with the enemy, spent a night under a Saxon roof, dreamed of his father and mother, been moved by the smell of a Saxon woman, carved a doll for a simpleton. So he had turned away from his quest; neglected the memory of Adele and baby Hugh – all right. All right!

But he had news. Something that Ralph did not. And he was going to share it with nobody. He was going to report it direct to Sir Baldwin. Maybe even Fitzosbern. Then let Ralph find fault with that, and let Bruno wag his long head.

Beams collapsed in showers of sparks.

William Capra raised his voice above the crackling and roaring. 'Do you think that will prise some silver out of him?'

Florens mounted his rangy horse. 'You will find that Fulk pays for work well done.'

Capra waved a hand behind him. 'Is that not well done?'

Florens cast a glance about himself from the saddle.

It was indeed well done. Not a body so much as twitched. He looked at Capra wiping his blade and smirking at brother Pomeroy. Did they have to enjoy it quite so much? Would they be so full of savage humour when they were called upon to do some proper soldiering? Could they not see that this was filthy work – more demeaning than mucking out horses? That the Duke was merely rubbing their noses in their contract?

Florens could not bring himself to agree with the barbarian at his stirrup leering up at him. Instead he pointed towards an unburnt wagon half hidden in a small grove.

'You have missed something.'

Capra looked round in genuine curiosity. 'Oh? Where?'

Following the direction of Florens' arm, he marched swiftly towards it, and began ransacking it, his jaw tight with greed. His brother followed close behind. They kicked aside two bodies in bloodstained black habits.

Torn clothes, bundles of kindling, sacks of apples were pulled out and dumped on the ground. Teeth set, eyes glittering, they delved deeper, breaking fingernails on the lids of boxes buried at the bottom.

Furious at what they found, they hurled books to right and left, and roared with delight as they pounced on two pewter candlesticks inlaid with coloured stones.

They rushed to gather torches of burning sticks from the collapsing ruins of the houses. Capra stuffed the clothing into small bundles against the wheels, and Pomeroy followed him, setting light to them. As they stepped back to survey their handiwork, they trampled on open, sprawling volumes, grinding them into the mud. They twisted their necks to see what was under their feet, bent down, and began tearing leaves out to feed into the fire.

'Stop!'

They turned in surprise.

'Stay exactly where you are. Do not move.'

Fulk walked slowly towards them. As he came closer, he lowered his voice. 'I said do not move – not a muscle.'

In only a few hours, they had come to understand that the more quietly Fulk spoke, the more he was to be feared. Pomeroy had a great weal under his left eye to remind him.

Fulk stooped and retrieved something from the mud. It was a broken-backed book. He picked it up as gently as if he were a nurse with a baby.

'At least I am in time to save this.'

Capra raised his voice in disbelief. 'But, Fulk, it is only a book.' He gestured with a crumpled fistful of parchment.

Fulk looked up from the page he was studying, his fingers spread across the lines of regular ink beneath the gorgeous illustrated initial.

'Your ignorance is surpassed only by your invincible vulgarity and your crass stupidity.'

Capra looked uneasily at his brother, and back at Fulk.

'There is nothing valuable in the wagon, Fulk. I checked. Only these. I was going to give them to you. Just look at that. Genuine. Look at the cut of the jewels.' He held out the two candlesticks.

Fulk glanced at them, and spat. 'If your taste is for coloured glass, I can not redeem you. But your disrespect for the written word will cost you your first day's pay. Let us see if that helps you to remember next time.'

Pomeroy stared. Capra almost hurled the candlesticks into the flames in his rage.

When Fulk was out of earshot, they complained to Florens. 'How were we to know he was a philosopher?'

Florens laughed. 'You were not. But you have learned something else of value.'

'What is that?'

'Fulk has a better eye for a bargain than you.'

Gilbert was pleased that he saw Ralph and Bruno before they saw him. They were bending over something on the ground. As he drew closer, he could see the signs of tragedy. Ralph looked up at the noise of his approaching horse.

'God's Breath, where have you been?'

Gilbert thought furiously. 'I – I had an accident.'

Ralph glanced at the bandage on his head. 'What do you mean – accident? Were you ambushed?'

'No. I mean yes. That is, a kind of ambush. I thought it was an ambush. I fell.' He put up a hand to his head. 'But it was not serious.'

'Serious enough to keep you out for a full day. Yet your horse looks in remarkably good order.'

'I had the flux as well. I could not travel.'

Ralph looked totally unconvinced. Bruno's face was a study in disbelief.

Gilbert began to sweat. 'Ralph, I could not even stand, never mind ride. What with that, and my head—'

Ralph gestured to the countryside around them. 'And you camped out here – alone?'

Gilbert clutched at a straw of dignity. 'It is not the first time.'

By now he had gained a better view of the horror around them.

'God – what is this?'

It was so awful that it drove all other thoughts from both their heads.

The first body was sprawled right across the track. The smock was caked with dried blood from huge gashes in the back. The tonsure was just visible around the split skull. Gilbert's jaw set hard. To kill a priest. What chance did a weak old man have, running from killers on horseback? And why crush his head with a mace when he was within a groan of death? Somebody had to dismount to do that.

Ralph came to stand beside him. 'Refugees. We saw them earlier. While we were looking for you.'

Gilbert was by now in such shock that he ignored the shaft.

The wagon was on its side, its contents strewn all around. The oxen struggled weakly in the broken yoke, their hamstrings slashed.

Gilbert rode about, his face ashen. One young woman, half naked, was spitted with a spear against the fallen wagon. The blood on her thighs showed that death was not the only horror she had endured. One child lay nearby, its sightless eyes turned away from its groping mother. Another was stretched, disembowelled, at the edge of the trees. An old crone lay with the arm she had raised in futile suppliance still fixed in the rigor of death.

If only they had been dispatched with a single skilful blow and laid out neatly, it would not somehow have been so bad. It was the wantonness, the obvious enjoyment of slaughter, that sickened him. It was unnatural, and it was so un-private, this gazing upon Christian souls frozen in the moment of meeting their

God; it was a sight for saints and confessors, not for humble soldiers.

Ralph answered his unspoken comment. 'It goes on. You know it goes on.'

Gilbert, his face still grey, thought of the family he had just left at the mill – thrown down in death like broken dolls.

'But like this? Does it have to be like this?'

'You can lose your long face,' said Ralph. 'It is the way of war. And it is the Duke's way of war.'

'Why? Kill the soldiers, yes. But to butcher old men and infants. What was their crime?'

'To be in the way,' said Bruno, as he put the oxen out of their misery.

Gilbert spread his hands. 'What is the sense? We shall need their labour when peace comes.'

'We shall indeed. The Duke kills not to create a wilderness but to create terror. Terror creates confusion. Confusion makes weakness. Weakness leads to defeat.'

Gilbert pointed downwards. 'Why do they have to enjoy doing it?'

Ralph spat. 'There are such men in any army. They are well paid for what they do.'

'They would need to be,' said Bruno.

'The Flemings.'

Bruno nodded.

Gilbert shuddered with loathing. 'I should rather have such men as enemies.'

Ralph gazed about him and sighed. A familiar image was raising itself before the eyes of his memory. Burning buildings, the sightless faces of his childhood friends, private boxes raped and pillaged, his mother whispering to herself in a corner, his father clutching the stump of his arm, and weeping more with impotence than with pain.

'There are no enemies, no friends – only survivors and victims, lucky and unlucky, those on whom God's Light shines, and those on whom it does not. War is the enemy, not the other side.'

'Do you feel nothing?' said Gilbert.

'Sympathy for the dead? Their agony is over. Rage? Can you take revenge on war? You might as well try to wreak vengeance on the weather.'

Hardly a word was spoken for the rest of the journey back to camp.

On the edge of it, they passed a pack of hounds being exercised. Great Jesus! thought Gilbert. Who would bring hounds on an adventure like this? He thought of the horror they had just left behind. He heard Ralph snort with disgust and utter one word.

'Beaumont.'

A whiff of latrines and stale bodies reached them. They forded one of the two small rivers that acted as natural fortifications on either side of the main camp. For several hundred paces the ground had been cleared of all timber and cover. Groups of sweating soldiers were dragging tree trunks towards the ever-growing palisade. They looked up at the new arrivals, and complained bitterly to them, cursing in the mindless, repetitive way of all soldiers. The sergeants in charge glared at them, in the way that all sergeants glare, and resumed their own loud swearing over the bent backs of their glowering workers.

Gilbert could see that the work was going well. The palisade was nearly up to its full height in several places, and there was already a catwalk for sentries on top of the square tower. The main building looked flimsy on its huge stilts, but the chief engineer had collected a sizeable party of Saxon prisoners. A few days of hard work with the shovel and the whip would get the gap underneath filled with earth, and it would look solid enough – as if it had grown out of its mound like a great wooden mushroom. Ranulf of Dreux was a miserable devil, but he knew his job. And for all his endless complaints about delays and shortages and other insuperable problems, he had found time to make a start on a hall for the Duke. Carpenters were carrying long planks through bare doorways to begin floors and benches.

Everywhere stood crude thatch shelters for livestock, grain, and other supplies. Sir Baldwin had already placed sentries on each one. Several wagons belonging to the Breton contingent had been moved to make room for more horse stalls – with extra shelter for the favoured destriers. That was Sandor's work. Two more armourers' smithies had appeared, and were working full blast. The Duke had been quick to take advantage of the charcoal-burning in the surrounding forest. Tucked away in a bend of a river, the archers sat over their fires, held up new arrow shafts to the flickering light, and ran thoughtful thumbs over feathered flights.

Behind the camp, on the far side, the land sloped gradually towards the sea, and the harbour, where the Duke kept his ships in constant readiness. Squads of Baldwin's men were engaged in regular altercations with those who were impeding free movement of supplies with their shanties and bivouacs.

The overall impression was one of bustle and purpose. Gilbert had been a soldier long enough to appreciate professionalism when he saw it. In another day or two the Duke's camp would be ready to sustain attack by a full army. Rumours were wild about the numbers of the English, but the more Gilbert saw of Baldwin's supplies, and Fitzosbern's direction, and Lord Geoffrey's training, the more reassured he felt. The more he saw of Ranulf's building, the less he worried about the arrival of the English. He had seen engineers like Ranulf at work in Brittany, in Maine, in the Vexin, and in Pevensey too. Normans understood castles. He hoped the English did not.

If the worst did come to the worst, the avenue of escape was assured. The ships were ready at any time, manned and victualled.

If the Duke's men were defeated – which God forbid – they would not have to turn and sell their lives dearly at the water's edge. Valhalla glory was all very well for Vikings, but it was not the Norman way.

Ralph and Bruno dismounted. Gilbert remained in the saddle. He did not wish Ralph to see him getting down with the bad ankle.

'I am going to make my report,' he said.

Ralph looked up at him. 'What do you have worth telling – the names of your nurse and groom?'

Gilbert flushed. The gibe made him angry as well as embarrassed. 'Damn you; you do not know everything. I have information. I go to report it.'

'I shall hear about it all sooner or later,' said Ralph.

Gilbert nudged his horse forward. 'But not from me,' he said over his shoulder.

Gilbert tethered his horse outside the tent of Sir Baldwin de Clair. He paused outside to warm his hands at the blaze, and to summon up his courage. To his surprise, Sir Baldwin was there too, sitting on a bench, munching. He spoke with his mouth full.

'What do you want?'

It sounded more like a challenge than a question.

'I – I have come to deliver my report, sir.'

'What – at this hour?'

'You said to come at any time, sir.'

Baldwin made a noise of annoyance. 'Oh, very well. Come on. Just getting warm too.'

Baldwin was so ready to grumble that it had not occurred to him to ask questions about the day's absence. He wiped his hands, threw the towel to a servant, and led the way into a tent that seemed better provided with the comforts of life than many a senior commander's accommodation. Sir Baldwin de Clair, like all quartermasters, seemed to spend half his time working to make himself comfortable, and the other half complaining about overwork and discomfort.

Inside, seated at a low table, crouched against the tent's sloping wall, a hatchet-faced monk scribbled endless lists, bent low in the guttering light of the mean candle-ends that were all that Baldwin allowed him

Baldwin saw Gilbert screw up his eyes in the gloom.

'It is all I have to spare.' He gestured towards the bowed clerk. 'Thinks I am as rich as Charlemagne.'

The monk sniffed.

Sir Baldwin could not have been more than sixteen or seventeen years his senior, but Gilbert thought of him as old.

He grunted like a grandfather while Gilbert reported what he had seen on his reconnaissance. He asked close questions on farm sizes, barns, oxen, stores, wells and other matters to do with supply and shelter. From time to time he barked dictation at Brother Crispin, who merely sniffed and continued recording the information without looking up.

Gilbert was impressed with Baldwin's professionalism. No anxiety about Harold's whereabouts showed. It was as if he treated the whole enterprise purely as an exercise in supply.

Well, thought Gilbert, perhaps he could surprise him. He felt the time was approaching for him to produce the choicest morsel of news. He almost licked his lips in anticipation.

Baldwin blew on his hands. 'Show me where you have been.' He saw Gilbert hesitate. 'Is it any good putting a map in front of you?'

Gilbert stammered, 'I – I am not used to maps, sir.'

'You are a scout.'

'Yes, sir, but I have not – I mean, I am not sure yet whether—'

'What are you, boy? Whose man are you?'

'I was with the Rouen garrison, sir. Before that, I served Lord

Geoffrey de Montbrai – the Bishop of Coutances.' Gilbert dropped the biggest name he could think of.

'Thank you,' said Baldwin. 'I do know who Geoffrey de Montbrai is. What did you do when you were with him?'

Gilbert cursed to himself. This was not how he had planned the conversation to go. 'I – I was in charge of the hounds, sir.'

Baldwin threw up his hands. 'Great Jesus of Nazareth! I ask for trained scouts and they send me kennel boys. All right, all right, just tell me, and Crispin and I will make sense of it.'

When he stopped grumbling, Baldwin asked sensible and searching questions. Using known landmarks and references to the sun, he pieced together a fair picture of Gilbert's journey. Crispin translated it into signs on the map.

Gilbert said nothing about the mill or its people. Nor did he mention the hill with the old apple tree near its summit. He was afraid that Ralph might report later, and it would come out that he had become separated from his companions, and there would be no end of trouble and shame. Moreover, he did not want anything to spoil the effect of the prime piece of military intelligence that he had been saving up. If he produced it with the right flourish, Baldwin might let his previous career with Lord Geoffrey's hounds slip his mind.

Baldwin blew on his hands again. 'First things first then. No enemy army?'

'No, sir.' Getting near.

'No sign of them?'

'No, sir.' A thumping of the chest.

'No information? No whispers? No rumours?'

Now!

'I think something has happened, sir.'

Baldwin stopped blowing. 'What do you mean? How do you know?'

'I encountered a group of refugees, sir. I overheard something.'

'How?'

'I am a scout, sir,' said Gilbert, relieved at last to make a point. 'It is part of my job to—'

Baldwin waved a hand. 'Yes, yes, all right, all right. What did you hear?'

'One of them was very excited, about some news he had just heard. When he told the others, they were, I should say, impressed.'

'What did he say, boy!'

'He spoke English.'

Baldwin glared. 'Then why did you not question them?'

'I have no English, sir.'

'You can manage a few words, surely. One of them might have spoken French.'

'There were several of them, sir.'

'Armed to the teeth, I suppose.'

Gilbert squirmed. 'No, sir. But I thought if I used force I should get nothing from them. By staying in cover I might hear more.'

'Did you?'

Confidence was evaporating fast.

'I think – only think, sir – that one of them said something about the north.'

'Is that all?'

'Yes, sir.'

'Think, man. How did he bring the news?'

Gilbert lashed his memory. 'He looked excited, sir, as I said. He – he waved his arms about.'

Baldwin scratched his chin. Making up his mind, he picked up a large cloak, fastened it round his shoulders, and beckoned. 'Come with me.' He paused at the doorway, turned, and growled to his secretary. 'Finish those returns from the Bretons and the Angevins before you kneel down for your Vespers or Compline or whatever it is.'

Crispin sniffed.

Baldwin paused again outside the tent, and looked up at the night sky. He pulled his cloak tighter. 'We shall have some frost, I should not wonder.'

The previous three days had been mild, but Gilbert decided it was better not to remind him of it.

Baldwin gestured. 'Is that your horse?'

'Yes, sir.'

'See to him. See the Magyar. Then meet me outside the Duke's tent.'

The Duke's tent! Gilbert was so excited that he did not trouble to try and hide his limp.

'Welcome.'

Despite the fading light, Gilbert could see Sandor's face shining with pleasure at seeing him. Sandor was one of those cherished people who always smiled when he met a friend.

Together they saw to the horse. Gilbert knew that there would be no more words until Sandor was satisfied that it was clean, dry, and comfortable.

He told as much of his story as he dared, following the little Magyar as he ambled to and fro in that rolling gait of his. Even when he was on foot, Gilbert thought, Sandor looked as if he ought to have a horse between his legs. Sailors were supposed to have a roll in their stride from their many hours on swaying decks as they crossed the sea. Did Sandor roll also because of his countless hours in the saddle when traversing the plains of his native Hungary?

Gilbert had heard many tales, and not only from Taillefer, about those monsters on horseback from the mists of time – the Huns. Their awful leader, Attila, was a fit companion for Satan and his devils in the fires of Hell. Whole cities, it was said, were consumed in the fires he lit on earth. Not even the mighty

Romans could stand against them. They had swept into the Empire like a human pestilence, destroying all before them. And then, like a pestilence, they had raged, and they had gone. Just as God in His mercy saved enough of His people from the fury of a pestilence to enable life to stagger on, so He had in His inscrutable wisdom saved enough of Christendom to rebuild itself when He had sent the Huns back into their distant plains of eastern darkness.

As he watched Sandor muttering soothing nothings to his horse, Gilbert wondered whether this grubby little goblin of a man were descended from those Hunnish warriors of the deep past. He was the right size. His clothes stuck out wildly. His skin was dark with dirt. He reeked of horses. He had a magic touch with them. He was never tired after the longest ride. He spoke an outlandish tongue, not one word of which Gilbert could understand.

Yet he was no devil. Imp maybe, but no devil; he laughed too readily. He had a great skill with language too. He conversed easily in French, though his natural eagerness with words led him sometimes into hilarious error. Gilbert had also seen him round campfires with Bretons and Germans. He had a gift for fellowship. He made even the flat-faced Flemings laugh.

His skill with horses was wonderful to behold. Gilbert, conscious of his own gift with dogs and other animals, could appreciate it more than most. Indeed, he had fancied he himself knew about horses, until he met Sandor.

Now, as he watched Sandor run his hands over his own mount, he stopped talking. It was as if Sandor could read, from the skin and the mane and hooves and harness, what had happened during the last two days, without any words of confession.

The little Magyar looked up. 'You have had the good luck,' he said.

'Yes,' said Gilbert. 'I have had the good luck.'

Sandor squinted up at him, causing spider-webs of wrinkles

to form round his dark eyes. Then he shrugged. 'I get some hay. You make your report.'

'Mark my words,' said Gorm. 'No good will come of it.'

Edwin sighed at Gorm's ability to look on the black side of everything. Gilbert had shaken hands. He was genuinely friendly. Of that Edwin was sure. Why else would he have carved that doll for Edith?

Rowena agreed with him. 'Father, he was grateful. And he took nothing.'

Gorm staggered towards the door, and looked back for a moment. 'He took knowledge. That will bring him back. And others too.'

He reeled out towards the mill house, and flopped on to a stool.

He had always solved his problems by moving on; it was easier. Now it was different. He was not the travelling jack-of-all-trades that everyone had always patronised and shunned and swindled. Making fun of his Danish accent. Now he was a miller; a man of substance. A freeman, holding land direct from the King himself. Sweyn now had an inheritance. He wiped sweat from his face. Dear God – was all this about to be taken from him?

Gilbert held his hands out to the blaze of the fire outside the great tent, and tried to look casual in front of the Duke's personal servants as they aired fresh laundry and heated pots of water. Very shortly he would be in front of the Duke, on his own. For a moment he half regretted not having told Ralph beforehand; Ralph would have had some advice to offer. Too late now. He hitched up his belt. He had got himself into this, so had only himself to blame.

He recognised Baldwin's voice, explaining. There was a short rumble of conversation. Then a pause.

'Come.'

There was no mistaking the harsh, throaty voice. A tent flap lifted, and a finger beckoned. Gilbert ducked his head and went in.

A row of stubby candles had been stuck askew in flat iron candlesticks along a large trestle table. At one end were piled the remains of a simple meal. There was one giant pot of cider in the middle. Gloves and spurs were strewn here and there.

Gilbert noticed that only the Duke had a proper chair. Most of the others around him were on cheap stools. A few were making do with sawn-off logs. It was obvious that the Duke's reputation for frugality and hard living on campaign was no legend put about to flatter the army. Baldwin's tent seemed far more comfortable than this.

'Step forward.'

Gilbert obeyed. He came closer to the light and could make out faces.

Bishop Odo of Bayeux, as usual, sat near the Duke. The candle flames scattered black smudges of shadow across his pock-marked face. His clerical tonsure made his undersized head look ridiculously small above the wide-shouldered episcopal robes.

Odo's face and head were the butt of endless camp jokes – 'His mother never knew she had dropped him; trod on his face when she stood up' – but he was a man to be wary of. He was intelligent, mean-minded, and he never forgot a grudge.

Gilbert also recognised the Duke's other half-brother, Robert, Count of Mortain. He had only half Odo's brains, but he was solid and reliable, and good at following orders. His men liked him; nothing he did ever took them by surprise.

Sir Roger of Montgomery was there, and Fitzosbern, and Count Alan, leader of the Breton infantry. Gilbert's old master, Bishop Geoffrey of Coutances, caught his eye and nodded faintly. A large man lounged in deep shadow at the back. No one sat near him. Oddly, he was the only one besides the Duke not drinking.

'Sir Baldwin de Clair tells us you have news,' said the Duke.

Gilbert swallowed. 'I – I dare to hope so, my lord Duke.'

There was a pause.

'Well, have you or not?'

The terse, impatient voice from the end of the table belonged to Sir Walter Giffard. Gilbert had good cause to remember it. He had once, at the gateway of Rouen castle, been rash enough to challenge Sir Walter as if he were a stranger. He smarted for days at the memory of the lashing he had received from Sir Walter's tongue.

There was a good chance that Sir Walter could not recognise him in the bad light, so Gilbert stood his ground and tried to explain what he meant.

The Duke questioned him on it. As Gilbert replied, William's restless eyes flashed to left and right, weighing and testing the effect the answers had on the men around him. Odo and Fitzosbern added their own enquiries. Gilbert surprised himself with his own nerve. Perhaps Sir Baldwin's grilling had stiffened his back just a little. He held to his story about a group of refugees, and to the one word – 'north'.

A general muttering followed, and the cider pot was passed round. The Duke did not take any. Neither did the big man in the shadows.

The Duke nodded to Bishop Odo, who banged on the table with the handle of his dagger. The company continued to lounge and drink, but all voices ceased at once, and all eyes turned to the Duke. Gilbert was impressed; it was a curious mixture of informality and absolute control.

William sat back, totally still save for the darting eyes. 'Fitz,' he said. 'Sum it up.'

Sir William Fitzosbern leaned forward, and put his hands

together like a judge. Gilbert, not sure whether to withdraw or to stay, looked for help to his old master, Geoffrey de Montbrai, and asked a question with his eyebrows. Geoffrey frowned and nodded for him to remain.

'Our scouts bring us mere threads,' said Fitzosbern. 'We can not yet weave them into a clear tapestry. Indeed we can make only outline patterns, and several possible patterns at that.

'First, nobody has seen Harold. Nobody has seen an army. When we crossed, nobody saw a fleet. Yet we know they exist.'

'The fleet does not matter now,' said Walter Giffard. 'We are here.'

'It will matter if they return to blockade us,' said a voice at the back. 'How do we get home?'

'We are here to discuss means of victory, not of retreat,' snapped the Duke. 'Fitz, continue.'

'Wherever the fleet has gone,' said Fitzosbern, 'it will not trouble us for the time being. At best Harold has disbanded it. If the weather broke it up, that suits our purpose too. If, as we suspect, they have moved to London, they will find it difficult to beat back to Hastings against the wind. It is most unlikely that they took the army on board with them. So we can discount the English fleet.'

'Harold and the army remain,' said Montgomery.

'And the northern earls,' said Robert of Mortain.

'Edwin and Morcar will not trouble us,' said Fitzosbern. 'At any rate not yet. Their charge is to watch the northern coast against Hardrada. It must be. Harold would not strip the north of all defences. The winds in September were from the north. Harold must have expected Hardrada's invasion first.'

'You mean he stripped the south of all defences?' said Giffard. 'Sounds just as stupid to me.'

'No,' said Fitzosbern. 'I think that is equally unlikely. Harold is too good a general for that. You all saw him in Brittany in 'sixty-four. Did he seem a fool?'

'He could be relying on a quick victory,' said Giffard, unwilling to surrender a point too easily. 'A forced march, a sudden attack, another forced march back.'

'Have you any idea, Walter, how far it is to Northumbria from Sussex? From our best information, it is more than two hundred miles. That makes a round trip of over four hundred miles, maybe five hundred. Could you march an army over five hundred miles in three weeks?'

Giffard offered no answer.

'I could not do it,' admitted Roger of Montgomery. 'But Harold might.'

'If he had enough horses,' said Odo.

'The English fight on foot,' said Geoffrey de Montbrai, unable to resist the temptation to correct his brother-bishop.

Odo rose with relish to the apparent challenge. 'There is nothing to stop them *travelling* on horseback, like anyone else. I should have thought that much was obvious.'

Geoffrey flushed, but kept his temper. 'We are indebted to my lord of Bayeux, as ever, for pointing out the obvious.'

Before Odo could think of a suitably stinging reply, his brother Mortain came in with another possibility.

'He could have gone north with a small detachment, just to take command.'

'No,' said the Duke. 'He is a sure leader. He knows how to delegate authority. His plan was sensible. He guards the south, and Edwin and Morcar guard the north. If he trusted them enough to put them there, he would leave them there.'

The company fell silent, unable or unwilling to challenge the firmness of the Duke's argument. Gilbert, stiff from much riding, and still in some pain, furtively eased his bad ankle as much as he dared.

Fitzosbern cleared his throat. 'Unless – the situation has changed.'

'You mean Hardrada has landed?' said Giffard, pouncing.

'Not only landed, but won a victory,' said Fitzosbern. 'Consider our information. Harold's army can not be located. Yet we know it was here during the summer. All our reports and interrogations confirm it. So we are driven to assume that he has moved. He can not move south without loading his troops on to his ships, and his ships are not there. He can not move east without our scouts knowing. He has no reason to move west; the west is under no threat either from us or from Norway. So he must have moved north. What we do not know for sure is, how far.'

'Waiting in London, ready to leap either way? Is that what you mean?' said Odo.

'That is one explanation,' said Fitzosbern.

'Sounds reasonable,' conceded Giffard.

'But not likely,' said Geoffrey, once again disagreeing with Odo.

'Why not?'

'If Harold were going to do that, he would have done it earlier.'

'He might have been driven there by lack of food in Sussex,' said Montgomery.

'In harvest time?' said the Duke. 'Never. There is food everywhere. You have heard the scouts' reports. Even we have good supplies, and we are the invaders.'

Baldwin felt it necessary to modify this unwarranted optimism. Like all quartermasters, he had a constitutional inability to admit to ample provisions.

'I can not say I am entirely happy yet, my lord. Reinforcements, though always welcome, constantly add to our problems.'

'Supplies or no supplies,' said Fitzosbern, 'my guess is that Harold has gone further than London. Look at the news we have. Whispers in Kent of a battle somewhere north. Our English-speaking scouts testify to this. That merchant ship we captured off Dover – fleeces from East Anglia. They told us of rumours about a Viking host. What was it? A fleet "more plentiful than the pebbles on the shore".' He smiled wryly.

'Always exaggerate, the English,' said Alan of Brittany.

Gilbert saw several grins. Count Alan, the commander of the wildest story-stretchers in the army, looked blank. The joke was lost on him.

Fitzosbern continued. 'Then comes the latest murmur in the wind, from – um – from this man.' He pointed at Gilbert. 'It confirms our suspicions about something in the north. And it may also help to explain Harold's absence.'

Giffard glanced significantly at Montgomery beside him. 'He has gone north to do battle with Hardrada. What I said.'

'True, Walter,' said Fitzosbern, 'but not for the reasons you think.' He paused to give effect to his next remark. 'I think it possible that Harold has gone north, not to fight the first battle with Hardrada, but the second.'

Giffard stared. 'What?'

'Look,' said Fitzosbern. 'We accept that Harold is no fool. I agree with his Grace that Harold would leave the defence of Northumbria to Edwin and Morcar.

'Now, suppose the Vikings land. Edwin and Morcar must attack, and quickly. They have no choice. Every commander must strike at an enemy beachhead with all speed, before supplies arrive and positions are consolidated.

'If Hardrada has landed, there must have been a battle. If Edwin and Morcar were successful, Hardrada is either a corpse, a prisoner, or a fugitive. There would be no need for Harold to move north. On the contrary, he would have every reason to move south with all speed against us. We should have Saxon war cries in our ears by now. The fact that Harold is nowhere near means he has received bad news. His northern host is broken. He has only one army remaining. He has moved to strike at Hardrada before Hardrada recovers from the first battle.'

Mortain frowned. 'But you said he would not take such a risk.'

'Not with two armies at his disposal,' said Fitzosbern. 'But with one? What choice does he have? To stay in Sussex and wait for us to land, knowing that Hardrada is spoiling the northern and middle shires behind his back? It would be intolerable. He is a king. He must defend his people. Why are we wasting so much land round here? Because we know that many estates here belong to Harold. We want him to strike at us in rage before his army is in full order.'

Fitzosbern sat back. 'No, as I see it, Harold has taken the only course open to him. To march that two hundred miles and surprise Hardrada. You never know; he might do it. Vikings are raiders; they are not campaigners. Harold might catch them unprepared.'

'Then what?' said Odo.

'Then,' said Fitzosbern, 'he comes south again. He must have heard of our landing by now. He will try to catch us too.'

'Never!' said Giffard, bristling.

'That will not stop him trying,' said Fitzosbern. 'He has no means of knowing how far forward our preparations are. His army, by all reports, is bigger than ours. Saints! He would have every reason for trying.'

Blank faces around the table registered doubt and disbelief. There were one or two mutterings of injured pride. Fitzosbern refused to be put off, and, unlike Odo and Giffard, refused also to become indignant. He reached out towards one of the iron candlesticks, and began twiddling it. When he spoke, it was as if he were communing with himself.

'Consider the temptation – not one lightning stroke, but two, and two invaders chased into the sea. It would give him a golden reputation for life.'

'We have no proof he has achieved the first yet,' said Giffard.

'We have one small hint,' said Fitzosbern. He stopped twiddling and pointed towards Gilbert. 'This man's report.'

Giffard looked sharply at Gilbert, as if trying to read some answer on Gilbert's face, and then back at Fitzosbern.

'All he said was "north".'

'And one other thing,' said Fitzosbern. 'He said the man who said it was excited. Excited. Not desolate.'

'So he knew about your "second battle"?' said Montgomery.

'And it was a victory for Harold?' said Geoffrey de Montbrai, clinching it.

Fitzosbern pushed the candlestick back into the centre of the table. 'That is the best sense I can make of it.'

There was a general stirring, such as an audience would make after a long story. Pots were raised and lowered noisily on to the table. The Duke, still and watchful, cast his eyes right and left to note reactions.

'Feasible, I suppose,' said Montgomery at last.

Geoffrey de Montbrai smiled to himself. As usual, Fitz had thought all of them right off the table.

There was another silence, broken in the end by Walter Giffard. 'So where do we go from here?'

'Nowhere,' said the Duke. 'We stay.'

Giffard gaped. 'With Harold on the march?'

Gilbert was surprised, and not for the first time, at the amount of plain speaking, even argument, that the Duke tolerated. He was too young to appreciate the ties that bound these hard men together. He had noticed the glitter of greed in their eyes easily enough, and the pride in their bearing; the bravery too, in their very presence in this country. When he stopped sometimes to contemplate the colossal gamble the Duke was taking, it made his throat dry. But it was the straight talking, the frankness, that took him aback. He could not yet see that they sprang not from insubordination but from common purpose, from the mutual confidence that arose from long, shared experience.

'We stay,' repeated the Duke. 'If Fitz is right, Harold will come to us in haste and he will come in fatigue. If he attacks in rage to avenge his wasted fields, he may also come to us in disarray. If he comes slowly, he will come to us in plenty of time. However he comes, we are prepared, and we fight on our own terms.'

'And we have the fleet in case,' said the same voice at the back.

The Duke looked round the table, his face a blank.

Nobody chose to speak to that idea.

'What if he does not come at all?' suggested Montgomery.

'We wait,' said Fitzosbern, who from long intimacy took up his Duke's line of reasoning. 'News will come sooner or later. It must. News travels faster than any army, if you have ears to listen.'

'So we just sit and wait for him to attack us,' said Giffard, beginning to bristle again.

'We have scouts, Walter,' said Fitzosbern patiently. 'We wait to hear news of Harold's army and news moreover of its condition. We have the resources for an open battle, and we have the supplies and the fortifications for a defensive engagement.'

Baldwin preened himself.

The Duke pushed back his chair. 'We are prepared,' he said. 'We wait now only for news. And that we shall seek yet more thoroughly. Fitz – more patrols. Meantime, the training continues. Brittany?'

Count Alan sat up straight. 'My swordsmen will be at the peak of readiness whenever you need them, my lord.'

'Coutances?'

Geoffrey nodded.

Odo pretended to look pained. 'Are we to be deafened by trumpets again, my lord? Is my lord of Coutances looking forward to the siege of Jericho?'

'They always sound louder in an empty head,' said Geoffrey.

'Enough,' said the Duke, heading them off. 'Coutances, get on with it.'

'As far as the ground permits, my lord.'

Giffard looked at Montgomery and shook his head.

William caught the glance, and reacted immediately. 'If Sir

Walter Giffard finds the task beyond him, now is the time to say so.' He allowed a short pause to strengthen his next words. 'So that I can allow his replacement time to accustom himself to the command.'

Giffard flushed with shame at the mere imputation. He rose formally. 'As God is my witness, and before these two princes of the Church –' he indicated Odo and Geoffrey '– I give you my solemn assurance that your Grace will never find me wanting in courage, honour, or loyalty.'

Gilbert swallowed. It was worth all the pain and nerves and discomfort just to see Sir Walter Giffard, of all people, thoroughly outfaced. For all the informality, there was no doubt about the Duke's authority.

As Giffard groped for his stool, William turned to Odo. 'Brother, you will take whatever spare infantry is needed for extra fatigues on the castle walls and interiors. The rest will be allocated for harbour work and further ground clearance. You will put your men at the disposal of Ranulf.'

Odo looked like thunder, but said nothing. Geoffrey smiled.

A voice spoke from the shadows, its tone a nice mixture of innocent enquiry and irony. 'And what are your Grace's orders for his loyal Flemings?'

William did not even turn in the speaker's direction. 'To wait until they are called upon, and then to obey. Meantime, to follow standing orders.'

He stood up.

Everyone rose, and collected gloves and spurs. One or two on the edge of the group drained furtive mugs. All paid their respects and withdrew. Baldwin pushed Gilbert out. The Duke's personal servants sprang to their feet, lifted the pots from the fire, and hurried inside with hot water and fresh towels.

Gilbert hung about, not sure whether he was dismissed or not. When Baldwin left him without further comment, he decided to drift away. Fitzosbern came out of the tent and called after him.

'Here, you.'

Gilbert hurried back. 'Yes, Sir William?'

'Come and see me early tomorrow. I want you to go again to where you heard that news of yours.'

Gilbert felt alarm. 'But, sir, they were only refugees; they may be miles away by now.'

'The news will not be,' said Fitzosbern. 'I want you to find some more.'

Gilbert searched for an excuse. 'I do not speak English, sir.'

'Take an English speaker with you.'

Gilbert tried another, more desperate tactic. 'Would it not be better, sir, to send a more experienced scout?'

Fitzosbern looked at him oddly. Modesty in young soldiers was rare, and therefore suspect. 'Who trained you?' he said at last.

'Ralph of Gisors, sir.'

'Ah, yes, the Rouen garrison. Works with – um – that tall man with the long face.'

'Bruno of Aix, sir.'

Fitzosbern nodded. 'Just so. Well, tomorrow you go together. You will show them the way. Bruno and your Gisors man can then use their "greater experience". Yes?'

'Yes, sir.'

Fitzosbern strode off towards his own tent. 'Remember that English speaker,' he shouted over his shoulder.

A large figure loomed out of the shadows and addressed Geoffrey de Montbrai.

'Greetings to my lord Bishop of Coutances. It is a long time, is it not?'

Geoffrey regarded the man with distaste, and pointedly did not offer his ring for the kiss.

Fulk the Angevin ignored the insult, and flashed a smile that his scar turned almost into a leer.

'Surely my lord bishop has not been deliberately avoiding me?'

Geoffrey stood his ground. 'I am one of the many who find no need to seek out your company. An opinion shared, it would seem, by his Grace the Duke.'

Fulk made a dismissive gesture. 'What of it? He has to be seen to assert himself. I can cope with that. Besides, he is a good general. I freely grant it.'

'Generous of you,' said Geoffrey.

Fulk bowed low to acknowledge the barbed compliment. 'My generous nature, my lord.'

Geoffrey half smiled at the man's effrontery. This was the creature who, fifteen or sixteen years ago, had ambushed him on the high road to Burgundy, and had come within an inch of killing him. For money. A hired killer. And here he was in England, doing substantially the same thing. In the intervening time, by all accounts, he had been fulfilling similar despicable functions over half Christendom, and beyond.

Fulk, who was watching his face, read his thoughts. 'It was a long time ago, my lord. I had a living to earn. No hard feelings, I assure you. It was nothing personal. Indeed, as a result of the episode, and of the skill with which you extricated yourself, my respect for you rose considerably.'

Geoffrey began to find him tiresome. 'What do you want?'

Fulk smiled devilishly. 'Only to give further proof of my generosity. Not, as formerly, to a contract victim, but to a comrade-in-arms. Strange, is it not, how Fate throws the most unlikely people together?'

'Get to the point,' said Geoffrey. 'It grows cold.'

Fulk produced a bundle from under his arm. 'If my lord would care to examine this at his leisure . . .'

He opened the cloth cover, and revealed a beautifully bound book.

Despite the flickering light of the fire, Geoffrey could

appreciate the standard of workmanship; the damaged spine was only incidental.

Fulk opened it at random, and held out the spread pages for Geoffrey's closer examination. 'The best English illustration, my lord. One of the finest schools.'

Geoffrey was enormously interested, but tried to appear wary. 'How do you know?'

'Does it matter, my lord? You know I am right; you can see for yourself.'

The devil *was* right, damn him!

'Where did you get this?'

Fulk looked as if he were about to savour the coming moment. 'Your lordship will not believe me, but, as I hope for eternal salvation, it fell off the back of a wagon.'

'What makes you think I should be interested in your lootings?'

Fulk raised his eyebrows. 'Is not your reputation as a connoisseur of fine scholarship and jewellery well known? Is not your cathedral at Coutances a byword for beautiful furnishings and venerable relics?'

The swine was well informed too.

'Since you appear to be aware of its value,' said Geoffrey, 'I expect you to name a robber's ransom for its price.'

Fulk pretended to look hurt. 'Come now, my lord – only a realistic bargain, between men of the world?'

'I do not buy without first examining the merchandise.'

'Willingly, my lord. I would, however, counsel reasonable expedition in coming to your decision. The morning tide is early, and your man Thierry returns to Normandy, does he not? Surely it would be safest for him to take it away from the theatre of war – in case any harm should befall it.'

Damn him – he was extremely well informed.

'You trust me to return it to you if I do not wish to buy?'

Fulk bowed. 'Your Grace is, as I said, well known. The very

soul of honour. A prince of the Church moreover. What better guarantee could I have?'

Geoffrey found himself admiring the man's total confidence. This criminal was capable of anything. If he had nearly murdered him for money fifteen years ago, he was equally prepared to murder him now for non-payment of debt.

'I shall think about it. You will have my decision first thing in the morning.'

'The word of a nobleman. I am answered, and most fairly. There remains only the trivial question of price.'

'Name it,' said Geoffrey.

Fulk did.

Geoffrey laughed. 'You know what you can do with it.'

'I do indeed, my lord. There is another bishop in this camp, who is equally anxious to enhance the beauty of his cathedral – at Bayeux, I believe, is it not?'

'The skin is a little charred with waiting, but it is good fresh meat.'

'Thank you, Ralph.'

Gilbert sat down, stretched out his tired legs towards the fire, and loosened the laces on his boots. His ankle still pained him. He began eating, but after a few mouthfuls, he was not sure whether he wanted any more. The nausea threatened from the very pit of his stomach. He tossed the remains into the fire.

'What did Baldwin say?' said Ralph quietly.

'He took me to the Duke.' Gilbert enjoyed saying that.

'Then what did the Duke say?' said Ralph, ignoring the pride.

'The Duke wants more patrols sent out. Tomorrow. You and I and Bruno must go together. With an English speaker.'

Ralph glanced at Bruno. 'Where?'

'Where I picked up my information.'

There was a pause. Ralph became impatient. 'You mean where your nurses groomed your horse for you?'

Gilbert flushed, and struggled to his feet. 'Damn you! Just see to it that you are ready. Fitzosbern's orders.'

'Do you know the way?' asked Ralph.

Gilbert whirled round, furious. 'You are ordered as company, not as guides.'

Ralph also became angry. 'You will have to tell me in the morning. Or I can find out now; I have only to ask Baldwin.'

'Then ask,' said Gilbert, limping away with his trailing laces. 'Ask – or wait until the morning.'

Ralph swore, and savagely poked the fire.

Bruno cleared his throat.

Ralph spoke without looking at him. 'Now what have I done wrong?'

'You know. You simply have trouble in admitting it.'

'Honour. His precious honour. Is that it?'

'If a man does not have that, he has nothing. Honour, pride, self-esteem – call it what you will.'

Ralph turned to face him. 'I thought you said he was not up to it.'

Bruno shrugged. 'Even dog-boys should be allowed to have their pride.'

'You bastard! And what about survival? Does that not count for anything?'

'Not at the cost of pride – no.'

Ralph flung an arm in Gilbert's direction. 'His precious honour and pride are crippling his life. He is so obsessed with them that he is blind to anything else. He will not live long enough to see his honour avenged if we do not . . .' He hesitated, having talked himself into a trap.

'If we do not nurse him,' said Bruno.

Ralph grimaced as the shaft went home. He wiped his forehead. 'Bruno, I am knightly born, like you. I know what honour is. But there are things more precious than that. I searched for years for the man who burned my home, killed my friends, sent my mother off her head, and turned my father into a cripple. And when I found him, what did I see? Fulk the Angevin had been ahead of me – tortured him to make the man's sister open the gates of the castle of Arques.' Ralph winced at the memory. 'A truncated, gibbering, wreck of a human being – no eyes, no ears, no nose, no hands, no privates. And do you know what sickened me? Not the sight of him. No. It was the knowledge that, in the long years of my search, I had wanted to do what Fulk had done to him. But when I looked down at this screaming, bloody mess, I knew that I could never have carried it out. I was grateful to Fulk for having shown me in time. Such revenge is pointless. It had crippled my life for years. If I had done it, it would have turned me into an animal. For what? Did it rebuild my home? Did it give my mother back her mind? Did it restore my father's hand?'

Bruno dipped the end of a cloth into some fat, and continued polishing a strap.

'Believe me,' continued Ralph, 'if I thought any action of mine would have made them whole, I would have raped a nun, spat in the Pope's face. But it was done, over, past. Just so with Gilbert. He can search the length and breadth of England, and never find the man he seeks. A wasted life. And one in danger. He is liable to notice nothing else.'

'And if he should find him?'

'What good will that do? Will it make Gilbert the true father of his wife's child?'

'It might help him to live with the fact that he is not.'

'No. It is a madness that could send him to destruction.'

If the boy did not improve, he could send them all to destruction, thought Bruno. However, he only shrugged and said, 'A man must have something to drive him – wherever it should take him.'

'Not blind anger. He is angry for what some man did before his wife married him.'

'You are angry for what God did to your brother before you left home. What is the difference?'

'Hail, sir knight!'

Taillefer held up a large, bony hand gleaming with gaudy rings. Beside him Sandor sprawled in some straw upon a pile of saddle-cloths. The fire painted shiny spots on his gnome-like face and danced in his dark eyes.

'Welcome to the lord of hosts,' declaimed Taillefer. 'What news bringst thou from darkest Scythia?'

However inappropriate or ill-timed his remarks, it was difficult to feel rage with Taillefer. Gilbert felt his bad mood beginning to evaporate already. He kicked Taillefer familiarly.

'Move over, you old sot. Drunk again. Where does he get it all from, Sandor?'

Sandor chuckled. 'Devils have more charm than saints,' he said. 'If they did not, Hell would be empty.'

Taillefer waved his hand again in another theatrical gesture. 'A soothing tongue can open more pockets than a sharp point.'

Gilbert joined in the joke. He pulled out his dagger. 'More pockets than this?' he said, pretending to jab it into Taillefer's skinny thigh.

Taillefer looked down at it for a moment, then raised his head. His bleary eyes seemed to sag with the weight of the bags underneath them. 'My dear boy,' he said, 'your knife will empty pockets only once. My voice will empty them many times.'

Sandor laughed, and so did Gilbert. They could never catch out Taillefer in moral argument. 'You and your stories.'

Taillefer coughed suddenly.

'Phew!' Gilbert recoiled from Taillefer's breath. 'Great Jesus, Taillefer – the onions!'

Taillefer professed surprise, his eyebrows pushing up a hundred wrinkles. 'What healthier diet could there be?

An onion every day for life,
And never fear the doctor's knife.'

Gilbert pushed him away. 'You eat onions only to take away the smell of beer.'

'Of course. And I drink beer to take away the smell of onions. It is an excellent arrangement.'

They laughed again.

Gilbert kicked up some embers and lay back on an elbow. 'Sandor,' he said, 'whom do we know who speaks English?'

'Why do you need such a man?' asked Sandor.

Gilbert explained.

'Carry your quest no further,' said Taillefer. He struggled to a sitting position. His long legs stuck out before him and his toes pointed straight up into the night air.

'You old fraud,' said Gilbert. 'You know not a word of English. And I have never seen you write anything in any language.'

Taillefer turned up his nose. 'A man does not parade his gifts until they are needed. As the great philosopher said – whose name momentarily escapes me – "Never uncover a blade before you mean to use it." However, since you disdain to make profit of my generous offer . . .'

Sandor and Gilbert laughed once more.

'He just wants a ride out to relieve the boredom and to get a chance of looting without danger,' said Gilbert. 'Come, Sandor. You know everybody. Who speaks English?'

Sandor pondered. 'He must be a knight? A Norman?'

'He can be a cross-eyed Jew, for all I care,' said Gilbert. 'Just show him to me and I will take him.'

Sandor's eyes sparkled. 'I show you – now!'

Gilbert blinked. 'Well?'

'I show you.'

'Where?'

'Here.'

Gilbert stared. 'You mean – you?'

'Sure.'

'You speak English?'

'Sure.'

Gilbert spluttered in his amazement. 'But – but you speak German and Breton. And French.'

'So why not English?'

'But that makes four.'

Sandor grinned. 'It is the first two or three that are difficult.'

'Ah, the gift of tongues,' murmured Taillefer to the tumbling flames.

Gilbert still found it difficult to get his voice. 'But – you never said.'

Sandor shrugged. 'A man does not put all his knowledge out for show, lest it go stale and be not remarked. Keep it covered and fresh, and it will be the more useful when it is needed.'

'Where did you learn it?' said Gilbert. He did not know much of Sandor's life; he could not understand how this little man from Hungary, on the very edge of heathen Asia, could come to speak a language from the opposite end of Christendom.

Sandor leaned across and retrieved a large pot near Taillefer's feet. He poured himself a full measure into a large hollow ivory horn, which he always carried with him. It was decorated with strange spiral carvings and bright mosaic chips of enamel. Gilbert waited while he drank. Taillefer slowly toppled backwards until he was totally supine.

Sandor wiped a hand across his mouth.

'You wish I tell a story, eh?'

'It is I who tells stories,' said Taillefer. 'It is my mystery.'

'You spin tales in the evening like a spider spins the web,' said Gilbert. 'One puff of morning truth and they vanish into fancy's air. Sandor tells stories with stones in the bottom.'

He had heard one or two episodes from his little friend's life, and was intrigued to hear more. He found it difficult to relate them to each other, but at least they were not impossible like Taillefer's fables.

Sandor let out an enormous belch far out of proportion to his size. 'Many year ago,' he began, 'the Vikings conquered England. There was a great king – Cnut. Perhaps you have heard.'

'Indeed,' said Gilbert. 'Lord Geoffrey spoke of him.'

Sandor made an expansive gesture. 'He was a mighty king. England, Denmark, Norway were his lands. Truly a great empire to rule from a longship.

'The old Saxon royal family was broken; its king was dead and its princes in danger. Two ran to Normandy – Alfred and Edward. You know this, no doubt. Alfred was murdered. Edward became King when Cnut died and his sons died.'

'He was the one who died this year, leaving no child,' said Gilbert. 'He was the last of his line.'

Sandor shook his head. 'There was another prince. He also was called Edward. He escaped too. He ran far, far. He came at last to my land.' His face softened. 'He came to Hungary. Our king made him welcome. He made his home with us. We have made a Magyar out of him. When he became a man we found him a wife – niece of an emperor, no less. We gave him lands and servants. And horses. In Hungary a lord must ride; he must have horses. He must have a good man to care for his horses.'

Gilbert stared. 'You?'

'My father. I too was there. He was a kind man, the prince Edward. But he was sad – sad.' Sandor sighed. 'To be sad in Hungary – truly a difficult thing to do.' He sipped thoughtfully.

'And then?'

'I teach him to ride. He teach me the English. It is a rough tongue. I learn with a stiff mouth. And he learn to ride with a stiff back. He was not one with the horse.' He made a gesture with his hand. 'He did not – he did not flow. Ah! It was great pity. I try very hard with him. But I learn more English than he learn horse.

'And then, one day – maybe eight, ten years ago – come messengers from England. King Edward has no son. He wishes Prince Edward to return, to take up the royal crown when it falls from the Confessor's head. Again Prince Edward, he is sad. Always he is sad. Ah –'

Gilbert and Taillefer joined in the chorus: '– to be sad in Hungary.'

Sandor laughed. 'He has a wife and children. He is forty years away from England. He will be a stranger. But the prize is great. And he is the lawful king. And England is his land. So he returns. It is a long journey – again through Bavaria, and Swabia, and Lorraine, and Flanders to the English Sea. He weeps to leave Hungary. I too weep. But my father is dead and I am master now of Prince Edward's stables. I have my duty.'

Sandor sighed again and took another swig. 'After many adventures we reach to Calais. There are many English nobles to meet him. He is received like a prince. He is given rich English clothes and many English servants. He is drowned in the English. He does not see his Sandor swept away in the tide of English.'

He shrugged. 'Sandor is alone, with only his horses. He must make his own way.' He finished his drink.

'Well?' said Gilbert. 'What then?'

Sandor grinned. 'I am not like Taillefer,' he said. 'I do not make stories that go on for ever.'

Taillefer snored loudly.

'Some day,' said Sandor, 'I tell another story. Now, we must sleep. Tomorrow you hear my good English and you judge. We go where your horse has the good luck, eh?

9 October

'Our greatest captain'

'Are you sure about this?'

'True as I stand here.'

'How do you know?'

'Gorm, I am a carter. I move about, I see people.'

'And have any of them been fighting?'

'No, but they had it from the King's rider himself. Horse nearly dead with running.'

'All right, all right. Tell me the whole story. Go on, surprise me.'

'Here, boy! Here!'

Berry came bounding down the hill, bursting with energy and goodwill. He skidded to a halt, his tail wagging furiously.

Edwin crouched beside him and ruffled the fur behind his ears. He looked at the paw that had been caught in Sweyn's trap. It was healing rapidly.

He clutched to his chest the sacking bag he was carrying, and pretended to growl at Berry.

'Are you a fine boy now? Eh?'

Berry, excited, jumped at him and assaulted his face with a long steamy tongue. In his crouching position Edwin overbalanced into the wet grass.

'Get off!' he spluttered, not really meaning it. 'You will break the mushrooms.'

The bag fell from his hand as he fought a mock battle with the dog. At last he pushed him off and struggled to his feet.

'Now – what have you done with those mushrooms?'

Berry crouched with a forepaw outstretched on either side of the bag, watching intently, his muzzle on the ground, his tail waving gently to and fro. As Edwin pounced, he bounded away.

Edwin retrieved the bag and followed Berry back towards the mill. It was such a glorious morning that he could almost have burst into song. What a blessing to the spirit was provided by God's fresh early air and the loving company of a good dog!

When he had risen in the chill dawn, cold and stiff, the world had seemed much less friendly, and God indeed a long way away.

Gilbert's departure the previous afternoon had depressed him. He hated the deception he had been forced to practise to hide Gorm's news, and he had hated Gorm for rushing in at the wrong time and spoiling what was a gentle moment, when two strangers stretched out in gratitude and hesitant friendship towards each other.

Edwin liked Gilbert. He was Gilbert's age and understood him. Gilbert had shown love to the creature he loved. Berry had whined a little when he rode away. He knew how Gilbert felt, alone in a foreign country. Only two years before, he too had known that loneliness and fear. Perhaps if Gilbert had stayed longer, he might have told him of his solitary, hungry, hunted journey through Normandy.

Then again, perhaps not, for Gilbert was also the enemy.

When he had stood in the doorway, what Edwin saw, and what Rowena and the others saw, was not a sheepish young man with a pale face and a weak ankle; they saw instead a strong, armed Norman soldier. Edwin knew better than anyone in that household that his lord and Gilbert's lord would meet in battle, and that they were well matched. During his stay in Normandy he had seen them both, had seen them talk to each other, watched them sizing each other up. Neither would give way to fear, or compromise, or bribery. The one might offer to parley with the other when the crisis came, but Edwin knew it would be a mere formality. Harold and William would decide their quarrel in open battle.

Gilbert would be summoned to that battle, on the other side. Worse, he – Edwin son of Edward – would not. Gilbert was a soldier; he, Edwin, was not.

It was not for lack of trying . . .

Harold had laughed.

'You, lad?'

'Please, sir, I have served you well, have I not?'

'In the kennels – yes.'

'Must I remain a dog-boy for ever?'

'You do not belong with my fyrdmen. Do you really want to be in that legion of middle-aged spear-prodders?'

'They are not all your army.'

Harold gaped, then laughed uproariously.

'Surely not one of my housecarls.' He jerked a thumb over the shoulder, and lowered his voice like a conspirator. 'Like Wilfrid here. Solid oak from the neck up. They would bore you to tears.'

Edwin could find no answer.

Harold put an arm round his shoulder. 'Believe me, my friend, you can best help me by keeping my hounds in good health for me. I can find plenty of men for a dirty day's work brushing away these flies from Norway and Normandy. But I can find very few good men with dogs like you. And I shall want you coursing the Downs with me till Domesday. What do you say?'

So Edwin said goodbye to his king. At least it was not the agony that the other goodbye had been in Normandy. He felt he could still stretch out his hand and touch the tears on her face. God, was it two years now? What had made it so much worse was that they had suffered their first quarrel just before he was told that he had to leave. Harold's orders again. It was a wonder that he still loved the man.

The days dragged when he returned to England. Luckily he was able to lavish all his love on a cheeky pup. Berry was a blessing, but he was not a cure. Edwin found himself spending more and more time at the mill, because Rowena was so kind. He had wept in her arms and told her of his loss. She tried to comfort him.

'Aud is fond of you.'

He almost tore himself away in his revulsion at the thought. He saw again her long rangy body, the bones in her chest, the large wrists.

'Aud! I never wanted her before, and now, after—' The tears flowed again. 'You must make her see.'

'Aud sees only what she wants to see. You are young. You are good. You have the strongest of all lords. What girl would not think what she thinks?'

'You do not.'

Rowena pushed away a lock hair from an eyebrow. 'Aud must look ahead. It is only natural.'

'So must you. You have Godric.'

'My father must give his word.'

'With that spoiled brat Sweyn in your way? And your father drunk half the time.'

Rowena took her arm away from his shoulder. 'They are my kin.'

Edwin knew at once that he had gone too far.

'I am sorry, Rowena. I meant no harm. But you are more loyal than they deserve.'

'I am no saint,' said Rowena. 'I think sin and I feel sin.' She pushed him away. 'But you will not hear of it.'

Edwin stood up.

'Thank you all the same for your kindness to me.'

'Well, be kind to Aud too. She has such a gap in her heart.'

Berry stopped, turned, and wagged his tail. It was not a morning for moping. Well, perhaps even Aud would appreciate the mushrooms he had picked.

'*Ite, missa est.*'

The ragged little congregation stood back to let the Duke leave first. Breath hung steamily in the dawn air. Geoffrey de Montbrai, Bishop of Coutances, had seldom felt so naked in front of an altar. There was little of the building visible beyond a few corner posts; not even beams and joists for a roof. Ranulf did not put chapels in outer baileys very high on his current list of priorities.

Two shivering chaplains helped him off with the episcopal robes. A servant fastened a long winter cloak round his shoulders and took the robes away for safe storage. The freezing faithful few kneeled at their final prayers, lips trembling and teeth chattering. The numbers would steadily increase as the battle approached. It would take a small regiment of priests to hear confessions on the battle eve.

Geoffrey looked over the hunched shoulders towards the two timbers that marked the doorway. How long would it be before he said Mass in a complete chapel, with a proper altar – not the Duke's portable box of relics? Would it ever be built? Would these defiant, lonely timbers one day soon be crackling in flames before a jeering Saxon army while daring, tense-jawed looters ransacked the reliquary for jewelled settings of the bones?

Geoffrey pulled the cloak about himself. No more thoughts

like that. They always crept in with the early chills of dawn, stiff joints and throats of leather. He should know better.

The Duke was already surrounded by a small knot of officers and servants, and was issuing commands in his usual brusque way. Fitzosbern and Baldwin were passing them on to subordinates.

'Ah, Coutances,' he said, when Geoffrey joined them. 'Get that man of yours.'

'Thierry, my lord?'

'Yes. I have some messages for him.'

It was typical of William's sharp, darting eyes that, despite the poor light, he had recognised Thierry among the bowed heads of the congregation.

Geoffrey had been surprised to come across Thierry's upturned face when he came forward to administer the Host.

Now he grabbed him as he rose from genuflection.

'What are you doing here? You did not come to confession.'

Thierry looked shamefaced. 'Your Grace will forgive, I am sure. I went to my lord Odo.'

He saw the immediate look of disapproval that appeared on Geoffrey's dark face.

'But you know all my sins already, my lord – and so well. I thought, if I confessed them to his Grace of Bayeux, it would somehow make it sound more – well, more contrite.'

Geoffrey growled. 'And you could avoid my lord Odo afterwards, whereas you could not avoid me. I see.'

'A state of grace before a journey, my lord. Would you deny me that?'

'And you have fasted since midnight? I do not believe it.'

Thierry spread his hands. 'It gives me no pleasure to say it, my lord. But consider what lies ahead of me. If I had eaten, I should only bring it all up within half an hour of sailing.'

Thierry was never stuck for an answer.

'Come,' said Geoffrey. 'The Duke wishes to see you.'

It was lucky for Thierry that his memory made up for the sins of his appetite. He listened with overhung brows to what William had to say.

Geoffrey stood apart, but watched. He knew the Duke's messages were likely to be largely for the lady Matilda, who was rumoured to be coming to the very port of St Valéry, so as to be able to hear the news at the first opportunity.

The army liked Matilda. She was tough, resilient, and did not suffer from the vapours so often attributed to ladies of noble birth. She mixed well, had a good sense of humour, and was not shocked by camp language. She was the perfect partner for the Bastard. She did not flatter, she did not whine, and she was no shrinking violet. Their domestic disagreements were loud, famous, and not infrequent. She shouted things to his face that senior vassals trembled even to think, never mind utter. It was clear to everybody that they were made for each other.

When William had finished, Baldwin grabbed Thierry's arm. 'Make sure you add my own good wishes to my lady,' he said.

Thierry ducked his head. 'And the lady Albreda, my lord?'

'What? Oh, yes – her too.'

Thierry threw a furtive glance at Geoffrey. It was common knowledge that there was genuine friendship between Baldwin and Matilda, and that Baldwin only tolerated Albreda. He had married her only on the Duke's insistence, and, having done his duty by fathering a son or two, had been content to let her lord it at Brionne while he went on summer campaigning.

He had long ago reached the conclusion that, all things considered, desire was a troublesome interruption to the steady tenor of a well-ordered life. He did not enjoy the usual boasting that occurred when women were discussed, and he did not initiate vulgar conversation. Indeed, his lack of interest in the opposite sex had occasioned much camp humour.

Once Agnes had entered a convent, he had not talked intimately with anyone. Only Matilda had come near him. Despite her teasing – 'Baldwin, why are you so old?' – she had become genuinely fond of him, and he felt the same towards her.

Outside soldiering, his main interest was his precious monastery at Bec. He had spent some time in one as a boy, and had learned to read there, even write a little. He found comfort in the daily round of a holy house, in the chapel bell ringing, endlessly, the hours of Divine Office. It was like being bound up in eternity.

He leaned earnestly towards Thierry. 'Now, I want you to go to Bec, and see to it that . . .'

Thierry nodded patiently. 'Yes, indeed, my lord. As usual. I understand.'

He had been doing this for years.

When Baldwin had finished, it was Geoffrey's turn. He called Thierry to his tent and picked up a parcel. It was double-bound in quality leather. 'This is to be delivered to Canon John – into his hands, and no one else's. Do you understand?'

Thierry drew back warily. 'It is not another relic, is it?'

None of Geoffrey's servants would touch a holy relic. When he had brought some back from Italy to grace the new altar in the young cathedral, he had had to carry them himself, all the way. His men had flatly refused.

'No, it is not,' said Geoffrey.

Thierry did not look convinced. 'It is well bound. It must be valuable.'

Geoffrey sighed and thrust the package at him. 'Here. Take the cursed thing. It is only a book. And I should not say valuable so much as expensive – cripplingly expensive. God help you if you lose it after what I paid for it.'

And please God that devil Fulk did not walk past any more upturned wagons at inopportune moments. Much more of this and he would be ruined.

*

Edwin watched Berry scattering dew on either side as he swaggered ahead down the path towards the mill. He snuffed the air deeply. What a tonic all this was. He stopped once or twice to touch spiders' webs in such a way that the dew fell without the thread breaking. He looked inside the bag of mushrooms, took out one of the biggest, and sniffed it. He turned it over and stroked the soft black gills. It was like the inside of a girl's thigh.

Rowena would be pleased. She would cook them in fresh butter, add some parsley and a few magic touches of her own, and they would soften the roughest bread into a breakfast fit for princes.

It was the least he could do to repay hospitality. And Rowena's kindness. And – be it remembered – Rowena's discretion. She never spoke of his lost love in front of anybody else. She kept her word.

Yet somehow Godric knew. Edwin was sure of it, but sure too that Rowena had not betrayed him. Thoughts passed between the two of them like magic; Edwin felt he could reach out and touch the bonds between them. Godric also had this uncanny perception. It gave Edwin shivers sometimes, and he could see that it frightened Gorm.

As they sat round the table and ate the mushrooms, he could feel Godric's eyes probing into every face while they talked again of Gorm's news.

'It was better than I thought,' said Gorm.

'Father!' said Aud. 'Those old fools make it up as they go along.'

Gorm waved a hunk of bread impatiently in the air. 'Not Saward and his gang. I do not mean them. Cripples and dotards. Gabbling sots, the lot of them.'

He took a large bite in the brief silence that followed, not noticing how deep it was.

'I got it from Algar. Now, he goes everywhere. I believe him. Think – the King's rider himself. He could not have made this up. I tell you there has been a great clash at Stamford. And the King has won.'

'Where is Stamford?' said Sweyn.

'Near York, son. There has been a big fight at a bridge. Hardrada is dead, and the King's brother, Tostig.'

'He always was a bad lot,' said Edwin.

Gorm leaned forward on his elbows. 'They say the King wept over him.'

Edwin could see half-chewed food in the miller's mouth as he spoke.

'The Viking host is broken,' said Gorm. 'There were not enough survivors to fill ten ships afterwards. And they came in hundreds – more plentiful than the pebbles on the shore.'

'There you go again, Father,' said Aud. 'More tall stories.'

'That is only half the fighting,' commented Godric.

There was a silence. Aud looked towards the sheepskins where Gilbert had lain, now piled tidily in a corner on a lath hurdle to keep them from the earth's dampness. Edith crooned over the stick doll that Gilbert had given her. Rowena put an arm round her shoulder and looked at Godric.

Only Gorm continued in the same vein. His own news, and the sense of importance it gave him, made him feel sure of the future.

'The King will be soon here. You will see. He marches fast behind the news of his win. The land of eastern Mercia is flat, with good tracks.'

'Winning can be as tiring as losing,' said Godric.

Gorm waved a hand as he belched. 'Bah! What do you understand? Ah, yes, I know, with brews and broths you are a master. Blind us all with craft. But you are a dreamer. You are not a man of the world. I have been far and I have kept my eyes open. And I tell you, Harold will be soon to London. He will gather the men of Essex and Surrey and he will be ready for the Bastard. His axes will trim them down. If Vikings could not withstand his housecarls, the Bastard's hired Flemings will go down like hay under the sickle.'

Edwin, on the other side of the table, was bored by his talk and sickened by the smell of his breath. He was also finding Aud's meaningful glances oppressive.

He got up, made an excuse, and went outside. He walked far enough away to escape the sound of Gorm's harsh voice.

He whistled for Berry, and collected a billhook from a shed. There was always kindling to be gathered, and the leaves were now falling freely. It was one of many services he could do to show his appreciation.

He paused to fasten a gate that had been left unlatched – almost certainly Sweyn's laziness again. Luckily, the pig had not escaped. He picked up a hazel stick from a pile of half-made hurdles, and gave the animal a friendly prod on the rump. He found himself leaning, with his arms draped loosely over the top bar.

If Gorm was right, Harold would return before very long. Would he wait in London for William to come, and let the Bastard waste his strength on the march? Or would he push on at once, catch him on the beach, and drive him into the sea? It did not appear as if the Normans had yet come very far inland. Gilbert was a scout, and must have been several miles ahead of the main army. So perhaps William was building a fortified camp near the coast somewhere, just to be on the safe side. From what Edwin had seen in Normandy two years before, it seemed very likely.

When Harold had returned from his season's campaigning with William in Brittany, he had praised the Duke's skill and bravery, and his generalship, but he had also remarked on his diligence and his caution.

'These Normans, lad! They think everything out. No wonder they love this game of theirs – what do you call it? – chess. They are thorough, but, by the Virgin, they are dull. They make war with a spare saddle on every horse.'

It was not Harold's way. The King was no fool, but he liked a decision. It was the urge for a quick decision that had made him march north, and, judging by the news, his instincts had been proved right.

Harold would be only human if he chose to rely on a method that had already destroyed one invader to destroy the other. Moreover, it fitted his character. He had come to know William's methods too, and would expect thoroughness and care in preparation. He would be right to guess that the Bastard had not moved yet.

The more Edwin thought about it, the more he felt sure that Harold would come south from London to meet William in Sussex. He must pass near. It would be only natural for him to march through or near his own lands, of which there were many close by.

Somehow or other, Edwin would meet him, and somehow or other, he would persuade the King to let him fight at his side. There was always someone at home to feed the dogs. Young Alwin would jump at the chance of some responsibility. Time he had some, really. Besides, Edwin would not be away for long. A week or so at most. Then they would return in glory. What feastings there would be! The King would be unable to deny him a place at his tables, especially after his great daring on the field of battle. He would miss the dogs. But what a career of excitement to fill their place. And surely the King would let him keep Berry.

He gave the pig a final jab.

He may have missed the first battle, but, by the Mother of God, he was not going to miss the second.

Ralph Pomeroy stood up when his brother approached. Though eager to know, he kept his voice down.

'Well? Was it enough?'

'Enough – and more. Archers, it seems, will haggle like Jews over arrows, but have no idea of the value of padded jerkins. I could have sold them three times over, and for twice the price. I must be slipping.'

William Capra pulled on the rein he was dragging until the horse was level with him. Another was tied behind.

'What do you think of these?'

Ralph whistled in appreciation, then glanced round furtively to see if they were observed. Capra reassured him.

'Do not distress yourself. Nobody saw me. Which was just as well.'

Pomeroy looked alarmed. 'You mean to say . . .?'

Capra shrugged. 'Not my fault. I went with a pocketful of silver, ready and willing to do some trading. But nobody was there. Giffard, apparently, has the flux, and is laid out. Not surprising, at his age. Must be past it. And the little Magyar was out exercising some of the new mounts.'

'What about the grooms?'

Capra made a dismissive gesture. 'A few bloody noses and a couple of tips saw to that.' He patted the wallet on his belt. 'So we have the horses *and* the money. Not a bad morning's work. Better than slaving away at fatigues with that bastard Florens breathing down your neck.'

Pomeroy looked nervous. 'Will he not know?'

'Know what?'

Pomeroy made a vague wave with his hand. 'You know – about the jerkins.'

Capra made a face. 'I expect so. But he can prove nothing. And he probably stole them himself in the first place. It will make up for them cutting our first day's pay. In any case, we are not going back, are we?'

Pomeroy looked blank. 'No?'

'No, my brother. We are going to take our new destriers, and we are going to find some proud detachment of knights – proper knights. No more of your mud-stained, foot-weary mercenaries. And we are going to carve out glorious careers for ourselves. I think I have rather taken a fancy to his Grace Bishop Odo of Bayeux. He looks a likely prospect.'

Ralph Pomeroy blinked. 'A bishop? Would not his brother be a better bet?'

'Mortain? No. Too stupid. I have seen them. My lord Odo has a head on his shoulders, for all that it is somewhat small. My lord Odo looks out for himself. I like a man who does that. Sits at the Bastard's right hand. Another point in his favour. We can do ourselves a lot of good there, my brother.'

Pomeroy looked at the horses. 'Suppose the Magyar comes looking for them? Suppose he tells Giffard?'

Capra snapped his fingers. 'Like Florens, he can prove nothing. He can not even guess. We change the shoes, refashion the mane, renew the tack, and pah! Who will take the word of a dirty little Hunnish barbarian against a knight of Normandy?'

Pomeroy still looked worried. 'I only hope you are right.'

Capra patted the neck of the leading horse. 'Your trouble, brother, is that you lack nerve and style. Confidence. That is the secret. You assume that everybody knows what you do. They do not.'

'I still think it is asking for trouble,' Pomeroy grumbled.

'Only if we stay and wait for it to catch up with us.'

Pomeroy looked up. 'What do you mean?'

'I mean, brother, that we kill two birds with one stone. For a day or so we nobly offer ourselves for the distasteful work of the wasting parties. Thus, we can stay out of harm's way, and you never know what tempting morsels we may pick up in the line of duty. When the hue and cry dies down, we seek out my lord Odo.'

He handed over the reins of the second horse.

'Which reminds me. How did you fare with the candlesticks?'

Pomeroy glowered. 'Everyone laughed.'

*

'Up there.' Ralph waved an arm towards the crest of the hill.

Gilbert hastened alongside.

'Nothing is there,' he said.

'Then we should get a good clear view,' said Ralph.

'Just an old apple tree,' said Gilbert lamely.

'Then we have nothing to daunt us.'

Sandor caught up beside Gilbert.

'Only old apples,' he whispered.

Gilbert flushed as he recalled his illness and its cause. He looked sidelong in guilt. Had he told Sandor? He could not remember.

They reached the tree and saw that it stood on a ridge just below the true summit, which lay a short distance to the north.

'Why do you want to come here?' persisted Gilbert, and instantly cursed himself for his mistake. Any scout naturally made for the high ground in a strange area.

Ralph looked at him oddly, but said nothing. He refrained from asking more questions, which might reveal yet other mistakes that Gilbert might have made. The last thing he wanted was Bruno's eyebrows saying 'what did I tell you?'

He dismounted and tied his horse to the lichen-covered trunk of the apple tree. He arched his back and stretched his legs. Gilbert, Bruno, and Sandor waited.

'That is the way we go,' said Gilbert, still nervous. He pointed north-westwards.

'So I see,' said Ralph.

'Shall we go on then?' suggested Gilbert, making to move away.

'All in good time.'

Something was disturbing the boy. Ralph did not know whether he wanted to find it or not. He walked slowly round the tree, not sure what he was looking for. To Gilbert his slowness was infuriating.

'I have made my report,' he said. 'I have seen all this.'

'And I have not,' said Ralph. 'But I intend to before I make mine.'

Bruno stood in his stirrups and gazed about him. With his great legs straight, he looked enormous.

'This would make a good position,' he said.

Ralph shook his head and trudged back to his horse.

'Depends rather on which way you are facing. If we occupied it against Harold coming from the north, we should have to cut down a lot of cover on our flanks. Behind us the ground declines a little too rapidly for an ordered retreat.'

'And look,' said Sandor. He pointed to a marshy stream that wound round the south side of the hill. It ran near the small grassy knoll close to its foot where Bruno had picked up Gilbert's trail the previous day. 'There is a sandlake.'

Even Gilbert joined in the laughing. Sandor looked surprised.

'But there is sand, is there not? And a lake?'

'No, Sandor,' said Gilbert. 'It is not a lake; it is a stream. But there is sand. If you like, a sandstream.'

Sandor shook his head. 'No. If I say that, I am like an angry snake.'

He looked down the hill again and watched the waters of the stream spreading in shallow side pools around the foot of the small knoll. Patches of yellow flashed between the green of the grass tussocks.

'No,' he said. 'I shall say "sandlake". It is gentle for my weary tongue.'

Ralph smiled, and patted him on the ankle as he stood beside the light pony that Sandor preferred to ride.

'Have it your own way, Sandor.' He grinned up at Bruno. 'What is it called, Bruno?'

'It is called a sandlake,' said Bruno solemnly.

Ralph continued his reconnaissance, and tried to ignore Gilbert's restlessness. What on earth was the boy trying to hide?

He remounted, and walked his horse to the true summit a little way further north.

'See a long way from here.'

Bruno nodded. 'Good, open ground.'

'Yes, apart from this damned gorse. Let us see if there are any tracks in or out of those woods.'

He pointed northwards, and kicked his horse down the shallow slope. Perhaps if they got away from the summit, Gilbert would become less anxious.

'Be careful!' called Gilbert. 'There is a ravine at the bottom.'

Ralph, with Bruno at his side, was too far ahead to hear him. 'I said, "Be careful!"' shouted Gilbert.

They cantered on, Bruno edging into the lead.

Swearing to himself, Gilbert kicked his horse into a gallop. Sandor, mystified, followed, after a careful glance behind.

'What the devil ...?'

Ralph was knocked aside as Gilbert overtook him.

'Stop! Stop!'

Gilbert galloped on, leaned out and snatched at Bruno's bridle. They came to a halt in a flurry of thudding hooves and flying tussocks of grass. Bruno's horse stumbled and nearly fell.

Bruno dismounted in fury.

'You fool! Do you want her to go lame? Can you not cry out?'

'I did. You were deaf. What else was I to do?'

'Explain yourself. That is what you do.'

Bruno examined Sorrel's legs.

Gilbert flung out an arm. 'Look! If it were not for me, you and Sorrel would be down there.'

Bruno peered. 'I see nothing, unless it is—' He broke off when he saw the tops of trees growing from the ravine's banks.

Ralph arrived and dismounted. He parted the undergrowth.

'God's Breath, that is well masked.'

'You see?' said Gilbert in triumph.

Bruno grunted.

'Is it steep?' he said to Ralph.

'Yes.'

'You should be grateful,' said Gilbert. 'Grateful.'

'Yes, yes, yes . . .' said Bruno over his shoulder as he moved to his left. 'There is an avenue of some kind here.' He walked his horse further. 'An old causeway, I should say. So there is a way across.'

Ralph joined him.

'It looks very old. Crumbling – see?'

Gilbert, indignant, watched them musing and pointing. He turned to Sandor, who had just arrived.

'Look at that. I save them from breaking their necks, and they take no notice. None at all.'

'Ah!' said Sandor non-committally. He wandered to the right. 'See?' he said. 'Somebody here did fall.'

He pointed to the gap that Gilbert had made two days before.

'Well, it was not me,' said Gilbert, and cursed his tongue once more.

Sandor said nothing. He dismounted, and clambered carefully down into the ravine. He called up, and pointed to broken stalks and twisted brambles.

'Here he fell.'

'Oh, yes?' said Gilbert as casually as he dared.

Sandor went right down to the tiny stream at the bottom. He looked about, and called up again.

'The man who was not you rested here – and crawled to here.'

Gilbert looked anxiously towards Ralph and Bruno, but they were still discussing their causeway.

Suddenly Sandor stooped.

'Come up, Sandor,' pleaded Gilbert. 'Now,' he added urgently.

Sandor scrambled back over the rim and pulled leaves off his jerkin. His eyes twinkled.

'You were lucky not to break the neck,' he said.

Having begun the lie, Gilbert felt bound to it.

'I tell you I did not fall.'

'Ah!'

Ralph came back with Bruno.

'We must move on.'

'I am all for that,' said Gilbert.

Ralph threw another searching look at him, and remounted. Bruno, after a further examination of Sorrel's legs, did the same. As they moved off, Sandor held Gilbert back. His other hand was inside his jerkin.

'You did not fall, you say?'

Gilbert looked furtively to make sure the other two were out of earshot. 'No, I tell you!'

'Ah! Then it is perhaps you will not want this, as it is not yours.'

Sandor took his hand from his jerkin, and held out a spur.

Sir Roger of Montgomery dismounted and handed the reins to a groom. A body servant took his helmet and gloves, and stood at a discreet distance. Bishop Geoffrey of Montbrai wiped his lips and held out a leather flask. Montgomery took it.

'Thank you.'

Detachments of knights waited, muttering in small groups. One or two sour looks were cast in their direction.

'Give them a rest,' said Geoffrey. 'Then we go again.'

Montgomery shook his head doubtfully. 'You will not get perfection, Geoffrey.'

'No harm in trying,' said Geoffrey.

Montgomery tossed the flask to the servant.

'Geoffrey, there you talk like a bishop, if I may say so. These are not saints, or heroes, but mortal men. I have to lead them; I know.'

'You do not see the whole picture,' said Geoffrey. 'You do not see what I see.'

'Seeing everything is not knowing everything. There are some things you know from inside, not from outside.'

Geoffrey sighed, and slapped his thigh with his glove in impatience. 'I am responsible to the Duke. I must get the very best out of them.'

'Geoffrey, they were good this morning – the best they have ever been. Surely you agree.'

Geoffrey inclined his head. 'Well, yes . . . But if only—'

'If only nothing! If we took them up and back a dozen more times, we should not improve on what we have already achieved today. Let them see some small sign of approval. Give them a change – a few hours for rest, for maintenance, gossip, drink – anything.'

Geoffrey did not look convinced. 'Now there, Roger, you talk like a squadron commander. If you were training a whole army of knights, you would talk differently. The vast majority of these men are stupid, vicious, and undisciplined, and well you know it. The fact that they sit astride a horse does not raise them above the animals in the infantry when it comes to military intelligence and initiative. Relax for one moment, and they revert to their basest habits.'

Roger gave a slight smile of irony. 'Are we not also knightly born?'

Geoffrey was not in the least put out. 'We have added talent and loyalty to our right to rule. That is why we command and they follow. And they will continue to follow only if we continue to rule.'

Montgomery tried a different line of argument.

'Geoffrey, listen. When you took over the training command in May, you had the worst task in the whole army. The Duke would not have entrusted it to you if he had not thought highly of your ability. I agree with his judgement. You have done wonders. I should think we now have the finest and best-organised corps of heavy cavalry in Christendom out there in front of us.'

'I thank you.'

'I mean it,' said Roger. 'Ever since early summer, we have followed your lead – and your instructions – even when we had misgivings about them.'

'You mean Walter and the trumpets.'

Montgomery made a dismissive gesture. 'If you like, yes. Walter believes in speaking his mind. But there are other things. Walter and I discuss them, but we do not trouble you with them because they are not your worry. This time, though, since Walter is not here, it is I who must speak out.'

Geoffrey was impressed. It was one of the longest speeches he had ever heard Roger make.

'What are you saying?'

'I am saying,' said Montgomery, 'that there comes a time when the man who sees the whole picture does not understand the whole picture. You have forged a brilliant weapon. None of us could have done it – I freely grant it. But it is we who must wield it. I and Walter, and young Beaumont, and Odo, and Mortain, and the rest. We are the ones who must lead. It is a question of fine judgement and fine timing, and appreciation of things that are apparent only when one does lead.'

Geoffrey looked distressed. 'Do you think I do not also wish to lead?'

'Of course. I know. I do not doubt your honour or your courage for a moment. But we must both accept the Duke's ruling. Just as we accept your authority in training and in deployment. Now you must accept our judgement when it comes to assessing the men's readiness for the biggest test of all – the actual instant of physical clash. This is a skill that is built just as your own skills are built – with time and experience.'

'To know when the sword is at its sharpest?'

'It is finer than that. Finer even than a thumb across a razor. Geoffrey, I bow to your judgement when it comes to preparing cavalry for the field. But our judgement counts too. I want to make sure that when I reach the Saxon line I can look about me and see all my knights there, with all their heart and soul. It is more than reason, more than training, more than practice. Call it instinct, if you like. It is closer than a hair's-breadth, and it is vital.'

Geoffrey was seeing a new side to his old comrade. He had known Roger of Montgomery for sixteen years, and valued his friendship. When Geoffrey had been struggling to make his way both as Bishop of Coutances and as vassal to the Duke, it had been Roger who had helped him with a hundred hints and suggestions. They were roughly the same age, and both saw clearly that the way to fortune was at the shoulder of the Bastard, for all the dangers that beset him. Geoffrey came to rely on Roger, as did the Duke himself.

Montgomery was undemonstrative, but his qualities became evident to anyone who campaigned beside him for a year or two. Geoffrey had come to share the view of him that was common to the rest of the Duke's commanders – a quiet, solid, courageous vassal. Not given to brilliant insights or to originality, remarkable only for his single-minded loyalty to the Duke, and for his patience.

These strengths had been most evident when he had shown willingness to marry Mabel of Bellême. Mabel was heiress to a vital frontier stronghold, the castle and fief of Bellême. She was also notorious for being a snob, and a cat of the very first order. True, it had more than doubled Roger's land-holding in Normandy, and it had strengthened the Duke's southern frontier, but there was nobody who envied him his success, because of the price he had to pay in the shape of Mabel.

He rarely showed impatience at this situation, or indeed at anything else. For him now give expression to such a profound statement of belief was remarkable. Possibly too it was a sign of the greatness of the moment that such a statement had been dragged from him.

Roger of Montgomery went on to provide yet another

surprise when young Robert of Beaumont rode up to join them. When the news had arrived of Sir Walter Giffard's indisposition, Beaumont had been deputed by the Duke to lead Giffard's detachment for the day.

Beaumont was everything one would have expected of a senior vassal's son – able, well trained, quick to display prowess, and full of the arrogant confidence that went with inherited wealth.

He talked of the squadron he had just led in the training manoeuvres as if it were his own. Montgomery looked askance at him. Beaumont did not notice.

'I am not surprised Sir Walter Giffard finds it hard to attend all these sessions. At his age. The men were saying the same.'

Montgomery now looked him fully in the face. 'I suppose you asked them.'

'Of course,' said Beaumont. 'It only confirmed what I thought anyway. Giffard ought to stick to his horse-breeding. His ideas are out of date anyway. I have heard him arguing with you, Lord Geoffrey.'

Geoffrey opened his mouth to reply, but was forestalled by Roger. For the second time that morning, the famous Montgomery patience ran out.

'Let me remind you that Sir Walter Giffard was leading knights when you were soiling your swadding clothes. His squadron is so well trained that a nun astride an ox could have led them this morning. You, you bumptious young cockerel, were only the pennon on the staff. Lord Geoffrey put you in simply to complete the picture – and to get you away from your precious hounds.'

Beaumont flushed.

Montgomery had not finished with him. 'And when Sir Walter returns to duty – as he will tomorrow – he will outlast you in the saddle on the day of battle. And a dozen like you.'

*

Gilbert slowed down as they neared the mill. Ralph understood at once.

'Lingering will not save you.'

Gilbert swore at Ralph's back.

Sandor came alongside. 'You have the good luck with these people?'

Gilbert hoped the mail coif would hide the worst of his blushes.

'I heard very little from them,' he said. 'There will be nothing else to find out.'

'We shall decide that for ourselves,' said Ralph, whose hearing was little short of miraculous.

Gilbert was stung. 'Well, I for one will be no party to torture. I am not one with the Flemings.'

'There is rarely any reason to torture nursemaids.'

Gilbert shouted in rage: 'They were kind to me. They saved my life.'

'Good of them,' said Ralph. 'Now they can tell us something that may help to save ours.'

Gilbert spurred his horse into greater speed. He drew level with Ralph and Bruno.

'Do you care about nothing?'

'I care about winning.'

'Is that all?'

Ralph kept his eyes on the trail as he replied. 'I also care about the two men we found an hour ago. They were from our army. Scouts too. Absent for three days. Stripped and mutilated. Good men. I knew them. Now think of your nurses; it was their countrymen who did that.'

Bruno made his only contribution. 'Think how lucky you were.' He sounded as if he half regretted it.

It was Berry who heard them first. Edwin laid down the bundle of kindling he had just tied together. He shook the remains of creeper bindings from around his feet, picked up his billhook, and crept to the edge of the copse.

'Here, boy!' he whispered.

Berry came and sat beside him. Edwin put an arm round his neck to quieten the soft growling.

Two faceless Normans trotted past. In their mail coifs and helmets, with the nasal guard hiding half their features, they all looked the same. True, one was very tall, but apart from that they could have been peas from the same iron pod. Their mail hauberks and iron-bound weapons jingled and creaked on polished leatherwork. Their heavy horses, each stronger than three bears, passed so close to Edwin that he could almost feel the air pushed against him with the impact of their passage. The ground shook with the boulder thud of their hooves. Berry recoiled in his arms.

A few paces behind came a third rider. Edwin's surprise and curiosity leaped up to challenge his fear. This one was different. No helmet. No mail. Only a leather jerkin and grubby leggings, cross-tied in the Saxon fashion. Yet he was clearly no Saxon. The strangely patterned knife scabbard and large ivory horn dangling from his belt told of a country far, far from England.

Thick, tousled black hair flopped over a face gnarled and wrinkled like the bark of an oak tree. He did not loom large like the other two. Neither did his horse. More pony than horse – rough, wiry, sure-footed.

Man and horse moved as one. The other two sat as if they had been riveted into their high wooden saddles by a blacksmith; this man seemed to have grown by magic straight out of the pony's back. The two Normans had control of their mounts, but by discipline; this strange, dark creature had not so much total control over his beast as pure harmony with it. Edwin had heard tales from the monks at Chichester about ancient creatures from the mists of legend, called centaurs, half man and half horse. As he crouched in the bracken and gazed up, he allowed that such stories could well have been true. He knew that he was looking for the first time in his life at true mastery over a horse.

It took only a blink or two for this odd little man to trot by, but the picture engraved on Edwin's memory lasted the rest of his life.

His prudence kept him from creeping out as soon as the man had gone. He listened, and heard nothing. He quickly twined a leash of plaited creeper round Berry's neck, grasped the end in one hand and the billhook in the other, and communed with himself as to the best route to take.

There was no hope of warning them at the mill, but he had to get there as fast as possible without being seen. He had little presentiment of mortal danger, because he could think of no reason why two solitary Norman soldiers and a horse goblin could be engaged on anything other than scouting. All the same, he wanted to be on hand, in case the suddenness of his appearance could be used to create a useful diversion.

He decided to leave the copse at the side away from the mill, skirt the far shoulder of the hill, and come down to the house from the far end, higher up the valley. He waited until the riders were well over halfway down the path towards the mill. Then, turning about, he raced through the copse, heedless of the noise of twigs and leaves. He burst out of the other side, and ran into another Norman.

Gilbert's horse reared, but Gilbert stayed in the saddle with an effort, offering silent thanks that neither Ralph nor Sandor had seen it.

Edwin fought for his breath.

'You!'

Berry wagged his tail.

Gilbert looked about him. 'Have you seen them?'

'Yes.'

Edwin stood still, his breath returning.

There was a long silence.

Gilbert thought of sheepskins beside a warm fire, and of two twisted, naked bodies sprawled beside the trail.

Edwin saw a young man his own age laughing at dog stories as he carved a little doll, and he also saw a third warrior encased in mail and helmet astride a staring giant of a horse.

'I did not wish to come here,' said Gilbert at last.

Edwin nodded. 'I believe you. What do they want?'

'News.'

Edwin became wary again. 'What news?'

'The news your miller carried.'

'There was no news.'

'There was news,' insisted Gilbert. 'You must realise. They know there is news. If you tell them, we will go away. If you resist, I shall not able to protect you.'

'Do they know you rested here?' said Edwin.

Gilbert looked down at the pommel of his saddle. 'They have guessed – yes.'

'Is there no debt then?'

'For me, yes,' said Gilbert. 'But not for them. And I must do my duty. We are enemies. And I know you are deceiving me. I give you only this one chance. Tell them what they wish to know. If not, they will try to – persuade. Your man Godric will fight to protect his woman. There will be bloodshed. Do you want that?'

Edwin hesitated.

Gilbert fidgeted.

'There will be a battle anyway, whatever you say and whatever you try to hide. Only hurry.'

Edwin came to a decision.

'We will go down together. Perhaps if I can speak enough French to them they will be satisfied.'

With any luck, he thought, he could forestall Gorm's craven fear. The miller could not speak to them unless he, Edwin, translated.

Gilbert read his thoughts.

'Do not try to deceive; we have a man who speaks English.'

Edwin gasped. 'You mean that dark rider at the back?'

'His name is Sandor. He is Hungarian. He speaks many tongues.'

'Then we must indeed hasten,' said Edwin.

Already he could see Gorm's tiny eyes and sweat-soaked face.

When Gilbert arrived, he felt as if he had stumbled on a tableau in a fair, so still was everybody. Gorm was indeed sweating as he cowered near the entrance to the mill machinery, his eyes small, like blackcurrants. Aud hung on his arm, the perfect image of the dutiful daughter. Rowena stood in front of the doorway, still holding the cloth with which she had been wiping her hands. Behind her, barely visible, lurked Sweyn. Edith was in her usual place by Rowena's skirt; the stick doll was in her right hand. Godric towered over them all, still as an oak on a summer's day, barely an arm's length from Rowena. He held a large spade as easily as if it were a kitchen knife.

In the strip between the house and the stream, Ralph leaned on a drawn sword. Bruno held the reins of all the horses. In between them was the Hungarian, squat and deep-chested, his hands on his belt, daylight showing clearly between his legs. Separated from his horse, he looked like an overgrown dwarf acrobat from a group of travelling tumblers.

The very stillness made the tension palpable. Gilbert felt that lightning was about to strike. He motioned to Edwin to stop by the gate. He himself dismounted and handed the reins to Bruno.

Ralph looked at Sandor. 'Ask them again,' he said.

Sandor raised his head. 'My friend, he say you have news of Hardrada, news of King Harold. We ask that you tell us. My friends they are three strong men. You tell us, I think.'

Messages flew from eye to eye across the yard like a flight of swallows. Rowena flashed a warning to her cringing father. Aud looked desperately at Rowena. Gilbert begged them with his eyes to say something. Edith's face lit up with recognition when she caught sight of him. Edwin tried to warn Godric against resistance.

Sandor echoed his thoughts when Godric made the slightest of movements towards Rowena.

'It would not be wise, big man. We do not wish to take lives, only news. But we will take both if you use strength.' He smiled and made a gesture to show his admiration of Godric's large body. 'To use your strength to no end – I think that would be pity.'

Ralph watched the messages fly, and knew that a chain of deceit bound these people before him. He had to find the weakest link in that chain. He looked from Edith's vacant expression to Sweyn's pout, from Godric's impassive stare to Rowena's flashing defiance. Then he turned to the couple by the mill door, and made up his mind.

He walked forward and grabbed Aud by the wrist. He was a little surprised by the quick flush of colour that came to her cheeks as he pulled her into the middle of the yard.

'Tell them, Sandor,' he said. 'Tell them that if they do not give us the news, we ride away with this young woman. We take her to our camp. Camp whores are few and far between. Many men are there who have scarcely seen a woman in three months. If they think Normans are barbarians, wait till she sees the Flemings. Tell them, Sandor.'

He waved his sword once or twice while Sandor translated.

Another swallow flight of glances passed between Edwin and Gilbert behind Ralph's back.

'No. Enough. I will tell you.'

It was Gorm. He came forward wringing his hands.

'Only, please let her go. Do not kill us.'

'When I hear your news,' said Ralph, and listened as Gorm spoke through Sandor.

'So,' said Ralph. 'Hardrada is dead, eh?' He glanced at Bruno, without releasing Aud. 'And Harold marches south again. Good. We shall be prepared for him.'

He looked for the first time at Gilbert. 'Your nurses wisely found their tongues.'

Gilbert nearly burst with rage and shame.

Ralph held Aud at arm's length. He heard her catch her breath, and saw again the flush in her cheeks.

'What shall we do with her, Bruno?' he called out with a laugh. 'Take her with us?'

'How can you?' said Gilbert, appalled. 'You gave your word.'

Ralph looked up, surprised. Seeing Gilbert so vulnerable brought out the hunter in him. A bantering smile spread over his face.

'A Norman's promise to a Saxon?' he said.

'Let her go,' said Gilbert, shocked and furious.

'Do not give me orders, boy,' said Ralph.

Both were now pushed by pride and temper beyond discretion. Bruno began to tie the horses' reins to a gatepost.

'You animal!'

It was Aud. She had thought they were quarrelling over her, and burst out in rage at Gilbert.

'You barbarian! You spit on the laws of hospitality. Is this what we get for our care of you? If it were not for us you would be dead.'

Gilbert froze, haggard at the thought of what she might have said.

Ralph shook her off as if she were a wet leaf. 'Great God in Heaven, Sandor, what is she saying?'

Sandor pursed his lips and looked at Gilbert.

Gilbert gazed back at him, entreaty glistening in his eyes.

Sandor gave a thoughtful hitch to his belt.

'She says her father tells great lies, and that he is a coward. She says she does not fear you and that you will burn in the fires of Hell. She says you are fit only for the Devil. She says—'

Ralph waved a gloved hand. 'Yes, yes, I follow the idea. She protects her father as he tried to protect her. She has more spirit than I thought. I was perhaps wrong about her.'

He sheathed his sword. 'Tell her she has nothing to fear. I respect loyalty.' He gave her a tiny nod. 'Away now. We have what we came for.'

He strode towards the gate, where Bruno, having decided that his intervention was not wanted after all, untied the reins. They both mounted.

'I shall follow,' said Gilbert. He made an excuse about a need of nature.

When they were out of earshot, he asked Edwin to translate what Aud had said. Then he turned to Sandor. 'Thank you.'

Sandor smiled and shrugged. Gilbert turned again.

'Tell them, Edwin, I could not stop them coming. I tried to keep them away.'

'I will tell them.' He pointed at Sandor. 'That is a good friend you have there.'

Gilbert sighed in relief. 'It is indeed. This is Sandor the Magyar.'

Sandor gave a slight bow.

'And I,' said Edwin, 'am Edwin son of Edward.'

Sandor repeated the name carefully. 'Ed-win.' He bowed again, making himself even more gnome-like.

Edwin returned the bow.

Sandor spoke in English. 'Where did you learn the French?'

Edwin replied in English, making a dismissive gesture. 'I went to Normandy two years ago with my lord. We stayed many weeks.'

Sandor's eyes screwed up. 'You learn very fast. You had a teacher?'

Edwin winced. 'I – I knew someone, yes.'

'That someone was kind to you?'

'Yes.'

Sandor nodded. 'That someone is now perhaps dead?'

Edwin shook his head. 'I do not know. I have not seen – them since.'

'Ah! A sad farewell.'

Sandor resumed in French: 'So! We too have a parting. Eh, Gilbert?'

Gilbert mounted, and looked down at Edwin. Two images still fought in his mind's eye – the sheepskins before the fire, and the two naked, spitted bodies.

'You have not travelled from here since I last saw you?'

Edwin looked puzzled. 'No. We rarely travel. I hope soon to meet – my lord. That is all.'

Gilbert sat back in relief; it was what he had wanted to hear. One of the two images was fading. He looked down again.

'You have told us the news. You will not be troubled again, I think. The wasting parties have done great havoc, but they will not come this far. There may be foraging groups, but they will take supplies, not lives. Tell Godric he must not place himself in their way. Then you will be safe. Now we must go.'

Sandor flashed his dark smile, and bowed again.

As he waddled beside Gilbert towards the horses, he spoke quietly. 'How can you make such a promise?'

Gilbert grimaced. 'How can I not? It is the best I can do.'

Sandor vaulted lightly into the saddle. Edwin shook his head in wonder; the dwarf had again become a centaur.

As they rode out of the yard, Godric moved for the first time and quietly laid down his spade.

Rowena wiped her hands again on her cloth and walked slowly into the house, pausing to rest a moment against the door jamb. She took a deep breath, and carefully pushed a lock of wayward hair from her forehead. Sweyn followed behind with

Edith, and, for no other reason than spite, hit her and knocked the doll out of her hand.

Edwin gazed after Gilbert and Sandor, thinking of love lost in Normandy and glory soon to be found in Sussex.

Gorm walked forward to put his arm round Aud's shoulder. She shook it off fiercely, puzzled at her own anger.

As they climbed the path towards the copse, Sandor spoke again.

'It is here you have the good luck?'

Gilbert nodded, tight-lipped.

'They are good people,' said Sandor.

'Mmm.'

'Good people – for farmers.'

'Millers,' corrected Gilbert.

'Farmers, millers, whatever,' said Sandor. 'They are down on the land.' He made a downward movement with the palm of his hand. 'They walk. We Magyars –' he patted his deep chest '– we are above the land. We ride.'

Gilbert did not reply. For the first time, Sandor had said something that annoyed him, and he did not know the cause of his annoyance.

Ahead of them, Bruno looked at Ralph and raised his eyebrows.

Ralph swore. 'I know, I know. That giant could have broken him in half. So he was lucky.'

'For how long?'

'He got the news.'

'Lucky again. A fat coward spills some words. How long do we depend only upon his luck?'

Two bare corpses in the woods stared sightless into Ralph's memory. They could so easily have been Gilbert. He had done enough things wrong to get himself killed several times over.

Bruno was right. Gilbert could not afford mistakes. He had to be made to learn, and all the best lessons were hard ones. The boy certainly could not allow himself to be distracted by his senseless search for revenge – revenge on a nameless man he did not know and was never likely to find, for a wrong that was not a wrong when it was committed. In war there was only one way to survive – to concentrate.

And Ralph knew that he too must concentrate. He could not allow himself the luxury of feeling fondness for Gilbert. Having him there was like having Michael with him again; it helped to soften the image of Michael's fever-ridden face; helped him to forget the patient Aimery, coughing his last breath as Ralph sat helpless at his bedside.

How did one avoid pain then? By never thinking, never feeling? Perhaps he should never have become a scout. They were the only ones in the army who were supposed to think. And that was what he liked about being a scout. Ralph felt wretched.

The Duke looked over the parapet into the seething bailey below. A train of empty ox-wagons was trying to make its way out of the gate and back towards the harbour for a second load. Whips, voices, and tempers were raised.

Fitzosbern leaned against the new timbers and watched William. The tension was beginning to show. Not visible to sweating soldiers, perhaps, or to grumbling knights, but the signs were there for the man who had the wit and the experience to see. Fitzosbern had had a lifetime to perfect his understanding of the pale-faced boy with whom he and Baldwin had sworn the oath in the gloomy little chapel at Vaudreuil twenty-six years before. To him it was as clear as spring water.

For one thing, the Duke was no longer teasing him. Fitzosbern did not like being teased, which of course was why William did it. When nobody was looking. It was a form of intimacy.

On their tours of inspection, he was walking more and more on his own, a few paces ahead. Fitzosbern watched his shoulders get tighter and tighter. When they were face to face, the eyes screwed up into pinpoints of darting light. A hand fidgeted with the pommel of a dagger; in better times, hands were often clasped behind the back, and there was the frequent tuneless humming. Now the humming had stopped.

Fitzosbern tried to help by indicating the obvious. He pointed down into the bailey.

'The curtain wall proceeds well.'

William said nothing.

Fitzosbern tried again.

'Montgomery reported. Said the training was the best it has been. Even Geoffrey was impressed, he said.'

William grunted.

'You saw the Bretons yourself this morning,' continued Fitzosbern. 'I saw Fulk's Flemings.'

'Flemings!' William spat.

Fitzosbern gave up. He turned as he heard the noise of heavy feet stumping up the steps to the parapet. Baldwin paused and wiped his forehead.

'More fresh vegetables. Just unloaded and safely stowed. We have enough for another two weeks, at a pinch.'

William whipped round as if stung. 'Knights, infantry, castle, supplies – yes. We have everything. Everything!'

Baldwin stopped short, as if slapped in the face. He looked blankly at Fitzosbern, who sent a warning with his eyes.

William stalked past Baldwin towards the top of the steps.

'Everything – except news!'

Baldwin stared after him.

Fitzosbern continued looking down into the bailey, not really seeing.

'He is trying to take the most difficult decision of all.'

Baldwin understood. 'To do nothing.'

'Just so,' said Fitzosbern. 'To wait.' He moved to the top of the steps. 'And he has no Matilda to tell him he is right.'

'We think he is right.'

'Not enough,' said Fitzosbern from half-way down. 'Even we two are not close enough. We believe in his decisions; she believes in the man.'

Then he is lucky indeed, thought Baldwin, as he picked at a splinter on the parapet.

Only one person had ever believed in him. Only with his sister had he been able to be himself. There was a radiance and innocence about her. He had always wanted to protect her, and she was no weakling. Indeed she was tall and big-boned for her age.

'Why do they always tease?' asked Baldwin.

Agnes stroked his hair. 'They see your softness and they think it is weakness.'

'You are soft,' said Baldwin, 'and they do not tease you.'

'They see me simply as a girl; I do not count. I shall become a wife, an old nursemaid, or a nun, simply as God and my family will it.'

Agnes as usual had spoken the exact truth. At thirteen he understood it. Even at eleven, so did she.

'Dearest Baldwin, do not be sad. We are given no choice about having life, and we are given no choice about how it is to be lived. I might as well be bitter that I have only two arms instead of three. Two is what God has given me. You are also what God has given me. I am happy with that.'

Baldwin gazed at her. 'How did you become so wise?'

'It is not wisdom; it is truth. Truth is always clear, if you look straight at it.'

'It is not clear to me,' grumbled Baldwin.

Agnes laughed. 'What does it matter? Whatever happens, we can always talk.'

But not for long.

That very night, their guardian, Osbern the Steward, who was also the guardian of the young Duke, was murdered. Arrangements had to be hastily made to keep the children safe.

The young Duke would ride tò the court of the King. Osbern's son William would go with him. Baldwin was to fly to Flanders, where his brother Richard arranged a place for him at the court of the Count. Osbern's wife, the lady Emma, was to go to the convent of St Amand at Rouen. Agnes was to go with her.

Dear saints, no! Agnes was his rock.

'It is as I said: girls do not count.' Agnes was accepting again, but this time she was crying. 'Oh, Baldwin, it really is hard.'

Baldwin felt his cheeks wet. 'I shall come back. By the bones of the Virgin, I shall come back.'

But he rarely did. No matter how hard he tried, the memory faded. As with a dream, he remembered that she represented something vivid and precious, but it became increasingly difficult to recall what it was. The few times that he managed to visit, the agony of fresh parting made him regret that he had re-opened such deep wounds.

Now Agnes was gone. And she was right: what choice had he but to accept?

He looked at the tiny wooden splinters he had been rolling between his fingers. He tossed them over the palisade.

The Duke had a point: the sooner something happened, the better for all of them

'Well?'

Again the hard, rasping voice. Gilbert was glad the question was directed at Ralph, not at himself. If he had had his way, he would not have been standing in the Duke's tent at all.

'I am not sure they will need me,' he had ventured.

Bruno had shrugged. 'Scared?'

'Damn you, no!'

'The experience will do you good,' said Ralph. 'You will not meet many generals like the Bastard. If you can stand up to him, you can stand up to anyone.'

'It is fine for you,' grumbled Gilbert. 'You are used to it.'

'I had to learn too. With Lord Geoffrey.'

'Not the same,' said Gilbert.

Ralph laughed. 'Try getting on the wrong side of him and see. I was younger than you when I started in his service.'

'A bishop is not a duke.'

'Enough,' said Ralph. 'Whoever it is, you must learn to look up and speak up and say your mind. A good general values an honest scout, and he will soon detect a bad one. If you are afraid in his tent you will be afraid on patrol. If you have taken risks to find the truth, you will take risks to speak it.'

'There will be so many of them,' said Gilbert. 'If it were only the Duke by himself. You never know where the next question will come from.'

'Have no fear. The Duke may not sit by himself, but he makes up his mind by himself. He is the one you must impress, not the others.'

Gilbert made a face. 'You try telling that to Sir Walter Giffard.'

'You do not realise,' said Ralph. 'They are all trying to impress the Bastard too. They want his trust and his favour just as you do.'

Gilbert shook his head. 'I prefer not to argue with Sir Walter Giffard if it is all the same to you.'

'You do not have to. You simply answer, when asked. Know your place, but hold your place. And watch them. Some day – you never know – one of them may be called upon to lead us. Anything can happen in battle – here or in Normandy. You must know which of them are worth following.'

As he marched behind Ralph towards the Duke's tent, Gilbert gazed at him in amazement. This extraordinary man seemed to regard no one as his superior. He walked as if he did not give a curse for anyone. They were going to be questioned by the most feared men in Normandy, under the command of the finest general in all France. They were going to be examined and judged.

And here was Ralph, swaggering in as if *he* were going to judge *them*.

He knew that Ralph's loyalty to the Duke was beyond question. Ralph would die for the Duke without a second thought. Yet he was capable of sizing up the men about him, just in case the unthinkable happened and he were to be left without a master.

Gilbert sighed. For all he knew, Bruno thought the same way as Ralph did, though he was never likely to find out for sure; getting ten connected words out of Bruno was like trying to pull a ferret's teeth. If he lived to be a hundred, thought Gilbert, he would never have as much knowledge as these two men.

'Ralph,' he would say, 'why do you always know?'

Ralph would look at Bruno and shrug. 'I am just good at guessing.'

'If it were all guesswork, you would make mistakes. But you are always right. Why do you know everything?'

Ralph would never give a satisfactory answer, and Bruno would only raise his eyebrows.

Gilbert sighed again. Would he ever be able to match these men in wisdom and ambling confidence? The miracle was that they even tolerated his presence. Whatever did they see in him? Or in each other, if it came to that? Each barely acknowledged that the other was there.

As he hovered in the shadows near the door of the Duke's tent, Gilbert began to regret his rash outburst to Bruno that he had no fear whatever of standing before the Duke. How he envied Ralph, waiting at ease in the candlelight. He gaped at his friend's genius for conveying respect, attentiveness, and total independence by his mere stance.

To Ralph it was simple. The men around him commanded by heredity; they fought from habit; and they acquired by instinct. But to do all three things successfully they needed news, and that was what Ralph specialised in providing. Every man, in whatever rank God had seen fit to place him in society, found his own way of expressing his rebellion against the men who lorded it over him. A priest could threaten Hellfire and browbeat with penance; a merchant could overcharge and take advantage of ignorance; a peasant had the weapons of delay and inertia. Men like Ralph savoured the moment when, as now, their lords and masters leaned forward, almost licking their lips, like a starving man before a feast.

'It is as we suspected, my lord Duke. There has been a battle, at a bridge near York.'

Gilbert could not see every man's face in the bad light, but he could sense that every eye was fixed on Ralph. The strained silence of the illustrious audience sent shivers down his back. If Ralph noticed the tension, he gave no sign of it.

'Hardrada is dead – an arrow in the windpipe. Tostig also has perished. The Norwegians are either destroyed or dispersed. Harold achieved complete surprise. Complete surprise,' he repeated, as if that were especially significant.

Gilbert frowned, the more deeply when he noticed the Duke and the men round his table nodding as if they took the point completely.

'You were right, Fitz,' said Count Robert of Mortain. 'Harold caught them off guard. It was just as you pictured it.'

Fitzosbern inclined his head slightly by way of accepting the compliment.

'Maybe,' he agreed. 'But I think our other news of today helps to explain it as well.'

'May I ask what news that is, sir?' said Ralph.

Gilbert swallowed. He would never have dared to ask questions on his own account.

Fitzosbern lit another stub of candle from a dying flame.

'Ah, yes. I was forgetting. You have been out all day.' He set the new stub in the candlestick. 'Within the last two hours we have had other intelligence from the Kentish side. Pedlars on their rounds from the Port of London had it from east coasters in the

Thames. The first battle was at a place called Fulford Gate, also near York. Edwin and Morcar tried to stop Norway and failed. They have retired to lick their wounds. Harold attacked about a week later. That fits in with your news. My guess is that Hardrada's host was weakened at Fulford, and was probably in no state to face a second engagement so soon. Quite apart from physical tiredness and casualties, they were probably short of supplies and low on weapons and arrows.'

'I quite agree,' said Baldwin de Clair. 'Good raiders but bad campaigners. Viking staff work always was poor.'

Ralph smiled to himself. Sir Baldwin was an awful old woman, and a self-satisfied one at that.

'Putting the news together,' said Fitzosbern, continuing to look at Ralph but in effect talking to everybody, 'the picture we have is this: the Saxon army of the north, under Edwin and Morcar, were defeated by Hardrada at Fulford, but we do not know how heavily. We know nothing of the state of their forces, or of their present position. Hardrada in turn was defeated by Harold. He was killed, his army was destroyed, and the fugitives have dispersed. But just as Hardrada was reduced by his first success, so Harold must have been reduced by his victory at your bridge, near York – um   ?'

'Er – Stamford, sir,' put in Gilbert, finding his courage and edging forward.

Fitzosbern looked up. 'Just so . . . Stamford. Mmm.'

'Sir?'

Ralph turned to him in amused surprise. Perhaps the boy was developing some independence after all.

Fitzosbern leaned forward on his elbows, twiddled the rusty candlestick, and continued in his patient way.

'Harold must now march south with all haste. Indeed, I am sure he is well on his way. If he can march north fast to face invasion and bad news, he can march south even faster with the trophy of victory in his belt.'

'His army will be that much more tired,' said Montgomery.

'I agree. And weakened from the battle at – um –' He snapped his fingers in annoyance.

'Stamford, sir,' said Gilbert.

Ralph smiled drily.

'Yes, Stamford,' said Fitzosbern. 'But he will not drag all his casualties with him.'

'What about Edwin and Morcar?' said Walter Giffard, who had dragged himself from his bed to attend, if only to put young Beaumont in his place should the chance arise.

'My guess,' said Fitzosbern, 'is that their army is too scattered. It would take too long to round it up again and reimpose discipline in time to be of use to Harold down here. After defeat, most fyrdmen run home, where they feel safer. Even professionals desert sometimes.'

'The difference is – they desert *before* the battle, not after. Much more sensible.'

The speaker sat back, savouring the laughter.

Gilbert looked fully at him for the first time. Now he remembered the sinister figure in the shadows at the previous council meeting. He saw again the casual, lounging attitude. He saw more clearly a veritable tree-trunk of a man, insolently confident in his own strength. A few days' growth of dark whiskers covered his heavy face. Thick hair fell to his collar. Black tufts sprouted from his ears and nostrils. A livid scar ran from the corner of his mouth right up to an eye. Where the skin had drawn tight in healing, it had dragged down the lower eyelid, laying bare a pink triangle of inner flesh. The eyeball and pupil were luridly discoloured.

Gilbert had heard much talk of this man. Most of it was bad, though he noticed that interspersed between the dislike and revulsion was a reluctant, wry admiration. If nothing else, this man was an excellent soldier. Gilbert had glimpsed him now and then, but had never been this close to him before. Now he got his first full taste of the massive captain of Flemish mercenaries, Fulk Bloodeye.

He knew too that the wispy little cripple standing behind him was his constant companion.

As the laughter rolled, this wraith leaned over Fulk's shoulder and proffered a dark drink in a small phial. Fulk waved it away.

After the laughter had died down, Fitzosbern resumed his summary. Gilbert noted how the Duke said nothing, but watched and listened.

'Harold will select his best men,' said Fitzosbern. 'His house-carls. He will get here as rapidly as possible, mustering whatever he can from county fyrdmen on the way. He will probably try to surprise us.'

'Never!' said Robert of Beaumont, blustering. 'He must be a fool.'

Bishop Odo reflected the more moderate views of the older men.

'He has seen us before,' he said. 'He campaigned with us in Brittany. Surely he knows we do not fight carelessly like Vikings.'

'True,' said Fitzosbern. 'But Harold is human. He wants victory, and he is willing to take risks. Why else did he come to us in Normandy in 'sixty-four? Everything he did there involved risk. And remember how successful he was.'

Montgomery looked at Giffard and chuckled reminiscently.

'The man was quite impossible.'

'Put yourself in his position,' said Fitzosbern. 'You have just used the stratagem of forced march and surprise attack and gained a complete victory. Would you, in the face of a similar threat, change that stratagem when it has been so brilliantly successful?'

Nobody could think of an answer. Gilbert began to understand why Fitzosbern sat so high in the Duke's councils.

'So,' said the Duke at last. 'He approaches. And quickly. So be it. We are prepared.'

'How do we proceed with him, sir? What is to be the manner of his – er –destruction?'

Fulk Bloodeye's smile was so disfigured by the scar that it became a leer. Gilbert could not be sure whether it denoted bloodthirsty anticipation or insolent enquiry as to whether the Duke had made up his mind.

William took it as a challenge, and turned slightly in his chair, so as to face Fulk directly.

'That is one of the things we are assembled to decide. These officers here – my tenants-in-chief – will discuss it. I may choose to listen also to your comments, but you will nevertheless wait until we come to a resolution. Then you will receive your orders. After our victory you will receive the balance of your pay. Meanwhile you will wait – and wait with respect – upon our decision. Whatever is the result, I tell you, by God's Splendour, that you will get what is coming to you.'

Fulk's smile faded, but not his insolent manner. He rose to his feet, towering over the company.

'In that case, your Grace, since I have no relevant advice to offer that I think your ... officers ... here would consider, your humble servant will await your Grace's pleasure by the campfire, with his loyal volunteers.' He picked up his gloves.

The Duke lowered his voice to a rasping whisper.

'The captain of Flemish ... contracted mercenaries ... will be excused from this council at his commander's pleasure, not at his own.'

The air went solid.

Fulk gazed at the stony faces round the table. Not one was looking at him. After a pause long enough for Gilbert to wipe his wet palms twice on his buttocks, Fulk shrugged, tossed his gloves on to the table, and sat down again.

If Gilbert's eyes popped at what he saw, his ears popped even more at what he heard.

The debate about strategy and tactics raged long and fiercely.

Nobody noticed him. Gilbert's legs ached after his day's riding, but he dared not ask permission to withdraw, especially after what had happened to Fulk. He looked questioningly at Ralph, who cupped a hand to his ear and nodded towards the table, as if to say 'listen and learn'.

Gilbert was impressed once again at how much plain speaking the Duke was prepared to tolerate from the men he trusted. He could afford to; it was obvious from the flurry with Fulk that there was no question about his total authority.

Gilbert remembered Ralph's earlier advice, and watched and judged, at least as far as his experience allowed.

Sir Walter Giffard and Sir Roger of Montgomery he knew. And Bishop Geoffrey, his old lord. Bishop Odo he did not know, but he could see at once that he was petty and small-minded. As for the rest, there did not seem much to choose between them – de Tosny, de Grandmesnil, de Montfort, de Warenne, and others deep in the shadows. Gruff, gritty, greedy men, with a keen eye to profit, and willing to take risks.

The odd one out was Beaumont. He was so young. What was he doing in this company?

Gilbert pulled himself together and struggled to concentrate.

The talk started quietly enough, with the question of what Harold might do when he reached London. Most of those present accepted Fitzosbern's opinion that Harold would press on at once.

'He must attack our bridgehead,' he said. 'Just as Edwin and Morcar had to attack Hardrada. Delay can only favour us. The longer he waits in London for the midland levies to arrive, the better equipped we become.'

'Will he not have a problem with fatigue?' said Montgomery.

'Fatigue? Exhaustion, I should say,' said Giffard. 'Yorkshire and back in less than twenty days and a battle intervening.'

'You forget two things,' said Geoffrey de Montbrai. 'One is the magic of Harold's personality. The other is the excitement of the time. The spirit of these men is moved, by victory and by concern for their native land.'

'Are you expert on these – er – inspired Saxons?' asked Giffard.

Montgomery smiled. His friend was beginning to recover.

'No,' said Geoffrey evenly. 'But I am a bishop. I know something of matters concerning the spirit. I tell you, if men are sufficiently moved, they can perform miracles, and I say these Saxons could be sufficiently moved. In normal times no army could get here so fast from Yorkshire, especially after what they have been through; but these are not normal times, and Harold is no normal general. I say they can do it.'

'At any rate we must be prepared for it,' said Fitzosbern.

'Suppose he picks up shire levies from Surrey and Sussex on the way?' said Beaumont, anxious to show off his geography.

'That is a chance we shall have to take,' said Fitzosbern. 'We can not commit our main force towards London without precise information as to his numbers and his position, simply in the faint hope of cutting off a few hundred fyrdmen from Surrey or Kent. It would expose our base camp and put all our fortifications at risk. Everything we have done since landing would go for nothing. Harold is no fool. At all times we must remember that. And my lord of Coutances has reminded us that Harold is a commander with great gifts of leadership. We all saw that in Normandy and Brittany two years ago.'

'Saints and angels, I should say so!' said Montgomery, looking at Giffard. 'He had *our* men eating out of his hand, never mind his own. Do you remember?'

The Duke brought them sharply to order. The infantry commanders were all for letting Harold come right up to the defences of the castle they had nearly completed. The chief engineer, Ranulf of Dreux, was brought in. He talked at great length, in his gloomy way, about fields of fire and tensions and stresses and killing ground. Much of it went over Gilbert's head. When

Baldwin put in his piece about supplies and reserves and siege ration planning, full of facts and figures, he found his jaw aching in the effort to suppress a yawn.

Fulk Bloodeye added his weight to the argument by suggesting that they should extend the deliberate destruction to a wider area.

'Waste in a wider circle,' he said. 'Harold will be provoked and will attack us in haste. He will have to travel over ravaged land to get here and will fight us on an empty stomach.'

Robert of Mortain was shocked out of his customary silence.

'How much of this land do you wish to destroy, by God? We shall have none left to be worth occupying.'

'I notice,' added Sir Walter Giffard tartly, 'that our captain of mercenaries sees himself once again as bandit and arsonist rather than as front-line soldier.'

'I notice too,' returned Fulk, 'that one of our ... captains of cavalry ... has not been anxious to commit his levy of knights to the business of meeting Harold in open battle before the castle.'

Giffard flared, and stood up.

'I should have expected such ignorance from a paid gang-master of foot soldiers. Any other member of this council could tell you that it would be insane to try and deploy cavalry in formation over such uneven ground bristling with tree stumps.'

'So it will be the old story,' sneered Fulk. 'Send in the infantry to break their strength and break our heads. Then send in the cavalry to carve them up and carve out their own glory.'

'Enough!' The Duke banged the handle of a dagger on the table, making the candlesticks jump.

Fulk shrugged again and resumed his careless lounging, Giffard glowered, until Montgomery tugged his sleeve.

'Walter!'

Giffard allowed himself to be pulled down.

Thereafter the council tried self-consciously to argue in

reasonable tones. If the cavalry could not be deployed before the castle, then suitable open ground had to be found elsewhere.

Ralph was questioned. So were several other scouts, who had been waiting patiently by the fire outside. All were agreed that the wide stretches of forest in the area did not make the task easy. The more they discussed the advantages of various fields of battle at a greater distance, the more the cautious ones reminded them of the dangers of moving too far from the base camp and castle.

Then Gilbert's old master, Bishop Geoffrey of Coutances, introduced a new idea.

'We must not forget,' he said, 'in all our talk of ground and of tactics, that we are dealing with a very special man.'

Fitzosbern grinned. 'Some more talk of the spirit, Geoffrey?'

Geoffrey smiled tolerantly. 'Spirit moves mountains faster even than your engineers, Fitz. Listen. If we are to win, we must not only outfight this man; we must out-think him.'

'Is he so clever?' said Odo. 'Are we not just a little bemused by his supposed talents?'

'I am well aware,' replied Geoffrey, 'that my lord of Bayeux, in his customary oblique way, means "you" when he says "we". And I will answer the ill-directed shaft.'

Odo glared, but said nothing.

Geoffrey continued. 'If being bemused by his talents means having a sound appreciation of our adversary's strength, then I am content to be called bemused. And I am sure our lord the Duke, on those terms, is equally happy to be so called. It is one of the principles of good generalship, in which art I am willing to give my lord of Bayeux the benefit of my not inconsiderable experience.'

'Get to the point, Coutances,' said the Duke. 'And do you, brother, stay dumb.'

Odo opened his mouth, thought better of it, and shut it again.

Geoffrey resumed. 'It is simple to find a man's weaknesses and use them. The trouble is that Harold does not have many. We must therefore turn not only his weaknesses against him but his strengths.'

'There you go again, Geoffrey,' said Montgomery. 'Talking in circles.'

'Be silent,' said the Duke sharply.

'Consider,' said Geoffrey. 'One thing we all noticed about this man when he was in Normandy was his charm. If I recall, Roger,' he said to Montgomery with a sly smile, 'you were as much – er – affected by this as anyone.'

Montgomery made a face. 'What if I was? As I said at the time, he—'

'"He was quite impossible,"' said Geoffrey. 'Yes. I know. You may recall that Harold relied greatly on this quality of – I repeat – his charm. If he could lead our Normans across the Couesnon under a rain of arrows, what can he not do with his own men, and in his own land?'

'So?' demanded Giffard.

Geoffrey, like Fitzosbern, refused to be rushed. 'Harold will demand prodigies from his men, and he will get them. Give him further to march, and he will demand more prodigies still. It never crosses the mind of a charming man that his charm will not work. A man who has worked one miracle will be tempted to work more. The greatest temptation placed before Our Lord was not lust, or avarice, but power. Most men, faced with the choice of creating victory by mere preparation or victory by miracle, will choose the miracle.'

'Geoffrey – please,' said Montgomery. 'What does all this mean in simple language?'

Geoffrey allowed another slight smile to appear. 'It means this, my friend: we must allow Harold to push his men to their very limits, so that by the time they arrive they are on the verge of exhaustion. It also means that Harold will scorn caution, and not wait for his extra levies from the central shires. It means that their elation of spirit will hide from them the fact that they are at the end of their strength. It means that Harold will be so anxious to take us by surprise that it will not occur to him that we might take him by surprise.'

'How do you propose to do that by staying put?' asked Giffard.

'I did not say stay put for ever,' said Geoffrey. 'Timing is all important. We wait. When he is near and hastening to attack us, we move at speed to attack him, on a field of our own choosing. There is our true killing ground – where we can deploy cavalry, not in front of our castle ramparts.'

Walter Giffard threw a scalding glance of triumph in Fulk's direction.

'Our entire cavalry strategy,' said Geoffrey, 'has depended for months on our ability to deploy large numbers of men – safely – on open ground. It is for this that I have been working, on his Grace's express instructions.'

'The cavalry are the shock troops,' said the Duke.

'You mean the élite,' muttered Fulk.

William heard him.

'I mean what I say. The cavalry are the very stomach of our plan. You and the archers are the limbs. You knew this when you agreed to serve.'

'On the assumption, my lord, that the cavalry, in their pursuit of the greater share of glory, take the greater share of risk.'

'Try riding with us, and find out,' said Giffard.

Fitzosbern, sensing trouble again, interposed.

'I have no doubt that each will do his part, and each will be eager to exploit his share of the profits.'

Before either Fulk or Giffard could reply, Fitzosbern swept on. 'I agree with most of what my lord of Coutances says.'

Geoffrey nodded in appreciation.

'However,' said Fitzosbern, 'it assumes that Harold's line of approach will rendezvous very conveniently with the battlefield we have chosen.'

Odo, glad at last to have a chance of criticising Geoffrey, said, 'We can hardly leave guides all over Sussex, saying, "This way to the battlefield."'

It was Montgomery's turn to head off Geoffrey from a dispute with Odo.

'Will he not come by the simple and obvious way? The old Roman road?'

'The fact that it is simple and obvious may be the very reason why he does not choose it,' remarked Odo.

'We must not be trapped by our own cleverness,' said Fitzosbern, 'or we shall waste our time guessing answers to problems we have created for ourselves.'

'Nevertheless,' said Geoffrey, 'I think it would be wise to choose more than one possible field, Fitz, and so do you.'

'We can not go all over Sussex,' said Odo, 'marking out dozens of them just in case.' He sniggered.

Geoffrey kept his temper.

'We do not have to. This is where our captain of mercenaries put his finger on a possible solution, albeit without intending to.'

Fulk raised his thick eyebrows elaborately, but continued to lounge.

'We begin to restrict our wasting activities,' said Geoffrey. 'We do not destroy farms merely to infuriate Harold. We also leave farms intact in order to lead him on. Any general marches where the tracks are easiest and the land is richest. So we create a pattern. We leave avenues of untouched land leading to the pieces of ground we have chosen. Harold will be a fool to himself if he does not follow one of them. He must make the journey easy for his men and he must provide food for them. When we know which route he is on, we prepare. When we know he is near, we pounce.'

Gilbert had been listening with his mouth open. He pulled

himself together when he and Ralph were questioned about possible avenues of approach and likely fields of engagement.

Ralph mentioned Telham Hill briefly, and let Gilbert take the questioning. Gilbert tried to sound knowledgeable about gradients and fields of vision and length of front. He wished he could remember all the airy thoughts that had gone through his mind when he had first considered Telham and had imagined himself as the Duke.

The council did not seem impressed, and Gilbert looked disappointed. Ralph knew well that the Duke and Fitzosbern were already acquainted with it. He decided to give Gilbert a second chance.

'There is another hill, sir. Just beyond. My partner here was the first to find it.'

Gilbert felt a glow of pride. Partner!

'Well?' said Fitzosbern.

Gilbert glanced at Ralph, who nodded for him to go on.

Gilbert described it as best he could, even to the detail of the old apple tree. The slopes, the field of vision, the woods on the far side, the sandy, marshy brook on the near side – all were included. He did not mention the ravine on the north side of the summit.

'Telham Hill we know,' said Odo. 'What do they call this one?'

'Sir?'

'This hill,' said Odo. 'It has a name.'

Gilbert began to flounder.

Odo pressed him. 'You interrogated the local peasantry?'

Gilbert licked his lips. 'Um – Sandlake, my lord,' he said at last. 'Yes. Sandlake.'

'Sandlake? What is that supposed to mean?'

Odo was making Gilbert feel awkward, and knew it.

'You remember, my lord, I – I said, at the bottom of the hill was a – a sandy—'

'Stream, you said. Yes, I remember. You said nothing about a lake.'

Gilbert sweated. 'Perhaps it was the Saxon accent, sir. He may have said "Sanlic" or "Senlac" – something like that – and I have translated it in error.' He grasped suddenly at an inspiration. 'We could call it "Grey Appletree Hill".' He subsided into silence, feeling a total idiot.

Odo opened his mouth to make a sarcastic remark, but the Duke cut in.

'A name is a name. "Senlac Hill" is the simplest. It will do as well as any other. Now – you both need food and rest. All of you will be busy tomorrow.'

'Sir?'

'His Grace means you are dismissed,' said Odo. 'Go, young Master Senlac.'

Everyone laughed – partly as a way of relieving the tension. What hurt Gilbert most was that even Ralph smiled.

Earl Leofwine replaced the tent flap, tossed his gloves on to the table, and flopped on to a stool.

'The last of the Berkshire levies are in. I doubt we can hope for any more.'

Harold held out a mug of beer to him.

'My feelings too. We can not wait any longer. It is time now that matters, not men.'

Leofwine nodded. 'So tomorrow then?'

'Or the day after. Give the Berkshire boys a rest. Then go. Three days should do it. A good thing the Bastard has chosen Hastings.'

'You mean, you know the ground.'

Harold grinned craftily. 'Yes. And I have an idea or two. Show you when we get there.'

*

'Welcome, my friend. A fine evening.'

Gilbert's cheeks were still burning.

'Is it? Ha!'

The pain on the Magyar's face cut through Gilbert's self-pity. He felt as if he had cuffed a faithful dog for wagging its tail.

'I am sorry, Sandor.'

'You are tired and hungry,' said Sandor. 'Sit and eat; that will stop you to be tired and hungry. And talk; then you will not be sad.'

Gilbert sat down against a log and eased his legs and back. The relief was enormous. Sandor plied him with titbits he had been saving specially.

'Now – talk.'

Taillefer opened his eyes and propped himself on an elbow.

Gilbert reached out for a mug with one hand, and stuffed food into his mouth with the other. Words tumbled out, mouth full and all: the Duke, the council, the argument; the hot tongue of Sir Walter Giffard, the slow tongue of Sir Roger of Montgomery; the bad feeling between my lord of Coutances and my lord of Bayeux.

'There is something crooked about Odo. You hear him telling you good reasons for doing something, and all the time you know he has another reason that he is not going to tell you. No wonder Lord Geoffrey does not like him.'

'With good reason,' said Taillefer. 'He has been a thorn in Lord Geoffrey's side for years.'

'But Lord Geoffrey is the better man,' said Gilbert.

'I agree again. He can see them all off at that table, except Fitzosbern. He has the longest head in all Normandy, save only Lanfranc of course. Even the Duke sits at Lanfranc's feet.'

'What was Beaumont doing there?' said Gilbert. 'He must be my age.'

Taillefer nodded and smiled. 'Too young, I agree. All dash and promise. Up in the saddle and down on the cheeks.'

Gilbert missed the hint. 'Yes. And did you know he brought a pack of hounds with him?'

'Who does not?' said Sandor.

'His father pulls strings,' said Taillefer. 'The old man dotes on him – thinks the sun shines out of his backside.'

Gilbert sneered.

Taillefer wagged a finger. 'Do not be hasty. Lord Geoffrey thinks highly of him. He may yet prove himself.'

Sandor proffered another little treat.

'And the Bloodeye. Did you see him?'

Gilbert shuddered. 'A monster. The very air around him is bad.'

Sandor nodded. 'Truly a bad man. A very bad man. But war too is bad, and he does war very well.'

'But the Bastard outfaced him. Without a threat or a gesture, without even raising his voice. I was sweating, and he was not talking to me.' Gilbert sat up in sudden recall. 'And who is that little cripple behind him?'

Sandor and Taillefer exchanged glances.

'He is a doctor of some kind,' said Taillefer after a pause.

'Why?' said Gilbert. 'Is there something wrong with Fulk? He looks as strong as a horse.'

Taillefer looked at Sandor again before replying.

'Because a man keeps company with a doctor, he is not necessarily an invalid. Rumour has it that their – association – is – of another nature.' He clapped his hands. 'But there! Because I associate with this diminutive Magyar horse-keeper, it does not mean that I am either a horse or that I need looking after.'

They laughed, which ended in Taillefer coughing until his eyes ran. Gilbert slapped him on the back until Sandor stopped him.

'Tell us the story,' said Sandor.

Gilbert stared. 'But I have just told you.'

'Tell it again. A good story deserves to become a friend, to be met many times. I like the stories.'

'I second the proposition,' said Taillefer, wiping his eyes.

'You?' said Gilbert. 'You dozed off in the middle, you wrinkled old wineskin. And before I finish, you will be asleep again.'

Taillefer made a grand gesture. 'Nevertheless...' He fished an onion out of his pocket. 'A knife, please?'

Gilbert recoiled. 'And carry that smell around on my blade?'

Taillefer held out his bony hand and waggled his wrist in impatience. 'Tut! Foolish boy. It cleans the blade; it does not spoil it.'

Gilbert grinned. 'Taillefer, you are impossible.'

He held out his dagger, and turned back to Sandor. In the firelight, with a blanket that Sandor had tucked round his knees, and with his stomach full, Gilbert relaxed. He told the story of the council all over again.

Sandor enjoyed most the talk of cavalry tactics and deployment.

'Walter Giffard is right. And your lord Geoffrey. We must have the room for the horses. They are not light and quick like our Magyar mounts in Hungary— Ah! There were some horses for you.'

He wandered for a moment, then pulled himself together.

'No matter. Norman horses must have room. They are heavy. It is for that also that we must use them together, as says your Geoffrey. For this plan the Duke has trained.'

'If the Duke already knows his plan,' said Gilbert, 'why does he request so much advice?'

Sandor smiled. 'The horses are the centre of his plan but they are not his whole plan. So he listens to his lords and he watches his enemy. His lords will tell him what is in their mind, and you and Ralph will tell him what is in the Saxon mind. When the enemy marches into battle, all the lords and all the scouts will think that the Duke is marching on their words, and they will be proud. Such pride is a strong rope to bind an army.'

Gilbert cocked his head and looked searchingly at the grubby, shiny face before him.

'Sandor? Where did you learn so much about horses?'

Sandor spread his hands. 'I think I tell you before. Prince Edward the Saxon, he—'

'No, no,' said Gilbert. 'That is all about riding. That was about Hungary.'

'Ah, Hungary—' began Sandor.

Gilbert headed him off. 'That was about your light cavalry. Where did you learn all about heavy cavalry? How do you understand so much of knights and their equipment? When I was talking about the council, you listened as if you knew what I was going to say next.'

'He is a devil,' said Taillefer in a low voice full of mock horror. 'He is a dark Hunnish devil who knows everything.'

Sandor gave him a friendly nudge.

Taillefer shifted painfully from one sharp elbow to another, and crunched the last of the onion.

'How did he learn all about shipping horses across the sea? Our lord the Duke does not employ fools. If he wants the best paid killers, he contracts with Fulk and his bloodstained Flemings. If he is in need of archers, he sends his agents with bags of silver into Artois and Picardy. If he is desirous of moving many thousands of warhorses across the Channel, he will seek out the finest horse ferryman in all Christendom.' He waved a hand. 'There he sits before you, my young friend – that devil-begotten little wizard knows more than Poseidon and Pegasus put together.'

Gilbert did not know the names, and even if he had, would have dismissed them as Taillefer's semi-drunken ramblings. But the drift of the remarks was plain enough.

'Sandor?' said Gilbert decisively. 'It is time now for you to tell me a story.'

Sandor's eyes sparkled. 'You wish I say a horse story?'

Gilbert nodded emphatically. 'A horse story.'

Sandor hitched his legs into a crossed position.

'Then be still,' he said, 'and pay attention.'

'And you, Taillefer, be silent,' said Gilbert, nudging him.

'Pooh!' said Taillefer, leaning back and pretending to sleep. 'I know all the stories there are to know. Sandor is a mere craftsman of stories. I – I am an artist, a weaver of spells. I—'

Gilbert dropped a folded blanket over his face.

'Now, Sandor.'

Sandor took a long, thoughtful swig from his ivory horn.

'It is a story of the South,' he said. 'A story of the sun, of a land of beautiful crops and a sea of beautiful blue.' He spread his palm across a calm, sunlit bay just in front of the crackling fire.

Gilbert drew up his blanket and lay back with his hands behind his head. He looked into the dancing flames, and saw white-laced waves swirling upon sands of gold on the edge of a garden of delights.

'Such lands,' said Sandor, 'as you never saw. Their fruits have juice in them to fill a wine goblet, of a sharpness to make the mouth tremble. And they make a cloth called cotton – soft like a maid's caress, cool in the sun. Softer still, they breed worms that spin like spiders, to weave something to make even cotton feel like the bark of a tree.

'They grow long sticks in the earth, and crush them to make a juice sweeter than any honey. They breed tall horses with split hooves and towers on their backs – long-necked horses, which drink but one day in seven ...'

'The horses, Sandor. Real horses.'

'Ah, yes.' Another huge gulp of beer. Gilbert watched the Adam's apple moving under the black stubble on his throat.

'I tell you before, the Prince Edward is drowned in the English, and taken from me. I am far from home. I was sad. Any man would be sad who is far from Hungary—'

'So what did you do?' said Gilbert quickly.

'I take service with a great man. Master Roger of Hauteville.'

Gilbert whistled. 'You worked for the Hautevilles?'

'Ah – you know of them?'

'My master Lord Geoffrey is their bishop.' Gilbert dropped his voice. 'It is said that he and the lady Sybil of Hauteville were once lovers.'

Sandor tried to look severe. 'Who is telling the story?'

'Sorry, Sandor.'

Gilbert did not hear the whole story, much as he wanted to. He drifted in and out of sleep, and each time he woke he had to try to piece together disjointed fragments

'Master Roger of Hauteville has a mind deep beyond his years. If I would tend his horses, he would promise me the adventure... Campania, Apulia, Calabria... I truly thought he was the greatest of men ... until I met one greater, who surpasses even his brother Roger in guile, who sleeps always with one eye open, like this... Robert the Guiscard, the mightiest of all the sons of Tancred of Hauteville...

'You think Bruno is tall? Or the Bloodeye? Pah! They could not kiss the Guiscard's shoulder ... His eyes can glitter like sparks off the anvil... His wild Normans follow him because he always is lucky, and he is his own man, and follows nobody... he has plans to move over the sea to Sicily...

'But they know only fighting on land, and they try to carry horses over the sea and it is a mess ... But the Guiscard is willing to learn ... he must be patient, he must prepare, he must think ahead. Your Duke has learned much from the Guiscard...

'He put his head on one side and he look from the corner of his eye, like this ... We learn before from the land, he says, so we learn now from the sea. We learn from those who know... we learn from the Greeks...

'He sends me to see a man called Alexius, who has travelled to Crete and Greece, to the land of the Golden Fleece and the golden city of Constantinople ... I think I know about horses, but I am like a child before him.

'Skander, he say to me – he call me Skander – you do not pour horses into ships; you build ships round horses. Engineer does not tell you where to put horses; you tell engineer how to build stables at sea. You do not take sailors and make them into grooms; you take grooms and make them into sailors. You must have space and time and food and water – plenty . . .

'We build the right ships and we take horses for the Guiscard and we have many adventures . . . One winter I travel home to Hungary, but my mother is dead and my brothers do not need me. I return to Sicily . . .

'And then, after the winter, comes a messenger from your duke. He has sent word that he prepares a great force for England. He seeks knights, good knights. But even more does he need knowledge. He must carry horses over the water. His messenger speaks with Alexius, but Alexius will not leave his sun in the south.

'The messenger asks where he can buy such knowledge, and Alexius says there is only one man, and this I know because I taught him . . .'

There was a pause. Gilbert woke up at the silence.

'And?'

Sandor shrugged. 'He found me.'

Taillefer snorted in his sleep, turned over, clawed his blanket up higher, and settled down again.

Gilbert gazed into the embers. He glowed with the Sicilian sun. He felt the juice of magic fruits on his tongue. He burned with longing – to sail with Alexius, to taste the salt of the Inland Sea on his lips, to set traps with the Guiscard, to conquer rich cities with Roger, to be the boon companion of those other brothers of Hauteville – William of the Iron Arm, Humphrey, Drogo, Geoffrey, Serlo. In that moment of magic conjured up by his friend, he was ready to neglect his duty, forget his duke; to banish Adele and Hugh from his mind, to cast out all thought of Adele's dishonour and his own shame; to turn away from the quest that had helped to bring him to England.

He was almost angry when the spell was broken by a dark shape looming out of the night shadows. It was hooded and it seemed to float. Gilbert screwed up his eyes. It stopped in front of him.

'You are Gilbert of Avranches?'

There was just enough flame in the fire to hint at the sharp features of Sir Baldwin's clerk, Brother Crispin.

Gilbert sat up.

'Yes.'

Crispin kept his hands folded in his sleeves.

'I come from Sir Baldwin de Clair. Perhaps you remember me.'

Gilbert nodded slowly. He could still hear the monk's sniffs of disapproval inside Baldwin's tent.

'I have news for you. A ship arrived today from St Valéry, carrying supplies. There were also many priests aboard. One of them came from your garrison at Rouen. You know Father Amaury, I believe.'

Gilbert nodded again, his mouth going suddenly dry. Great Jesus! Was it Adele or was it Hugh? Babies could be carried off so easily. How many strong men had he seen weep at the death of their first-born in the cradle. Tiny and helpless, they were like fledgeling birds teetering on the edge of a lofty nest; the smallest chance, the slightest whim of an angry God, could sweep them away like leaves in the wind, and no grief could bring them back.

He struggled to keep his voice level. 'I have heard him say Mass, yes.'

He did not wish to admit that Father Amaury had heard his confessions of shame and guilt and jealousy and cruelty, heard them many times. Was he now to receive God's punishment for his savage emotions? Adele had suffered enough from them. Was it now his turn? Had his prayers and fasts not been sufficient?

He strained forward to catch the faintest glimmer of emotion on Crispin's hatchet features. After an eternity, he fancied he saw something that could be called a twinkle in the eye. Then a tremor ruffled the corners of his mouth.

'Be of good cheer; it is good news. You have a son called Hugh?'

'Yes. Yes.'

'Your wife sends you a message. She says that, God willing, and in the fullness of time, you will have a second son. She asks you to think of a name, and she sends her love.'

Gilbert looked this way and that.

'Are you not pleased?' said Crispin.

'What? Oh. Yes. Yes. I am pleased.'

Sandor laughed. 'He looks as a man does when a horse kicks him.'

Brother Crispin allowed himself the luxury of a smile. 'I have noticed a similar effect many times in these circumstances. The condition is rarely serious and usually cures itself. Father Amaury warned me to expect it.'

Gilbert felt his face burn.

'What did Father Amaury say? What did he mean? Why is he not here?'

Crispin drew himself up.

'I have told you all that Father Amaury told to me, almost word for word. He is not here because he crossed the Channel today, and Father Amaury has not crossed the Channel before. When I last spoke with him, he told me he is not looking forward to crossing the Channel again.' Another glimmer of a smile flitted across Crispin's bleak face.

'When he is well again, you may speak with him yourself. Now I must go. I have duties with Sir Baldwin. He wants the new supplies counted and recorded. Then I have my daily obligations to fulfil. The Blessed St Benedict allowed a certain flexibility in the timing of Holy Office prayers for those brothers whose

174

duties carry them beyond the walls of their monastery, but he did not allow unlimited time for clerics under the vow of chastity to revel in news concerning motions of the flesh, however righteously connubial they may be.'

He pursed his lips, bowed slightly, and faded into the night.

Sandor gazed after him, smiled, and shook his head.

'I thought he was dry like an old stick. But the sap runs in him. It is good.'

'You mean you understood all that?' said Gilbert in amazement.

'No. Not the words. But the man – him I understood. He is good. He is a man who sees. Is your priest Amaury like that? Does he see?'

'Yes,' said Gilbert awkwardly. 'He sees.' He tried to change the subject. 'Why is he here? Brother Crispin talked about a boatload of priests. Why, in God's name?'

'You have answered yourself. You said, "in God's name".'

Gilbert frowned. 'I still do not see.'

Sandor began bustling him towards the rough sail-canvas shelter he had built near the horselines.

'There will be soon a battle. You have not fought in a big battle before?'

'No.'

'I tell you – before a battle a man thinks. On the morrow I may meet my God. I must be ready. There are many thousands of men in this camp. Your Bishop Geoffrey and Bishop Odo can not hear the confessions of all. Duke William is a good captain and a good son of the Church. There is a time for a captain to stop thinking of a man's weapons and to think of his soul. William has provided these priests for the souls of his men. He wants them at peace in their mind when the battle comes, ready to go to Heaven. If they are not ready to go to Heaven, they will be afraid of going to Hell, and they will avoid death. They will run away, and the Duke will lose.'

Gilbert felt his first real twinge of mortal fear. Such thoughts had not come to him before. Now, in the dark, with the memory of Crispin's black, looming figure in his mind's eye, and Sandor's words in his ears, he began to think. Of a hundred black, looming, faceless figures. Of horrible wounds. Of pain inconceivable. Of the pit. The scarlet, roaring pit . . .

This would never do. Fear was a fact – that was what Ralph said. A man had to learn to live with it. Like the weather.

He caught sight of Sandor smiling.

'What is it?' said Gilbert, annoyed.

'Where I come from,' said Sandor, 'men laugh at Christians.'

'Why?' Gilbert now felt annoyed in another way, and he still did not know the cause of it.

'Why?' said Sandor. 'Because their Creator of the World is poor and humble and weak. Because they pray for help in battle to a man who surrendered to his enemies and let them kill him.'

Gilbert stared. 'You mean you are not a Christian?'

Sandor put up both his palms in mock horror. 'Ach! I do not say that. I live with Christians. I share their God as I share their food. It is a way to friendship.'

Gilbert frowned, not entirely satisfied.

Sandor fussed round him and tucked under his head a pillow that smelled like a saddlecloth.

'And now I must do my last duty. Two horses have been stolen – maybe more. I must be watchful. I have my ideas about the thief.'

Gilbert now smiled. 'Sandor, you can not stop thieving in an army.'

As he stood up, Sandor showed one of his rare traces of anger.

'I can stop thieving of my babies. I worry and I watch. And I care all the time. As the Duke thinks of his men and their souls to keep them content and so win, I too think of my horses and their souls.'

Gilbert stared again. 'Sandor, horses do not have souls. Any priest will tell you that.'

Sandor looked solemnly down at him. 'There are souls and spirits in all things.'

Gilbert had just enough light to see the Magyar's eyes glow. The squat, bow-legged figure looked a grotesque, stunted mass from where he lay. A ripple of unease ran along the back of Gilbert's neck.

Sandor's voice sank to a whisper. 'Have you never stood in darkest forest, lone, beside a pool? Or waited on a hilltop, chill, above the silent mist? Or listened in a cave that hides deep in a mountain's heart? The spirits are always there for the man who has eyes and ears and an open head.'

Gilbert swallowed. 'If you say so.'

'You talk to your dogs?'

'I – I did – yes.'

'You know why. So you know why I talk to my horses. Sleep now. You have much to do in the dawn.'

When Sandor left, Gilbert searched hard for sleep. His body was certainly ready for release, but his mind would not grant it.

Sandor's misshapen figure loomed over him once more, whispering in the shadows. Brother Crispin, and a hundred other Brother Crispins, reared up in the darkness beside the burning abyss. In an effort to escape, Gilbert raced again through the Duke's council meeting, and saw the hard, tense faces in the flickering candlelight round the table. No mercy there either.

Fear changed to rage as he remembered the Bishop of Bayeux; Odo's spotty face seemed well built for sneering.

'Master Senlac.'

Gilbert's face burned. Let him jeer while he had the chance. Just wait till the battle, and Odo was unhorsed and facing a maddened Saxon housecarl with one of those hideous axes that could cut a man in half. He would be only too grateful then to have Gilbert of Avranches straddling his body and fighting off the enemy. There would be no more 'Young Master Senlac' then.

Gilbert shut his mouth tightly. He would have the measure of Odo, just as the Duke did. Odd that it was the Duke's voice that he recalled first – that, and his darting eyes. They had come to rest only when he turned to deal with Bloodeye.

Gilbert shuddered. There was something evil about Bloodeye. He had seen mercenaries before, and he had seen cruelty, and he had seen death. Men like the Flemings he understood; he hated them only as he hated the savagery of a wild boar. He expected little else.

Loutish young Normans like Capra and Pomeroy did not puzzle him either. Probably dragged up as pedlars' bastards or cottars' brats, with no decent family background, they had never known anything else except avarice and deceit and violence. They revolted him, but they did not frighten him.

Fulk was different.

For a start one could not despise him. His size, his immense strength, his brimming confidence, even his insolence, all proclaimed him to be a man. Gilbert knew his fighting record too; nobody could accuse him of cowardice. He had served in the armies of King Philip of France, and the Emperor himself – in Flanders, Franconia, Saxony and Swabia, as far as the Eastern Mark and Poland. Further still, some said. Sandor claimed that Fulk had once fought against the Magyars. There were many camp stories about him – that he could read and write; that he had had his own mother locked up because she was mad; that he did not drink.

Then too he had the natural habit of command, and wore it as naturally as a monk did his tonsure. His own men obeyed him without question.

Yet Fulk's soul ran deeper than that. In a man from whom one would expect boasting, one found that he said rather less than he meant. There was a light in the eyes that was not simply lust or avarice or humour – though he could be funny, very funny. It was as if . . . as if, in the middle of his duties and his commands and his jokes, he was thinking of something else all the time; as if his present life and everything in it did not really matter. Mystery stared out of him through his eyes – one blotched and disfigured, the other pale, staring, fish-like.

Gilbert could not explain, and so he feared with a superstitious fear. If he had been forced to put it into a few words, he would have said that he knew Fulk to be evil as surely as he knew Rowena to be good. He had no other way to express it.

It was not mere gratitude for what she had done for him. Nor was it lust, though he had to admit that he found her body rich and desirable. He had lain on those sheepskins and watched her, and Godric, and Edith, and the others. He had seen patience before, and kindness, and love, but this was different, and he could explain it only by calling it goodness. He saw it, and he knew that Godric saw it.

Perhaps he was simply far from home. He turned restlessly. He felt sick at the thought of what might happen at the mill if the wasting parties decided to destroy it. There was a good chance, of course, that it would be on one of the avenues to be left in order to draw on the Saxons. The building and the machinery would be valuable, and the valley was rich with food.

Would such a consideration deter a man like Fulk? Orders or no orders? He turned over again. And what of his quest? Should he not stay loyal to that too? How much attention had he given to it in the last two or three days? Crispin's news had brought it all bubbling to the surface.

Somewhere in England was the man who had forced Adele. When she first told him, he had not known how to vent his rage. Because Adele was there, and not her ravisher, she had been the one who suffered . . .

'Why did you not tell me at the start?'

'I – I hoped it would not be necessary.'

Gilbert struck her.

So that was why she had been so passionate, so demanding, so consuming. She had made his senses spin with excitement and desire, taunting him with novel delights even as he lay back spent. There had been no caress, no trick, no sensation that she had not been willing to lavish upon his trembling body.

Not only was he possessed; he was flattered. To think that she loved him that much. He heard garrison louts boasting of the love feasts they enjoyed in the brothels of Rouen, and bemoaning the dull primness of their wives, and all the while he hugged himself with secret delight. He put up with coarse jibes from his fellows about his tiredness and lack of energy because he knew they were only jealous. When Adele told him she was with child, his pride knew no bounds.

It was then that the whispers began to reach him. At first he paid no attention. He knew Adele was no virgin; in a garrison town like Rouen, it was difficult to find one. She had made no secret of that. Indeed, they laughed at what she called her first try, and he boasted of one or two clumsy young conquests of his own.

But soon the trickle of rumour became a steady stream, from stable boys and kitchen maids and valets and grooms and women-in-waiting. It reached the stage where he could not lean on a bridge or rest by a pump or drink in a guardroom without seeing winks or nudges or hearing broad hints dropped. just loudly enough for him to hear.

Each time he made up his mind to ask Adele, when they were alone, she drowned his senses once more with her intensity, and her vows of undying love. When they rested together afterwards, she talked incessantly of the coming son – she was sure it was going to be a son, because she knew he wanted a son – until he fell asleep.

She was right, and she knew how much. And Gilbert knew that she knew. Getting a wife was not hard; getting a son was. He knew that his mother would disapprove of any woman he married because she would not be good enough for her son. But any grandson, he knew too, would bring tears of joy and pride to both his mother and his father. Wives did not make a man immortal; sons and grandsons did. It was because Adele understood him so well that he felt the anger rising within him. She was using his own deepest cravings against him.

When her stomach began to swell so early, his suspicions grew, but Adele brushed them aside with a flurry of old wives' tales about forward-looking wombs and slender bodies and irregular rhythms of her unclean times. Still he could not bring himself to challenge her outright.

Her labour was long and painful. It drove all thought of infidelity from his mind. All he could think of was her agony. He had tried to see her in the early stages, but had been driven out by the wildness of her eye and the restless, sweat-soaked body, and the waiting women flitting like ghouls about the bed on errands of mystery. He waited nearby, but was flung from the castle by her screams.

Ralph tried to get some drink into him.

'Great Jesus, Ralph! Just let it be pulled out dead. Anything to stop her screaming.'

When he first saw the child, he forgot everything he had thought and said.

After the gentleness and the baby talk and lumps in the throat came the ribald jokes from Ralph and Bruno, and drinks in the guardroom and reminiscences and back-slappings.

When it was all over, the whispers and the nudges began again. With them returned Gilbert's fears and worries. He wanted the story to be untrue, yet his brain told him it was all too likely. He wanted to get at the truth if only to put an end to the torture of doubt, but he was afraid that the truth would tear away his immortality.

A score of times he screwed up his courage to raise the

question. He prepared whole scenes of conversation, planning to steer it carefully towards a well-laid trap where Adele would have to admit the truth. Each time she slipped away, her face watchful, her eye wide, her chatter about baby Hugh faster than ever.

When the moment came at last, it took them both by surprise. Each felt enormous relief, even though Gilbert struck her, even though tears ran down both their faces.

'Who was it?'

'It was nobody here.'

'Who was it?'

'It was not my fault. He forced me.'

'And you did not complain?'

'He was not Norman. He was one of the Saxons who came with Harold. How could I complain? They were all the Duke's guests. We were supposed to be kind to them.'

'Kind!'

'He forced me, I tell you. The next day he was gone. What could I do? Plead with the Duke to go to England and bring him back?' . . .

That would not now be necessary. He was in England, and he, Gilbert of Avranches, would find the man who had dishonoured his wife. The man whose bastard he could not help loving. At least it would stop the wagging tongues.

The wretch could not be far. Most of the Saxons with Harold on that trip had been from his estates in Sussex. Castle gossip had told him that too. It was possible, of course, that he had already been killed by the wasting parties. Possible, but unlikely. This swine had been able-bodied – very able-bodied. Most of those killed by the likes of Capra and Pomeroy and the Flemings had been very young or very old. He could have marched north with Harold to face Norway, and he could be lying in a stagnant ditch near the bridge at Stamford, gazing up at the moon with sightless, glazed eyes. Or he could be on the march southwards again. If so, Gilbert would find him. On the longest patrol, in the deepest forest, in the thickest battle, Gilbert would find him. And when he found him—

'Still no sleep? Truly your mind is heavy more than your body.' Sandor dropped down beside him. 'You should sleep the good sleep. You will soon have another son.'

'Oh, Sandor . . .' Gilbert groped for words.

'Too full, eh?'

Gilbert nodded miserably.

'It is time, I think,' said Sandor, 'that you tell me many things. They will make your mind light like air and you will sleep. But start slowly.'

Gilbert started slowly, but it all came out in the end.

'So,' said Sandor, 'now you must – repair your honour?'

'I shall find him,' said Gilbert. 'I shall . . .'

While Gilbert slept, Sandor lay awake.

When his young friend had talked of his love, his face had creased in pain. It reminded the Magyar of something earlier that day. A young Saxon had grimaced in the same way when he talked of someone he had known in Normandy, someone who had taught him much in a short time.

Truly an odd coincidence.

10 October

'Perjury he hates'

'Top of the morning to you, Sir Baldwin. I hear you want some good wasting done today.'

Baldwin de Clair looked at them with disgust.

'Enjoying it is not a requirement.'

William Capra gestured to his brother. 'We just like doing our duty, Sir Baldwin. At a bit of a loose end today.'

'So Bloodeye kicked you out?'

'Not at all. On temporary transfer, as you might say. Come on, Sir Baldwin, you need the men. I heard you say so.'

Baldwin did not have the time to argue.

'If dirty work is so much to your taste, you can come with me.'

Capra threw up a parody of a salute. 'We shall no doubt learn a lot, sir.'

Baldwin looked at their horses. 'Where did you get those?'

Ralph Pomeroy began to sweat. Capra looked Baldwin straight in the eye.

'Fortunes of war, Sir Baldwin – fortunes of war.'

*

Ralph glanced at Bruno. God's Breath! It was all coming down to them. Well, to them and a few other trusted scouts. It was the most vital commission of the entire enterprise: find the English.

Fitzosbern could hardly have made it more obvious.

'Draw as many rations as you want. Stay away two days – three. *But come back with something.*'

'I understand, Sir William.'

'I only hope you do.'

A rare sign of nerves from the imperturbable Fitzosbern. Defences, food, equipment, training at a peak – they had everything. Except an enemy. They had provided for every conceivable tactic on the part of the English except their absence. It must have entered any thinking man's head that they and their duke could soon be looking faintly ridiculous.

'Go as far as London if you have to.'

Bruno allowed himself a lift of his expressive eyebrows. Ralph did not bother even to look at him again, the tension was so palpable. While they were away, the whole army would have to wait. They had been driven to exhaustion to get themselves ready, and now they *were* ready, but they could not *stay* ready for much longer. They had to have a battle, and the Duke relied on his scouts to provide the wherewithal for that battle.

'Report as soon as you are back – day or night.'

'Sir.'

Fitzosbern turned away, then turned back.

'Oh – will you be taking that boy with you – the one who – um—'

'Gilbert of Avranches, sir.'

'Just so. Well – are you? Deep in enemy territory. Could be useful.'

What a temptation! To have the approval of Sir William Fitzosbern himself. That would be one in the eye for long-faced Bruno.

Even as he thought it, Ralph knew it was impossible. On their work in the next two days the whole invasion could depend – win or lose, all or nothing, life or death, a kingdom or a grave.

Gilbert had so often asked him why he, Ralph, always knew. Now he, Ralph, was asking the same question about Bruno. It always hurt, but Bruno was always right.

Gilbert's face came up clearly before his mind's eye – a face alight with eagerness, innocence, the passion to please. Gilbert 'of Avranches', as he loved to call himself. And shining through Gilbert's face was the glow of Michael.

Bruno cleared his throat. Ralph tore himself away from his visions.

'No, sir. We shall move better as a pair.'

'Have it your own way.'

When he had gone, Ralph turned at last to Bruno.

'Satisfied?'

The wasting parties did their work with dread efficiency. Gilbert, bitter and cast down, had to watch them. After the first few burnings and killings he did not bother to turn away his head. What was the use? The sounds assailed his ears just the same – the rushing and crackling and screaming and thudding. Every time he heard the rasp of a dozen sword blades leaving the scabbard his throat went dry and his stomach went tight.

But he knew that it had to be borne. He could hear Ralph saying, 'What do you want – soldiering or looking after dogs?'

At least the horror drove from his mind his bitter disappointment at being left behind. He had tried – oh, how he had tried ...

'Ralph, please. Take me if only for company.' He pointed at Bruno. 'You will get none from him.'

Bruno said, 'I say one thing to Ralph every day.'

'Just one, eh?' Gilbert sneered. 'What is that?'

'The truth.' He swung round and gave Ralph's horse a sharp slap on the rump.

As they trotted off with bulging saddlebags, Ralph shouted over his shoulder, 'Look after that hauberk.'

The Duke had accepted Bishop Geoffrey's plan of calculated destruction along definite paths. Under Fitzosbern's direction, Sir Baldwin and Brother Crispin had produced maps of the area simple enough for a handful of the more sensible senior knights to follow – though he detailed a scout to go with each group just to make sure that they did not go the wrong way, or, worse, ambush each other.

Baldwin had decided to lead one party himself, if only to get away from the stores for a day and see some of the terrain with his own eyes. What he actually said was, 'Anything to get away from Brother Wormwood.'

By the look on Crispin's face, the relief was mutual.

'You know the north-west sector,' said Baldwin to Gilbert. 'Take us to Senlac and then on from there.'

'Guided from Senlac by young Master Senlac,' smirked Capra. 'How nice!'

Ralph Pomeroy sniggered.

Gilbert hissed to Sandor beside him. 'How did he know? Who told him?'

Sandor sighed. 'My friend, you can not stop the wind rustling through summer trees, and you can not stop stories running through a camp, when soldiers have nothing to do but listen.'

Gilbert bared his teeth. 'When I get the chance, I shall ram those words down his throat.'

Sandor laid a gnarled hand on his arm. Every crease in the fingers was black.

'My friend, you must learn patience. Revenge is a dish that must be taken slowly.'

'You are not the one who is aggrieved.'

'You make the mistake,' said Sandor, jogging easily beside him.

Gilbert looked puzzled. 'You, Sandor? Why?'

Sandor lowered his voice. 'I lost two good horses. For a day I suspect. Now I know.'

'How?'

'I offer to come with you to watch the horses when the soldiers ...' He made an expressive gesture. 'While I watch and wait, I look at horses. Now I know the thieves.'

Gilbert's face cleared. 'Ah! You mean—'

Sandor put his finger to his lips. 'The two dirty ones. So I say – watch and wait. And think of the good things. It is well that it is not Fulk who comes with us. Would you fight him so quickly if he had said the joke?' Sandor looked innocent. 'Or if he were to burn the wrong farm?'

Gilbert blushed, and fell silent. As usual Sandor had understood not only what he had said, but what he had not said. He was furious at Capra – true. And he was disgusted at the killing and the burning. But all the while the fear fevered his thoughts – would they waste the mill? After he had assured Rowena that they would not.

He had tried to read Baldwin's map but had failed. He dared not ask in advance without arousing suspicion. He took comfort, as Sandor suggested, only in the fact that Capra and Pomeroy would at least be likely to follow Baldwin's order if he said 'no'. Unlike the beast Bloodeye.

Gilbert's respect for Fitzosbern went up; that wise commander had avoided possible trouble by detailing most of the Flemings that day for camp and castle fatigues. It was also quite possibly the Duke's punishment of Fulk himself for his insolence the night before.

Gilbert took refuge for the time being in abuse of Taillefer.

'Why are you with us, you old bag of meal? More plunder?'

Taillefer looked as if he needed hands beneath the bags under his eyes in order to hold them up.

'Tut! A gross slander. Can a minstrel not go for a ride in God's fresh air without incurring such base calumnies?'

He snuffed deeply, and doubled up over the saddle with coughing.

Gilbert and the nearby soldiers laughed.

They ambled easily between bouts of havoc. Capra and Pomeroy took over the conversation. They shared tastleless jokes about tricks for making houses burn faster, about the best use of an axe for maiming sheep, about the body odour of Saxon women. They compared their meagre haul of loot with each other, and looked forward to better pickings later on in the day.

The valley of the mill came nearer, and Sandor watched Gilbert's face become tighter.

At last they breasted the rise, and paused for a moment, scanning the valley for any sign of Saxon columns or patrols.

Baldwin's professional eye took in the mill, the cluster of houses lower down, the clear stream, the well-filled gardens and ample fields. He fished the crumpled map from the inside of his jerkin, peered at it, and looked up again to confirm his whereabouts.

Gilbert saw the mill wheel moving smoothly and knew that Gorm was at work. He heard Aud's voice shouting from inside the house. Edith was squatting in a corner of the chicken run. Something small was in her podgy hands. He felt sure it was her stick doll. He swallowed hard.

Then he heard Capra's vulgar accent breaking the silence.

'Never burned a mill before.'

Pomeroy hawked and spat. 'Should make quite a blaze.'

Gilbert looked helplessly at Baldwin.

Rowena came out of the house and collected some water. One of the men-at-arms nudged Capra and pointed.

'Well, Sir Baldwin,' said Capra, 'what about one more, just to give us an appetite before we eat, eh?'

Baldwin stuffed the map back into his jerkin.

'Why so eager?'

Capra leered. 'Just seen something interesting, Sir Baldwin.'

Baldwin picked up the reins. 'When I have seen what I want to see, then I shall give the word – not before.'

Pomeroy joined in. 'Come now, Sir Baldwin, we have been riding and – working – all morning. Give the lads a bit of fun to finish off with.'

'You heard,' said Baldwin. 'Do as you are told.'

'She looks nice and ample from here,' said Capra.

'Shut your mouth,' said Baldwin, blushing.

Gilbert looked at him in alarm. Was he losing control? Capra, sensing a cheap triumph, pushed him further.

'You can have first bite if you like, sir. Privilege of rank.'

'You are insubordinate,' said Baldwin, but he did not make it sound convincing.

Capra looked round at the others and smirked.

'Tell you what, sir – you have her all to yourself and just give us the mill.'

The men-at-arms grinned.

'Just so long as you let us watch,' said Pomeroy.

There were throaty cackles.

Baldwin was now flushed and embarrassed. He dug his heels in his horse and rode on ahead.

Gilbert could contain himself no longer.

'Great Jesus, hold your filthy tongue! Or I shall cut it out and feed it to the crows.'

Capra opened his eyes wide in mock surprise. 'My, my! Young Master Senlac to the rescue. Whose virtue are you protecting – hers or his?'

Everyone roared.

If Baldwin heard he gave no sign. He was probably too far ahead.

Gilbert half drew his sword and urged his mount forward.

Suddenly a thin, scrawny horse placed itself between Gilbert and Capra.

'My lusty warriors,' said Taillefer, 'let us not quarrel over the goods before we have ascertained their worth. A wise merchant does not put a price on an article before he has judged its value.' He smiled devilishly. 'Should you require a connoisseur to assist you in coming to a wise price, I am at your service.'

He contrived to produce a dignified bow from the saddle.

Everyone laughed again; the edge had gone. They spurred their horses cheerfully after Baldwin. Gilbert glared, but at last slammed his sword back into the scabbard.

Sandor patted him kindly on the shoulder. 'Save your sword; you may yet need it. Watch and be patient.'

As Gilbert rode down the hill, he saw Rowena shade her eyes in order to see more clearly where the noise was coming from. He urged his mount forward so as to be at the front with Baldwin.

Until now, he had been in some awe in the quartermaster's presence. Now he had seen a lout like Capra tear great holes in his authority. Baldwin's awkwardness where women were concerned was a camp joke. Gilbert himself had laughed at it.

He had worried before about Baldwin stopping Fulk. Now, it began to look as if he could not stop Capra or Pomeroy either if they should take it into their heads to disobey him and destroy the mill. Could he, Gilbert and Sandor, and that posturing wineskin Taillefer hold them off? And to what purpose? Suppose they did destroy one farm too many. Would it affect the overall plan that much? Would the Duke bother even to investigate?

'Watch and be patient,' Sandor had said. Very well. He would watch, but that swine Capra had better watch too.

'Father!'

Hearing Rowena's voice, Gorm laid down a lever and came to the door of the mill.

'Fetch Godric,' said Rowena, without taking her eyes off the Normans.

Gorm took one look and bolted towards the barn, where Godric was sorting apples.

'They are here again,' he said, panting with exertion and fear. 'Why have they come back? He said they would not.'

Godric stood up and dusted his hands. 'Then he was wrong.'

Gorm wiped his palms on his thighs. 'Where shall we go?'

Godric looked out of the doorway. The Normans had almost reached the stream.

'It is too late.'

Gorm almost moaned in his fear. Godric pushed him towards the house.

'Edwin and Aud are inside. Tell them. Perhaps they will have time to hide Edith and Sweyn.'

'What about Rowena?'

Godric picked up an axe. 'She is my trust,' he said.

Gorm gaped. Never before had he seen Godric with a weapon in his hand. He looked as frightening as the Normans. When Gorm hesitated, Godric turned sharply.

'Go!'

Gorm puffed away. How he hated Godric then for his calmness and decision. Why was it that Godric always knew what to do? How was he always able to take in a whole situation? And never a thought for him, the man who brought him up – oh, no! He could think of Aud and Sweyn and Edith – even Edwin, an outsider. But not a flicker of interest in him. Only one thing on his mind now – that arrogant daughter.

He fumbled with a gate latch. Between the two of them they would do for the whole household. Godric would provoke them with the axe and Rowena would push out her chin and flash her eyes, and where would that get her?

And when he had once before suggested a more – well – friendly attitude, what had she said?

'Would you rather your daughter was a Norman whore just to save your skin?'

Of course he had not meant it like that. Trust Rowena to see the worst possible meaning. Now Aud – she had understood. Aud would be willing to – make sacrifices – in the interests of all. But not Rowena – oh, no!

His breath came shorter. God, how he needed a drink!

Aud looked up in alarm when he burst in. She nearly dropped the platter she was placing on the table. Edwin took one look at Gorm's face, laid down his knife, and rushed to the doorway. The Normans were splashing across the stream. Berry growled quietly.

'Get them to the loft, under the straw. Quickly!'

Gorm had to carry Edith up the ladder. Sweyn whimpered. Aud tried to get a glimpse of the Normans through the door before Edwin pushed her up too.

Then he went to the threshold, forgetting his knife.

'Where are you going?' said Gorm in alarm.

Edwin turned on him in surprise. 'To be with Godric, of course. Where else? Are you not coming?'

He was not being heroic. It was simply that, if they were going to die, he could not think of a better place to do it than beside Godric.

Gorm writhed and sweated and made feeble gestures. 'I – I must guard my family.'

He clambered up the ladder. Edwin gave him one glance that made him feel worse, then went out to join Godric and Rowena.

He reached them just as the two leading horsemen dismounted. Godric, who had placed himself in front of Rowena, put out an arm to keep him back. Berry came and sat at his heels.

Edwin picked out Gilbert, who made a small but helpless sign.

Baldwin summoned Sandor forward and began to question Godric through him. Godric was surprised; the queries were about mill machinery and sacks of corn and local bread ovens.

There followed others about animals and stocks of winter food.

Godric answered evenly enough, without taking his hands off the axe. The Normans could find out easily anyway; asking him was only saving time. Answering them might get them away faster before any of them thought of mischief. Judging by the numbers, this was more than a mere spying patrol.

Edwin had noticed the numbers too, and had seen the hard set of the faces. He had seen that look on Norman faces before, when he had been with the King in France. He had attended on Harold and the Duke on campaign in Brittany, and he had seen looting and wasting in the captured towns of Dol and Rennes and Dinant.

He felt a great sadness, not only because his beloved friends might die, but because he too would die without a weapon in his hands. How stupid to have left his knife on the table. The one time above all that he needed it. He had so wanted to fight beside his king in the coming battle. It would surely be a glory to die protecting one's lord; what faithful servant could hope for more? It seemed such a waste that he should fall here, cut down by a Norman sword from behind, and left to bleed to death, alone, sprawled among dried cow dung.

Gilbert watched in alarm as Capra and Pomeroy dismounted. They took no notice of Baldwin as he put his questions and peered at his map, but walked slowly about the yard. Capra tore staves out of a fence and stooped to gather handfuls of straw to tie about the ends of them. All the while he whistled tunelessly. Pomeroy wandered off towards the buildings. Gilbert again felt loathing rising in his throat.

He edged towards Edwin and whispered, 'I am sorry. It is not my doing. I will try and—'

He broke off when he saw Capra looking straight at them and frowning.

Capra tossed two prepared torches to the men-at-arms.

Baldwin replaced his map, walked to his horse, and pretended to fiddle with saddle straps.

Here was a fat valley indeed. The trouble was that he could not be sure from the map whether or not it was on one of the avenues they were planning. He did not wish to betray his confusion, so it meant coming to a decision on his own initiative. He pressed his face against the horse's belly and puffed as he tugged at the girth.

There was plenty here. His quartermaster's instincts told him that it would prove an excellent camp site. When the Duke moved on London after the battle, the valley could possibly take the whole army. There was an ideal water supply, and the mill would provide flour for fresh bread, a rare luxury on campaign. He had seen orchards and beehives, and the large Saxon had confirmed his estimates of other supplies and livestock.

On the other hand, those louts Capra and Pomeroy had challenged him once, and would probably challenge him again. Would the Duke back him if he punished them? All for the sake of a Saxon mill? *Was* it on one of the avenues? He could not be sure.

Would it not be easier to go along with them? If he gave way, they might be more amenable, and more tired, when it came to leaving the next farms untouched on a confirmed avenue. After all, they were all the Duke's men, and the Saxons were the enemy. Out here in an unknown Sussex vale, who was to record what happened? It would be better for his authority if the decision were to come from himself. If he did not lead them, he might have to follow them.

'Just give us the word, Sir Baldwin.'

The back of Baldwin's neck went redder.

Damn the man's insolence!

Gilbert whirled on Capra. 'You animal!'

Capra paused, looked round to make sure his audience was attentive, and smirked.

'Master Senlac to the rescue again?'

Gilbert drew his sword, almost spitting with rage.

'Touch this place, and I kill you.'

Sandor came forward; Gilbert swept him away with an arm.

Capra's eyes narrowed. 'No Norman does this for Saxons without reason. You know this place. You have been here before.'

'He is a scout,' said Sandor. 'It is of course he knows it.'

Capra was not so easily put off.

'I saw him speaking to one of them. He knows them. There is more here than we have seen.'

'He spoke with them,' said Sandor. 'Asked many questions. It is thanks to him the Duke knows of this place. It is part of the Duke's plan,' he lied valiantly.

Capra hesitated for a fraction, then sneered. Gilbert's temper, which Sandor wanted to damp down, flared again.

'Never mind whether I have been here or not. They are people; you are an animal. Touch one of them, and I shall kill you.'

Capra spat. 'You are getting above yourself, dog-boy. Do you think you could match me? And what about these men here?'

He pointed to the men-at-arms, crowded near on jostling horses and thoroughly engrossed.

Gilbert, still hot with temper, surprised himself with the sharpness of his answer.

'I am in rage, and I care not what happens. I may die, either by your hand or by theirs. I may not have your skill at killing, but I am stronger than you, and, I promise you, you will die too.'

He grasped his sword hilt with both hands.

Capra swallowed, and changed his tactics. He looked past Gilbert and spread his hands in dramatic appeal.

'Well, Sir Baldwin? Who commands here – you or this ... kennel boy?'

Baldwin licked his lips. He had been in war and in authority long enough to know that the situation could suddenly change, and had. He had found an unexpected ally. That brought fresh difficulties. If he accepted Gilbert's support and forbade Capra to go ahead, he knew Capra would taunt him about 'leaning on Master Senlac'. If he rejected Gilbert and gave the word, he was playing into Capra's hands, and losing Gilbert's loyalty as well. They were several miles from camp. He might need Gilbert, and that scruffy little Magyar of his.

Screams came from the house. Rowena's hand flew to her throat. Godric turned to look, but stayed with her. Everyone forgot Gilbert and Capra for a moment.

First Edith rushed from the doorway. Then Sweyn. Then came Gorm, prodded from behind by Ralph Pomeroy, who paused on the threshold to pull something after him.

'Look at this, lads.'

He dragged Aud after him by a bony wrist. He was so pleased with himself that he did not notice Gilbert's agitation or Capra's unease.

Gorm fell to his knees. 'I am a poor man, sir. A poor man.'

Aud continued screaming until Pomeroy dumped her on the ground beside her father at Baldwin's feet.

'Well, Sir Baldwin, you have a choice now. Which one do you fancy?'

Aud crossed her arms over her chest as if she were naked. She was still panting, and there was a dark flush on her cheekbones. She was surprised at the sudden stillness. Sweat stood out on the stretched skin below her throat. She looked at the hard faces round her as if she were not sure which one to scream at.

Baldwin swallowed.

'I should go for this one,' said Pomeroy. 'She is hot and sweaty already. She will make a lot of noise, but I think she half wants it anyway. What do you think, Will?'

William Capra was glad of the diversion. He sniggered. 'I agree. Just right for you, Sir Baldwin, especially since you are not used to it.'

The men-at-arms roared with laughter.

'Good for learning on, sir,' said a stray voice from the back.

The goad snapped Baldwin's temper.

He walked across to the group of men-at-arms and stood before them. He pointed to one man.

'Down.'

After a furtive glance at his companions, the soldier dismounted.

'Sir?' he said, with as near an innocent voice as he dared. He was still holding one of Capra's prepared torches. He put it hastily behind him.

Without warning, Baldwin hit him with his gloved hand so hard that he fell, and turned away before he hit the ground. Gorm stopped his frightened gabbling and watched. Baldwin strode back to Aud, who still crouched in excited fear. He stooped and held out his hand.

'Rise.'

Aud gazed up at him, still not moving. Her lips parted. The flush deepened on her cheeks.

Baldwin shouted to Sandor over his shoulder. 'Tell her I want her to stand up. Nothing more. Tell her nothing will happen to her.'

Sandor translated.

Aud looked at him with wider eyes.

Suddenly Baldwin felt sorry for her. Something else too. He was conscious of an odd familiarity, and groped in his mind for an explanation. Recognition came with a shock like a physical blow.

Agnes! She reminded him of Agnes.

It was uncanny.

Baldwin took off his glove and again held out his hand. The first time he had meant it to be a gesture of defiance to Capra. Now it had a totally new dimension.

Slowly, very slowly, she too put out a hand. All the while she kept her eyes on his. At the first contact, fingers clasped tight, with feverish intensity.

As he raised her slowly to her feet, Baldwin found himself wanting to soothe her hot cheek. For the first time in his life he did not feel awkward with a woman, despite the language barrier, and he knew she was not awkward with him either. Rowena had never known till that moment that Aud could make such a graceful movement.

Without taking his eyes off Aud, Baldwin shouted over his shoulder again. 'Sandor? Tell her there is no danger. Tell her we shall soon be going. Tell her no suffering will come to her family.'

Sandor translated again.

Aud withdrew her hand, but slowly. For each of them it was like gold dust running away between their fingers.

Baldwin watched Aud stride to stand beside Rowena and Godric. She took Edith's hand.

Without looking at Gorm, she said, 'Get up, Father. There is no fear now.' She could not understand why she felt so sure.

Gorm, his face glistening, his brow puckered in disbelief, scrambled to his feet.

William Capra would not yet admit defeat. 'You know you punished the wrong man there, Sir Baldwin.'

Baldwin stood up straight, pulled on his glove, and looked at Capra. 'Oh, no. I am just about to deal with the right one.'

A small part of him stood back amazed at his coolness. He could not explain it, but he suddenly knew exactly how to deal with the situation, instead of hovering with worry between two ghastly possible results.

'Your orders are as follows. You will refill your flasks and water your horses. You will stay in formation beside your mounts. You will not go near the buildings, you will break those torches across your knees, and you will not lay a finger on any of the people who live here. Is that clear?'

Capra looked straight back at him.'

'Why have you changed your mind – sir?'

'I have not changed it,' said Baldwin. 'I have simply not told you before of my decision. This valley lies on one of the avenues that we have decided to leave open for Harold. He can not be more than a few days away by now.'

'We have only your word for it,' said Capra.

'That is all you are going to get,' said Baldwin.

Capra once more tried a mass appeal.

'Who cares what happens to this place anyway?'

'I care,' said Baldwin, meeting him head on. 'Because I have my orders. And I have just given you yours.'

'And if I do not carry them out?' said Capra, coming out into the open.

'Then I shall give orders for you to be whipped – here – now. Just look around you. As you are more stupid than you are insubordinate, I must point out the obvious. I have the Magyar with me, and young Senlac, the Saxon boy here, and that giant with the axe. He alone could cut you in half with one hand if I gave the command. As for your ... audience ... one already has the marks of my glove on his cheek. The others will be pleased to seek my favour when I tell them how many more camp fatigues await them when we arrive back. I can not see your ... loyal comrade Pomeroy here risking his dirty neck against all of us, just for you. Can you? Not even Pomeroy is that much of a fool.'

Capra hesitated. Baldwin drove him back.

'I should not bother to think of telling his Grace the Duke either. Use what little intelligence you have. Whom will William trust and believe – his quartermaster, of many years' service, kin to the ducal line, oath-bound comrade of twenty-six years? Or a pedlar's bastard fit only for scavenging and petty terror?'

Baldwin spat at Capra's feet and turned away to Sandor.

'Tell them we shall water the horses, take a little food and water ourselves, and then after a rest we shall move on. My men will not enter the house.'

Nevertheless, it was an uneasy time, to begin with.

Godric never moved from Rowena's side, and never let go of the axe. His body was not tense, but his eyes were constantly alert. Nor would he pay any attention to Gorm's nervous chatter.

Gorm forgot most of his fright in his indignation. Could this great oaf not see that the whole place was in danger? Had he no care for the safety of anyone else – Sweyn, or Edith, or Aud, or himself, for that matter, who had taken him in and raised him?

Aud – by some mystery that he could not divine – had somehow secured some sort of reprieve for them, and this ox was about to shatter it with his misplaced idea of gallantry. Did he fancy himself as some champion from Charlemagne's court of heroes? What a fool! Could he not see that any one of those Normans could slash his hamstrings from behind and then dispatch him at leisure as he wriggled helpless like a dog with its back broken? It would give the rest a taste of blood; before you could turn round the other soldiers would have run berserk and killed everyone. With his stupid devotion Godric would have done for them all.

Gorm's forehead wrinkled in bafflement. Why? Why? Godric had never shown the slightest sign of possible violence before. Gorm could still see the patience in the boy's dark eyes as he put a hand up to his cheek where the marks of Gorm's drunken fingers still glowed. Even as Godric grew to full strength, Gorm had found it difficult to break the habit of striking. His foster son steadfastly refused retaliation either of word or of deed. It baffled Gorm and annoyed him, so much so that he often struck again.

In his drunken musings Gorm put it down to lack of spirit, poor breeding, or even stupidity, and sympathised with himself for being stuck with such a pudding. But when Godric read his thoughts, or cured him of his many stomach ailments, or simply looked at him in the firelight, he knew that behind his eyes lurked spirits and passions of a nature and depth totally beyond his reach. It was then that he was not only baffled but frightened.

Godric, he decided, was not wholly human. He showed no violence, no temper, no fear, no worry. There was no weakness that Gorm could seize upon and use. Godric owed his upbringing and his livelihood to him, yet Gorm sensed that in the right situation, none of that would matter. He raged inwardly that Godric never showed himself; there was never a glimpse of his soul.

Until now.

Gorm raised his eyebrows, then lowered them again. Had this been going on under his nose and he had never seen it? Was this dark-spirited, silent young ox a prey to common human feelings after all? And was he daring to climb above his social status by lusting after his benefactor's daughter?

Gorm wiped the last of the sweat off his palms. Well, he would see about that. Nobody was going to deprive Sweyn of his inheritance – nobody.

Sweyn!

Gorm suddenly remembered, and looked round for him. Sweyn and Edith were crouched before the very tall, lanky Norman – the only one who was not properly armed. Gorm had spent many years of his life on the road; he knew a minstrel when he saw one.

Taillefer stopped making patterns and boxes with string, and pulled a thin pipe from his wallet. He sat down and put it to his lips, watching the two children out of the corner of his eye. He played a note or two.

Edith giggled. Sweyn edged forward in curiosity. Taillefer played a snatch of tune. Edith clapped in pleasure. Sweyn's pout was for once lost in a smile.

Taillefer stretched out his long thin legs, leaned against a gatepost, and played a song. The men-at-arms, lounging and munching, listened contentedly and grinned at each other as they recalled the vulgar words of the guardroom version.

William Capra looked round and swore quietly to himself. He nudged Ralph Pomeroy.

'Idiots – think only of their stomachs.'

He flung a stone at Berry, who jumped, and then snarled at him.

Edwin put an arm round the dog's neck and looked accusingly at Gilbert.

'They are no friends of mine,' muttered Gilbert, staring straight ahead and trying to conceal the fact that he was talking. 'You saw.'

'I did. And I honour you for it. It was brave. Perhaps you have saved our lives.'

Gilbert saw Capra gazing at him and frowning once again. He stood up and pretended to stretch his legs after the meal.

Sandor had no such scruple. He cut some cheese and passed a piece to Edwin.

'The big man would have fought. Many would have died. Truly the woman is fortunate to have such devotion.'

Edwin nodded. 'Their love is very strong.'

Sandor pursued an idea which had occupied his mind for a day or so.

'You have a love too?'

The question was so unexpected that Edwin lost his voice for a moment.

'She was – she is – not here.'

'Far, perhaps?' said Sandor innocently.

'Not of this land,' said Edwin. 'I have not seen her for – for many months.' He blinked. 'Two years – about.'

'Ah.'

Sandor spat out a piece of rind. 'Gilbert has a love. He also has a son.'

'Then he is truly lucky,' said Edwin with more decision. He looked up suddenly, and his eyes were wet. 'Tell him from me.'

Sandor thought it wise to change the subject.

'See how Taillefer leads them in a dance.'

Taillefer, now on his feet again, was doing a disjointed little jig, playing the while. Edith and Sweyn danced too, in a parody of his movements. They followed him in swaying line across the yard, through the gate, and towards the house.

Baldwin moved to stop him. Aud put a hand on his arm.

'He will do no harm.'

'My orders,' said Baldwin. 'I gave orders – nobody to go near the house. Near the house.'

Aud pointed at the lounging soldiers. Two were even dozing.

'There is no danger now. This minstrel of yours is cunning. His pipes have charmed your men and put them to rest. Let him go on with his work. Besides, see these apples I have brought you. They are the very best of the season. Godric was sorting them in the barn when you came.'

Was it really less than an hour ago? She was living now in a different age.

Neither could understand what the other was saying, but the meaning of each was clear.

'Here,' said Aud. 'Take them quickly. We can not afford to give to everybody.'

Baldwin took off his glove again. Aud's body came close to him as she slid the fruit into the satchel at his waist. As he held open the flap, their hands touched, then clasped as tightly as before.

They looked at each other. Baldwin did not know whether he wanted to prolong the silent moment or bring it to an end. From inside the house came the notes of Taillefer's pipe and the high treble of the children's voices.

Baldwin cleared his throat. 'Thank you.'

Aud ducked her head. 'Thank you for being kind to us.'

She helped him to fasten the satchel.

'What a touching scene!'

Baldwin whirled round. Leaning over a gate was Fulk Blood-eye.

'A truly affecting moment.'

Aud gasped in horror when she saw his face. She gasped again when she saw the person with him.

He was undersized; beside Fulk he looked dwarf-like. His stoop and his misshapen shoulder made him smaller still. His hair was black and long, not like a Norman's at all. Nor did his skin have the pocks and stubble common to most campaigners. It was smooth and dark, soft almost like a woman's. The thin moustache down either side of his mouth glistened with good grooming.

His hands, folded like a monk's before him, were small and delicate, with fingernails trim and clean. From the way he held his head, slightly back, it was clear that, like many cripples, he was vain, and fastidious about his dress.

Everything about him was smaller, lighter, and smoother than normal. The leather of his jerkin showed fewer gashes and burred edges. His helmet had not the sharp outlines of the Norman pattern. Tinkling ringlets of mail hung loose from the headband. The dagger was curved, not straight; the sword was shorter and lighter. The handles of each showed curious patterns. Around his waist and under his belt was a great silken sash in bright red.

The eyes were gleaming pinpoints of light. He said nothing, content to let Fulk do the talking. Aud looked desperately from one to the other, not knowing which one to fear the more.

Fulk swept a prodigious bow. 'Greetings to my lady. My congratulations, Sir Baldwin. I did not know you were a diplomat as well as a – soldier. A courtier too. Anticipating harmonious relations after the conquest, perhaps?'

With a furtive squeeze of Aud's hand, Baldwin stepped towards him. Recovering from the shock of Fulk's arrival, he still had enough residue of confidence from his reprimand of William Capra to be able to go on the offensive.

'What are you doing here?'

Fulk glanced at Aud. 'I might ask you the same question.'

Baldwin ignored it. 'Your Flemings were on camp duty. I arranged it.'

Fulk smiled easily, adding another crease or two to the scar on his face. 'My Flemings, maybe. But not myself. Captains of mercenaries do not perform menial tasks.'

'They were William's express orders – after your insolence to him.'

'Yes,' said Fulk. 'I thought as much.' He yawned elaborately. 'However, I became bored watching my men humping logs, and rode out in search of interest.' He glanced about him. 'I seem to have found it.'

Baldwin refused to be drawn.

'How did you get here without being noticed?'

Fulk waved a hand towards the olive-skinned statue behind him. 'My Matthew knows the ways of the hunter,' he said with heavy irony.

Matthew smiled till his eyes became slits.

'Besides,' said Fulk more brusquely, 'you were taking no precautions – lazing all over the place. Half an army could have walked in. I wonder if his Grace the Duke would care to hear that?'

'The Duke will receive my report,' said Baldwin. 'And half an army could not walk in because half an army is not here. Not a single soldier is here in this valley, and well you know it. There is nothing here except a quartermaster doing his duty and a captain of mercenaries neglecting his. Would "his Grace the Duke" care to hear that, do you think?'

Fulk scarcely heard him as he cast his eyes around.

'I take it this is one of the farms that we must not burn.'

'Intelligent of you,' said Baldwin.

'Hmm. Pity.'

He stooped, picked a stalk of grass, put it between his teeth, and ambled off with his hands behind his back. Matthew followed silently. As he walked past the door of the house, Taillefer came out and nearly bumped into him. The merry piping ceased at once. Sweyn and Edith, tumbling after him, stopped laughing and stood still. Edith cried out in fear. Matthew turned his yellowing eyeballs in their direction and smiled. Sweyn backed into the house again.

When Fulk appeared at the edge of the yard, the men-at-arms sat up. Fulk patted a door jamb and looked up at the lintel.

'Truly a fine barn.' He peered inside. 'Plenty of thick, strong oak beams.' He looked round at the men, who were now brushing the crumbs from their laps. 'Not like you, lads, is it, to be taking things so easy?'

Ralph Pomeroy looked uneasily at his brother Capra. They could not run now.

'What do we do?' he muttered out of the corner of his mouth.

Capra showed no signs of unease. On the contrary, his eyes shone with anticipation.

'Nothing. Worry about that when it happens. Right now things look as if they are going to get interesting.'

Pomeroy persisted with his furtive whispering, never taking his eyes off Fulk. 'But the horses. And the jerkins. Suppose he—'

'Shut your mouth! Control yourself. Watch and be ready.'

'Yes, indeed, a fine establishment – worthy of Saxon building at its best.'

Baldwin, who had followed closely, could see that Fulk was spreading tension with every step and every word. Each man in the yard was now tight like a stretched bowstring, waiting for a sign. Only Fulk seemed relaxed.

Baldwin clapped his hands. 'On your feet. Time to ride. We have much work before sunset.'

Fulk turned in mock surprise. 'Why such a hurry, Sir Baldwin? Could we not think of something to – er – give their stomachs a glow before we ride on?'

The men hesitated, looking from one to the other. Capra's lips moistened and parted.

Gilbert swallowed. A whole family's lives lay upon a knife edge.

'Just a little something to warm them, Sir Baldwin. Eh, lads? It would not take—'

Fulk caught sight of Rowena for the first time. He stood stock-still for a moment, then walked steadily towards her.

'It was as if she were pulling him on a string,' said Gilbert afterwards. 'As if he could not help himself.'

Fulk stood before Rowena and raked her with his eyes. Nor did he miss the whitening of Godric's knuckles over the handle of the axe. The silence seemed so long that Gilbert found time to offer up a prayer.

At last Fulk shrugged and turned away. Gilbert let out a sigh of relief.

Suddenly there was short rasping sound, and Fulk's dagger was at Rowena's throat. Everyone had been caught unawares. He had moved very fast for a big man.

The dagger shone in the autumn sun.

'Drop the axe.'

There was something unusual about the way he held her; Gilbert could not make out what it was.

Godric hesitated.

Fulk pressed the point until a drop of blood showed on Rowena's neck.

Gilbert whispered to Edwin. 'For God's sake, make him drop it. He will do it. Jesus help us, he will do it.'

Edwin made a sign.

Slowly, very slowly, and without taking his eyes off Fulk, Godric bent and laid the axe on the ground.

'Take him!'

It was Baldwin who now took everyone by surprise. A dozen hands seized Godric. Someone produced a rope from a saddle horn, and tied his hands behind his back.

Fulk tightened his grip on Rowena. The dagger gleamed at her throat. He looked awesome in his strength and menace, but Gilbert could not help thinking that he looked awkward too.

Fulk blinked.

'What does this mean, Sir Baldwin? Do you want her tied up too?'

'It means,' said Baldwin, 'that we must be on our way. I had him bound so that you will have no excuse for indulging in your usual . . . practices. Torture in self-defence.'

Fulk blinked again. The light off the knife blade troubled him.

'This farm stays untouched,' said Baldwin. 'Those are the orders of William himself, who will pay your wages when you have fulfilled your contract, and when I report that you have fulfilled your contract. I repeat, no one here will be hurt and no damage will be done.'

Fulk raised his eyebrows. 'Do you propose to leave these two able-bodied men here, give them the chance to warn the . . . the . . .' He seemed to grope for the word.

'Saxons,' said Matthew, who appeared at his elbow. 'My captain is concerned that the Saxons might learn our plan of the avenues.'

Baldwin glanced at Fulk, then waved a hand airily.

'They have no idea what we are talking about.'

'He has,' said William Capra, pointing at Edwin. 'I saw Senlac talking to him. The minute we leave here he will be off to warn Harold like a coney out of corn under the sickle.'

Fulk looked several times to his left, then dropped his knife hand. He loosed Rowena in order to pass his other hand across his face. Rowena, shuddering with loathing, sprang away from him.

Baldwin pointed at Edwin. 'Bind him too.'

Edwin had his arms pulled back. Gilbert tied the knots firmly enough to hold but not to bite. As he did so, he squeezed Edwin's wrist reassuringly.

Fulk tried several times to get his knife into the scabbard, thrusting and missing. Matthew took his wrist gently.

'It is well, my captain. Do not worry. Shall I help you?'

He eased the weapon from Fulk's hand and secured it.

Fulk mumbled something unintelligible, and allowed Matthew to lead him away to a large log, where the cripple eased him gently down.

Capra moved towards Rowena. 'Do you want us to bring her as well, Fulk?'

Fulk did not seem to hear him. Nor had he given the slightest sign of recognition. Instead, with his head down, he was absorbed in his clothes, and began pulling tiny pieces of straw and leaf off them. Matthew leaned down and loosened the laces at his neck.

Capra, puzzled, raised his voice. 'Fulk! Do you want the girl?'

Fulk raised his head. His eyes looked in Capra's direction, but even the good one was blank.

'Close the wagons!' he said. 'Close the wagons. Ready to move. Close the wagons.'

Capra looked in alarm at Pomeroy.

Matthew was fumbling in a waist wallet. Godric, though tense with worry for Rowena, found himself curious.

'I said leave her alone,' said Baldwin. 'No hurt to anyone here.'

'I agree, Sir Baldwin,' said Pomeroy, trying to behave like his brother. 'We shall not do anything to her here. Let us take her back with us. That way we shall all be – er – satisfied.'

The soldiers sniggered.

Baldwin glanced again at Fulk. Matthew had pulled from his wallet a canvas package, which he opened out on a flat stone.

Inside, it all looked to anyone else like bundles of withered weed, but Godric recognised them at once. It was obvious by the way Matthew turned them over that he knew exactly what he was doing. He carefully selected some dried leaves and held them to Fulk's nose. All the while he murmured soothingly to him, encouraging him to breathe deeply. A small brown hand rested softly on Fulk's shoulder.

Baldwin turned back to Pomeroy. 'Pomeroy, you take a long time to learn, by the spirits. Then, with a mind like a midden, it would take a long time for things to sink in. Still, try and comprehend this. When we return I shall report to Duke William that one soldier only was too stupid to grasp or to obey his Grace's plan. Had it not been for me, he might have ruined it. Because of you, the Saxon army could have come at us from an awkward direction, and the whole enterprise could have been put at risk – all because of one empty-headed, lust-ridden cottar's brat who could not obey orders. What price would you give for your skin when William hears that?'

Pomeroy let his eyes stray towards Fulk. The big captain of mercenaries had lifted his head, but was peering in different directions as if he did not recognise where he was. Matthew's arm was round him.

'Do not expect support from that quarter,' said Baldwin. 'He will not even hear you. Ask the hunchback if you do not believe me.'

Matthew flashed a black glance at him, but he said nothing.

Pomeroy grimaced in frustration.

'You will guard those two prisoners,' said Baldwin. 'Watch them well, and deliver them to me, unhurt, at Hastings. One attempted escape, or one mark on either of them, and watch out for your back.'

Silent and tight-lipped, Pomeroy turned away.

'Now, mount,' said Baldwin. 'We have wasted time enough here.'

As he settled on his horse, he saw Aud standing by the corner of the house.

'Tell her they will not be hurt,' he shouted to Sandor. 'Tell her they will return when I have questioned them.'

Sandor translated, and heard Aud's answer.

'She believes you,' he said.

Baldwin winced. 'Thank God for that.' He would cross the next fence in that course when he came to it.

'What about Fulk, sir?' said Gilbert.

'Damn Fulk,' said Baldwin.

He had heard camp rumours of Fulk's illness, but had never before seen it for himself. He felt none the wiser now, and the symptoms seemed oddly unrelated and unsensational. Nevertheless, he felt a curious urge to put himself as far away from it as possible. As for leaving him deep in enemy territory, there was the dusky cripple at his elbow. They would survive; the Devil always looked after his own. If they did not, Baldwin could think of no one who would mourn. He dug his heels into his horse.

'Come.'

'Where is Taillefer?' said someone.

Baldwin swore. 'Damn that minstrel too. We are a military detachment, not a troupe of travelling tumblers.'

'Pray to not distress yourself on my account, Sir Baldwin,' called Taillefer, emerging from the house. 'Only a call of nature.'

'Inside the house?' said Pomeroy. 'You lying old lecher. With an idiot girl too.'

Taillefer spat. 'For shame, Pomeroy. I did not think even your mind could stoop below the midden.'

Pomeroy glared. One soldier laughed.

'Taillefer would not have the energy. More probably he has been sleeping. That is his call of nature.'

Taillefer ignored the jibe. He turned, and bent down to Edith, who had followed him out.

'Here, child.' He held out the tiny pipe.

Edith cried out in pleasure, and seized it. Aud came up and put a hand round her shoulder. Gorm poked his head furtively round the door.

'When you have finished giving alms,' shouted Baldwin, 'perhaps we can get on.'

Taillefer managed a bow, coughed with the effort, and took his horse's reins.

'Ever at your disposal, Sir Baldwin.'

'Move the prisoners.'

Rowena had time to place a hand over Godric's heart.

'I shall come back,' said Godric. 'Watch and wait. Hide if need be. But watch. I shall come back. Give me your hand.'

Rowena raised her fingers to Godric's lips and pressed them gently. Gorm saw Godric's eyes glow.

Pomeroy pushed him on, and wrenched Edwin after him.

Berry snarled.

Capra dismounted suddenly and rushed back.

'We may hurt no person, but by the Blood I shall have that hound!'

He pulled out his sword, swung it viciously, and broke Berry's back.

Edwin cried out in pain, but was pulled again by Pomeroy. He kept turning his head to keep Berry in sight. As they passed a bend beyond the stream, he could still see the dog's legs twitching.

Aud rushed suddenly to the stream and called after him. 'Be at peace, Edwin. I shall see to him.'

Edwin heard her, and stumbled on, blinded by his tears.

Gilbert pulled in beside Sandor, still furious. 'The beast! To kill a dog!'

Sandor shrugged. 'A Saxon dog?'

Gilbert whirled on him. 'Sandor, how could you? Any dog! Capra is less than human.'

'No, my friend,' said Sandor. 'He is very human. He lost face. How could he regain it? Only by killing, if only a dog. Ask yourself, which is better for you – the dog alive, or the family alive?'

Gilbert swore. 'He is still a wild animal.'

'That is may be,' said Sandor. 'But you tamed him. I do not think you could tame the Bloodeye.'

Gilbert shuddered at he knew not what.

'What was it? And what stopped him?'

'Sir Baldwin,' said Sandor. 'You saw. You heard.'

Gilbert tossed his head. 'Sandor! You know what I mean. What was wrong with him?'

'It is a sickness. He has it many times. Excitement can cause it, they say. Danger. Passion. That woman was very . . .' Sandor gestured expressively. 'They also say in camp he is mad. Or that he is possessed by the Devil.' He shrugged. 'But then your Devil is always the mover of mysteries.'

Gilbert frowned. 'What do you mean?'

'Is what I say. When you have great happenings which you understand – war, death, pestilence, a bad winter – you say it is the Will of God. When you have happenings which are myster-ies, you have fear, and you say it is the work of the Devil. So I say – the Devil is dark, and God is open. And the Devil is very busy,' he added.

The Devil! Gilbert stiffened as an answer to a problem flew almost within his grasp. When he strained his mind to capture it, it flew away again. He took up his original enquiry.

'What does Matthew know about this – this sickness?'

Sandor smiled. 'My friend, he is no "Matthew". He is a Turk.'

'An infidel!'

'So it is said. In Christendom we see little of infidels. That is why you gasp. But this "Matthew" has much knowledge in places that are dark to us.'

'Knowledge of the Devil, you mean.'

Sandor spread his hands. 'You see? Is exactly what I say. You do not understand, and you blame the Devil.'

Gilbert turned away, as the fugitive answer flew once more within his grasp. He reached out and this time caught it.

'Of course!'

Sandor looked at him.

Gilbert slapped the top of his thigh. 'The Devil. The Devil's hand. I knew there was something odd about him. Did you see how Fulk held his dagger? He is left-handed. Devil-handed. Great Jesus!'

Sandor was not impressed.

'It is God who gives a man two hands, not the Devil. If a soldier injures one, must he tie the other to his side? Does your Bible decree it thus?'

Gilbert shook his head in despair at his friend's ignorance. 'Sandor, it is well known.'

Sandor shrugged.

Gilbert muttered a brief prayer under his breath and crossed himself.

'They make a good pair – one with the hand of the Devil and one with the knowledge of the Devil.'

'I did not say that,' said Sandor. 'The Turk knows much of medicine. Did you not see the herbs he prepares for the illness of Fulk? Did the Devil make the plants grow? Matthew is never far from the side of Fulk. Like a shadow.'

Gilbert remembered that he had seen Godric watching intently as the little Turk ministered to Fulk. He remembered too that he owed his own recovery to Godric's secret knowledge. (Was it only three days ago?) Was Godric privy to the same dark science as this infidel? But then he, Gilbert, had been cured, and he was quite sure that Godric was a good man, as he knew that Rowena was a good woman. He could still see the blood on her neck at the end of Fulk's dagger.

He shook his head. It was all too confusing. Sandor had not helped.

'Why does Fulk call him "Matthew"?' said Gilbert.

Taillefer dropped back beside them. 'Do you think it would be good for the spirit of a Christian army, marching under the banner of His Holiness the Pope, if its best doctor were known as "Selim-ud-din from Damascus"?'

Gilbert snorted. He thought of the cat-like grace, the lurid red sash.

'Selim or Matthew, he still makes my flesh creep. Those yellow eyes!'

'When you are wounded you may change your mind,' said Taillefer.

Gilbert gave a nervous laugh. 'I suppose you know all about wounds and actions, you old trembler. I notice you were well hidden when Fulk drew his dagger.'

Taillefer looked down his beaky nose. 'I was in the house, blessing the children.'

Gilbert gazed at him in disbelief, then remembered the gift of the pipe.

'Yes. I must admit that really was generous, Taillefer.'

Sandor chuckled. 'Have you seen the payment he took for his playing?'

'What do you mean?' said Gilbert.

'Show him,' said Sandor.

Taillefer fished three small onions out of his wallet.

'And the other payment,' said Sandor.

Taillefer delved once again.

Gilbert gasped as he recognised Edwin's dagger.

'Taillefer!'

Taillefer pulled down the corners of his mouth. 'I needed something to cut the onions, and you were not, as I recall, a willing lender. This was lying on the table. Nobody seemed to have need of it. Then Sir Baldwin called.' He lifted his shoulders in a heron-like shrug. 'I forgot it was in my hand.'

'Taillefer, you are impossible!'

Bruno paused on the edge of some forest.

'Rest here. Good cover. We shall see them first.'

Ralph raised his eyes Heavenwards.

216

'It speaks. It actually speaks.'

'What is it you want? If I tell you the truth, you are in rage. If I tell you lies, you will be in rage again. I can not please you.'

'Company. I want company. The English will be better company than you.'

'You have too much company already – in your own head. There is no room for me. I hope you can make room for the English when we find them.'

'Suppose they have scouts out as far as this,' said Earl Gyrth.

'Then they will probably see us,' said Harold.

'Does that not worry you?'

Harold chuckled. 'Brother, they have known we were coming ever since they landed. And I am sure they are ready for us. The only doubt concerns when.'

'Are you not taking a chance?'

Harold shook his head. 'It is William who has taken the chance by coming here in the first place. And in two or three days I intend to show him just how big a chance that is.'

Tears and sweat stained Edwin's face as he stumbled along behind Pomeroy's horse on the weary way to the Norman camp. Godric stumped doggedly on the end of a rope behind William Capra. He neither spoke nor looked back. Edwin could tell nothing from his huge shoulders of what was passing in his mind.

Dully he recognised the landmarks they traversed. He had coursed here many times with his hounds and the Earl Harold, as he was then, especially in the happy times before the fatal voyage.

When they had left Bosham he had guessed that Harold's captain had set course for Hastings. They had done the same journey several times; it was often quicker than the pit-strewn roads of Sussex. But they hated doing it; they feared and loathed the sea. How they had cursed Harold for never feeling seasick. They cursed even more when the storm arose, and more still when it blew them onto the Norman coast. Cursed it and blessed it at the same time – for marooning them and for saving their lives, even though the waves took his beloved dogs.

Edwin would never understand the ways of the Almighty. Why should God see fit to wreck them, not on the English coast, but on the coast of Normandy – stranded game, waiting to be snared by the bandit Guy of Ponthieu? Then, at the very moment of capture, Edwin blessed his God that he had lain exhausted among some rocks, and had escaped notice by Guy's soldiers.

In the midst of his hungry wanderings from Ponthieu to Rouen, he cursed his God yet again. Then, fed and warmed in the Duke's great kitchen at Rouen, he forgot his misery and his fear.

For Adele was there.

At once all the wretchedness and worry and loneliness became worthwhile, because they had led him to her. God's Wisdom suddenly became blindingly clear. In the long days of high summer, while his master, the Earl Harold, and his captor, the Duke, dallied and feasted and hunted and made war together, he breathed joy and fire with Adele, and learned French faster than any monk of Fécamp or Jumièges could have taught him.

When they made love, he forgot his master, his country, even his beloved dogs lost overboard. When they lay softly together afterwards, each murmuring endearments that the other only half understood, he knew that God had singled him out for special favour.

When the sudden embarkation came after Harold's oath to William, Edwin had little chance to say a proper goodbye, and he knew just as surely that God had marked him instead for special pain.

And yet – when God gave him the dog Berry, his sun shone once more.

And now his beloved Berry was dead, and he was being dragged by a rope from the saddle of his murderer – at any rate, his murderer's brother. He cried bitterly in his despair, and swore in mindless, endless monotone.

As they drew nearer the Norman camp, he noticed the burned farms and stiff bodies, only to swear all the more. He took no fear from the hard stares of the Norman sergeants or the sweaty glowerings of the fatigue parties, still at work on the soaring fortifications. He now expected to be killed anyway; the method, whether torture or hanging or a speedy knife-thrust, did not really matter. In any case, he would be relieved of his suffering. The only pity was that his king would not arrive in time.

The one thing he was not prepared for was for nothing to happen. Pomeroy tied him to one of the few remaining trees. Capra did the same with Godric, then took his horse and his brother's – despite Sandor's grinning offer to look after them – and went to find some food. Pomeroy waited in surly silence. When two idle Norman archers came by and loitered to ask the obvious questions, he swore at them and they slouched off in ill humour.

Baldwin dismissed the rest of the detachment, and went to make his report to the Duke. Sandor made straight for the horse lines. Taillefer felt the need for a good sleep.

As he stretched his long body on some of Sandor's horse blankets, he pushed to the back of his mind the knowledge that he was sleeping more and more as the weeks went on. It might be significant, but he could not be sure. He was frankly too tired to worry about it. Life was hard enough in any case, without adding to it by fruitless speculation. God, he had discovered in a long and eventful life, was not kind to thinkers and philosophers. He punished those who pondered His ways overmuch by leaving too many conclusions behind in the mind when the thinking was finished. It was altogether too disturbing.

Oblivion was preferable every time, if not from drink, then from sleep. As he lay back he dandled Edwin's knife in his bony fingers, but decided that an excess of conscience was also too disturbing. As conscience faded, so did consciousness. Sleep, regretfully, did not taste as good as wine, or even English beer, but at least one did not wake up with a headache.

He did not move when Gilbert flopped down nearby and began making up a fire. There was a comforting blaze going by the time Sandor came back from his beloved horses. He pulled some food out from inside his jerkin.

Gilbert thanked him, but ate in silence.

After a while, Sandor fidgeted. 'Are you still angry?'

'What do you think?'

'Anger brings only misery.'

Gilbert took another moody bite. 'What do you suggest?' he said with his mouth full, gazing into the fire.

'Revenge.'

Gilbert looked up. Sandor's eyes were twinkling. He stood up and picked up the remains of the food.

'Where are you going?'

'Follow.'

Sandor took the food to the prisoners. Gilbert hung back because he did not wish to face the jibes of Capra about his friendship with Edwin. He stood out of Capra's sight and watched as Edwin and Godric ate.

Sandor rejoined him. 'There it is,' he said.

Gilbert blinked. 'What?'

'Your revenge.'

He pointed at the prisoners. Beside them Capra and Pomeroy munched at the food Capra had obtained.

Gilbert blinked again. 'I do not follow.'

Sandor put a finger beside his nose. 'You want revenge?' he said quietly.

'Yes. Yes. But how?'

'I too wish revenge – for my stolen horses.' He looked over his shoulder again at the prisoners.

'Well?' said Gilbert impatiently.

'Time and patience. Patience and time.'

Gilbert narrowed his eyes. 'Sandor? You have an idea. What is it?'

Sandor screwed up his face in a simulation of deep thought. 'In this moment, my plan is only a light in the eye. But it will grow, and then I tell.'

'Oh, Sandor, tell. You must tell.'

Sandor cautioned him to a quieter voice, and grinned. 'I tell you this much. For my plan I need three good liars. I am devilish good liar. This is one. Can you be two?'

Gilbert hesitated.

'To punish Capra? For the dog?' prompted Sandor.

Gilbert set his jaw. 'Yes.'

'Good. Then go and finish your food. And pray to the Devil to make you a good liar.'

As Gilbert went off, Sandor smiled wryly. The Devil would have a big job.

The Duke, as always, was a good listener. He sat patiently through Baldwin's report. When it was over, he turned to Sir William Fitzosbern.

Fitzosbern, reading his thoughts, nodded. 'That completes it,' he said. 'For nearly twenty miles around we have prepared the ground.'

Baldwin grimaced to himself. It jarred on his quartermaster's nerves that they had to destroy so many valuable supplies solely in order to win a victory that would increase their need for food.

'And the avenues?' pursued the Duke.

'All intact, and according to plan. If Harold desires to surprise us, he must march twenty miles before battle, with no food available on the way. I do not think even he will risk that. If he does, his army will be hungry, foot-sore and leg-weary before the first arrow is fired, and his wagons of spare weapons will be miles behind. If he wishes to feed his men, he will come by way of the avenues, and we shall be prepared for him; our ground is chosen.'

William nodded. 'Yes. Now – where is Ranulf?'

There was a slight murmur of anticipation among the members of the assembled council of officers. With any luck, there might be a modest measure of entertainment to be extracted from the next few minutes.

Ranulf of Dreux limped in to make his report. His leg had not been properly set after he had fallen off a ladder on a half-built tower in the Vexin, and it always pained him in damp or chilly weather.

The experience served only to add doctors, ladders and autumn to the long list of things he regularly complained about. When asked why he put up with the hard outdoor life of a castle-builder, he had answered by claiming that any alternative could only be worse. When asked why he had chosen to work for the Duke, he said that it gave him scope for experiment. 'It certainly was not for the money,' he would say, and to the Duke's face.

Ranulf saw all choices in life as finding the lesser of two evils. Commanders put up with him because he was a fine engineer, probably the best fortifications expert between Brittany and the Rhine. William could recognise talent when he saw it, and understood leadership deeply enough to know that Ranulf's ill humour sprang from natural pessimism and not from insubordination. Though William rarely laughed at a joke himself, and even more rarely made one, he appreciated that Ranulf's gloomy manner made men smile, and that was good for morale. He was prepared to tolerate his outspokenness, safe in the knowledge that nobody else would dare to try and emulate him.

'Well?' said the Duke.

Ranulf shrugged. 'I am sure your Grace is aware of the appalling difficulties under which I am labouring—'

William interrupted him. 'I want progress, not difficulties.'

Ranulf winced at another spasm of pain in his leg, and eased it into a better position.

'If your Grace would take the trouble to—'

This time it was Bishop Geoffrey de Montbrai who interrupted.

'What my lord the Duke means is that, while he is fully aware of the diverse problems you have to deal with, he is so confident in your ability to overcome them that he is anxious to hear of the many and imaginative ways in which you have done so.'

'Ah. Well. In that case...'

Sir Walter Giffard and Sir Roger of Montgomery smiled furtively at each other.

When Ranulf talked about his profession he was forthright and precise. He gave a long list of tasks still to be completed, and made dismal forecasts about the possible effect of future bad weather slowing the work, but to William and his senior commanders it was clear that the castle was substantially complete. They could see that the hall around them was already well advanced, a sure sign that Ranulf was secretly satisfied with the progress of the military features of the building. He went so far as to admit that Baldwin's fatigue parties had laid in 'adequate' supplies of fresh building timber, though he could not resist an aside about its 'questionable quality'.

Baldwin harrumphed in disgust, but the Duke ignored him.

'So we are ready.'

Ranulf made a face. 'I should not go so far as that, my lord. When one considers the many unknown factors – the size of Harold's army, the possible speed of his attack, whether or not he will be equipped with siege equipment, the questionable loyalty of mercenary soldiers in an unfamiliar defensive role, the attitude of civilian labourers ... and even if we win the battle, the whole business of a military occupation is teeming with difficulties.'

William leaned forward.

'Are we ready?'

Ranulf grimaced again, as if admissions were like bad teeth being extracted.

'Well, my lord, the situation is far from satisfactory, but, given the many difficulties that are at the moment insuperable and therefore must be borne, and bearing in mind that we know nothing – nothing – about the scale of the enemy's operations, I should say, on balance, taking things all round, we are about as ready as we are ever likely to be.'

William sat back satisfied.

Giffard glanced again at Montgomery. That was a major statement from Ranulf. Things must be going very well indeed.

Giffard turned back to the Duke. 'Well, sir, what do we do now?'

'We wait.'

Messages had arrived from my lady Matilda on the evening tide: 'You followed your instincts with me; now follow your instincts with England.'

'We wait,' repeated William.

'Is that all?'

'Any better ideas, Walter?' asked Fitzosbern.

Giffard gestured vaguely. 'Well, no ...'

'Good,' said Fitzosbern.

When Giffard still looked dissatisfied, Fitzosbern spoke again.

'Look, Walter, we have our defences complete, thanks to Ranulf.' Ranulf inclined his body slightly in stiff deference. 'Baldwin has built up good supplies of fuel, fodder, weapons and food.' Baldwin preened himself. 'We have a plan, we have defence, we have good training, and we are masters of the local ground.'

'And we do not know where in Hell the enemy is,' said Giffard.

'Just so,' agreed Fitzosbern blandly. 'But we have had patrols out in all directions, some halfway to London. Harold will come, and when he does we shall know, and we shall be ready.'

'And we shall win,' said the Duke.

Geoffrey de Montbrai put a hand on Giffard's arm.

'I am sorry, Walter. All we can promise you is a victory, not the date of it. You will have to be content with that.'

Everyone chuckled, and the mood of the meeting relaxed.

A pot boy appeared with food and drink, and another made up the fire in Ranulf's new hearth.

'Where is Taillefer?' said someone. 'Time for a story.'

William and Fitzosbern exchanged glances. William's eyes suggested it might be a good idea. Fitzosbern's replied that there was nothing else, under the circumstances, that they could usefully do.

'Taillefer!'

Gilbert shook him for the third time.

'Wake, damn you, wake!'

Sir Baldwin had made it clear: 'I do not give a curse where he is, or what state he is in. The Duke wants him. Get him.'

'But, sir, he is not young any more. We have had a long day.'

Baldwin remembered he had an ally in Gilbert. He took the edge out of his voice.

'Look about you, son. This army is poised, strung tight like a bowstring. We have everything we need except a battle. At this moment our enemy is not the Saxons; it is boredom. If there is one man whose life is given to fighting boredom it is Taillefer. '

Gilbert nodded, and made off.

'Besides,' shouted Baldwin after him, 'he will do anything for a free drink.'

At last Taillefer stirred.

To Gilbert's surprise, he made no complaint. He sat up slowly, and opened and closed his baggy eyes several times. He flapped a wrist.

'A cloth soaked in cold water. And a drink.'

'Taillefer, they do not give free drink at the Duke's kitchen.'

'Bah! Tell them it is I, Taillefer, the Duke's minstrel, who has need of it.'

The normal weariness in the voice was being replaced with authority. After a brief worried glance back at him, Gilbert did as he was told.

When he returned, Taillefer was standing up. Gilbert squinted at him in the bad light. He looked different. It was not merely that he had picked the wisps of straw from his clothes or pushed the straggling locks of grey hair from his high, veined temples. Nor even that he was wearing a richer cloak. There was a gleam in the eye, a tension in the body, that Gilbert found oddly exciting.

Without a trace of shame, Taillefer stuck Edwin's dagger into his scabbard. He adjusted the folds of his tunic and gave a decisive hitch to his belt.

Suddenly a fit of coughing doubled him up. Gilbert put down the water and the beer and rushed to help him. Taillefer waved him away.

'Only a minute,' he managed to gasp between the seizures.

Gilbert waited helpless until the attack passed.

Taillefer stood up again and motioned for the water-soaked cloth. He held it to his forehead, his cheeks, his drooping jowls, the back of his neck, even his wrists. Then he shut his eyes and began taking wary, long breaths, as if testing to see how deeply he could inhale without the cough catching him again. At last he opened his eyes, and caught sight of Gilbert's anxious gaze.

'I must get it right, do you see?'

'But surely, Taillefer, if you are ill, the Duke will understand. You have had these attacks before. I know. Sandor has told me.'

Taillefer shook his head. 'No one will "understand". I am a minstrel; I must perform. If I do not, why am I here?'

'You may die if you do not rest,' said Gilbert. 'I have heard of this coughing sickness. One of my cousins died of it.'

Taillefer looked directly at him, and for the first time smiled almost fondly at him.

'We all have our duty to do. Your duty is to find the enemy. The soldiers' duty is to fight the enemy. Your lord Geoffrey's duty is to train a man's body and his horse. The priests prepare a man's soul. And I – Taillefer, prince of minstrels – lift a man's heart. What would you have me do – leave these men to face death alone because I am afraid to take the same risk, albeit in another way? Where is the honour in that? A soldier can not miss a battle and keep his honour. I am a performer; I can not miss a performance and hope to keep mine.'

He took some deep breaths again, and seemed satisfied with the result. 'A soldier keeps his weapons in good order,' said Taillefer. He pointed to his own chest and took an impressive breath. 'This is my weapon. Without it, I am no minstrel.' Then he checked the silver clasp at his neck, and held out his hand for the beer. He drained the cup, wiped his mouth, and composed himself.

'And now,' he said, 'lead me on. When we arrive, you announce me.'

'What?'

Taillefer's eyes gleamed. 'Bang with your sword hilt on the door.'

Gilbert gaped. 'What do I say?'

'You will think of something.'

Gilbert led the way, in a sweat of doubt and worry.

The hall was full to bursting. The word had flown fast. Men of all ranks had crowded in from every corner of the camp.

The Duke did not have his usual raised platform; Ranulf's carpenters had not had the time to construct one. Instead he sat at ease in an improvised chair, deep amidst his senior vassals. He did not say much, as was his custom, but he listened in quiet, slightly amused contentment to the ribaldry that was going on around him. To the careless glance, he was relaxed; to the shrewd gaze, his eyes, sharp and restless in the still head, were proof of bowstring tension.

Gilbert was again struck by the amount of familiarity the Duke was prepared to tolerate, yet amid all the closeness and laughing and thigh-slapping there was not one flicker of disrespect.

On either side of the Duke sat his two half-brothers, Bishop Odo of Bayeux and Count Robert of Mortain. Sir William Fitzosbern was close by; so was Gilbert's old master, Bishop Geoffrey of Coutances. Behind him Sir Walter Giffard was sharing a joke with his old comrade, Sir Roger of Montgomery. Behind them again, Count Alan of Brittany was deep in a garrulous story with young Robert of Beaumont. All around them were the men who had led their levy of knights to swell the Duke's cause – and their own fortunes – in the great enterprise of England: Sir Ralph de Tosny, Sir William de Warenne, Sir Hugh of Grandmesnil, Count Eustace of Boulogne, Hugh of Montfort, William of Evreux, Turstin Fitzrou, and a score of others. All of them thought the supreme prize worth the supreme wager.

Beyond their benches and stools was packed a dense mass of soldiery. The Duke had raised no objection.

'Let them come,' he said, shrugging. 'It is cold outside. Get out some more drink.'

Baldwin was appalled. 'But my lord . . .'

'Get out a barrel. Two.'

'Two!'

'We have plenty. You said so yourself. If they have not yet earned it, they soon will.'

Baldwin could have cut off his own tongue for breaking the

cardinal quartermaster's rule. never admit to having a full cupboard.

So they squeezed in by the score, cursing at the splinters on the rough-hewn jambs. They joked and jostled and spilled half the free drink – knights, swordsmen, spearmen, archers; grooms, valets, wagoners; Normans, Bretons, Picards, Angevins; Hollanders, Gascons, Burgundians; men of Brabant, Hainault, Lotharingia, and Franconia; Bavarians, Swabians, and Lombards; a few stark men from distant Calabria and Apulia, their faces still brown from the Italian sun, their memories full of hair-raising exploits with the Guiscard. There was a noisy knot of men clustered around Fulk Bloodeye, now apparently recovered, for he was making them guffaw with his jokes. Matthew the Turk hovered darkly behind him.

After shouldering their way through the press outside the hall, Gilbert took a deep breath and hammered on the door with the hilt of his dagger. Drawing his sword was out of the question.

The hubbub died down. To his horror he realised that the next person who had to speak was himself. To his amazement he found himself speaking.

'Be silent, be silent for the Duke's noble minstrel, Taillefer FitzArnaud of Prades.'

There was a hush, as if they were expecting him to say something else. But he could not think of anything else to say. He felt terrible. Then he saw Taillefer looking at him in amazement.

'How did you know that?'

Gilbert felt better then.

'Sandor told me.'

Taillefer patted him on the shoulder and took him forward with him. They bowed together. There was such a roar that Gilbert thought Ranulf's new roof was coming off. He seized the chance to get a seat right by the fire.

Gilbert stared at Taillefer. He had never seen such peace settle on a man's face, save in death. He was no longer weary and old.

Gilbert swore afterwards that the bags under his eyes disappeared ...

Taillefer stepped forward without bothering to see whether he was treading on anyone. In that great press, men still found room to wriggle out a path for him. When he reached the blazing hearth he paused, and looked at the front few rows. Walking along the length of them, he looked at each man in turn. At the end of the line, he swung about, making a great swirl with his cloak as he did so. Walking to and fro now, with the firelight glittering on his clasps and buckles, his whole figure underlit by the flames, he swept the whole hall with his lofty gaze, regardless of status and rank.

Gilbert stared again. Taillefer was looking at every man and telling them without words that he was the master. It was as if he were casting a net with his eyes.

Taillefer stopped. A few stray dogs – who came from God knew where – lifted their muzzles and looked curiously at him.

The only sound now was the crackling of the fire.

Taillefer fixed a young Breton with his eye, raised his brows, and allowed a look of disapproval to settle on his face. The Breton stopped peeling the carrot in his hand and looked in alarm at his comrades on either side. They had their eyes fixed on Taillefer, who now shook his head in mock despair.

One or two soldiers sniggered.

Taillefer stepped forward and took the carrot from the young man's hand. From his own pocket he produced two onions.

Gilbert would not have believed it possible that a man could do so much with a carrot and a pair of onions. Great Jesus, he was vulgar! But funny! He had men rolling helpless on the ground. And the noise! Each new joke raised a laugh like a clap of thunder, and just when it was dying away, somebody would be heard coming up for air, and they would start all over again. Taillefer could stand there doing nothing at all, and men were falling about.

Then he acquired a pair of shepherd's shears from somewhere, and held them with the blades downwards so that the resemblance was obvious. He started teasing the carrot between the blades, and telling such stories. Everyone jumped when the blades sliced it. Men became hysterical. When he got to the onions, of course they made him cry, and the stories continued relentlessly. Sergeants were holding their sides and the tears were streaming down their faces. Sir Walter Giffard was begging him to stop.

Taillefer appeared to take notice, and stood still while the gales of laughter subsided. Suddenly he was different. The remains of the onions were missing from his hand. The shears were gone. The eye was dry. The head was lowered slightly. One hand was spread across his chest; the other rested lightly on his hip.

The laughter died. Men sighed and blew and shook their heads and wiped their eyes, and smiled in reminiscence. Taillefer waited for complete silence. Then he began to recite.

> Now hear me all. You all know who I am.
> Taillefer my name. I do not need to brag.
> Who knows the minstrel who can be my match?
> I pause. You see? No answer comes me back.

Men grinned at each other, but there was no laughing now. Instead they fidgeted like children about to receive a treat. And Taillefer, like a wise parent, knew how to whet their appetite. 'I take you now, far from this foreign camp.

> I take you far, far to a distant land.
> I take you all, I take you by the hand.
> You march with me, and with King Charlemagne.
> You march with us, and battle in Espagne.
> Defeat the Moors, return in glory clad,
> And leave to guard the pass, the mountain track,

Our greatest captain, greatest in the land.
I tell you now, in this short interval,
Of mighty Roland, his blade Durendal.
I sing of Roland in the Pass of Roncesvalles.

Such were the cadences in Taillefer's speech that it amounted almost to singing. Gilbert had no idea that the human voice could be so varied, could encompass so many moods and characters.

A ripple of excitement spread out to the edges of his audience. Men hitched up leggings and adjusted jerkins to make themselves comfortable. They knew exactly what was coming. They thrilled to every detail of the story. Older sergeants growled in contentment at the description of Charlemagne.

The Emperor Charles, long-bearded, white with age,
Champion of Jesus, lover of God's Name.
All Christians bow, all men accept his sway.
In Christendom, he is the suzerain.
For virtue he is soft; for evil wrath is great.
Justice he loves; perjury he hates.

A few glances were cast in the Duke's direction at the mention of perjury. If Taillefer's voice put the memory of Harold's broken oath into William's mind he gave no sign.

'Was he thinking it?' Gilbert asked Sandor later.

'He was,' said Sandor. 'And he knew other men were. And Taillefer knew. I tell you, my friend, Taillefer is a cunning merchant in words; he delivers what the Duke wishes.'

Taillefer lingered too over the darkness of Ganelon's treachery.

Thrice-deeply dyed with base betrayal's black,
In envy lost, with jealousy gone mad.
No sacred vow could ever hold him back;

No love of friend could stay his wicked hand.
He bears in Hell the Devil's "traitor" brand.

'Bastard!' muttered someone under his breath. This time nobody glanced at the Duke; everyone knew at once what the soldier meant, and murmured in agreement.

When Taillefer told of the bravery of Roland, of the nobility and good sense of Oliver, of their great friendship, even unto death, young soldiers sat like boys with their arms round their knees, looking up at him with glowing eyes.

They thrilled to every detail of the battle.

Roland rode out, tossing his sword up high.
Blade Durendal shone bright against the sky . . .
Archbishop Turpin lifts his staff right up,
And prays for all. 'God's Will this day be done.'
Twenty thousand Frenchmen place their trust.
Twenty thousand voices shout as one,
Prepared to fight a million if they come . . .

'Cheer up, my lords,' shouts Roland to them all.
"The Holy Banner flutters out before.
A place in Heaven for you if you fall;
For those who live, the booty is the more.
Fat lands, rich gold, fine treasures are in store.
Such wealth, my dears, adorns your bloody swords.'

Gilbert's mouth went dry with excitement.
Taillefer's voice grew stronger.

We meet them, lads, we fight them face to face;
We strike them down, those cushion-couching knaves.
Our spears strike home, our arrows find their places.
Our swords hack holes in massy Moorish mail.

The voice swelled and rose.

> Their heads shall fall, their bodies fold and break.
> We shall kill all, for are we not the greatest?

'Yes!' came back the answering roar.

Each time one of Roland's peerless warriors killed an infidel in single combat, there were outbursts of aggressive approval.

Every champion had spurs of gold, a noble steed, a gilded shield.

Still the Moors came on. Roland, with the flower of French knighthood dropping dead about him, at last sounded his horn to recall Emperor Charlemagne and the main army. Putting his famous Oliphant to his lips, and gathering all his strength, he took a mighty breath, and blew. The deep tone boomed and echoed through Spanish canyon and Frankish vale for thirty great leagues. On and on it went till the hillsides rang, till the blood ran from Roland's mouth and the veins burst in his temples. It reached at last the aged Charlemagne. Even then Ganelon tried to pretend that the Emperor's old ears were playing him tricks.

But Charlemagne understood the message, and, pausing only to decree the arrest of Ganelon, gave the order for the army to turn about. They spurred and galloped like madmen to the rescue, hoping against hope that they would not be too late.

They were.

The hall fell silent as the ranks of champions thinned. First Oliver, then, Archbishop Turpin and finally, Roland himself died, after his despairing and unavailing effort to destroy Durendal.

Taillefer paused and looked about the hall. The flames burned silently. Red tears gleamed on stubbled cheeks.

Judging the moment to a nicety, Taillefer raised his hands high.

'What do we desire, my children?'

A great shout made the new beams shiver.

'Revenge!'

Revenge was what Taillefer gave them in full measure. As the grim-faced host of the Emperor bore down in righteous fury on the fleeing Muslims, some of the younger men cheered. There were grisly details of separate acts of vengeance, as angry Franks paid out the enemy for their dead friends in Roncesvalles. No Saracen, no Moor, no infidel escaped the wrath of God and His servant Charles; they died with cowards' wounds on their backs, or they drowned in their armour trying to swim the swollen River Ebro.

The world of Christendom was made safe again, as Charlemagne himself bestirred his aged bones to split the skull of the Great Emir, and the remaining captive paynims were baptised at point of sword. The wicked Ganelon had his arms and legs tied to four high-mettled stallions, and four lusty sergeants urged them at full stretch towards distant running mares.

Taillefer lowered his voice to match the spent silence in the hall.

> And oh, my dears, the victor Charles is sad.
> Roland is gone. No glory brings him back.
> And yet – and yet – his spirit lives perhaps,
> And courage brings, to each and every man.
> When battle comes, he strengthens honest hands.
> Look hard, my sons, and there, before the van,
> You shall behold the gleam of Durendal.
> And hearken always, those of you who can –
> The horn of Roland sounds in Roncesvalles.

The fire was almost dead. A dog whimpered in its sleep.

Gilbert blinked. Taillefer was gone.

The hall emptied itself in utter silence.

When Gilbert found Sandor, the little Magyar was putting Taillefer to rest as if he were a baby.

'Sandor – he was magnificent!'

Sandor put a finger to his lips.

Gilbert caught sight of a dark stain on a cloth that Sandor hurriedly stuffed under a saddle.

Sandor changed the subject.

'I have taken food to your Saxons,' he said.

'They are not my Saxons,' protested Gilbert. Sandor brushed it aside.

'I have taken food also to their guards. Drink too. I take drink to these two bad men. I help them to guard when we take prisoners to the privy pit. I tell them you are no friend of the Saxons – just a foolish boy who has a fancy for the fair-skinned one. A long time in camp, away from women – you understand.'

'Sandor!'

Gilbert was spluttering in rage. Sandor was unmoved.

'They think it very funny. Already they make jokes about you.'

Gilbert felt himself blushing in the cold darkness.

Sandor patted him on the arm. 'Now they think you weak. That is good. Now we can surprise them. I told you I was a good liar.'

'But Sandor, how could you?'

'To be a good liar, you must choose your lie. All men will not believe all things. With dirty minds, you choose a dirty lie. Now, they believe me. Tomorrow they will trust me.' He grinned. 'You see? A smile and a pot of beer and a good story – together they make a good trap.'

Gilbert spat. 'Animals!'

'Patience, my friend. Patience, and no pride. If you want to catch your fly, you use not vinegar, but honey.'

Gilbert was far from convinced.

'What is the rest of this . . . plan of yours?'

Sandor glanced down at Taillefer. 'For that we need a minstrel, a teller of stories. Tomorrow maybe, after a good rest.' He pulled the blanket tenderly up under Taillefer's chin.

Gilbert sighed and stretched out near him. Sandor wriggled in between them.

Gilbert turned up his nose and rolled over. If only Sandor would wash just now and then. It was not merely the smell of horses either.

Gilbert hunched his shoulders against the cold.

Why was Sandor so kind to Taillefer? There was another story somewhere. One day he would find it out.

Sandor was already snoring.

As Gilbert closed his eyes, he thought of Adele and her unborn son. At least that was his. It had to be. The thought of Adele being unfaithful again was impossible, intolerable. Besides, having scoured England for one ravisher, he could hardly go back and scour Normandy for another.

Great Jesus! – and they said it was a man's world.

Ralph sighed, shivered, and wriggled deeper into his blanket. They dared not light a fire, for fear of Saxon patrols. The cold, the lack of cheer from a fire, the absence of any chink of uncertainty in Bruno's armour – all added to Ralph's gloom.

'You miss him, then?' The question came out of the blue.

Ralph was stunned. He had forgotten how good Bruno was at reading his thoughts. He was also angry that his thoughts showed.

He had tried to hide them – God's Breath, he really had tried. Just as he had tried with Michael. For months after Michael had died, he had put his heart and soul into his father's holding. If anything, he had tried too hard; the effort sapped his patience, and left him with no reserve of control. His elder brother, Aubrey, was a fault-finder, a tale-bearer, a goad, a tease, a bully. Sooner or later, Ralph was forced to tell his father, they would come to blows. He had too much love for his family to burden them with the pain and shame of such an encounter.

His father listened in sad silence, and agreed. He knew, without Ralph telling him, that the ache of Michael's death could be assuaged only by doing something that freed the spirit. Aubrey was a cage. Ralph would have to go.

He had taken service first with Fulk the Angevin, of all people. A much younger Fulk, unscarred either outwardly or inwardly, but possessed even then of the capacity to inspire fear, and of the curious detachment that looked so much like boredom. A born leader of men, but without scruple or conscience. When they had taken the contract to ambush a party of travellers, it was Fulk who had pushed the knife into Ralph's hand and told him to show his commitment by killing the chief captive.

He had found himself looking into the face of Geoffrey de Montbrai, Bishop of Coutances – the man who had given the last rites to his dying brother, Michael, who had sat with him and helped him out of his agony and into Paradise.

Ralph could not do it. It cost him his employment, almost his life. Geoffrey had saved himself in the end. Fulk laughed at the irony, and, almost as an afterthought, had stabbed Ralph in the stomach by way of payment for his disloyalty. Had it not been for Bishop Geoffrey, he would have died.

So he took service with a bishop, and soon found a partner in one of Fulk's ex-soldiers, the portly and talkative Aimery. Aimery made no demands, he spoke enough for both of them, and he was totally loyal. Then Aimery died after a skirmish on a lonely road in Burgundy, and the agony for Ralph began again. Its only cure, as before, was in flight. Lord Geoffrey was sad, but he understood.

Ralph went on his travels again. He took his ghosts with him – two of them this time – and spent the next few years seeking a way of burying them.

Then Bruno had appeared. He helped towards the burying. The ghosts haunted only on bad days. And this was one of them. He shivered again.

'You miss him then?'

And now Gilbert. It was Michael all over again – and curiously without the pain. Of course he missed him. It was because of Bruno's relentless common sense that he was now deprived of him.

'Oh, shut up.'

Bruno continued collecting dry ferns and packed them down beside his saddle.

'I leave you to your misery. But reflect now and then. Are you the only person in the world to lose anybody? Must you wear your grief like a leper's sores?'

Ralph almost jumped with the shock. It was the nearest he had ever come to Bruno's feelings. But he continued to look bad-temperedly up at him.

'Does nothing bother you? Does nothing agitate you?'

'Many things distress me. But I can do little about them. If I could, they would not distress me.'

Ralph shifted his attack.

'Does it not bother you that we can not find the English?'

'Not much. Harold will come. We all know he is coming. He will take little caution. And he will use one of the main roads out of London.'

'Do you not want us to be the ones who find him?'

Bruno patted the final ferns into place.

'Yes. But I shall not feel bitter if we do not. Get some sleep. I shall watch first.'

Ralph gave up. But Bruno was right, damn him. They might find the English; they might not.

11 October

'This foreign camp'

Bishop Odo of Bayeux said early Mass. Bishop Geoffrey of Coutances assisted. On the express orders of the Duke. Nothing else would have made him do it.

The attendance was poor. Odo was scathing.

'Clods! Idiots! They decide that the enemy will never come. Can they not see beyond their own noses?'

'They can see at present only one monster stalking them,' said Geoffrey. 'It is not death; it is boredom. But like death, boredom can also look eternal. A man can be equally afraid of both. But he does not fight boredom with the sacrament.'

'Ever the student of the human spirit, my lord?' said Odo with heavy irony.

Geoffrey, although badly in need of breakfast, kept his temper.

Odo levered off his bulky episcopal robes, and dumped them casually into the arms of a servile attendant.

'May I offer you something? I should like to show you a most handsome reliquary that has come into my possession. It will look well in my cathedral.'

If he had not been so hungry and cross, Geoffrey might have

smiled at Odo's lack of subtlety. There was one thing about Odo you could always rely upon – he was never rude to you by accident.

The reliquary had turned up in some looting around Hastings. It was handsome work, in the finest Saxon tradition. Geoffrey had tried to secure it, but, by bribes and intrigue, Odo had beaten him to it, and now wanted to gloat.

If Geoffrey accepted the invitation and exchanged barbed remarks over a cup of tepid broth, he knew it would be only a matter of time before Odo raised the stakes and began talking about his son, John, knowing full well that Geoffrey still grieved for his own son, Raoul.

Geoffrey excused himself, and walked towards his own tent. There was a heavy dew. Tent ropes quivered and showered him as he brushed against them. From inside came the usual mindless swearing as late risers bestirred themselves. Outside, in the avenues between bivouacs and half-dead fires, men stretched and scratched themselves, shivered and cursed, blinked and looked vacantly about them.

Geoffrey glowered as he picked his way between half-hidden tent pegs.

How long had Raoul been dead now? Fourteen years? And it still hurt. Worse, it showed, as Odo had proved. Whenever he visited Sybil, neither of them talked about it, even after all this time.

They were still good friends. No passion any more.

He had had other women since. Sybil had foreseen that. But he had not talked to them as he talked to Sybil. They were now totally at ease with each other; they liked, respected, understood, and admired each other. Neither feared that any untoward demands would be made beyond the limits of the relationship that each of them, and circumstances, had helped to forge over the years . . .

They had found it hard at first, especially Geoffrey. As he

struggled with the unwelcome vocation that had been forced
upon him, he hammered away at Sybil's decision to take the veil.
What did she expect? How many bishops these days lived like
monks? Or were expected to live like monks?

'More and more. Listen to the instructions of the Holy Father.
Listen to Lanfranc. Listen to the Duke. It is the way the world is
going, Geoffrey, like it or not.'

'Look at Odo. He has fathered a brat.'

'Exactly,' said Sybil. 'A brat. Is that what you would have
wanted for—' She grimaced to hold back the tears.

Geoffrey felt tears too. For the son he had barely seen.

'Then marry me.'

Sybil shook her head, still in pain. 'You know we can not out-
face the whole world.'

As the years passed, Geoffrey slowly came to realise why, as
God and the Duke held his nose against the grindstone of the
vocation he had not sought and did not want. Every time he sat
at the bedside of a man in fever or a woman in blood after child-
birth; every time he raised his crozier over a huddled little flock
in a chilly, dark castle chapel; every time he kneeled beside a
broken body on a battlefield and looked into terrified eyes – he
crept snail-like towards understanding.

And she would have been the perfect companion, passion or
no passion.

Now it had to be company only when his duties and his
travels permitted. A healing balm of rest and ease at random
intervals in his life of ceaseless travel, duty and danger. With
each year, further cares clamoured for his attention – the
episcopal estates, the never-ending building and furnishing of
the cathedral at Coutances (please God it would be finished
before Odo's at Bayeux), the ceaseless search for relics and books
and fine works of art with which to embellish it, the rebuilding
of the town and – who knows, one day – the aqueduct. Visits to
councils, meetings with Lanfranc and the other bishops, longer

journeys to Rome and to the south to seek more funds from his most famous and most wealthy parishioner – the Guiscard. More recently, as his reputation for training soldiers spread and grew, increasing demands from the Duke.

Work had shown him, over the years, the truth of Sybil's words. Work was now the only remedy. If God sent the Holy Spirit to him in the shape of sweat and blisters and a busy brain, who was he to question the method? What right had he to expect visions and revelations and miracles?

As he looked about the camp, and saw men purposeless and bad-tempered, he became more convinced than ever that God was making a valid point.

When Gilbert waylaid him just after breakfast and begged to be taken back into his service, he sent him packing.

'I have failed, my lord. I am no longer trusted. Bruno thinks I am a liability. Ralph agrees with him. What future is there for me?'

'If you knew what was waiting for you further along the road, there would be no point in travelling it. Right now you have your duty. You tried hard enough to get yourself into this position. Do you think Ralph was born an expert? Be about your business and do not trouble me with trivialities.'

Gilbert's face puckered in anguish. He thumped a fist into his other palm.

'You are like Ralph, sir. Why is he so sure? Why are you always so sure? Why can I not be sure?'

'Be off with you. You are a soldier, not a philosopher.'

As Gilbert stumped miserably away, Geoffrey shook his head. Sure!

Later that morning, Roger of Montgomery complained again about his relentless pursuit of perfection. Geoffrey had his answer ready.

'Are you never satisfied?' said Roger. 'Are they not good enough?'

'Yes. But not occupied enough. Never mind your knife edge, Roger. If we do not work them, there will be no knife.'

Armourers lost their tempers more often than ever. Noisy rows erupted from trivial accidents like tripping over tent ropes. Knives came out between Germans and Hainaulters over an armful of kindling. The fatigue parties had stopped grumbling; sergeants muttered over their mid-morning pots of beer.

Fulk Bloodeye left Florens to do the swearing and the nagging – the dirty work. God's Face – war was a tedious business at the best of times, but now!

Fully recovered, he roamed listlessly, struggling to recall the images that were last in his mind before his attack of the day before. With nothing else to devote his wits to, this problem loomed suddenly large and important. It was also an exercise in self-reassurance. There was nothing wrong with his memory – not really. Nothing that could not be put right by some concentration and some self-discipline. Nobody had laughed at him for it – not yet. Certainly not to his face. There was nothing wrong with his capacity to strike fear; he could see that every day on the faces of his younger soldiers. Some of the newer ones, like young Dietrich, took obvious steps to avoid him.

So be it.

Fulk scratched his chin and fingered the scar on his cheek . . .

There was a woman. A fair woman. A proud one. And a big man. That was right – a big man with an axe.

'Matthew?'

He turned about from force of habit to ask a question, but the Turkish shadow, for once, was not there.

Fulk shrugged off the feeling of unease, and continued his walk.

He passed a clump of hazel half strangled by briar. Higher up there still grew a few nuts that the short-limbed Saxon peasants and Norman foragers had not reached. With his great height he could stretch out and pick them. A tough brown thorn caught the underside of his exposed wrist. As he withdrew it sharply, it scratched him.

He cursed and examined the damage. Nothing serious. Then he looked away, frowning. The blood on the softer skin under his wrist brought back another image – a dagger, blood on a soft neck, a trembling woman, a flashing eye, the feeling of warmth against him.

He raised his head as if snuffing the air in search of further recall.

Just then he caught sight of Sir Baldwin making one of his rounds. The prisoners! There were prisoners – two of them. The picture began to fill out.

Taking care to stay out of sight, Fulk followed.

Baldwin hated armies with nothing to do. He had lost count of the fights over gambling losses. He was not a specially fastidious man, but he never could shed his disgust at the hideous things that some men did to pass the time. He was no dog-lover, but he hurried to get away from the clumps of leering louts torturing strays that they had caught with tempting morsels of rotten meat.

On his way to check up on the two Saxon prisoners, he skirted the camp for a while to get away from the smells, and came upon the burst carcass of a dead horse beside a flooded privy pit. Some bawling Bretons were beating the bloated body with sticks and betting on the number of rats that ran out into the seething mud.

Baldwin roared at them. They looked at him in surprise, and went off at last with surly mutterings. It would be only a matter of time before they found some other nasty things to do, but at least he would not be there to see them.

He was not in the best of tempers when he found his prisoners and their unwilling guards. William Capra and Ralph Pomeroy received the sharp side of his tongue.

Baldwin walked up to Edwin. The boy looked cold and tired, but otherwise not unwell.

Baldwin began hesitantly. 'You – you are the one who speaks French?'

Edwin nodded.

'You have been fed?' said Baldwin.

'Yes, sir. The little Hungarian.'

Baldwin jerked his head to where Capra and Pomeroy slouched in surly watchfulness.

'They have not hurt you?'

'No.'

Baldwin nodded in satisfaction. He glanced awkwardly to and fro, then coughed once or twice.

'Your – er – your sisters. What are their names?'

Edwin looked surprised at this unexpected line of questioning, and glanced at Godric before replying.

'They are not my sisters.'

Baldwin swallowed. 'Then one is your – your wife, I should not wonder.'

Edwin shook his head. 'I am a friend. I was visiting. The fair one, Rowena, is loved by Godric here.'

'And the other? The slim one?'

Edwin knew just enough French to appreciate that Baldwin avoided using the word 'thin'. He glanced again at Godric.

'Aud. Her name is Aud. She is unmarried.'

Baldwin nodded. 'Ah. I see, yes. Yes. Aud. Hmm.'

He put his hands behind his back and kicked a stone.

'Yes. Well, I must be on my rounds. I will come again later. I will see the Magyar and tell him to come again with food.'

As if searching for a way to end the interview tidily, he turned and found fault once more with Capra and Pomeroy before marching off.

Fulk lounged nearby.

So – her name was Rowena, was it?

*

Taillefer opened his eyes a fraction.

Feeling a draught, he looked down. His clothes were gaping open. Matthew the Turk had his hands upon him.

Taillefer's immediate reaction was to recoil from the touch of an infidel, but the hands were oddly soft and reassuring. Matthew, or Selim, or whatever his name was, clearly understood his business. Taillefer had seen Moorish doctors at work in Spain, and knew that their skill was far in advance of anything in Christendom. Indeed, one of them had once been captured and brought to the court of Navarre, where Taillefer was employed at the time; the man was appalled by what he saw the Christians doing to cure their sick and wounded.

Matthew saw Taillefer stir. He flashed a charming smile under the silken black moustache, a smile that was curiously not reflected in the eyes.

'It was like being blessed by a snake,' said Taillefer afterwards.

'You must rest,' said Matthew. 'I will prepare a medicine for you, and your friend will heat it. I will tell him when to give it to you. Now, sleep.'

Matthew pulled his clothes together again.

Before he shut his eyes, Taillefer glanced at Sandor, and saw the concern in his face.

When he heard them whispering in Greek, it was his turn to be concerned. He did not speak Greek, and Sandor knew he did not.

He opened one eye just enough to see, without perceptibly lifting the lid.

Matthew was asking a lot of questions, which Sandor answered readily enough. He then pulled out the bloodstained cloth from under the saddle. Matthew nodded as if that was what he expected, then gave what was obviously his medical opinion, for Sandor listened attentively.

When the Turk had finished, Sandor sat in silence for a while, then asked one question. By way of reply Matthew pulled down the corners of his mouth and shrugged. Some coins changed hands, and Matthew was gone, his red sash glowing brightly amid the drab colours of dirty straw and mud-splashed timber.

Taillefer shut both his eyes properly and sighed deeply. If he were honest with himself, it came as no surprise to him. All the same, it was ... well, it was a pity. He would have liked to see, just once more, the summer flowers blooming on the upland meadows of the Pyrenees.

'God's Breath, where are they?'

'On their way,' said Bruno patiently.

Ralph eased his back, took off his gloves, and flexed his fingers.

They were in cover at the forest's edge, blankets over their mail hauberks to prevent any glinting in the fitful autumn sun. They had rubbed their helmets several times in dirt to hide any metallic shine.

The further they ventured away from the camp's operations area, the more peaceful and normal the countryside became, and so the more numerous and careful had to be their precautions to avoid being observed.

Ralph cursed again. 'So we just sit here.'

Bruno pointed down towards the open Thames Valley. 'Do you suggest we show ourselves down there?'

'So we sit?' repeated Ralph.

Bruno shrugged. 'We have come as far north as is practical. They must come south from London, and they must come through the forest. Whether we stay, or move from side to side, they must pass us sooner or later. If we do not see them, other scouts will. You can not hide several thousand men, even in a forest.'

Ralph swore once more. 'This is as bad as waiting with the

army. Fighting over gambling debts all day, and sitting round the fire all night listening to old sots like Taillefer telling tales of treachery and revenge.'

Bruno looked at him. 'You do not think revenge an honourable cause?'

'No, I do not. And you know why. I have told you enough times.'

'The Duke does not share your opinion.'

Ralph spat. 'The Bastard may talk of broken oaths, and he may wave his precious Papal banner. That is only to put himself in the right, to make invasion a virtue. To turn himself from a usurper into an avenging angel. Revenge for him is merely a means to an end. I say there is no point in revenge for itself.'

'Try telling that to the Duke.'

'Try offering this to the Duke: tell him he can have one or the other – revenge or England. And see which one he chooses.'

Bruno pointed up towards the sun. 'I think your mind is like that,' he said. 'It throws a great light on many things. You do indeed see very clearly. But you do not see everything. Like the sun, the greater your light, the greater the shadows. You miss things too.'

Ralph raised his eyebrows in imitation of Bruno. 'Oh? And what am I missing?'

'You see what drives men,' said Bruno. 'You do not see what inspires them.' He turned his horse away. 'Shall we satisfy your impatience and take a look at the Rochester road? We have seen all the others.'

'Who says it cannot be done?'

Robert of Beaumont's face glowed with sweat and triumph as he reined in his destrier. He tugged off his helmet and pulled the mail coif from his head.

'Full kit too. Full battle order.'

He tossed the helmet to a puffing servant who had just come level with him.

Sir Walter Giffard and Sir Roger of Montgomery looked at each other and smiled. Geoffrey and his trumpets!

Beaumont flushed deeper still. 'You may mock, my lords. But you have seen the evidence of your own eyes – which I presume are still good enough.'

Giffard glared, but said nothing.

Beaumont flung out an arm towards the squadrons of knights that were regrouping under the direction of Bishop Geoffrey and his provost-sergeants.

'An ordered retreat. A tactical withdrawal. Advance and retire on demand. It can be done.'

'In the mind,' agreed Montgomery.

Beaumont stared. 'But you have just seen.'

'Yes,' said Giffard. 'Here.'

Beaumont took a deep breath. 'My lords, we have done this in the morning, the afternoon, and the evening. We have done it on open ground and over broken ground. We have done it forwards, backwards, uphill, downhill—'

'Sideways?' suggested Montgomery innocently.

Beaumont paused. 'Sir Roger, do you accept nothing that is new?'

'I accept anything that is useful. And may I remind you that it is I whom the Duke has placed in command on the right, not you.'

Beaumont patted his horse's neck. 'And may I remind you, sir, that we are all committed to the plan of the Duke and Bishop Geoffrey. If we are to break a line of infantry, and we can not do it by impact, we must do it by guile and manoeuvre.'

'Young man,' said Giffard, 'we shall all be following the Duke's plan. And you will be following Sir Roger's orders – whatever they may be.'

Beaumont gestured again towards the resting knights. 'You are determined that this idea will fail.'

Walter Giffard shook his head. 'Not at all; it will require no assistance from us.'

'God's Blood, man!' said Beaumont. 'What more proof do you want? How many more times do we have to do it to make you see? Do you want yet another of these push-and-shove messes that we have always had? Have you no sense of refinement? Have you no sense of subtlety?'

'Maybe not,' said Giffard. 'But I have my common sense. And my *common* sense tells me that it is not yet proven.'

'We have tried it under every conceivable condition.'

'Yes,' agreed Giffard. 'You and Geoffrey have put every ingredient into your training except one.'

Beaumont looked puzzled. 'What is that?'

'The enemy.'

Beaumont recovered instantly.

'At least we are trying something new. We believe in being creative.'

'We believe in winning,' said Montgomery.

'You won in the past, I grant you. But this is now. I am a man of now. I am not a man of the past.'

He wheeled his horse, nearly knocking over his servant, and cantered off.

Giffard was purple with rage.

'Insolent whelp! What does he know?'

'About as much as you did at his age,' said Montgomery.

Giffard growled.

Montgomery smiled. 'And you have to grant, Walter, that he did stand up to us. And who knows? He might – he might just – be right. Ideas have to change some time.'

'What does the Bastard see in him?'

'Rest assured, Walter, that William does not promote Beaumont simply because his father makes a fuss about him. There must be talent there. William would not jeopardise the expedition just to do a favour to an old vassal.'

'Geoffrey does think well of him too,' admitted Giffard, somewhat unwillingly.

'There you are then. And Geoffrey is the finest judge of a fighting man I know.'

Giffard grunted, unconvinced.

As they ambled back to their tents, Montgomery recalled some gossip about Robert of Beaumont's courtship of a young but plain orphaned heiress. Did the boy really need to chase land and money like that, when he stood to inherit so much from his father?

Montgomery grimaced. Mabel, with her passion for scandal, and her spiteful tongue, had dug under the news in order to find the dirt. Bellême, after all, was not all that far from the Beaumont fief . . .

'She is under age; I think it is disgusting. A limp and a squint too, they say. He hovers round the convent like a tom cat on the tiles. Just wait till her guardian finds out.'

Montgomery had long since learned to take Mabel's utterances with a large pinch of salt. It struck him that if a vain, good-looking, wealthy boy like Beaumont took notice of an under-age, cross-eyed cripple in a convent, there must be some genuine affection there. Quite strong too, he would guess.

So – once again it seemed that there was more to this young man than met the eye.

Beside him, Walter Giffard wondered how his friend Roger could take such insolence from a puppy like Beaumont with such patience. Must come from living with a shrew like Mabel. It also meant that Roger had no doubts whatever about his ability to handle the likes of Beaumont when the time came.

Even so, whoever heard of a worthwhile victory that was not expensive? Where was the honour in cheap success? Five minutes of battle experience could overturn weeks of training theory. Geoffrey knew that well enough; it was only young, unbled puppies like Beaumont that were completely bewitched by it.

Giffard sniffed. Living in the past, eh? Eyesight furring over? Not stand up to a full day's fighting? Well, we should see about that.

'Follow me.'

That is precisely what Fitzosbern did. William kicked his horse forwards without waiting. They made their silent way from the castle right down to the shore. William took no notice of the glances and the whispers and the salutes. One look at his face, and the fatigue parties and ox teams and groups of loafers went silent, even fell back slightly. Near the beach, the Duke dismounted, handed his reins to a groom, and walked onto the shingle. Fitzosbern followed.

William commandeered a boat.

'Take me out to the *Mora*.'

'Sir?'

A boy gaped. A man cuffed him.

'His Grace's ship, you idiot. Jump to it.'

William motioned to Fitzosbern to join him. The oarsmen, their excitement a mixture of surprise, gratification, and fright, pulled with a will. In the entire procedure, the Duke did not utter a word.

He walked to the rail and looked out to sea. A hesitant member of the crew came forward, but Fitzosbern waved him away.

'Keep everybody back. If we need anything, we shall call.'

Fitzosbern came and stood beside his duke, and still said nothing. The breeze was blowing towards the shore. What a joy it was to be free from the smells of thousands of men and horses. Free too from the noise. Fitzosbern's manner had told the crewman that his Grace wanted not only privacy but silence. Word sped around the nearby ships. Men went almost on tiptoe. Heavy loads were humped in stifled, cheek-bursting scuffles. Clumsy ship's boys enjoyed the rare pleasure of being sworn at in whispers.

William and Fitzosbern both leaned on the rail, snuffed the air, and sighed with relief. With nothing to look at but the sea, William's eyes for once ceased their restless shifting from side to side. He brushed some invisible dirt from the rail into the water.

Fitzosbern glanced at the Duke. The last time William had looked so awkward had been over fifteen years ago . . .

'Marriage?'

Baldwin blushed, but stuck to his suggestion.

William scoffed. 'To some grizzling daughter of a scheming vassal with ideas above his rank?'

Baldwin came back. 'Would the niece of a king be high enough for you?'

William suddenly remembered that Baldwin had just returned from exile with the Count of Flanders.

'You surely can not mean Matilda?'

Baldwin blushed again. 'Why not?'

'She is a dwarf, so they say.'

'She is not a dwarf. Short maybe, but not a dwarf.'

'And a face like a gargoyle,' snorted William. 'Besides, she is a child.'

'She is seventeen years old. And by no means uncomely.'

'Then you marry her.'

Baldwin was still unwilling to give up.

'She has great spirit.'

He thought it a good idea not to refer to Matilda's temper and her rich resources of swearwords. Besides, he had always enjoyed her company; it was impossible not to. They were genuine friends. It was natural for him to want to bring together the two people who had been near him during his youth. It so happened that he thought they were well matched.

Baldwin turned to Fitzosbern, who looked inscrutable. William turned to him as well.

'Out with it, Fitz.'

Fitzosbern cleared his throat. 'Can you think of a neighbour better connected than Count Baldwin of Flanders? Brother-in-law to the King, and soon to be brother-in-law to Earl Godwin of Wessex. To say nothing of a flourishing cloth trade.'

William for once looked hesitant. 'What have I to offer?'

'Yourself. You are a good prospect.'

William made a face. 'Suppose she is awful?'

'She is not awful,' said Baldwin, right on cue. 'Unusual, maybe, but not awful.'

'Meet her and see for yourself,' said Fitzosbern. 'You do not have to propose marriage from here.'

William looked awkward again. Fitzosbern glanced at Baldwin, then gazed innocently at the ground.

'Of course, if you are afraid of a dwarf with a face like a gargoyle ...'

Within days of meeting each other, the two were behaving like a married couple.

Now William scratched some peeling varnish with a fingernail.

'So close, Fitz.'

Fitzosbern continued looking towards Normandy as he spoke.

'Which would you rather do – carry this through, or court Matilda all over again?'

William stood up, and slapped the rail with his palm.

'By the Splendour of God, Fitz.'

As they walked up the shingle, Fitzosbern noticed that the Duke had begun humming again.

*

Fulk Bloodeye finished his inspection and closed the tailboard of the last wagon. Florens had done his work as reliably as ever. Fulk nodded.

'All right. Tell them they can rest.'

Florens passed the word.

'About time too,' muttered a soldier, flopping onto some old sacks. 'Christ, he drives you hard. The battle will be a holiday after this.'

'I doubt it,' said an older man.

'We have packed and repacked those Devil-begotten wagons three times. Are we in some kind of competition?'

'Yes, we are, Dieter. It is called surviving.'

Dietrich hawked and spat. 'I thought we were hired to fight a battle, not load up for market. What are we – professional soldiers or camp lackeys?'

Florens of Arras drew out a whetstone and began honing the blade of his dagger. He spoke over his shoulder.

'Both, soldier, and plenty more if need be. Forgotten the wasting, have you?'

Dietrich looked alarmed; he had not thought Florens could hear him. Florens took no offence, and carried on in an even voice, in time with his sharpening.

'When you have campaigned with Bloodeye as long as I have, you will see the sense of what he does. I tell you, before the week is out, you will be on your knees for what is in those wagons.'

'Half of it is stolen,' said someone. 'I hope to Christ the Bastard never finds out.'

Florens grunted. 'You should have seen what we did to get the other half.'

'We have to do that sort of thing in battle, to earn our money. Why do we have to do it to find our food? De Clair is a good quartermaster.'

'Baldwin de Clair is a very good quartermaster,' said Florens. 'He is also a terrible old woman. You try getting something out of him once the action really starts. Besides, he is a Norman. We are Flemings.'

'The Bastard's wife is Flemish,' said Dietrich.

Rainald of Delft sat beside him and stretched out his long legs. 'What Florens means, Dieter,' he said, 'is that we are mercenaries.'

Dietrich pouted belligerently. 'We are as good as they are.'

Rainald and Florens looked at each other and smiled.

Dietrich pouted again. 'What is it?'

Rainald patted him on the shoulder. 'It is your first season, son, so we make allowances for you. You will learn soon enough.'

'What?'

'That everyone needs us and everyone hates us,' said Rainald.

'We go everywhere and we do everything – for money,' said Florens. 'The others do it for excitement or land or power or bloodlust. That is all right.'

'The Lord will smile upon you,' continued Rainald, 'and His Holiness the Pope will give you a sacred banner to fight under. But do it for money and you are lower than the dogs.'

Florens took it up. 'If they want dirty work done that their precious scruples will not allow them to do, they hire us to do it, and then hate us for doing it.'

Rainald spat out the end of a broken fingernail. 'It is noble to die for your lord, killing Saxons right and left. But do the same thing and stay alive for your pay – that is mean.'

'We are professionals,' said Florens, examining the edge of his blade. 'They fight for dear life; we fight for a living. And we do it for hard cash. They hate us for being here; they hate us for what we do; and they hate us for having to pay us to do it.'

'And they hate us for surviving,' added Rainald.

Florens slid the knife back into the scabbard, and put away his whetstone.

'And if you do not carry out Bloodeye's orders to the letter, you will not survive. And serve you right.'

Dietrich glared. 'I know how to take orders. I am not afraid of battle.'

Rainald and Florens both burst out laughing. Dietrich looked blank.

'You will be, son, you will be,' said Rainald.

'Any fool can survive a battle,' said Florens. 'Even you – with a bit of luck. It is before and after that is difficult.' He patted the wagon behind him. 'That is where Fulk is miles ahead of them. They do not come any better than Bloodeye – take it from me.'

Dietrich shuddered. 'Evil bastard! Devil-handed as well. Gives me the shivers.'

'I should have more shivers if he were not here,' said Rainald.

'I should try living with your superstitions if I were you,' said Florens. 'Did it ever occur to you to wonder *why* he uses the left hand?'

Dietrich blinked in surprise. 'Well, I . . . Well, no, not really. You just see the left hand and—'

'Yes,' said Florens. 'You just see, and you let the old wives' tales take over. You still have the mud of the furrow on your boots, boy.'

Dietrich blustered. 'I signed on, just like you. I am a professional.'

Florens sneered. 'Call yourself professional? Let me tell you something. When I first knew Fulk, he was the finest with the blade I had ever seen – with the right hand. But he kept having trouble – it went back to the wounds he had received.'

Dietrich fidgeted to interrupt. 'The face! Right into his brain, they say. That is why—'

Florens held up a hand. 'Forget the rumour, and hear the truth. I am talking about the wounds you never see – in the body.'

'Where?'

'Never mind. He recovered, thanks to Matthew.'

Dietrich smirked.

'You may have cause to be thankful for that infidel before the week is out,' said Florens. 'Matthew saved his life, but every so often Bloodeye would have trouble with his right arm. Something about an arrowhead they could not get out. It would come without warning, and the limb would lose its strength. Just for a few minutes at first. Then the attacks became longer. Matthew warned him they could get worse.'

Dietrich looked at Rainald. 'Is this true?'

Rainald continued lounging. 'Listen, and learn.'

'So what did he do?' said Florens. 'Give up? Weep? Kneel at holy shrines and beggar himself at collection boxes? Retire, become a gaoler or gatekeeper, and bore one and all with a hard-luck story? No. He worked at it. A hand, he reasoned, was a hand. He needed only one to swing a sword. The Almighty had given him two. Very well – he would learn to use the other. For a whole year, he lay low. The stories flew about – Fulk the Angevin was a cripple; Fulk was a prisoner; Fulk was a coward, a drunk, an old man, dead. He put up with all that And he worked.' Florens leaned forward. 'And now, he is still the best with the blade I have ever seen – with the *left* hand.' He spat at Dietrich's feet. 'And you talk about being professional. Boy – you have not begun to learn what it means.'

Dietrich made a noise of unwilling agreement. 'I still say he is an evil bastard. And as for that ghostly little cripple that shadows him ...'

Rainald grimaced a silent warning.

Dietrich glanced round furtively, but Fulk had not heard him. He sat apart, eating and gazing into a vacant distance.

Dietrich turned back, but whispered his next words: 'Is it true he drinks only water?'

Rainald grinned. 'Why not ask him?'

Dietrich blushed, mumbled something about a call of nature, and made off. Florens and Rainald chuckled together once again.

Fulk still heard nothing. He gave up trying to work out where

Matthew might be, and found his thoughts being dragged back yet again to the mill, to the fair woman, to the big Saxon prisoner.

Nearby, some voices were suddenly raised over disputed bets, and there was the usual scuffle. Fulk had only to get to his feet; the crouching archers looked up at him, and settled down once more to their game, continuing their dispute in hoarse, fierce whispers.

Fulk turned away. Games of chance held no interest for him; he did not have enough control over the outcome.

He was not short of entertainment in the shape of torture as he wandered about – dogs, dying horses, even birds. It did not hold his attention for long. It was always done by clods, and clods had no imagination. Little skill either; death came too soon.

Rowena.

Out of the blue, the name came back to him.

It was too late to go to the mill now. Tomorrow, maybe, if the English had not arrived by then.

But the Saxon peasant. The giant. There ought to be possibilities there.

He took out a dagger and flicked a finger across the blade. A picture of the Saxon's still, dark face came into his mind. Instinctively he knew that no threat would make him cringe; no pain would make him beg for mercy.

Rowena! Fulk lifted his head sharply as a thought struck him. His bloody eye narrowed as he turned the idea over in his mind. The scar on his cheek twisted as he smiled in satisfaction.

He put away his dagger, dusted his hands, and went in search of a camp whore.

She could not understand why he wanted her to walk so far. 'Much nicer here,' she whined.

Fulk said nothing.

She scuttered along beside him, glancing shyly at the watching faces that they passed. She slipped her hand into the crook of Fulk's great arm, and flung back her head in defiance. The soldiers grinned just the same. Fulk took no notice.

'You must not get yourself too tired first,' she simpered.

'Shut your mouth. You will be well paid.'

As they neared the edge of the camp, she became uneasy.

'Here. Where are you taking me? And what are them chains for?' She began to hang back.

Fulk grabbed her wrist and pulled her along.

When she caught sight of the two men tied to trees, she protested again.

'What is this, anyway? They are Saxon.'

Fulk turned on her. 'So are you, my precious. Or half Saxon. Probably the result of some French fisherman's night out in Dover or Rye. No airs and graces, please, my dear.'

A whole series of alarming prospects flashed through her limited mind.

'I do nothing funny,' she declared. 'And certainly not in the open air. Freezing out here.'

Fulk towered over her. Still holding her wrist, he pulled her towards him, and tilted her chin with his other hand.

'You will do whatever I say.'

She pulled back her head, away from the livid scar and the sagging eye; she was now afraid as well.

Fulk took the chains dangling from his shoulders, and tossed them to William Capra and Ralph Pomeroy. He gestured towards Godric. 'Him. One end to his ankle and the other round the tree. Put this one round his wrists. Then undo the ropes.'

Capra was glad of the diversion, and began at once to grumble about Baldwin. Fulk, still keeping a firm hold on the girl, drew his dagger. She began whimpering in fear. Capra saw the weapon, stopped grumbling, and hesitated.

'Have no fear for your back,' said Fulk. 'I shall not put a mark on him. Do as I say.'

More from curiosity than from anything else, Capra and Pomeroy obeyed. Edwin and the girl watched in tense silence.

When Godric was secured, Fulk motioned him forward, until he stood at the limit of the ankle chain. Half an arm's length of links dangled between the fetters on his wrists. Fulk had judged the distance so that he stood just out of Godric's reach. This was a refinement he had thought of at the last minute. To allow him greater physical freedom, and so increase the frustration in the mind.

First he would parade the girl, pull off a strip or two of clothing. Then he would say the name 'Rowena'. If Godric did not at once catch his meaning, he would when the knife came up to the girl's throat and drew a spot – just a spot – of blood. Fulk did not intend to be clumsy about this and spoil it by cutting the bitch's throat too early.

Then some more clothes would come off. If she protested, he would tie her down – not too tightly; he wanted a good lively struggle. He could rely on Capra and Pomeroy to catch the general drift and make some tasteless remarks. It would all add to the entertainment.

He had never had a girl watching another man's face before, but it should provide a novel sensation. All the time, he would say 'Rowena'. Get the other two to say it as well. Come to think of it, why not let them have her too, when he had finished?

That was the first half.

The second half, the part he was really looking forward to, would come the next day. Parade with the horse, mount it, lean down, and say 'Rowena' once more, just before leaving. And, as a finishing touch, bring him back a scrap of clothing, a bloodstain or two?

He pulled the girl round so that he held her facing Godric. He put the dagger to her throat and looked at Godric.

'Rowena,' he said. 'Remember? Rowena.'

He knew from the flash in Godric's eyes that he had caused a reaction. It was a thrill like seeing the quarry break cover. He felt his heart leap with excitement. This was infinitely better than listening to old stories or tearing birds to pieces.

Looking down, he was partly dazzled by the sunlight catching his blade. He blinked and looked again. Was the point against her neck or not? He blinked and squinted once more.

Perhaps he would not bother with the knife after all – just have the girl and finish. Get her to the ground first – that was the best thing. Less trouble. He looked down. Piles of leaves swirled around in a blurred black circle. The ground came up to meet him . . .

The girl stepped back quickly, her arms clasped about her, her eyes wide with horror.

Fulk's face had gone grey, almost blue. His body was rigid. Saliva trickled from the corners of his mouth.

Edwin felt a thrill of fear, and jerked at his bonds as if they were suddenly going to be merciful and allow him to escape this Devil-possession.

Capra and Pomeroy looked helplessly at each other.

'Bring him to me,' said Godric. 'Bring him here!'

They looked at Godric, but thought Godric wanted to finish him off. Besides, it meant touching that huge . . . thing on the ground.

Godric turned in desperation to Edwin. 'Tell them to do as I say. Tell them I want to stop it, not kill him.'

'Look at their faces,' said Edwin. 'Look at mine.'

'There is nothing to fear. If they will not touch him, tell them to let out this chain. It is only two paces more that I need.'

Edwin looked at Fulk, rigid, foam-flecked, and blue.

'Godric! After what he has done?'

'Threats, threats,' said Godric. 'You punish a man for what he does, not for what he threatens. This is interesting. Hurry!'

Edwin stared. 'Interesting!'

Godric shook the chains impatiently. 'There is little time. Tell them I can help him. Tell them I can stop it spreading to them. Tell them anything. Only get me to him.'

Edwin at last succeeded.

On Godric's instructions Capra was sent for warm water and a small cup. Pomeroy packed off the girl. He and Edwin watched fascinated as Godric, still carefully chained, laid his hands on the body.

Fulk was jerking and twitching all over. Godric undid the jerkin at the neck, and told Pomeroy to cut a strip of material from it. He tied two or three knots in it and eased it between Fulk's teeth. He moved the dropped knife away from the head as it thrashed from side to side, and tossed it to the amazed Pomeroy.

As the movements became slower and gentler, he turned the body on to its side, and pulled the dark hair away from an ear.

The girl was still watching from a nearby clump of bushes. Pomeroy leaped up and smacked her across the rump with the flat of his sword. She fled squealing. 'What about my money?'

Godric searched hastily through the contents of his waist wallet. He had very little that was suitable. He would have to make do.

Capra came puffing back with water and the small cup.

Godric tested it. Half cold. It should have been wine too; he had not thought in time. Still, no matter; it would have to do. He squeezed some juice from the herb into the water, threw in the rest, and stirred it. Then he strained it off into the small cup. He looked at the two Normans.

'Hold him softly, but not loosely.'

They hesitated.

Godric reassured them. 'He will soon be still, but I am in haste and do not wish to spill any. He does not know what you are doing and he will not remember when he wakes. Tell them, Edwin.'

They swallowed nervously, but obeyed.

They watched, interested in spite of themselves, as Godric carefully poured the contents of the cup into Fulk's ear.

The twitchings subsided, and Fulk lay still.

'It is over,' said Godric. Edwin translated.

'You mean, dead?' said Capra, alarmed.

'No. Sleeping.'

Just then Gilbert and Sandor arrived.

When they heard what had happened, Sandor was the quicker to take advantage of the situation.

He took Capra aside and offered him a large mug.

'Try this,' he said. 'It is the best, from the Duke's own kitchen.'

Capra was very glad of it. Sandor noticed that his hand shook slightly. Strange, he thought, how sickness sapped a man's courage much more than death.

He leaned his head close to Capra's and lowered his voice. 'My friend will help you to carry him. To the Turk – quickly – in case the big Saxon has given the wrong medicine. I will stay and help your brother to guard the prisoners. Also I must talk with the fair one. My friend is a little shy, so I must arrange the – the affair. You understand?'

Sandor gave him a nudge. Capra, his courage revived by the beer, let out a snigger.

Sandor became even more confidential. 'I am thinking,' he said. 'You have been on guard a long time. It is maybe you would like relief – a good rest, a story or two.'

Capra looked interested.

'I have a friend who tells good stories,' Sandor continued innocently. 'The best.'

'You mean Taillefer? Stupid old sot!'

'I speak of when he is sober. Last night he tell stories to make the hair walk about on the neck.'

'So?'

'So – I can arrange for him to tell them to you. He is not greedy; just a few silver pieces. Think about your loot after the battle. You can have a rest, a good meal, a good drink, and a good story. My friend Gilbert and I will guard for you, and Gilbert can see to his – um – tender matter. Sir Baldwin will never know. Is it a bargain?'

Capra hesitated. 'When?'

Sandor spread his hands. 'When better than now? My friend is, shall we say, eager. Ask what your brother thinks. I can send word to Taillefer.'

Capra and Pomeroy muttered together.

'Hurry!' said Sandor, pointing to Fulk.

Capra turned back to the Magyar. 'Only three pieces, mind. No more.'

Sandor nodded vigorously. 'It is a just price. It is not easy to get the better of you, I can see. So be it.'

Sandor walked over to Gilbert.

'It is arranged,' he said solemnly. 'You go with Capra now. You carry the Bloodeye to his Turkish shadow. I stay with Pomeroy to guard, and I pretend to talk with the Saxon for you.' He placed himself with his back to Capra, and gave Gilbert a broad wink. Then he whispered, 'Warn Taillefer to be ready.'

'He is your third liar?' said Gilbert quietly.

'I hope,' said Sandor. 'If he is awake. And bring tools for the chains.'

When Capra and Gilbert had staggered off with Fulk slumped between them, Sandor offered a drink to Ralph Pomeroy, who gulped it greedily.

'You hear the bargain,' said Sandor. He jerked his head towards Edwin. 'Now I go to talk to the fair one about – you know—'

Ralph leered.

Sandor became confidential again. 'I must speak with him in English. You must know, it is a little delicate. I have to settle a price.'

The Norman lifted his head in agreement.

Sandor ambled casually to where Edwin was tied.

'Listen with care. I must cause you to look in surprise and also in shock. You understand? So that the guard is deceived.'

Edwin nodded.

'So,' said Sandor. 'We – Gilbert and I – help you to escape. Soon. Be ready.'

As Sandor had expected, Edwin registered the necessary surprise.

Ralph Pomeroy smirked to himself.

Edwin frowned. 'Why are you doing this? We are Saxon.'

'Gilbert is my friend,' said Sandor. 'He is also your friend, and he remembers what you did for him. He wants no harm to those at the mill. You must warn them before he does anything bad.'

'Who?'

'The big man with the scar, the one who fell.'

Edwin still looked puzzled. 'And you? Why are you doing this?'

Sandor inclined his head slightly towards Pomeroy. 'They stole two of my horses. Two of my babies. I want revenge. Is that enough?'

Edwin nodded. 'So I use you and you use me – is that it?'

'Just, is it not? And now, remember. I said I must cause you shock. It is part of our plan.'

'How?'

'It would take too long,' said Sandor. 'Just listen and answer.'

Sandor stirred some leaves with his foot, his memory toying with a thought that had struck him when he had first visited the mill.

'You had a love,' he said. 'Across the sea, in Normandy. She is dead?'

Edwin's jaw dropped.

Sandor stole a glance at Pomeroy, who turned away to chuckle to himself.

'You miss her?' said Sandor.

Edwin nodded.

'You still love her?'

Edwin nodded again, his face ashen.

'Is it possible your love had a child after you left?'

Edwin looked thunderstruck. It was a while before he found his voice.

'I have no idea. I have had no word since – since—'

Sandor spoke quietly. 'You are doing well. I am sorry for the questions, but it is for the plan. The guard must think that we want you to stay here, not to go. You see?'

'Yes,' said Edwin, distressed and confused.

Sandor glanced once more at Pomeroy. The plan was going very well indeed.

All they had to do now was wait for Gilbert and Capra to return. Then there was only one anxious moment when Sir Baldwin looked in on his rounds. Sandor kept in the background while the two brothers were questioned.

Surly but satisfied, Baldwin hung about afterwards. Sandor and Gilbert began to fidget. At last Baldwin went up to Edwin.

'Um – your friends at the mill. They have always been there?'

'Yes,' said Edwin. 'Gorm – he is the miller – occupied it about twenty-odd years ago. He married the old miller's daughter.'

Baldwin harrumphed. 'I see, yes. Yes. This Gorm – what manner of man is he?'

Edwin thought of the sweaty palms, the beery breath, the bad temper, the tiny, fear-shot eyes.

'He is a skilful miller. He is a Dane from East Anglia. A freeman.'

'A freeman? Ah! Hmm. A freeman. Yes. Well, I must be getting on.' He turned to Capra. 'Keep your eyes open, you two, or watch out for your backs. For your backs. Carry on.'

Everyone sighed with relief when he had gone.

Gilbert passed round the food and drink that he had brought with him. Sandor was careful to see that Capra and Pomeroy were served first, and amply. While they munched and guzzled, he threw a question at Gilbert with his eyes. Gilbert nodded.

'So,' said Sandor, turning to the two brothers, 'all is in readiness. Gilbert says that Taillefer awaits you, with his eye bright and his tongue sharp.'

'And his hand open,' added Gilbert, catching the spirit of it.

Pomeroy belched. 'He will be paid when he is finished.'

'And if we feel like it,' said Capra.

Sandor inclined his head by way of agreement. 'Good sense, good sense. Many times I tell my friend here how sensible you are. A hundred minstrels could not deceive you.'

Capra growled.

Sandor clapped his hands. 'And now, be rested. You have deserved it. And you are very generous to allow my friend the chance to . . .' He pointed to the blankets under Gilbert's arm and gave a most expressive gesture.

Pomeroy and Capra went off in a gale of raucous laughter.

'There is no haste,' called Sandor after them.

'Slow starter, is he?' bawled Capra, as they disappeared towards the main camp.

Gilbert was still blushing. 'Sandor, how can you do it?'

Sandor was still gazing after them. 'Remember, my friend – more honey and less vinegar.' He waved a hand in their direction. 'Now they are not only deceived; they are content. Truly flattery is the best weapon of the Devil.'

'Oh?' said Gilbert vaguely.

Sandor looked surprised at his ignorance. 'It is the one chosen by the Devil against your Lord. Come.'

They loosened Edwin's ropes. Gilbert dug out some tools from inside the blankets. Sandor broke the fetters on Godric's wrists and ankles.

'When do we go?' demanded Edwin.

'Patience,' said Sandor. 'First you eat. Then you get warm. Gilbert, the blankets.'

Gilbert wrapped one round the shoulders of each of the two prisoners.

Edwin huddled down into it, suddenly more conscious of the cold and stiffness in his joints.

'Why do they not suspect? Why did they not question you about the blankets?'

Gilbert and Sandor looked at each other. Gilbert felt himself blushing again.

Sandor put on a solemn expression. 'It is a very deep plan, you understand. It would take much time to explain.'

Gilbert blew quietly in relief.

'So,' said Sandor. 'Eat, and be warm. Then walk about. You will not get far if your legs will not bend nor your ankles turn. Keep the ropes close by, and watch. I go for a while.'

'Where?' said Gilbert.

'Horses,' said Sandor. 'You must have horses. Two Saxons walking near a Norman camp – men will suspect. But two Saxons riding – there must be a good reason. So they will not suspect.'

While Sandor was gone, nobody could think of anything to say. Gilbert paced nervously. It seemed hours before Sandor returned. He had five horses with him, fully equipped and ready for travel.

Gilbert almost fell on them in his relief.

'At last!'

Sandor put a hand on his arm. 'We wait for Taillefer,' he said. 'To make sure of the plan.'

It was further agony for Gilbert. Even Sandor began to show signs of agitation.

When the minstrel finally arrived, he did not look well.

'It is a long way without a horse,' he wheezed.

There were spots of dried blood on his jerkin. Taillefer also seemed to be having trouble with his back.

He waved away Sandor's look of concern.

'Our two friends were a little impatient. When I told them my voice was tiring, they beat me with the flat of their swords to – er – revive it.'

'And you have been coughing,' said Gilbert.

Taillefer looked down at the stains on his clothes, then raised his head and eased his shoulders painfully.

'At first I joined Sandor's plan for mischief. Later, for money. Now, I am in it for revenge.'

'You remember the plan?' said Sandor anxiously.

'I put it in,' said Taillefer.

'Put what in?' said Gilbert.

'The last touch,' said Sandor. 'I ask the Turk to give me a medicine; it goes in the drink to make a man sleep. We use it in Hungary, in my country. We get it from the old priests of the wide plains. It is very strong. The Turk, who knows many things, knows also of this. You do that, Taillefer?'

Taillefer nodded emphatically. 'Indeed, my friend, in the fullest measure. And I added a small touch of my own. Your Turkish doctor also gave me some medicine, to purge the bowel. Our two gallants refused to pay me. Since they refused to loosen their pockets, I have taken the liberty of loosening their stomachs.' He lifted his eyebrows expressively and looked at everyone in turn. 'I should estimate that our two additions to their liquid refreshment should prove sufficient to immobilise them for a while.'

Everyone laughed.

'Which one acts first?' asked Gilbert.

Taillefer spread his hands. 'Does it matter? They wake up lying in it, or they drop off and fall in it. Either way, we leave them in a most satisfactory situation – *dans la merde*. Shall we be on our way?'

Besides taking the straight route out into open country and not through the camp, there was, as Sandor had said, scant need of further precaution. Edwin and Godric pulled up their hoods to hide their long hair. To any but an inquisitive observer, they were most likely a small group of troopers and grooms exercising horses. They did not go fast; Taillefer was clearly unwell, and Godric was no horseman, certainly not on a Norman destrier. If any stray sentry or lounger threw a remark at them, Gilbert dealt with the answers.

'Truly,' said Sandor with a smile, 'you are becoming a better liar. You see? All you need is practice. Eh, Taillefer?'

Taillefer grunted in agreement, but said nothing. His face was grey.

'What is it, Taillefer?' said Gilbert.

Taillefer tried to smile, not very successfully.

'I am afraid that repeated blows on the back with the flat of the sword are not conducive to comfortable riding.'

Sandor looked anxiously at him, then said to Edwin, 'It is perhaps we can not escort you very far. We become slower and slower. See that hill, the one with the sandlake at the bottom?'

'That? I think it is called Caldbec in English.'

'We call it Senlac,' said Taillefer, in between coughs.

Sandor glanced at Gilbert, who remained stony-faced, then back at Edwin.

'I think we leave you by Sandlake,' he said.

'I am well enough,' said Taillefer. 'I do not wish to spoil a good plan.' He coughed. 'Well enough. I can go further.'

When they reached the stream he collapsed.

Godric carried him to some dry ground. He was now bringing up blood again, and seemed feverish. Godric began undoing his upper clothes. Sandor moved to stop him, but Gilbert laid a hand on his arm.

'Leave him. He knows what he is doing. He did as much for me.'

After his examination, Godric stood up and looked at Sandor.

'He is very weak. I think maybe there is a rib broken; at least it is badly bruised and therefore painful. This causes more strain on his breathing. He can go no further on horseback.'

Edwin translated for Gilbert.

'Then we camp here,' said Sandor.

Godric shook his head. 'He must have warmth and dryness. Out here – a frosty night perhaps – no good.'

There was a silence.

Gilbert scanned the land around them. There was no one in sight.

Edwin was the first to speak.

'It is still several miles to the mill. Delay could be dangerous. If we are recaptured we will all suffer. Taken together like this.'

Sandor beseeched Godric with his eyes.

Godric handed the reins of his horse to Sandor. 'Little man from Hungary, you have done enough. You have no debt to us. Besides, I am a bad horseman. Sling him between his own horse and this one. Take him back.'

Sandor wiped an eye. 'Big man, for you I go back and I lie like the very Devil. We will keep your trail hidden as long as we can.'

'Good. Now, tell us – where can we hide until dark?'

Sandor pointed up the hill. 'See that old apple tree? Go beyond and down a slope. You will find a ravine hidden in trees. No one will dare to follow there. We know – eh, Gilbert?'

'Yes,' said Gilbert gruffly.

'If news of your king comes in the morning, every Norman will be too busy to chase two Saxon prisoners.'

Edwin looked at Gilbert. Suddenly they were enemies again. How did he say goodbye?

There was an awkward silence. Sandor resolved it. He held out his hand to Godric.

'I get my revenge; you get your woman. Is it a fair bargain – between enemies?'

Godric's huge paw engulfed Sandor's hand.

'A fair bargain.'

Edwin and Gilbert shook hands in red-faced silence.

From the shoulder of the hill Edwin and Godric watched Gilbert and Sandor fashion a sling for Taillefer. As they moved off, they turned one last time and waved.

Godric waved back.

'I hope we do not meet again.'

'Amen to that,' said Edwin. Then, becoming practical, he asked Godric. 'Will you ride behind me?'

Godric shook his head. 'No. I have had enough of wooden saddles. And we shall attract too much notice. I shall come behind on foot. You will go faster, and I can watch our trail. Look for a good place to hide.'

'And tomorrow?'

'Tomorrow, you go ahead again. Tell Rowena I shall not be far behind. That is all she needs to know.'

Good lying came with practice. Gilbert discovered the truth of Sandor's philosophy; he got better as he went along.

First they had to see to Taillefer. Sandor knew where some archers had a wagon in a corner of the main camp.

'It is near to us and away from the Capra. I do them some favours. They will let us use it for Taillefer.'

'Will they not search the whole camp when the alarm is given?' said Gilbert.

Sandor shook his head. 'Sir Baldwin will not waste good soldiers chasing Saxons who escape. If they do search, the camp is the last place they will look. Or ask questions.'

'And if they come here last?' said Gilbert, still not reassured.

Sandor shrugged. 'They find a minstrel who is sleeping off his drink – as he always does. While he recovers from a fall.'

Sandor went off to the horse lines for routine duties. Or so he said. It was really that he was concerned about theft. About an hour later he returned. He clambered hastily over the tailboard into the wagon.

'Haste!' he said to Gilbert. 'Our friends are out of *la merde*. They have told Sir Baldwin.'

Gilbert sat up in alarm. Sandor put up a reassuring hand.

'Now it is time to put them back in it again. Sir Baldwin is coming. Remember, enjoy your lies, and you will enjoy your revenge.'

He took the ivory horn from his belt and poured some beer into it. He spilled some of the contents over the straw on which Taillefer was lying. He was bending over the minstrel and cradling his head when Baldwin pulled back the cloth at the back of the wagon.

Taillefer rose brilliantly to the occasion.

He had been drinking again, he was ashamed to say, with his friends the archers. Gilbert, amazed at his own inventiveness, joined in. They had taken him up one of the new castle cat-walks – Sir Baldwin was no doubt familiar with them – and he had fallen down the steps. All the way, added Taillefer. That explained the bruises on his back. Perhaps Sir Baldwin would care to see them for himself, suggested Sandor. No, Sir Baldwin would not care to see.

So, Taillefer admitted, he had lain prostrate all day, punished for his sins with many pains and with the bloody flux. Numerous bloodstained cloths were displayed. Baldwin's nose wrinkled at the smell of beer inside the wagon.

Taillefer thanked his God that he had had the company of his two faithful friends all day, here, in the wagon. Apart, of course, from the time when they took food to Sir Baldwin's prisoners. How were they, by the way?

Escaped? Great Jesus! How could two watchful men like Capra and Pomeroy allow such a thing, especially with the threat of a flogging hanging over them? How could they be so stupid? Their story was what? Oh, Sir Baldwin must be joking.

Gilbert thoroughly enjoyed himself.

Baldwin satisfied his conscience that he had made all

reasonable efforts to secure recapture. If they had gone, well, there was no great harm done. If they had any sense, they would go home and get the women out of the way. Frankly he rather hoped they did. The battle would not be long now. And there was Fulk.

'Where is Bloodeye? Have you seen him? William wants him.'

Sandor pretended to cudgel his memory.

'I did see him earlier, Sir Baldwin. He was – um ...'

'... at a bit of a loose end,' said Gilbert. 'Off duty, as you might say.'

Baldwin read it wrongly. He thought at once of the mill. Of two young women. Of Fulk's leering face. He wrenched his mind back to the spot.

'I go now to arrange two floggings.'

It was the nearest he could get to striking a blow at Fulk.

When he had gone, Gilbert and Sandor wrung each other's hands, and nearly exploded with silent laughter. Taillefer lay back and held a cloth to his mouth.

Gilbert suddenly remembered something.

'Tell me, Sandor,' he said between stifled snorts of delight, 'where did the horses come from?'

Sandor looked innocent.

'Horses?'

'There were five – mine, yours, and Taillefer's nag. Who did the others belong to?'

Sandor grinned from ear to ear.

'I take from two who do not need them because they are *dans la merde*. Did I not say that it was a very good plan? Besides, they were my horses anyway.'

'Here?'

'Yes,' said Ralph. 'We are out of reach now of their short-range scouts.'

'Enough for an hour.'

They tethered their horses to a tree at the edge of the clearing. Ralph decided to risk a fire. It would be their last hot food till well into the next day. It was now dusk, and hard to distinguish a campfire from a charcoal-burner's smouldering.

While Ralph cooked, Bruno saw to the horses. He was not happy about one of Sorrel's legs. They ate and relaxed in silence.

Ralph felt curiously flat and without spirit. He had expected to feel excited, full in the chest, pleased with himself. After all, they had done it; they had found the English. They had done the one thing that the Bastard had been dying for.

'We show him the enemy. Now it is up to him.'

Trust Bruno to put it bluntly. It meant, as he and Bruno both knew, that their work was over. There was a long, hard ride back to Hastings, but that was mere drudgery and boredom. Once they had announced their news, they dropped out of the picture. Up to this very hour, they had been the most important men in the entire army – the only men who could give the Duke what he wanted. News. The minute they announced it, they became expendable. There would be barely time for a gruff word of thanks, and they would be brushed aside.

Then it would be all rush and command – 'Fitz' this and 'Fitz' that; Giffard and Montgomery and Beaumont and Odo and Lord Geoffrey and all the rest barking orders; Bloodeye, his sagging eye gleaming with relief at the prospect of something at last to do. No more gossiping and grumbling and nagging and moaning. Archers and swordsmen and knights, tense-jawed over final clippings and fastenings of equipment, swearing at last-minute losses and breakages and failures, beating the nearest valets and servants and grooms. Sir Baldwin, totting up his sheaves of spare arrows and squeezing yet more barrels of water onto his wagons until the axles threatened to buckle.

He, Ralph, and Bruno would not be part of that excitement. They would watch, from the outside.

Ralph dangled some rind above the flames and watched it sizzle.

'Do not distress yourself. The Bastard will need us again.' Bruno as usual had read his thoughts.

'He will not let us fight,' said Ralph.

'Of course not. He will need us to get him to London after the battle.'

'More drudgery.'

Bruno shrugged. 'It is work. Battles like this are fought once in a lifetime. Work like ours comes every day. You should be grateful.'

Ralph dropped the rest of the rind into the fire and wiped his fingers.

'Is that how you see it? Do you not mind?'

'It is my trade, and it is yours. Battle or no battle, there is always a campaign. And that means work. You chose it too.'

'It chose me really,' said Ralph.

Bruno shook his head. 'This is no time for changes of heart. You are empty and drained because you have achieved your object – like a lover after passion. Have no fear – you will feel desire again. You are a scout because you are a scout, and there is an end of it.'

'Is that really the end?' said Ralph. 'After the conquest, do you see nothing different?'

Bruno ran his tongue over the front of his teeth. 'One battle will not do it all. It may gain the Bastard the crown, but it will not make every Saxon bend the knee. We shall still be outnumbered hundreds to one. There will be fighting and campaigning for years, or I do not know the Saxons. We shall not be short of work.'

Ralph looked into the fire.

He had not thought as much about it as Bruno clearly had. The Bastard had attracted most of his army by promises of land – land beyond their wildest dreams of grandeur and greed.

Ralph had vaguely supposed that a small portion at least of that landed loot would fall his way, but he had not stopped to think whether that was what he really wanted.

The idea of settling down crossed his mind as frequently as it did everyone else's. All men on the move dreamed of stopping, just as all men on the land dreamed of travelling. His father had been a landed knight, and so was his elder brother, Aubrey. If God had decreed that he should be the first-born of his father, he would have been settled for years by now at Gisors, like Aubrey, and generally content to be so.

The last time the thought had occurred to him was at the mill. The tall daughter, the fair one – she had put ideas into his head. Of course, it was quite out of the question; she was humbly born. And he had been campaigning long enough to know that she was sort of young woman with whom every man fell in love when he was far from home.

No doubt there would be celebrations after the victory. He had seen that too. He had caroused and whored with the best of them – or the worst. The trouble was that one forgot the pleasure so quickly. He had nothing against whores on moral grounds; army life made them indispensable. What he resented was that they offered only relief for the symptoms; they did not cure the disease. They left him with only an ache in his body, and did nothing for the ache in his mind.

Michael dying of fever, with his large, frightened eyes; Father waving his stump of an arm after the raid; Mother singing to herself in a corner; Aimery gasping to death in the infirmary at Cluny – the only remedy he could find was to move.

And Gilbert? Would he take away the pain of Michael? Unlikely. Now. Bruno was making him see the truth. Perhaps the boy really was not up to it. So the sooner he went back to his precious Adele and his baby, probably, the better for all concerned. What did it matter who the father was? In these troubled times, any father was better than none at all. Besides, it was clear that he loved the child, despite what he said. It shone out of him like a light. Just as Michael's goodness had shone out of him.

He fidgeted; this was intolerable. Much more, and he would be crying his eyes out. He began to scoop earth on to the embers.

Bruno said nothing, but collected his gear, and went to have another look at Sorrel's leg.

'Well?' said Ralph, as he packed the saddlebags.

'It will do,' said Bruno. 'We can not gallop in this forest. A good steady pace will cause no harm, I think.'

'With the miles in front of us,' said Ralph, 'that is the best we can hope for. You know we must aim to be with the Duke by morning – midday at the latest.'

Bruno pulled on his gloves and grasped the reins.

'Then let us be on our way. Being still seems only to make you miserable. Let us hope our news does not have the same effect on the Bastard.'

'You wait. You just wait.'

Gilbert passed the back of his thumb over his lips. Sandor and Taillefer looked at each other.

'"Dog-boy." "Kennel boy." "Master Senlac."'

'Words,' said Taillefer. 'Only words. They are worth nothing. I am a wordsmith; take it from me, they are worth nothing.'

Gilbert gave a wobbly wave of his beer mug.

'It is all very well for you. The words were not thrown at you. They do not hurt you. Nothing hurts you, you old wineskin. You can not bruise a wineskin.' He chuckled. 'That is clever. Clever. Can not bruise a wineskin.'

He reached out for the pot. Sandor started to move it away from him, but Taillefer stopped him.

'Let him,' he said softly. 'What else can he do but wait?'

Gilbert squinted in the bad light of the candle-stump.

'What are you two whispering about?'

'Taillefer asks me about medicine,' said Sandor.

Gilbert waved vigorously. 'No. You are lying. Lying. I know what you talk about. "Poor Gilbert," you say. "Left behind while Ralph and Bruno do the real work. Not up to it, poor lad. Farm boy, you see. Not up to it. Not like sons of knights. Not like Ralph and Bruno." Oh, no.'

The beer dribbled down his chin. He wiped it.

'Well, you wait. I shall make them all eat their words. Bishop Odo – Bishop clever Odo. And high-and-mighty Bruno of Aix, with his great wall of a face. And Ralph, most of all . . .'

His face puckered at the onset of tears. He fought them down. Sandor put out a hand. Gilbert beat it off.

'There is a battle to come,' said Taillefer, from his bed of straw. 'A chance for all men.'

'Ah! Now there –' Gilbert waved the empty pot again '– there you say something.' He hiccuped. 'There can a man – a real man – prove himself. Not a mere scout.' He spat over the tail-board. 'Not a spotty bishop. You wait. Everyone will see me; there will be no argument. No remarks. Then let Bruno the Great Talker find something to say about that.'

Sandor and Taillefer looked at each other again. Gilbert caught the expression that passed between them.

'Sympathy! Last of all do I want sympathy.' He struggled to his knees, and clambered to the back of the wagon. He fumbled with the catch of the tailboard, failed to undo it, and tried to climb over. The mug clattered against something metallic. He slipped and fell right out, picked himself up, and lurched off.

'I go to talk to men. Men, do you hear!'

Sandor retrieved the mug, refilled it, and passed it to Taillefer. He gave himself another full measure in his ivory horn. For a while they sipped in silence.

'He reaches up so high,' said Sandor sadly.

'All to no purpose,' said Taillefer. 'He calls himself "Gilbert of

Avranches" when he comes from a nearby village. He strives to
be a soldier when he is gifted with animals. He bursts to be a
scout when he works best with others.'

'Is it so wrong?' asked Sandor. 'Wrong to wish to please your
friend? To make him proud?'

Taillefer shook his head. In the guttering light, the shadows
under his eyes and the lines in his forehead showed thick and
dark. The bony fingers that clasped the mug glinted from the
gaudy rings.

'It is not Ralph he seeks to impress. Or Bruno, or Odo, or the
Duke, or anybody else. It is himself. He searches for a means of
being proud of himself.'

'His honour?'

'Yes, if you like. Honour helps a man to cope with fear. In the
end it is fear that is the bane of all. Fear of the dark; fear of the
forest; fear of the Devil; fear of Hellfire; fear of famine, disease,
pestilence, pain; fear of failure; fear of the enemy; fear of death.
These are great truths, which anyone with eyes can see for himself. This is God's pattern. This is all that God chooses to show
us of His purpose. What chance does a man have? Can he alter
this pattern of the world set by Almighty God? Can he alter the
place that God has fashioned for him? Can he remove a single
one of the dangers that surround him? But honour can rescue
him from despair. Honour can give a man pride. And pride can
be a shield against fear.'

'Stronger than hope?' said Sandor.

'Yes. Hopes are too often dashed. Pride is the wreckage to
which a man can cling in the shipwreck of his hopes. But it must
be the right pride. The pride in a man's own position as decreed
by God. That is where Gilbert is wrong. He can find a hundred
armies in the dark; will that make him a professional scout like
Ralph? He can kill a thousand enemies; will that make Bruno see
him as knightly born? He can lead a squadron into battle and
win the day for the Bastard; will that bring the respect of Bishop

Odo? He is in distress because he searches for other men's honour. He needs to find his own.'

Then let him find the man who dishonoured his wife, thought Sandor.

'There is a devil that drives him,' he said. 'I remember it today, when we make our plan. Something the Saxon say to me once. About his love.'

Taillefer sighed, lifting yet more wrinkles in his forehead. 'Ah – love.'

Sandor grinned. 'You want I tell a story about love?'

Taillefer smiled. 'You? You horse prophet? You saddle-imp? What do you know of love?'

Sandor scratched the stubble under his chin.

'I am a very deep man,' he said with mock solemnity. 'Be silent, and I tell you ...'

'The Holy Banner flutters out before'

'Father! Father, you must wake!'

Rowena shook him roughly. She was past patience now. For nearly two days she had tried to get a decision out of him.

Gorm raised his heavy head from the table. The boards round his sprawled arms were blotched with stale beer. He hated Rowena for waking him.

He looked at the well-strapped bundles by her feet. He saw Edith, scrubbed and dressed for the road, her moon face lifted patiently to await Rowena's word. In her podgy hand she clutched her stick doll and her pipe. Trust Rowena, he thought, to truss her up like a sack of wheat. He hated Rowena for being so ready, so capable.

He hated her too for what he knew, even in his stupefied state, she was going to make him do.

'Father, you must make up your mind.'

Sweyn and Aud hovered in the background.

Gorm looked desperately this way and that.

'Where is Godric?' he said. 'Where is that ox? Never here when you need him.'

Rowena shook him again.

'Godric is gone. The Normans took him, with Edwin. They may come back at any time. We have wasted enough hours as it is. We are ready to go. All we need is your word. You must give us your word.'

Gorm frowned in the effort of recall. Godric and the axe . . . Godric at Rowena's side . . . Rowena pressing her fingers to his lips . . .

'Godric,' he said. 'That lust-ridden serf. He wants you. And you – I remember now. You love him.' He pondered this in deepening disgust, and repeated with heavy irony, 'Love.'

Rowena tossed her head in despair. 'Father, we must leave – now.'

'You do love him,' insisted Gorm, unable to forsake his one coherent thought. 'See?' He turned to Aud and Sweyn. 'She does not gainsay it.'

'She has been making eyes at him for years,' said Aud. 'You were too – too blind to see, Father.'

Gorm turned back to Rowena. 'You fool!' he said. If he had been on his feet, he would have struck her. 'Do you think I will give a portion for my eldest daughter to marry a bastard foundling?'

'He is not a foundling. You told me once you knew exactly who he was.'

'He is nothing,' shouted Gorm. 'Nothing. Do you hear? He shall not become my kin.' He stretched out an arm for Sweyn's shoulder. 'He shall not share my son's land. On free tenure, mark! Direct from the King. That ox shall have none of it.'

Sweyn nestled against his father and looked smug.

Rowena tried again. 'Father, if we do not move, there will be no land, and no one to share it either. The Normans are coming from one way, our army from another. You saw what those men nearly did. We can not hope to be so lucky next time.'

'She is afraid of being raped,' said Aud. 'That big man with the scar and the knife.'

Rowena turned wearily to her. 'My sister, all women fear it, but we do not all think on it all the time.'

Aud glared.

'Father,' said Rowena, turning back, 'It is not our honour but our lives. You saw how close we came. You are our father. I will do your bidding, but *you must say*.'

Gorm seized on it as one who looks forward to a meaty argument. 'You have not done my bidding since your mother died. I fathered an empress in you. You will only do it now if I say what you wish.' He looked intently at her.

Sweyn gazed expectantly at Aud; there was another good fat row in the offing.

'I am not such a fool as you think,' said Gorm. 'I know why you wish us to leave. Godric will come back to an empty house and will take it over. A few months' living here, and the local court will deem him the owner, especially if you have planned for something to happen to me.'

'Father!'

'A child could see that. No court will uphold me here – a mere Dane, an outsider. It has always been the same.'

He wandered off into garbled recriminations from the deep past.

Rowena stood firmly before him and shouted at the top of her voice.

'Father!'

Gorm looked up, surprised. Rowena composed herself.

'Father, hear me well. I am leaving and I am taking Edith. We shall not go far – probably the first of the King's manors that will take us in. Edwin told me to use his name. He is known in many places where the King hunts. For the last time I beg you to come with us, and tell Aud and Sweyn to do so as well.'

Gorm struggled to his feet, dimly aware that a show of dignity was required. His clothes were awry. An expanse of hairy white stomach bulged over his sagging belt.

'This is my mill,' he said. 'I am a freeman. I hold this mill from the King. My son Sweyn will do as I say. Aud is – Aud is a dutiful daughter. Not a beautiful daughter, but a dutiful daughter. Not beautiful, but dutiful.' He sniggered at his own joke. 'I shall not give up what is mine. Mine. Not yours. You are not a dutiful daughter,' he said, returning to his theme.

Rowena turned to her sister.

'Aud,' she said. 'I can not take Sweyn against his will, or against his father's will. But you – you are a grown woman. I ask you now – use your own mind. Are you coming with us?'

Aud drew herself up. When she did not stoop, she was taller than Rowena.

'You have always been headstrong,' she said. 'I think you are headstrong now.' She waved an arm. 'All round us we have strong walls. We are safe. What safety would we have on the road? How are you going to look after Edith? Out there are two armies, refugees, deserters. You call that wisdom? Here is your home, your father, your family. Even Godric said, "watch and wait".'

'He also said "hide if need be." He expects me to use my own mind.'

'You are running away to save your own skin for Godric.'

Rowena turned away and put out her hand.

'Come, Edith. We go for a nice long walk, yen?'

'Yes, yes.'

'You have your doll?'

'Yes, Edis' doll here. And Edis' pipe.'

She blew a jarring note or two. Sweyn winced.

Rowena tried to kiss her father, but he brushed her aside. Sweyn cowered away.

'Father, will you put the ox to the cart for us?'

'No. Neither will Sweyn.'

Sweyn made a rude face.

'Then we walk.'

*

'How long?'

'Hard to say, my lord duke. But certainly not tomorrow. Nor would any normal general be ready by the day after. Then Harold is no—'

'Splendour of God, man!' William burst out. 'I want better than that. Call yourself a senior scout?'

Ralph took the rebuke without flinching. He met the fierce gaze; for once the eyes had stopped their restless shifting, and were almost afire with their intensity.

All about them each man was frozen in total stillness. All those months – and now! Ralph brushed his palms together as if he were dusting away the last vestiges of uncertainty.

'My lord, if Harold marches hard he could be within striking distance by tomorrow evening.'

There was a buzz of excitement.

Ralph looked round at the effects of his remark. Bruno allowed himself a private grin. Ralph could swagger even when he was standing still.

The meeting had clearly been summoned in a hurry. Nobody was wearing mail. A few were still eating. One or two had been interrupted in shaving. Sir Walter Giffard had cut himself in his haste. It had not improved his self-control.

'You mean a night attack? Have some sense, man.'

Ralph met him head on too.

'No, Sir Walter. I do not think even Harold will try that. His men will be too tired. They must have a night's rest.'

'And attack in the morning.'

'Yes, sir. Try and take us by surprise – early.'

The Duke slapped his knee. 'Then we rise yet earlier. You agree, Fitz?'

'Yes, sir,' said Fitzosbern. 'And we go to him.'

'But our castle is finished,' said Giffard, dabbing at his chin. 'Even Ranulf admits it. Why not let Harold beat himself to pieces on it? He will have no siege machinery.'

'Because it provides him with the initiative, Walter. We would then be waiting for things to happen.'

'That is what we have been doing since we arrived,' said Giffard.

'Now it is time for a change,' said the Duke.

Giffard threw up his hands in bafflement. Beaumont, who had squeezed in at the back so as not to miss anything, decided it was time to get himself noticed.

'I agree with his Grace. I am for moving, not for waiting. At a time like this, standing still is for old men.'

Giffard could have strangled him.

Montgomery tried to calm him down.

'Walter, listen. Harold has campaigned with us. He knows we are good at castles, good at waiting, good at preparing. Being a man of rapid decision himself, he tends to look down on what he sees as overcaution. He thinks us overcautious. I heard him say once that Normans make war with a spare saddle on every horse. Maybe we do. But we can change when it is necessary. Now it is necessary.'

Giffard growled.

'Roger is right,' said Fitzosbern, though he intended the remark to be for everyone. 'All the preparation in the world is no use without the right timing. Nobody here has attained his senior position without being aware of the paramount importance of timing.'

Beaumont looked proudly at the men on either side of him.

'Timing will give us surprise,' said Geoffrey de Montbrai. 'If we move against him we shall be going against our own habit, our own usage. We shall catch him on one foot.'

'And we shall win,' said the Duke.

'I agree,' said Beaumont. 'Let us move fast and strike! We shall crush him like a beetle.'

His seniors smiled.

Montgomery looked thoughtful. 'There still remains the problem of their numbers. We do not know their strength.'

'That is a chance we must take,' said Fitzosbern. 'It is the price we pay for the advantage of surprise. Harold is taking a far bigger chance by going for us with a tired and depleted army.'

'Yes, but how depleted? How do we know he has not made up his losses?'

Fitzosbern turned to Ralph. 'Do you think he has recouped after that ... bridge engagement at ... um ...'

'Stamford, sir.' Ralph considered. 'I should say there was still a sizeable army. As for numbers—'

The Duke interrupted. He had long since learned to distrust any estimates of large enemy forces, even by his experienced scouts. Few scouts saw an army conveniently drawn up together in one place; they were usually strung out on a line of march. Nor did the Duke want Ralph coming out with wild over-estimates; it was bad for morale. One could sometimes gain more precise figures from high-ranking traitors, but they were also suspect for obvious reasons. William sought instead useful information.

'What sort of personnel?'

'A lot heavy infantry, sir.'

'That will be the housecarls,' said Beaumont, showing off knowledge that everyone else already shared. 'The élite of the army. Axemen. Professional, and hard as nails.'

William ignored him.

'Any more?'

'Like swordsmen?' said Alan of Brittany, whose Bretons prided themselves on such skill.

'Swords, yes,' said Ralph, 'but no separate sword detachments. And not much in the way of horse, so far as I could see. No bows either. A sprinkling of spearmen. As for the rest, remnants mostly, armed with everything but the garden spade.'

Fitzosbern nodded. 'Harold has made up his numbers by

collecting whatever he can on the way, and he can not afford to be fussy. All the same, I should be surprised if he does not have a goodish number of fyrdmen with him as well, and they are not armed with garden spades.'

'Fyrdmen?' said Beaumont, puzzled.

Giffard glanced in triumph at Montgomery. So the puppy did not know everything.

'The fyrd,' said Fitzosbern, 'is the English annual military gathering – the host. You know – "the realm is in danger". We have knight service; Harold has the fyrd. It is rather more amateur than our system, and not so regular, and they are hardly in the first flush of youth. But it seems to work. At least the English have always made it work. They pride themselves on their amateurism.'

'It goes back long before Cnut,' said Geoffrey de Montbrai, adding a touch of scholarship.

Bishop Odo, anxious to nullify any credit that might accrue to Geoffrey, and keen to show off his military knowledge, asked a question.

'What sort of shape are they in?'

'Hard to tell, sir,' said Ralph. 'Armies never look their best on line of march. But they are keeping up a good rate.'

'Which brings us back to their estimated time of arrival,' said the Duke, deciding that everything useful had been said.

He turned to Fitzosbern. 'Fitz, I want scouts out towards the English night and day. Work them in relays if necessary. Work them singly if need be, and damn the risk. We must cover twice the ground, all the ground. We must know if they keep up the present speed of approach. We must know if they come along the avenues.'

'And if so, which one.'

'Yes. See to it. Take Odo with you to brief them. I shall go through the drills again now for the knights.'

He waved a hand round the ring of his senior commanders,

who wiped the last of the soap off their cheeks and thought of breakfast getting cold.

The Duke turned to Geoffrey de Montbrai. 'Coutances – send word to de Clair that he must have his supply wagons ready to move by tomorrow night. Tell him to come here as soon as possible. Send for all the archer and crossbow section leaders, and the senior armourer. Ask Ranulf how many men he needs for a security garrison—'

'And divide it in two,' said Geoffrey, grinning.

'Yes. Yes. Appoint a commander. Turold of Vermandois will do – unless you can think of a better.'

Geoffrey stood up. 'Turold would also be my choice, my lord. But may I remind you that I too have responsibilities at this time, as does my brother bishop of Bayeux. It will be a time soon for the curing of men's souls.'

William waved a hand. 'I have an army of priests for that.'

'Nevertheless, my lord Duke, they have to be allocated.'

'Time enough for that tomorrow. Men will not begin to fear until the darkness before a battle, and that is not tonight. You told me yourself that attendance has been poor. But you can arrange for yourself or Odo to say Mass for me tomorrow as usual.'

'As your Grace pleases.'

'See to it, Coutances. You are a man who can carry many instructions in his head. And it now needs your authority. After so many days of rumours and false alarms, it will take high rank to make men move.'

Geoffrey bowed and left.

'Oh – and find the Fleming Bloodeye,' the Duke called after him. 'It is time his money-men began earning their keep.'

At the end of the hall, Odo and Fitzosbern issued instructions to the assembled scouts, and divided them into watches. Men grumbled when they were assigned to night duty.

Ralph looked around for Gilbert. 'Where is he?'

Bruno shrugged.

Just then Gilbert tumbled in through the door, and stopped abruptly when he saw Odo and Fitzosbern. His hair was awry, his face was grey, and there were shadows under his bloodshot eyes.

'I – I am sorry, my lords. I was in a distant part of the camp and I had a sick companion to see to. I came as soon as I could.'

Odo raised an eyebrow. 'Well, well, young Master Senlac.'

Gilbert writhed.

Ralph tried to come to his rescue. 'He has a gift for late arrival, my lord. But the gift is often fruitful.'

'Indeed?' said Odo, ignoring the irony. 'Always late in? Then he can be late out for a change. He is on the night watch.' He looked directly at Gilbert. 'Get to your bed again; you look as if you have just left it.'

Fitzosbern pursued the idea rather more practically. 'Rest well, then ride. We must have instant news of any change – speed, direction, apparent design. Understand?'

Gilbert nodded vigorously. 'Yes, my lord.'

'The minute you have anything, you return at the gallop.'

Fitzosbern looked at Ralph and spoke as if Gilbert were not there. 'Can he manage a night reconnaissance by himself?'

Gilbert, his heart now pounding as hard as his head, waited dry-mouthed.

As Gilbert felt Ralph's gaze, so Ralph was conscious of Bruno's expressionless face.

The boy was pale with tension and pain. Whatever he had been doing for the last two days, it had not been pleasant. Probably finished up drunk with that old soak, Taillefer. Hardly to be blamed, after the rejection he had suffered. And now, the lashing from Odo's tongue.

He knew what Bruno was thinking – could almost hear it. He had listened once before, and it had hurt him as much as it had hurt Gilbert. For the life of him he could not do it again – not kick him while he was down.

Could he manage a night reconnaissance by himself? Every scout in the army would be out there as well. The boy had to be given a chance.

'I should think so,' said Ralph.

And damn Bruno to Hell!

Fitzosbern grunted. 'So be it.'

He turned to the other scouts. 'Go now, and see to your horses. If you are on the night watches, you can obtain rations from Sir Baldwin de Clair. The first relay leaves at noon. The second at nightfall. The third at midnight. The fourth at dawn. Report back in person to me or to my lord bishop Odo.'

Odo opened his mouth to say something sarcastic to Gilbert, but Fitzosbern placed a hand on his arm.

'Come, my lord. The Duke's council. We are needed more there.'

Odo contented himself with a lofty smile, and followed.

Gilbert glared after him.

'You wait. You just wait – Bishop bastard Odo of Bayeux.'

Ralph nudged him. 'Careful, careful. Mistress Arlette of Falaise may have neglected to marry the Duke's father, but she did marry Odo's father.'

Gilbert spat. 'He is still a bastard.'

'You can endure the edge of Odo's tongue. Be thankful instead that Fitzosbern trusts you. His is the judgement to watch for.'

Gilbert softened. 'Yes. Yes, I know.'

What was far more important was that Ralph now trusted him.

Ralph patted him on the back. 'Go now. Get something to eat. And rest well; you look awful.'

Bruno favoured him with a comment. 'And stay away from Taillefer; he is getting you into bad habits.'

Gilbert grinned, and put his hand to his head in mock agony.

'Warn Sandor,' said Bruno. 'Tell him I wish to see him about Sorrel.'

'When you ride out, remember what I have told you,' said Ralph. 'You seek information, not glory. Glory is for heroes.'

'And heroes die,' said Bruno.

Gilbert smiled. He looked about fifteen when he smiled like that. Ralph poked him softly on the jaw with his fist.

'Look after that hauberk.'

Bruno came to stand beside Ralph. They watched Gilbert go.

Ralph, as usual, felt Bruno thinking.

'Well, what else could I do? There is no harm at this stage, is there?'

'Not to the army,' said Bruno.

Ralph looked up sharply. 'To him? No. Not even Gilbert—'

'– "of Avranches"—'

'– "of Avranches" – will fight the whole English army by himself in the middle of the night. With any luck he will not find them at all.'

'And tomorrow?'

Ralph tucked his gloves into his belt. 'Tomorrow – we can keep an eye on him.'

'And when the battle comes?'

'When the battle comes,' said Ralph, 'we hope Almighty God will keep an eye on all of us.'

Bruno grimaced.

'Now,' said Ralph, 'shall we find Sandor? Let us see what he thinks about Sorrel's front leg.'

Sweyn recognised the Norman horse before he did the rider. He came rushing into the house.

'Father! The Normans!'

Gorm barely stirred. Sweyn tried shaking him. Gorm flung him off. Sweyn looked at Aud.

'It is no use,' she said. 'You will not move him.'

She nodded towards the door. A slight flush had appeared in her cheeks. 'Where are they?'

'On the hill, by the wood.'

In the silence that followed, Sweyn began weeping in his fear.

'What do we do?'

Aud glanced down at her father sprawled across the table. Even as she looked at him, he slid from the stool and slumped on to the rushes. His feeble attempts at rising sickened her.

She looked quickly round the house, deciding what she could take in a hurry. Sweyn followed her with his eyes, content to wait for her initiative. Now that Rowena was gone and her father was helpless, Aud did not stop to think how odd it was that she should be taking the decisions. When she later recalled that time, she was surprised to remember that although she felt fear and excitement, she did not sense panic. The flush was gone from her face too.

Having collected what she felt was vital, she flung Sweyn's heavy cloak towards him and indicated Gorm's travelling stick in the corner.

'It is Father's,' said Sweyn in awe.

Aud glanced at Gorm, then back at Sweyn.

'Take it.'

She motioned Sweyn to wait by the rear door. Fastening her own cloak at the neck, she crossed to the front entrance and looked carefully out.

Edwin was crossing the stream.

Aud was puzzled that her surprise and relief were tinged with annoyance, and it was not simply annoyance at Sweyn's having misled her. Someone else had arrived to take decisions again.

Nor was she overjoyed at Edwin's first question.

'Where is Rowena?'

'Gone. She has taken Edith and gone. She has left us.'

Edwin ignored the sneer in her voice. There was not time now for family squabbles. He tethered the horse.

'Where did she go?'

Aud continued to look disdainful. 'She said something about the King's manors and Chichester.'

'Yes,' said Edwin. 'I told her to go there. Why did you not go too?'

Aud turned about and stalked into the house. Edwin followed her. Aud pointed at her father, who had struggled to a sitting position.

'He would not go. We felt we were safer here.'

'Then why are you dressed for the road?'

'We thought you were the Normans. How did you get away? Why are you riding a Norman horse? Where is Godric? Is he dead? Did they torture him?'

Trust Aud to turn to the most lurid possibilities. As her questions beat at him like tiresome windblown leaves, Edwin thought of Godric stumping along the trail behind him.

'Go ahead,' Godric had said. 'Ride as fast as you can, but take care; there will be Norman patrols everywhere. And the English army must be closing by the hour.'

'What about you?' Edwin asked. 'English patrols could be just as suspicious as Norman ones.'

'You forget. I lived on trails for the first ten years of my life. I shall be delayed, but I shall not be stopped. I have no fear for me. Our fear is for those at the mill.' He clasped Edwin's hand in his great paw. 'Now ride. And tell Rowena . . .'

He searched for words.

Edwin smiled. 'There is no need, my friend. It is enough for her to know that you are on the trail. She will understand.'

Edwin had been prepared to find them all there, or nobody. Finding the family split was upsetting. Aud was no help.

'Why are you on a destrier? How did you steal it? Are you being followed?'

Edwin held up a hand. 'Aud, please. It is a long story. Godric is well. He comes behind. Have you something to eat and drink?'

'How close are the Normans? Should we not be going? Where will you take us?'

Edwin began to sense that feeling of unsatisfied demand that was always in the air whenever he was alone with Aud. He did his best to avoid the trouble that he could see was coming.

'Aud, I have been a prisoner. I have escaped and travelled far. I am hungry and thirsty. Before we do anything I must eat and drink. Please see to it while I water the horse. The Normans sit still and wait for news of the King's army. An hour here more or less will make no difference.'

Aud tightened her lips but made no reply. She took off her cloak and flung it across her travelling bundle. Edwin did not wait to exchange further words. Time enough for that after he had seen to the horse. He had not bargained with having to deal with Aud on her own; he had relied on Rowena or Gorm being on hand to take the lead.

He held a rein and watched the horse drink. As his eyes wandered round the yard, they fell on a small mound of freshly dug earth to the side of the chicken run. Aud had kept her promise; he was at least grateful to her for that. Now he felt no tears. Too much had happened. Too much lay ahead.

The reminder served only to make him all the more determined to find the army and fight at the King's side. True, he would not be among the housecarls, but he had spent many hours hunting the boar with his king, and his spear arm was as strong and as sure as that of any freeman in the fyrd. Let them only give him an armful of spears, and he would send some Normans to the Hell they deserved. If God was kind, maybe He would send Berry's murderer to gallop towards him in the first charge. Already he could see the surprise and horror on the man's face as the shaft thudded in and drove the rings of mail into his chest. As the swine fell, Edwin would leap forward to finish him off with his knife. He put his hand to his belt.

His knife! The Normans had not taken it when they bound him. He had left it on the table. God! Was it only the day before yesterday? Well, at least it would be a useful way of starting to talk with Aud. He tethered the horse again, hitched up his belt, and took a deep breath. He could not talk about knives for long. He would have to tell Aud what he was going to do, and he knew what she would say, and he knew he would handle it badly.

Aud placed food and drink before him without a word. He consumed it in silence. Gorm had fallen asleep again. Sweyn fidgeted, but Aud stilled him with a gesture.

Edwin wiped the back of his hand across his lips.

'What happened to my knife?'

'The minstrel stole it. Or so Edith said.'

Silence fell again. Aud made it worse by putting on her cloak once more.

Edwin clutched at his final straw.

'Thank you for – for seeing to Berry.'

Aud picked up her bundle and waited by the door.

Edwin glanced at Gorm, and saw no help there. He would have to deal with Aud alone.

Before many minutes, Edwin was in exactly the position he had foreseen, and knew he was powerless to prevent. Aud's voice had risen so high that her father woke up again.

Edwin was a coward, a cheat, a traitor, a deceiver. When she, Aud, was dishonoured and dead, then perhaps his conscience would strike him, and she hoped it would give him no rest.

She was past reason. Nothing Edwin said was any good.

'Follow Rowena. Go to the King's manors.'

'How do I know which way she went?'

'Go to any royal manor and say my name in the kennels or stables. They will take you in.'

'And be killed in open country? With a helpless child to protect?'

A podgy, strident boy had become a helpless child.

'Why can you not take us with you? There are women with the army.'

'Have you any idea what sort of women? In any case, you are wrong. The King's army will be moving too fast. They will have hardly any baggage, never mind women. And I have only one horse.'

'Two can ride on one horse.'

'What about Sweyn? Would you leave a "helpless child" behind?'

'You could walk. You are still man enough for that.'

'I have no any idea where the King is. We might be walking for days.'

'Then hitch up the ox. We all could sleep in the cart if necessary.'

'Aud, I must get there quickly. The battle must come soon.'

Aud sneered. 'And you must win your honour and glory while we, your kin, lie dead in this wreckage.'

Edwin passed his hand across his brow. 'Aud, there is no wreckage here. '

'There will be.'

'And yours is not my kin.'

'We were pledged once to each other. It was understood.'

'The understanding was on your side only.'

'You never said so.'

'You were never willing to listen.'

'It was all right until you came back from Normandy. You were never the same after that.'

Edwin moved in desperation towards the door.

Aud pursued him. 'There was someone. Admit it. Look me in the face and admit it.'

Edwin could not stand it any more. He rushed towards the horse.

'She must be Norman,' Aud shouted after him. 'Going with the enemy. A fine tale to tell the King; no wonder you do not want to take me to him. And if the Normans catch you they will punish you as well.'

Edwin took the reins, mounted, and turned his horse up the valley.

'Follow Rowena!' he shouted, without looking back. 'Take Sweyn and follow Rowena.'

'Adulterer!' screamed Aud.

Edwin dug his heels into the horse's flanks and urged it to the gallop. Anything to get away.

Aud returned to the house. Sweyn watched her anxiously, but her anger passed quickly. She was in charge again.

For a moment she stood very still, deep in thought. Then she snapped her fingers.

'Come, Sweyn. Get your stick.'

'Father's stick.'

'Yours now. Come.'

'What about Father?'

Aud paused in the doorway. Gorm was barely stirring. She made one last effort.

'Father. We must go – now. Can you walk? Can you get up?'

He raised his bleary eyes to hers.

Aud slapped him in temper.

'Father. We are going. We are leaving you if you can not get up.'

A flash of anger appeared. 'You do not go. I forbid it.'

He looked round vaguely. 'Where is Rowena?'

'She has gone and we are following.'

'Craven flight. Forgotten us. Left us. Wrong to leave the home.'

'No, Father. Rowena was right. Edwin has been here to warn us. The Normans are near.'

'I forbid you, forbid you . . .'

'I am taking Sweyn.'

Alarm followed anger. He reached out to clutch her. Aud stepped back quickly and he fell forward. He raised himself and began crawling across the rushes on all fours. Scraps of straw caught in the thongs of his shoes; others were stuck in his hair. Sweat stood out on his brow.

Sweyn stood transfixed. Aud thumped him across the shoulders and drove him towards the door. The delay in getting him and his bundle outside enabled Gorm to catch up with her. She felt his hand drag at her skirt. He clawed his way up her clothing until he was upright. He grabbed both her shoulders.

'You shall not go. I forbid it.'

She recoiled in loathing from his noxious breath, and struggled to release herself. She heard something rip. Her father was now running out of breath. With a desperate heave she pushed him away. He fell against the door jamb, and his head whipped back against the wood with a loud thud. Winded and dizzy, he slid down to the ground.

Aud clambered over him, collected her bundle, and skipped quickly outside again. Sweyn was still gazing fascinated at his father. Aud pushed him along.

'Hurry. We must hurry.'

Sweyn followed, looking often over his shoulder. At the turn of the track he looked back for the last time. His father had fallen out of the doorway.

As they fumbled with the latch of the gate, his voice was carried to them.

'Here is your home. I forbid you to go. I forbid it!'

They rushed on, gradually slowing to a steady walk. Neither said anything. For once Sweyn did not complain about the effort of carrying a load.

Gorm struggled again to a sitting position. Something was in his hand. He looked down. It was a piece of Aud's dress. He used it to mop his brow, then stuffed it absently into his jerkin.

So he was alone again. Well, he had been alone before. Let them go. Let them traipse all over the countryside. They would come crawling back soon enough. They would have to admit he was right. He was a freeman, and a freeman stood by his property. Besides, Normans needed mills as much as Saxons did. And he would see through their swindling ways, exactly as he saw through those of the Saxons. He would drive just has hard a bargain, and they would have to pay. He was a good miller, a good miller ...

If they did not come back? They would have only themselves to blame. He had tried to warn them. And when that lump Godric returned, what would he not say to him! Lusting after Rowena. What pride, what presumption – a freeman's daughter!

Gorm gritted his teeth, but after a moment relaxed his jaw. A gleam entered his eye as a thought struck him. After all these years he had a means of getting at Godric. At last – to be able to shatter that massive stillness!

It never crossed his mind that Godric might not return.

Sir Baldwin de Clair leaned against a tent post and looked at the two bodies stretched out inside. The white of their backs contrasted strongly with the deep tan on the back of their necks.

'Jesus of Nazareth, what a handsome pair of lilies,' he said, pulling off his gloves. 'Ha!'

Ralph Pomeroy and William Capra looked at each other, but neither moved from their prone position.

Baldwin stepped forward and peered at the livid marks across their shoulders.

'You will live,' he said. 'You will live.'

Capra growled.

Baldwin touched his back very lightly with the end of a glove. Capra cried out.

'Hurts, does it?' said Baldwin. 'Well, that comes from letting prisoners escape.'

He leaned down till his mouth was beside Pomeroy's ear.

'Learned our lesson, have we?'

'Yes.'

'Yes – "Sir Baldwin".'

'Yes, Sir Baldwin.'

'"And thank you, Sir Baldwin, for sending Brother Crispin and the buckets of salt water."'

'Thank you, Sir Baldwin, for the salt water.'

'I trust that Crispin administered the treatment – er – satisfactorily.'

Pomeroy winced. 'He did it with relish.'

Baldwin smiled in satisfaction, and stood up.

'I relied on Brother Crispin to show God's Mercy to the wrongdoer.'

'Is that what he called it?' said Capra.

'Count yourself blessed that I had you whipped only down to your waist, or Jesus and Brother Crispin would not be the only people turning the other cheek.'

William Capra propped himself on his elbows and tried to ease his shoulders.

'We made a mistake, Sir Baldwin, and we have paid. Is that not enough?'

Baldwin paused on his way out. 'Oh, yes, I nearly forgot. No, it is not enough. At dawn you will report to Sir William Fitzosbern's tent and pay the fine that the Duke has fixed.'

'What? Ah!' Capra tried to turn in a hurry, and cried aloud in pain. 'We have already been punished.'

Baldwin smiled hugely. 'Ah, no. That was only my punishment, for insubordination and incompetence. The fine is the Duke's punishment for disobeying the orders of your superiors and gross dereliction of duty. Allowing two prisoners to escape at this time could have endangered the whole army.'

'We did not allow them,' protested Pomeroy. 'We were deceived.'

'Clearly a very simple thing to do,' observed Baldwin.

'Save your breath, brother,' said Capra.

Baldwin pulled on his gloves.

'Report to me for duty – both of you – as soon as you have seen Fitzosbern. You have tonight to rest and meditate on your own stupidity.'

'How can we get jerkin and mail on to backs like ours?' complained Pomeroy.

'Think of something,' shouted Baldwin over his shoulder. 'Send for the Turk. He will empty your purse too.'

When he had gone, Pomeroy cursed steadily to himself, until Capra silenced him.

'Shut your mouth. I have to think.'

Pomeroy blinked, but obeyed. He rested his chin on the backs of his hands, and tried to ease his shoulders into a less agonising position. He was always content to let his brother do complicated things like thinking.

After a while the silence began to get oppressive. Pomeroy fidgeted.

'Well?'

'It is time we moved on, brother.'

Pomeroy frowned. 'Where? You mean, to Normandy?'

'I said "on", not "back".'

Pomeroy's frown deepened. 'How can we escape Fitzosbern and the Duke?'

'We can not. We pay. But what we do afterwards is our business.'

'You mean, leave Sir Baldwin?'

'Do you wish to stay – and risk another beating? I see you are calling him "Sir Baldwin" now.'

'Well, no. But—'

'Afraid he will come after us? Bloodeye did not bother.'

'He probably forgot. They say his illness—'

'Yes, yes, I know all about that. But de Clair made no effort to go after the prisoners. When the English arrive, he will have no time to go after anybody. The hour can not be far distant. This camp is buzzing like an angry hive.'

'So what do we do?'

'We seek our fortune, brother. We look out for the main chance. I see none of that with de Clair, do you? Nor with his friend, the Bishop of Coutances. We should finish up drilling all day with those trumpets in our ears.'

'There are others,' said Pomeroy.

'Bah! Giffard would not have the patience, Montgomery does not have the space or the money, and Beaumont does not have the authority.'

'Where then?'

Capra rubbed his chin. 'We need a leader who, like us, has an eye to the main chance. He must have authority, status, influence in high places. Ideally he should have a hearty dislike of Bishop Geoffrey and Bishop Geoffrey's friend, Sir Baldwin de Clair. You never know when the occasion of revenge will present itself.'

Pomeroy gaped in admiration. 'You mean, Odo – like you said?'

Capra sucked his teeth. 'His Grace, the Bishop of Bayeux, no less. Should have done it before.'

Pomeroy looked doubtful. 'Aiming high.'

'Nothing venture—'

'Risky.'

'Look at us now. De Clair will give us nothing. If Fulk finds us and remembers, he will cut our throats. Where would you rather be – waiting for one of them to catch up with us, or serving loyally in the contingent of a prince of the Church – a prince of the Church who is moreover brother to the Duke himself? Brother to a possible King of England.'

Pomeroy swallowed. 'I still say it is risky.'

Capra allowed himself his first chuckle in many hours, and put up with the pain.

'That is where you lack style, brother. And confidence. Too many adventurers on the run move down the social scale instead of up. Nobody expects you to have the nerve to go that way.'

Pomeroy knitted his brows in the effort to take in the argument. At last a valid objection occurred to him.

'But Odo is a swine. The whole army knows that.'

'I agree,' said Capra blandly. 'He is also a cheat and a liar.'

'Well, then.'

Capra grinned. 'In that case we should take to him like a duck to water.'

'My lord, I – I cannot put into words.'

Geoffrey was almost in tears of mortification.

The Duke waved his anguish aside. 'Could have happened to any one of us. I sent you with orders to the castle, so you were the one who fell. It is as much my fault as yours.'

'But I should have been looking.'

'Stop torturing yourself, Geoffrey,' said Fitzosbern. 'The Duke sent you to give orders to the garrison commander, not to count how many steps had been cut out by scavengers for firewood.'

Geoffrey stirred painfully on his bed.

'I suppose if the Turk fashions a strong enough splint ...'

'I do not want heroes,' said the Duke, 'and I do not want liabilities.'

Geoffrey ran a hand through his dark hair, which stuck out like straw round his tonsure when he was agitated.

'But what about the – you know, the whole thing? If I am not there ...'

Fitzosbern was unmoved. 'It will still work.'

'Fitz is right,' said the Duke. 'If a cart is well fashioned, it does not need its wright to drive it. '

Geoffrey flopped back on to his pillow, thoroughly depressed.

'I am much obliged to your Grace.'

Nobody spoke while the Duke paced up and down. The space inside Geoffrey's tent was limited; Giffard, Montgomery and the other senior commanders huddled into a corner to give William enough space.

The Duke stopped at the foot of Geoffrey's bed, and motioned everyone to come closer.

'The cart is still sound; we simply change the drivers. Fitz – you will take over operational command in place of Coutances. Montgomery – you keep overall control on the right. I shall remove the Flemings from central command and put them directly under you. That will make Fitz's job easier. Brittany?'

'My lord,' said Count Alan.

'You still take the left. My brothers will come under your orders.'

Bishop Odo and Count Robert of Mortain looked chagrined, but said nothing.

'Thus we will balance our strength – a cavalry commander on one wing, with spare infantry, and an infantry commander on the other with spare cavalry – and so balance our chances. Possibly improve them. It will give Fitz more flexibility. Giffard – you will take the centre in place of Fitz.'

'Delighted!' said Giffard, glancing in triumph at Montgomery. One in the eye for the puppy Beaumont.

'Hmm! Good. Well then.' William began humming as he left the tent.

The others followed, except Fitzosbern, who remained for a moment in the doorway.

Geoffrey eased his bad leg into a better position.

'If you are going to say how sorry you are, I shall excommunicate you.'

'On the contrary,' said Fitzosbern. 'I was going to suggest that you stop feeling sorry for yourself. You are lucky you did not break your neck. You are also lucky the Turk understands broken bones; how many cripples have we seen made because simple falls were followed by bad treatment, or no treatment at all?'

'Anything else?' said Geoffrey sourly.

'Yes. You should feel flattered.'

Geoffrey gaped. 'Flattered?'

'Yes. It is honour enough that your schemes of training and tactics should be followed when you are there. It is an even greater compliment that we should be following them when you are not.'

'And I have to lie here and sweat and wonder,' said Geoffrey.

'Then do that,' said Fitzosbern, as he dropped the tent flap. 'There is no pleasing you.'

Outside he nearly bumped into Fulk.

'You are late. The Duke wishes to see you at once.'

'On my way, Sir William. Just visiting the patient.'

Geoffrey greeted him with more ill humour.

'What do you want?'

Fulk spread his hands in mock appeal. 'What do I have to do to gain your gratitude? I supply you with rare books for your church. I send my doctor to set your leg. I come in person to enquire after your health.'

'And you once would have had me killed – for a fee.'

'I keep telling you – it was nothing personal.'

'And your word is your bond, of course.'

Fulk still refused to take offence.

'Very well, I am going. But reflect, my lord; we have more in common than you think. We are both at odds with the world in our respective ways.'

Geoffrey reached for a cup of wine. On impulse, he offered a cup to Fulk.

'Thank you, no. But I take the gesture as a sign of goodwill – at last. By way of returning the compliment, may I say that I shall, as a fellow-professional, regret your absence in the coming conflict.'

Geoffrey held up his cup in token of acceptance of the favour.

When he had drunk, he said, 'You remarked that we had something in common.'

Fulk smiled, not in friendship, but in irony. 'Yes. I said we both know what it is to be at odds with the world.'

'Is that all?'

Fulk smiled again. 'I think it would be rash to pursue the search for similarities in men so unlike as ourselves. We might both find surprises.'

Geoffrey put down the cup and looked intently at him. 'Would you by any chance be getting round to the subject of confession?'

Fulk laughed. 'Oh, a deadly shaft, my lord bishop.'

He moved towards the door, still laughing, and paused at the flap.

'Let us leave it at this, my lord: you are impatient with the world; I am merely bored with it. That is enough affinity for both of us, I should say. Rest well. I shall send Matthew tomorrow.' He twisted his scar in one last ironic grin. 'After all, you have many faculties beyond your military ones, and we owe it to our noble cause to try and preserve as many of them as possible.'

Geoffrey had hardly lain back again when another request came from outside.

'Permission to enter, my lord.'

It was Thierry. No mistaking the voice. Back already – he must have made good time. Coutances and Rouen, and two crossings of the Channel. News of Sybil!

But Geoffrey still refused to abandon his sour temper completely; it was too comfortable.

'Come in, come in. What is this – a private tent or the Pope's audience chamber? Not a moment's peace. You took long enough.'

Thierry wiped his mouth to remove the traces of gravy. His Grace was as grumpy as ever, but then, with a broken leg . . . He tried to put the best shine he could upon the situation.

'At least the lady Sybil will not have to worry about you on the day, my lord.'

*

Matthew's dark eyes glowed. Capra and Pomeroy swore at him; they heaped insults on his faith and on his professon; they passed vulgar judgement on the softness of his flesh and the smoothness of his hands. His face showed no further emotion.

When he named his price they swore again.

By way of answer he took a silk kerchief from his cuff and trailed it delicately across one red weal on Capra's ribs.

'You must attend the Duke at dawn, I hear – wearing mail.'

Capra cried aloud once more. 'All right. All right. We agree. Get on with it.'

Matthew held out his hand.

'Yes, yes, yes, we shall pay,' said Capra impatiently.

Matthew stood up. In the bad light of the tent's interior his crippled shoulder and gleaming eyes gave Capra a twinge of fright. The tinkling ringlets of mail around the rim of his helmet added to the unearthly effect.

'You promised to pay Taillefer after. You pay me before.'

He held out his hand again.

Capra grumbled tearfully, but propped himself on an elbow. Wincing with pain, he fished coins out of his waist wallet and counted them out. Even in his agonising position he took care that their hands did not make contact; he dropped the coins one by one, his chipped and blackened fingernails poised gingerly above the moist brown palm. The delicate fingers snapped shut like a cat pouncing, and flew to a secret fold of his huge red sash.

A silken smile spread under the thin black moustache.

'Now – lie still. This will give pain at first, but later you will be at rest.'

'Just get on with it, you perfumed idolater.'

'One thing more,' said Matthew, his voice softening almost to a purr. 'My ointment works best in silence. If insults poison the air, the ointment will catch the evil and sting for longer.'

Pomeroy frowned. 'What does he mean?'

Capra growled. 'He means, brother, that we must hold our tongues.'

They lay in silence while Matthew, enjoying a private joke, tended their backs. They could at least stand and move when he had fastened their bandages, though they cursed the smarting.

'You wear only wool tonight,' said Matthew, 'so that the marks breathe. Then leather tomorrow. Mail if you can stand it.'

He packed his canvas case. Pomeroy wondered what was the meaning of all the strange signs embroidered on it.

'Now,' said Capra, 'we must have horses for tomorrow. Our destriers were stolen.'

Matthew stood up.

'Yes,' he said. 'I heard. The biters have been bitten.'

Pomeroy was annoyed.

'We have stolen nothing.'

Capra tossed his head at his brother's obtuseness.

Matthew smiled at the ease with which Pomeroy had fallen into error.

'You will of a certainty steal nothing more; everyone will be too watchful.'

He made to go, but Capra seized his arm.

'Horses. Tell us.'

Matthew recoiled from the physical contact. He wriggled to escape.

'I am called away.'

'Oh? Where?'

Matthew glared. 'Captain Fulk. You wish me to tell him whom I have been treating?'

'In between treating him?'

Matthew at last disengaged himself, but looked slightly flustered.

'Captain Fulk is well. He has been riding.'

Capra sensed a chase. With the instinct of the hunter, he pounced on weakness.

'Where?'

'Riding.'

'To that mill again.'

'He has been riding.'

Capra smiled; the quarry was about to break cover.

'I bet he has. Riding more than the horse too. God – he recovered quickly. Then he would, with you near him, eh? A magic pass here? A black spell there? How does it feel – to cure him only for that? All your skill, and he spends his energy that way.'

Matthew began to look distinctly uncomfortable. Capra pursued him.

'Did he tell you what it was like?'

Matthew's face darkened. 'He went riding. Now he rests. That is all.'

Capra guffawed. 'God's Face, was it that strenuous? Did she struggle that much?'

'He did not go to the mill.'

'Liar!'

'He did not. He told me.'

'And you believed him? Ha!'

Matthew hesitated. 'He was – he was near the mill only. He went only to see.'

'And he caught her running away. Made it more exciting, I suppose. Pity the Saxon giant was not there to see it. Still, the idiot was. Or perhaps he had her too. No wonder he is resting now.'

Matthew raised his voice a tone or two. 'Captain Fulk will be on duty tomorrow for many hours. Now he is resting. He needs – to rest.'

Capra thrust his face close to Matthew's. 'You hate the idea. You hate the very idea of his being with a woman. Go on – admit it.'

Matthew's eyes flashed. 'I shall tell Captain Fulk. I shall tell him where to find you. Tomorrow he will come. But he will not have whips, like Baldwin. He will have chains and knives, and he will have Florens and Rainald and Dieter. And I shall watch!' He almost spat the last words, his chest heaving with excitement.

Capra and Pomeroy laughed at the success of their chase.

Matthew drew a deep breath in the effort to control his emotion.

'And when Captain Fulk has finished with you, you must obtain horses. Only this time you must pay, as you paid me. You will have to go to the Magyar.' His eyes gleamed in triumph. 'You need medicine from a Muslim; now you need horses from a pagan.'

He left them staring at each other in furious impotence.

Godric needed all his patience. His journey was dogged by delays and bad luck.

A score of times he was forced to hide when he heard hoofbeats or voices. He praised God for the sprawling size of the Wealden forest, though he cursed the number of false alarms. Only twice did he nearly run into genuine Norman patrols. Most times it was bedraggled groups of refugees, fleeing they knew not where. Nor did they care, so long as it was away from the invaders.

In his head all the while was the image of Fulk – Fulk lounging, Fulk leering, Fulk with his knife at Rowena's throat, Fulk taunting him as he strove in chains, Fulk twitching on the ground, his head lolling with sightless open eyes.

Edwin should be at the mill by now. He would warn, but he would not stay to protect; his destiny, and his duty, as he saw it, lay with his king. Godric understood that. All the more reason to make haste himself.

Suppose Rowena did not take flight? Suppose she were prevented? Suppose the rest of the family united against her?

Suppose Fulk . . .? Fulk was capable of anything; it would not be simple murder or swift, lancing dishonour.

Yet another disturbance up ahead forced him to climb a nearby tree. Into the clearing straggled a line of more fugitives. The man was nearly at the end of his tether. A thin child clung round his neck, and another stumbled by his side, clutching his hand. In his spare hand he carried a pitchfork, the knuckles white with unnecessary tension. Behind him came a haggard woman, bowed with a bundle too big for her. Behind again staggered the grandfather, using both hands to support himself on a long stick.

As they passed below Godric's tree, he could hear their laboured breath. At the end of the clearing, the man stopped and turned to allow his wife and father time to catch up. When they reached him, they paused in relief. He merely turned away and went on. The woman and the old man looked at each other, then they too began again, their legs stiff with the effort of renewed movement. Nobody said a word.

Godric watched in silence – born of helpless pity as well as of necessary caution. There was nothing he could do for them, and if he had appeared, the suddenness would have shocked the man into violence or the grandfather into collapse.

Nevertheless, when they had gone, Godric allowed impatience, for the first time, to get the better of him. Instead of climbing all the way down, he jumped from too great a height. As he bent his legs with the impact, he felt a savage pain in his left knee that made him almost cry out.

Suddenly, even standing became agony.

He hobbled to a clump of young trees and broke off a small bough. Having no knife, he snatched at the twigs down the length of it with his bare hands.

He turned to look up the trail to the end of the clearing. It seemed very far away. And he still had miles to go. A moment ago he had felt sorry for the old man.

Taking a deep breath, he resumed his journey, leaning and hopping, leaning and hopping.

'Ah, now, that is interesting,' said Sandor with a straight face. He had listened solemnly to William Capra's tale of woe. Capra, he noticed, did not accuse him of anything, and he was not going to protest an innocence that had not been challenged. Pomeroy hovered sulkily in the background.

Sandor continued polishing some girths. Capra waited impatiently.

'Well?'

Sandor spoke without looking up. 'It is true: good horses can be procured at any time for cash. Half in advance,' he added thoughtfully.

'Then get them,' said Capra.

Sandor spat on to the freshly applied polish, stuck his finger inside a fold of cloth, and began rubbing small circles on the leather.

'First there is the question of price.'

'Name it.'

Sandor waggled a little finger in his ear, then quoted a figure.

Capra opened his mouth to argue, but realised that he was in no position to bargain. However, he did not wish to give in at once.

'Proper destriers?'

'From Sir Walter Giffard's own stock at Longueville.'

'Fully broken and trained?'

'Ready for battle tomorrow.'

'Equipped?'

'To the last buckle, if you wish.'

Capra pretended to ponder deeply.

'I suppose, for two good destriers, in time of war ... Still unreasonable, but under the circumstances ...'

Sandor looked up. His eyes showed the faintest glimmer of a twinkle.

'I think you make a small error. The price is for each horse.'

'Each!'

Sandor bowed his head in solemn assent.

Capra leaped to his feet, wincing at the pain, which in turn made his temper worse.

'You dirty little Hunnish horsethief!'

Sandor shrugged.

Capra spluttered in anger. 'I should not put it past you to sell our own horses back to us.'

Sandor privately agreed that it would be a neat, and most apt, resolution of the situation, but out of the question, since Edwin ought, by now, to be at the mill. The other mount, the one Godric had returned, was too good to be allowed back into the possession of a lout like Capra. Besides, they had both belonged to Sandor's herd in the first place, and he was not going to allow his babies away again.

Tucked away in a separate enclosure were the frightened, staring arrivals from the last Channel crossing – almost thrown into ships in Normandy in response to the Duke's urgent appeals for spare mounts. They were immature and unstable, their training schedules a mess of compression and half measures, their readiness for battle a matter for fortune-tellers.

Sandor cleared his throat.

'I have a hundred horses for sale – all of them of the finest breeding, the highest training, the greatest strength, the like of which you will not find anywhere in England.'

Capra snorted. 'Do not be so sure.'

Sandor spread his hands. 'Then go and seek. Search the stables from here to London. You will find good horses, well-bred horses, large horses, fast horses, perhaps even clever horses. But a horse to carry a knight in full gear – war saddle, mail, helmet, sword, spears, and a shield to flap over his left ear? A horse to

turn, wheel, advance, retire and keep a line in the noise of battle? A horse trained to obedience for constant fighting?' Sandor shook his head. 'Such horses do not grow on English trees.'

Capra grumbled, swore, and threatened.

'You must be mounted by tomorrow morning,' said Sandor, who seemed to be very well informed.

The coins were flung at his feet.

Aud stopped, and rested her load against a boundary stone. For the last mile or more she had felt her footsteps dragging. Yet it was not normal fatigue; she was sure of that.

Sweyn had hardly uttered a word, not even to complain. He came now and perched himself on Aud's bundle, nursing his own in his lap. For once she did not scold him.

She stood for a while with her hands on her hips, looking back the way they had come. Then she wandered to and fro, picking bits of grass and dead leaves from the hem of her skirt. Finally she squatted by the side of the track, took up a stick, and began making doodles in the bare chalky earth. All the time Sweyn watched her in silence.

At last Aud stood up. She tossed away the stick, dusted her hands, and motioned to her brother to stand up as well. She picked up her bundle and set off in the direction from which they had come.

Sweyn ran after her.

'Where are you going?'

'To get Father, of course. Go back for your things and catch me up. We must be home before dark.'

Sweyn took one look at her face and obeyed. He had always been used to her being loud and dissatisfied. This quiet resolution impressed him. He ran to obey her with such a will that his fat face was red with effort by the time he drew level again.

'I thought you said – said – it was – was dangerous to stay.'

'It is. It is even more dangerous for Father in his state.'

'But he can not go far.'

'He can if we use the cart. It was silly of me not to think of it before. We can rest well under a roof tonight, which will give him time to lose the drink. Early tomorrow we can fill the cart with food, and Father can go at ease.'

'He will complain about his headache,' said Sweyn.

'He will complain about his headache anyway.'

'What if the Normans come tonight?'

Aud shook her head. 'No. They will not. They are only men. At night they will seek shelter under their own roof – be it timber or tent. Edwin said they sit still and wait for our army. If they come out tomorrow to meet the army, we shall be before them and gone, and we shall have with us everything we value.'

'That means I have to yoke the ox,' said Sweyn in his usual whine.

Aud boxed his ears.

'You are right!'

'What do you think, Sandor?'

The little Magyar rose from the squatting position he had adopted while examining Sorrel's leg.

'She has been ridden far.'

'What choice did we have?' said Ralph.

'More than she did,' said Sandor. 'You decided. She obeyed.'

Bruno stood at Sorrel's head and murmured apologies and endearments. Ralph had never seen him so distressed.

'If she rests tomorrow,' said Sandor, 'perhaps she can carry you the next day.'

'The Duke wants us out at dawn,' said Ralph. 'The English are very near.'

'I know,' said Sandor. 'That is an easy matter. I can find a patrol mount for Bruno. It will carry him tomorrow. The next day after that, he can ride his Sorrel. But only scouting. No fighting – too much strain.'

'The battle will almost certainly be on that day – on Saturday,' said Bruno. Not that he or Ralph seriously expected to be in it. Though they could hope.

'Then you will either miss Sorrel or you will miss the battle,' said Sandor.

Bruno swore.

Sandor, seeing his chagrin, stooped and felt again at the weakened leg.

'See,' he said, standing up. 'There is heat and swelling. To ride her in battle is a big risk, a big risk. If you love your horse . . .' He shrugged.

'I love my horse,' said Bruno.

'I am pleased you say that,' said Sandor. 'And now, for tomorrow. Go to the third stable behind the Duke's hall. Speak to Serlo – a thin man with hair the colour of sand. Say Sandor the Magyar speaks with your voice. He will choose you a fair mount for tomorrow. He will also stable Sorrel for you under good cover and feed her. I shall visit later.'

'And the next day?'

'We do not know what the next day brings until we open its bag in the morning,' said Sandor.

Bruno thanked him and pressed a coin into his hand. Sandor tried to decline but he insisted.

'That is for loving my horse and telling me the truth,' he said.

He led Sorrel away, still talking gently to her and patting her neck.

'Where is Gilbert?' said Ralph, when they had gone.

'He rests in a quiet place along with Taillefer. Come.'

'What is wrong with Taillefer?'

Sandor told him.

'How does he react?' asked Ralph.

Sandor lifted his whole body in a shrug. 'Who can tell? He lies and sleeps, then he wakes and stares into air. Then he drinks and laughs. And he sleeps again. It is hard to know.'

They wove their way through the usual maze of smoky fires and sizzling spits, overfilled wagons and wattle lean-to's, fresh horse droppings and head-spinning privy pits.

Ralph made an explosive noise of disgust with his lips. No wonder he preferred being a scout – out of all this.

'God's Breath! Come fast Saturday. I shall be pleased to get away from all this, victory or no victory.'

'Ah,' said Sandor non-committally. Smells rarely bothered him. Smells gave him information, not offence.

As they passed a knot of Bretons round a fat-dripped carcass suspended over glowing embers, he sniffed deeply, and cast a remark over his shoulder.

'One of the Beaumont's hunters has become the prey.'

He paused beside a wagon and greeted a group of archers. In answer to his query, one of them jerked a thumb towards the tailboard.

'All is well,' he said. 'No visitors. Only the boy.'

They climbed inside the wagon. Taillefer, propped on an elbow, put a finger to his lips and pointed to Gilbert, still asleep before his night patrol. One candle stub gave enough light to throw large shadows on the crude awning, through which came wicked draughts for the unwary.

'How is he?'

'He enjoyed the revenge,' said Sandor, trying to head him off.

'What revenge?' said Ralph, frowning.

Sandor told the story of the prisoners and the escape.

Ralph whistled silently. 'And Baldwin had them whipped?'

'And fined,' said Taillefer. 'Then Matthew emptied one pocket for his medicine, and Sandor emptied the others for two more horses.'

Ralph chuckled softly. 'Serve them right. I saw them when

they arrived. Worthless, both of them. Not only poor soldiers, but poor conspirators, too, it seems.'

Taillefer pointed at Sandor. 'They were in the presence of a master.'

Sandor's eyes sparkled.

Ralph frowned again. 'But why help Saxons to escape?'

Again Sandor explained. 'When Gilbert was sick, this big Saxon maybe save his life. He carry him like a baby, Gilbert says, and nurse him and make him well. I want revenge on Capra for stealing my horses. We use the prisoners and pay a debt – that is all.'

'Hmm.' Ralph nodded towards Gilbert. 'How is he now?'

Taillefer glanced at him. 'Sleep rescues him from his miseries and his ghosts.'

'That bad?' said Ralph.

'You should know,' said Taillefer.

'I had no choice,' said Ralph. 'I had to leave him. I owed it to Bruno.'

Sandor interrupted. 'If we are to argue, let us go another place. Gilbert needs to rest.'

'I shall come with you,' said Taillefer. 'A call of nature.'

'You old soak,' said Ralph. 'It is not your bladder; it is your throat that needs attention.'

Taillefer looked straight into his eyes, the bags under his own falling deeper than ever.

'It is both, if you must know. Now – shall we find a fire and a pot?'

Three or four drinks later, Ralph turned to Taillefer again.

'What did you mean by "ghosts"?'

Taillefer blinked. 'Ghosts?'

'You said "miseries and ghosts". Miseries I understand. I help to cause them. But the ghosts.'

'The same that haunt any man – fear. In his case, many of them.'

Ralph undid the laces on his boots.

'All men fear.'

'Death, yes. And oblivion. The second rescues you from the first. But Gilbert fears living deaths, from which there is no rescue. He fears that he will not live up to your standards, not come up to your expectations.'

'He tries. I see that.'

'You do not know how much he thinks of you. You do not know the depth of his desire to win your approval.'

Ralph swallowed. 'I gave him the hauberk.'

'He treasures that,' said Taillefer. 'And more than you will ever know. But he yearns for more; he wants success; he wants to see admiration in your eyes.'

Ralph found his eyes pricking. He could also see Bruno's face.

'I am agreeing with Taillefer,' said Sandor. 'You and Bruno found the English. He found only a Saxon family who cared for him when he was sick and fell off his horse.'

Ralph heard Bruno's voice: 'The boy is a loser.'

He made a vague gesture. 'I do what I can. Believe me, I do what I can.'

Taillefer scratched a cheek. 'I take it you know about the other devil that drives him.'

'Are you now his confessor?' said Ralph drily.

Sandor refilled his ivory horn with beer.

'If you offer a fire, a blanket, a supper, and a willing ear, you catch many things that tumble out of men's hearts.'

'This devil,' said Ralph.

'You know of Gilbert's secret desire in England?'

'Make yourself clear.'

'You know he is not the father of his son?'

'There was castle gossip. What of it?'

'It troubles him deeply,' said Sandor. 'His wife tell him, after many questions. She say a Saxon forced her.'

'A Saxon?'

'When Harold visit Normandy. One of his men.'

'Ah, yes – I remember,' said Ralph.

'So now Gilbert scours England for the man who forced his wife.'

'So what? He is not the first man in this position. He will not find him.'

Taillefer leaned forward eagerly, as if he had been waiting his opportunity.

'But suppose he did?'

Ralph snorted. 'Impossible. A million to one.'

'But do you not see the importance of it? To avenge his honour. Honour will carry him through the fears – fear of letting you down, fear of dying, fear of everything else. You and Bruno – you have your own knightly pride. Our leaders have their own code of vassal and lord. Our priests and bishops have the ear of the Almighty. What does Gilbert have, apart from this?'

Ralph shook his head. 'Too philosophical for me. Too clever by half. The boy does not know and he is never going to find out, and that is an end of it. And you know my views on revenge.' He pointed to his stomach. 'I could show you the scar made by Bloodeye's dagger sixteen years ago. But I shall fight alongside him if need be. The past is the past.'

'As a comrade?'

'I shall not lift a finger to save his life, but I shall do nothing to take it. Neither action will remove my scar, nor the chills I suffer in the cold weather. Look at your stories. Did Charlemagne's revenge bring Roland back? Look at my family. Did Enguerrand's mutilation restore to my father his hand, or to my mother her wits?'

'It is not the revenge; it is the honour.'

'But it *is* the revenge,' insisted Ralph. 'Honour is only the skin; revenge is the tasty fruit. It is the pride of fools.' He flung out an arm in the direction of the wagon where Gilbert slept. 'And in any case, there was no dishonour. She was not unfaithful. The offence took place before she was married.'

'She deceived him.'

'Rubbish. She did what any terrified girl would have done. What choice did she have? And now this young man has a pretty wife, a son he loves in spite of himself, and another son soon to be born. If he survives this battle, he will have land and rewards and all the glory he can imagine. Why poison it with senseless revenge for a dishonour that is no dishonour?'

'And if he does not survive?' persisted Taillefer.

Ralph did not know what to say; the prospect was beyond even pain to contemplate. He waved an arm in a falsely dramatic way.

'There are the priests. The Bastard has imported enough to fill a cathedral.'

'They can remove the fear of death; they can not remove the fear of dying, of pain, of mutilation. I have seen men before battle – far more than you have. I have looked into their eyes, into their hearts.'

'More philosophy,' said Ralph. 'And in any case irrelevant. He knows nothing and neither do we.'

Taillefer looked at Sandor. 'Tell him what you told me.'

Sandor repeated his story of what he had heard from Edwin. Ralph was totally unmoved.

'Coincidence – pure coincidence. You do not know the name of Adele's ravisher, and you do not know the name of Edwin's lover. And yet you connect the two? Ridiculous. Put it into one of your romances, Taillefer.'

'It matters not,' said Taillefer. 'Can you not see? It will give him purpose over and above his fears.'

Ralph shook his head. 'At best a fancy; at worst a lie. Would you have a man die for that?'

'Not for knowing it is a lie, no. For believing it is true, yes. What are my stories but fancies? Lies, if you like. But they inspire. Believe me, I have seen it. Did not Our Lord admit to his apostles that he spoke in parables? That is all I do. If I can create my small portion of faith or courage, where is the harm?'

'For a lie?'

'For belief. My friend, we are not talking about absolute truth; we are talking about faith, confidence. About moving men to unwelcome action.' Taillefer waved an arm to take in the whole camp. 'Men, I know, will fight out of lust or greed. I prefer them to fight out of honour, out of a trust in something over and above themselves. So I tell my stories. Who knows if they are true? Who cares? Men believe because they want to. They need something to get them through the coming day of trial. They *have* to believe. What else do our priests do but help us to get through a life of trial? Surround us with a fence of hopes and fears. Who knows – who really *knows* – if they are true? And if they did, how many others could they convince?'

'So you would spin this romance in Gilbert's young head?'

'You have your code,' repeated Taillefer. 'I only wish to give him the same chance as you, the same courage. Bruno says he is a loser; this could make him a winner. Would you not want that?'

Would he not want it!

Taillefer laid a bony, bejewelled hand on Ralph's arm.

'Think, Ralph. If he sees his honour there, it is there. If he lives, he will be exorcised. If he dies, he dies justified. Would you have him a broken survivor, a self-soiled failure still in pursuit of a man he can never find?'

Ralph ached with the pain of willing peace of mind to Gilbert, but into his mind's eye came the familiar sight of Bruno's face, the still slab of eloquent flesh below the vociferous eyebrows. Into his ears came the familiar flat voice: 'the boy is a loser'; 'Michael is dead'.

All his instincts, twenty years of wary treading, made him cry out against flights of imagination such as Taillefer described. A battle was a battle; fear was fear; dying was dying.

He did what he did when the pain of Michael's death was too much in the company of brother Aubrey's bullying; or when the loss of his friend Aimcry gave him no peace in the continued service of Bishop Geoffrey – he took himself away.

'The boy does not know,' he muttered. He retied his laces and stood up. 'If he does not know, he does not know, and there is an end to it. Far better to concentrate on his duties.' He gained assurance as he moved on to the familiar ground of his own work.

He gazed down at Taillefer. 'Good night, philosopher. When he wakes to go out, tell him I wish him well.'

'Anything else?'

Ralph deliberately ignored the hint.

'Yes. Tell him to look after the hauberk.'

William Capra counted his money. It did not take him long. He lay down very carefully, and rested his chin on his hands.

Ralph Pomeroy came in from a scavenging trip.

'Want some nuts?' He held out a bulging bag.

'No.'

Pomeroy made a face, and eased off his leather jerkin with many grunts and curses. He saw the open pouch beside his brother's hands.

'How much do we have left?'

'Not enough.'

'Ah.'

Pomeroy glanced at his brother's face, and could see that he was thinking again. He too lowered himself gently onto his stomach, and began cracking some of the nuts.

Capra reached out for a mug of beer and sipped thoughtfully.

'Ralph?'

'Yes?' said Pomeroy, spitting out bits of shell.

'Someone will pay for all this.'

*

Taillefer coughed. He lit a fresh stub of candle from the old dying one, and peered at the stains on his kerchief.

He preferred knowing the truth about himself. It would help him to face the battle day.

He looked at Gilbert stretched out beside him. He had it in his power to give the boy something that would help him to face it too. Belief. Was that not even stronger than truth?

He pushed his fingers through a rent in the wagon awning and peered out at the night sky. It was time.

He shook Gilbert.

'Wake now. Wake.'

'Mmm?' Gilbert woke a start.

'It is nearly the hour. No, no, lie still for a few more minutes. I said, "nearly". There is something I must tell you before you go.'

Sandor went prowling among the horse lines.

'No Capra? No Pomeroy?' he asked.

'Not a sign of them,' said Serlo. 'Have no fear, little man from Hungary. They have burned their fingers. They will not try again. Sir Walter Giffard has placed extra sentries.'

'Did the tall one come to you?'

'Bruno? Yes. I gave him a spare horse. Sorrel is resting. See?'

After the frantic activity of the day, the camp seemed to be sleeping the sleep of exhaustion. Would it be like this tomorrow night, the probable eve of battle?

As he picked his way back to the wagon, Sandor wondered idly what chance of success Harold might have if he could launch a thousand determined men on William's camp at a moment like this. He dismissed the thought almost at once. Even if his army could overcome the depression of night; even if the Norman castle, sentries and scouts never existed; even if the house-carls were all immortal heroes of iron who could consider such an attack immediately after a fifty-mile march from London –

there was the simple problem of darkness. Sandor knew from experience that is often difficult for a couple of horse-thieves to keep contact with each other over any distance during an approach in darkness. For an army to find its way, stay together and act together would be impossible. Though it did not stop him worrying a little about William Capra.

He climbed over the tailboard and into the wagon. Gilbert had already gone. Taillefer was asleep. A stained kerchief was crumpled in his bony hand. Sandor eased it tenderly from his fingers, and pulled the blanket right up to his ears.

Sandor wriggled down into the still warm place where Gilbert had lain, curled up, and fell instantly asleep.

Gilbert steered his horse past the last sentries.

'Good luck, son. Go get them.'

Gilbert did not reply. He had something else to find now besides the enemy.

13 October

'Twenty thousand voices shout as one'

A heavy dew soaked what grass was left after a fortnight of constant traversing by feet, hooves, and wheels. A few early fires were already sending up wispy plumes of woodsmoke like ghostly shivering poplars. Spangled spiders' webs trembled below dripping ropes and awnings.

Sandor offered cheery greeting to chilly sentries, who, after the coldest and loneliest watch of the night, did not share his good humour. As he tramped round to the horse lines, a hundred swear words floated towards him. Men cursed the cold, the damp, the stiffness of limbs, the staleness of the food, the English, the Duke, the man in the next row who snored, the smell of the pits. Anything and everything had an obscenity stuck to it; it was a soldier's way of saying what he thought of soldiering.

Sandor talked to grooms, tested halter ropes, patted steaming noses, murmured in Magyar to twitching ears. Satisfied once again that all was well, he returned to the wagon. He paused outside for a moment, and glanced up at the sky. Gilbert should be back soon, or at least by full daylight. Sandor climbed in beside Taillefer, curled up and went to sleep as quickly as before.

Gilbert breasted the rise and came out of the woods above the mill. There was just enough light to see it.

There was no smoke. He rested in the saddle, as if half expecting to see Rowena come out to collect eggs. He would not be able to distinguish faces at this distance, but he would know her walk anywhere. He knew Edith's dumpy little gait too, and he would recognise Aud's voice if he heard it. In his mind's eye he could also see Gorm's laboured step; despite the sharpness of the air, he fancied he could sense the fetid staleness that the miller carried around with him. It came as a shock to realise that he felt more comfortable with the sights, sounds, and smells of this household than he did with any other since he had left his family home near Avranches.

He shook his head vigorously, as if to waken himself from a dream. This would never do. They were Saxon; they were foreign. For all that they had shown him kindness, they were the enemy. It was his task now to question them and extract information from them. Without cruelty, maybe, but not without firmness. He was no vomiting weakling now, out of his senses, prostrate in the evening dew. He was a Norman scout, searching out news of the enemy army, and following, moreover, a fresh trail left by an escaping prisoner. He had a duty to do, a task to fulfil, a reputation to make.

Then why was he still sitting here?

He looked furtively over his shoulder, as if he expected Ralph to be there, his mouth already framing questions that cut through his every defence and artifice.

'God's Breath! Why do you chase a single quarry for some petty private grievance when you should be carrying out your orders and searching for an entire army?'

Gilbert could almost hear him saying it.

'Does the Duke care about your precious honour? Does Fitzosbern? Does anyone?'

Gilbert writhed in indecision. Ralph's voice hammered away in his head.

'And what of me? How do I face the Duke now? I – who told Fitzosbern you could be trusted alone. How do I tell them that you deserted your duty, disobeyed your orders, endangered the whole expedition – all for your pitiful honour, for an act of adultery that was no act of adultery? Thousands of lives put at risk because a dog-boy is disturbed in his tiny mind.'

Gilbert lashed himself far more viciously than Ralph could ever have done.

He was quite sure that Ralph knew everything. If Taillefer knew, you could rest assured that Ralph did, and the whole army would know before long. That stupid old wineskin could not keep a secret to save his life. He could not resist telling Gilbert himself. How could he resist telling the world?

Gilbert flushed at the thought of the crowded hall in the fire-light. Taillefer would not need any onions or carrots; he would have them falling about with a much better story. Gilbert could see even Sandor laughing.

Tears pricked his eyes. How could Sandor have betrayed him? Sandor, of all people. Well, it just showed you; you should not trust foreigners – Magyar or Saxon. To think – less than a day ago, he had shaken the wretch's hand! No wonder he had looked awkward. How he had had the face to—

Gilbert started as a figure came to the door of the mill. He screwed up his eyes; the figure's back was turned.

They would all know at the mill too. Sandor and Edwin had talked more than once. And he – Gilbert the Great Fool – had gone along with that disgusting 'plan' of Sandor's. All the time he thought they were hatching it, they were laughing behind his back. And when Edwin was able to reach the mill again, it would be too good a story to keep to oneself.

'Here, listen to this. You know that clod-wit Norman who got the flux and fell off his horse? The one we cleaned up and packed off to the Duke again? Well, guess who his wife is . . .'

The figure looked as if it was dragging something heavy. As it cleared the threshold, Gilbert recognised Aud's angular body. It was her father she was trying to carry. The boy staggered out with a leg couched under each arm. They were trying to reach the ox-cart. It was piled high with bundles, which protruded at both ends from the badly fitted awning.

The miller was not completely unconscious either. He flapped his arms, and appeared to be protesting. Disjointed, strident phrases floated up to Gilbert.

They would never get him to the cart at that rate.

He dug in his spurs. With no pretence at caution he cantered down the hill.

It was Sweyn who saw him first because Aud had her back turned. He dropped his father's legs none too gently and whispered, 'The Norman.'

Aud dumped her father's body. One hand flew to her throat.

Gilbert entered the yard, dismounted swiftly, and tethered his horse.

'Where is Edwin?'

They looked blankly at each other.

Gilbert, in the manner of all foreigners trying to make themselves understood, raised his voice.

'Where is Edwin? Ed–win. Where is he?'

They still showed fear, so he tried to reassure them. He made signs to show that he was alone, but still extracted no answer. He tried another line of approach.

'Where is Rowena?'

He saw Aud's lips tighten, but she offered no reply.

'Edwin!' he roared. He could think of no other way. It never crossed his mind to draw his sword or strike them even with his hand.

Gorm stirred and blinked his eyes.

Gilbert rushed to the water butt by the barn, snatched a bucket off a hook, and filled it. He came running back and hurled the contents at Gorm's head.

While the miller was still spluttering, he seized him by the shoulders and shouted into his face. 'Where is Edwin?'

Gorm's eyes seemed to recede. With consciousness had returned fear. Despite the dripping water, Gilbert could smell sweat and beer on him.

The miller stretched out an arm towards the north. Gilbert glanced up the valley and back to Gorm.

'He has gone to find the army. He has gone to join the King.'

Gorm had picked up some words of French in his many travels, more than he cared to admit, probably more than he consciously remembered. Under the stimulus of fear, some now came back to him. He gaped at Gilbert, who tried again.

'He has gone to join the King.' Gilbert shook him. 'Tell me!'

Without shutting his mouth, Gorm inclined his head.

'Was he mounted?'

Gorm frowned. Gilbert enunciated clearly.

'Mounted. Was – he – on – a – horse?' He made clicking noises with his tongue to imitate hooves.

The head dipped in agreement.

'Did he go that way?' said Gilbert, flinging an arm in a northerly direction.

Gorm nodded again.

'When? Today? Yesterday?'

Gorm's brow puckered.

'Today?' said Gilbert.

Gorm shook his head.

'Yesterday?'

A nod.

Gilbert flung him away, walked swiftly towards his horse, and mounted. Something made him pause. He turned to Aud.

'Take him. Take him and the boy. And go.'

He made gestures to indicate men coming from behind him, and to show urgency.

Aud ducked her head.

Gilbert rode off up the valley, and soon picked up Edwin's trail. It was very unlikely to be anyone else's, he reasoned. Now that he was using his professional skills, he was thinking more clearly. Very few peasants owned horses, and even fewer had them expensively shod like a Norman destrier. In any case, nearly all the horseflesh for miles around would have been either saddled to carry men to the English army, or requisitioned by Norman foraging parties to provide spare mounts and haulage for supply wagons. If they were not fit for that they would have gone into the pot long before now.

The large shoe imprints stood out sharply against all the other split-hoof marks. Gilbert had rarely followed such an easy trail. He was lucky too that Edwin followed the main tracks and lanes; since he knew the country so well, he could stick to them because he knew exactly where each one went. There was no need to strike blindly across open land or thrash through virgin forest.

After three hours he rested. As he munched at the rations that Baldwin's storemen had issued to him, he found it easier to reconcile his duty with his desires. If he was right, and if this was Edwin's trail, and if he did not lose it – they were all 'ifs', but, now that he was doing something he understood, he felt confidence returning – he would achieve one of two things sooner or later. He would either catch up with Edwin or he would locate the English army. If God were kind to him that day, he might do both. He could return to camp with his honour restored in his own eyes, and his reputation made in everyone else's. And see what misery-monk Bruno made of that.

He swallowed the last piece of cheese.

For once he did not see how he could go wrong.

'Spare arrows?' suggested Fitzosbern. 'The English are not expected to use many archers. We can not rely on collecting spent enemy shafts.'

'All taken care of,' said Baldwin de Clair. 'I have not been up half the night for nothing. For nothing.'

Fitzosbern, as usual, refused to take offence. He knew perfectly well how thorough Baldwin was; he had spent the last hour, listening while he dressed and breakfasted, going through countless details with him. Moving the supplies and spares of a whole army at a few hours' notice was a gigantic task, yet as far as Fitzosbern could see Baldwin had not missed a thing. Fitz did not really think Baldwin had forgotten the arrows; he simply wished to find a way of indicating that he had been following closely, a way of showing his appreciation for Baldwin's efficiency. He did not really listen to Baldwin's answer.

'Every man will start with at least thirty. If we can get the wagons near enough – depending on the ground – the archers can retire through the cavalry and draw fresh issues when they need them. As long as they receive proper authorisation from yourself or William.'

Fitzosbern did catch the last remark, and allowed himself a small private smile behind his cup of broth. Like all quartermasters, Baldwin had an aversion to issuing stores without direct orders from on high, preferably God.

'What is the water situation?'

'I have briefed William's own cellarer. Nine coopers have been working at full effort since we had access to a smithy. There was some trouble with the Breton armourers; claimed their swordsmen had priority. I nearly had a row with Count Alan.'

Fitzosbern growled. 'Why do smiths and armourers always consider they are a law unto themselves?'

Baldwin shrugged. 'We have enough now – that is the important thing. And the cellarer has not suffered from lack of instructions. We are as ready as we can be, Fitz.'

Fitzosbern nodded. 'I am sure we are.'

He offered a cup of broth. Baldwin accepted, took a mouthful, and wished he had declined. Back in his own tent, Brother Crispin was no doubt enjoying something infinitely better while he recovered from the sharp side of his master's tongue throughout hours of lists and checks.

Baldwin made a face. 'Time you found a better cook, Fitz. This is awful.'

Fitzosbern nodded gloomily. 'I know. I keep meaning to get round to it. Slips my mind.'

For a minute or so they sipped and slurped, and wiped wayward drips from their chins.

'How is William bearing up?' said Baldwin at last.

'Pretty well, considering,' said Fitzosbern. 'He had a bad few hours a day or so ago, but he pulled round. Now that we have firm news, he is better. Then Geoffrey's man – I forget his name – arrived yesterday, with news from Rouen and St Valéry. So he heard from Matilda. That helped. Matilda sends her best respects to you, by the way.'

Baldwin felt warm; Matilda did not forget friends.

'How is the lady Emma?'

'Mother? Well now, thank you. Well.'

There was another silence.

At last Baldwin said, 'How do you think it will go?'

Fitzosbern gave him a typical Fitzosbern answer. 'We are here. We are here because we wanted to be here. It is up to us to make it go.'

Baldwin grunted. He had expected nothing more.

Fitzosbern then surprised him with a rare show of emotion.

'But I will say this: if anyone in Christendom can make it go, William can. And I for one wish to be nowhere else at the moment.'

Baldwin sensed for the first time a whiff of drama. It had begun as a wild dream when the Confessor had, so William said, offered to make him the heir to the throne if there should be no children of the royal body. Then, as the years passed and the Confessor showed less and less interest in Queen Edith (if indeed he had shown any in the first place), what had been a vague project steadily became a constant aspiration – though not taken entirely seriously by the ducal court, any more than one took entirely seriously a prince's vow to make a pilgrimage to Jerusalem.

But when the Confessor died, it had taken a leap into the realm of possibility. By the time Fitzosbern had argued doubting vassals into joining the expedition, it had moved towards distinct likelihood. The celebrations and wet throats of the departure from St Valéry had turned into sick stomachs and dry mouths as they approached the pebble beach of Pevensey. From then on it was the absence rather than the presence of the English that had produced the worry – the lack of news. For a while nerves were pushed into the background as every muscle was strained to make ready for every possible eventuality – building, gathering, collecting, piling, practising, planning.

When they were ready, poised, expectant, there had come the waiting, the boredom, the wondering, the self-doubt. Mercifully, that had not lasted too long. News of Harold's approach had fired the whole camp into frantic activity. Now that too was nearing a conclusion. All that was needed was definite knowledge of the time and place of Harold's arrival, and the reckoning would soon come. All those years of hopes and plans and efforts were narrowing down to a single pinpoint of decision. Small wonder the drama of it had touched even a literal man like Fitzosbern.

Baldwin set down his cup on the trestle boards.

'Did my two lilies come to pay their fine?'

Fitzosbern nodded. 'Just so. William somebody-or-other and his brother. What are you doing with scum like that?'

'Putting them in their place. Excuse me; I must go to the harbour. Another ship dropped anchor overnight. Now that we have enough light, the sooner we unload the better. Supplies have a way of melting into thin air. Thin air.'

'Go then. Come and see me again in the afternoon. If we have news of the English, come at once. Sorry about the stew.'

Baldwin looked round outside for Capra and Pomeroy. There was no sign of them. Baldwin was not entirely surprised. Pity, though. He had had a fine job lined up for them, unloading salt-soaked sacks and heavy wooden crates. Still, on balance, good riddance. They could go and be a curse to some other commander.

He called for his horse, and went to collect Brother Crispin. If he did not reach the ship quickly, the supplies would disappear faster than cheese by a rat-hole. However many trusted men he posted on deck night and day, all sorts of things just seemed to slide away. He had also seen small groups of Flemings drifting innocently in the direction of the harbour. News of fresh arrivals drew them like flies to honey, but he could never catch one with anything on him. Fulk boasted openly that his men were the best equipped in the whole army, and Baldwin knew he was flaunting his success, defying him to detect it.

'Come on, you,' he said sourly to Brother Crispin.

Crispin was not a good horseman, a fact partly accounted for by the dreadful nag he had to ride. It was as lean and bony as he was; if you gave both of them a good shake, their legs would drop off. Baldwin tilted his head slightly in mirthless humour. What they said was true: a man sooner or later came to look like his horse, or the other way round. It was a miracle it had escaped the pot.

If Brother Crispin felt that the continued existence of this bone-rattling relic of horseflesh was a proof of Divine generosity, he gave no sign of it. To him, any journey on horseback was one of the many scorpions sent by an inscrutable Providence to scourge man's sinful body.

So they rode in silence. Crispin, after failing to derive spiritual uplift from the mortification provided by an ill-fitting saddle, shut his eyes and tried to console himself with memories of distant hours spent toasting his chilblains in the warming room of his monastery at Bec. It was a great test of the imagination.

Baldwin escaped his countless pressing worries for a short while by allowing his mind to slip away to the place whither it had been pulling for nearly two days.

It was ridiculous. He knew only two things about her: her name was Aud, and her father was a freeman. That was something; servile status would have been unthinkable. Aud . . . The name sounded Danish. Well, that was better than Saxon. Danes tended to produce more freemen than the English. Viking blood, you see. Like his own ancestors, the founders of Normandy. And God knows, they had started with little enough, barely five generations back.

Perhaps Aud was descended from some Danish adventurer chieftain; that would put her almost on a level with himself. And with Albreda. Albreda! How far away she seemed, and how – how foreign! They had never had much in common. It was a mistake to assume that members of the same family group were likely to make better marriages. Suddenly Albreda, with her screwed-up eyes and her sharp tongue, was more than a burden; she was a barrier.

Baldwin sighed. He knew he was thinking outrageous things. If only he had somebody to talk to. Matilda would have teased him. Only Agnes would have listened . . .

He understood very little of what Aud had said. He had been quite unable to convey to her what he had thought or felt. And yet – and yet – something had passed between them. How often had he praised God that he had thought to take off his glove before offering her his hand. If he had not, their flesh would not have touched, and then ... He knew that she was concerned for him. He *knew*. Why else would she have offered the apples? Their hands had touched again. His mind told him that hers was thin and hard from much kitchen work, that his own was pitted and rough from a lifetime in camp and saddle. Yet his heart assured him that they had touched with the softness of children in prayer.

He could not put into words then what he felt, and he could not now. All he understood was that the moment had been unbearably tender and indescribably precious.

It had been shattered by the Devil-begotten Bloodeye. Not content with that, he had gone on to taunt him in public. Pomeroy and Capra had been led on by him; their insubordination was as much Bloodeye's fault as their own. But Fulk's motives were different; he seemed to take delight in crime for its own sake, as if he derived pleasure not from the profit of crime but from the crime itself and from the evil that produced it.

As for the yellow-faced, misshapen little cat of a man who shadowed him ... A fine pair they made. Theirs was an unnatural partnership, hinting at depths of darkness to make the imagination tremble.

And yet, on the surface, Fulk gave the impression that nothing mattered. This indifference, this lack of apparent effort, could be infuriating. A rare man indeed – who could inspire deep fear and provoke intense irritation at the same time.

Baldwin crossed himself in reflex self-protection.

A nudge on the elbow from Brother Crispin jerked him back to the misty morning.

'Hmm?'

Crispin pointed.

An altercation was in full swing between Baldwin's sentries

and a handful of Flemish mercenaries. As Baldwin and Crispin hastened closer, one or two knives came out.

'Enough of that!' snapped Baldwin.

Men on both sides paused and looked over their shoulders.

'Put them away, lads.'

Fulk appeared from nowhere, and lounged against a cartwheel, whittling a stick. Baldwin was furious. Fulk had deliberately timed his remark so that their obedience would appear to come from his own command, not from Baldwin's. And the swine had almost certainly put them up to it in the first place.

Baldwin rode right up to him, still seething, though he had the presence of mind to remain mounted. On foot Fulk would have towered over him. Baldwin waved a gloved hand.

'Dismiss them.'

Fulk did not even lift his shoulders from the solid wheel.

'I thought you would be grateful for the extra labour, Sir Baldwin. The ship must be unloaded quickly, in case thieves get at the cargo.'

The gall of the man! Baldwin struggled to keep his temper.

'I have my own fatigue parties for this. I know my job and do not need to be reminded of the priorities of it.'

Fulk shrugged elaborately. Dietrich, Rainald and the rest stood still, looking to him for a lead.

Baldwin jostled them with his horse.

'Go on, move!'

Fulk tried one more dig.

'Do you think his Grace will be pleased to hear that you rejected the chance of assistance to finish the job quickly?' He looked innocent. 'Hardly the act of a careful quartermaster, one would have thought.'

Dietrich smirked at the others. Bloodeye was an evil bastard, but you had to hand it to him; he was usually good for a bit of fun.

Baldwin rose to the occasion.

'I should not expect a mere captain of mercenaries to be fully conversant with the many tasks that require attention in a military camp before a major engagement. All he has to do is to present his men in line of battle at the right time, collect his money afterwards – and do as little as possible in between.'

Fulk made a grand gesture to acknowledge the sharpness of the thrust. Baldwin was not finished.

'As a matter of fact, since you so kindly offer me the services of your – er – men, they can report at once to Turold at the castle. For a start they can go round all the walls doing some skin-soaking.'

'On a morning like this? Did you miss the dew? It would take the fires of Hell to set the skins alight, never mind the walls.'

Baldwin leaned slightly forward. 'If I say the skins on the walls need resoaking, they need resoaking. When they have finished doing that, they can fill all the fire buckets and get them up on the catwalks. When they have done that, I am sure Turold will find plenty more for such – willing workers. You would not like William to reduce your final payment because of dereliction of duty barely hours before the battle, now, would you? Dereliction reported by none other than his quartermaster – and kinsman.'

Fulk looked hard at him. Baldwin did not enjoy the gaze of the disfigured, bloodshot eye, but he tightened his jaw and held his ground.

At last Fulk relaxed. He slammed his knife sharply into the scabbard, tossed away the stick, and brushed some invisible dirt from his hands.

'Do as Sir Baldwin says, lads. And think of your pay after the battle, when *everyone will get what he deserves.*'

The eye looked more baleful than ever.

The Flemings trudged off, Rainald hunching his high shoulders and savagely kicking a stone. Baldwin dismounted and began checking supplies with Crispin. Fulk left the cartwheel and came over.

'Plenty more arrows, I see.'

Baldwin said nothing. He knew that Fulk was not loitering simply to talk about arrows. He tensed in expectation.

Fulk tossed a stone into the water.

'I hear your Saxon prisoners escaped.'

'Yes,' said Baldwin. 'Two sore backs told you that.'

'I expect they will return to their mill.'

'Yes. I expect they will.'

'Interesting place, that.'

Baldwin refused to be drawn.

'Worth a second look, I should say,' said Fulk.

Baldwin struggled to concentrate on Crispin's recital of figures, but they were going in one ear and out of the other.

'I found it much more interesting on a second viewing,' said Fulk. 'So were its inhabitants.'

He tossed more stones so gently that they barely made a 'plop' as they entered the water.

'Have you noticed how the most unlikely people improve on – er – closer acquaintance?'

Baldwin tried a counterattack; he could not put up with this all morning.

'If you are trying to vaunt that you raped the fair one, why not come straight out and say so? Then we can all applaud your bravery and continue our work.'

Fulk pretended to look surprised. 'Oh, her? Oh, yes – ripe and juicy, I agree. A fine romp. But one tires of routine conquests. Being a gourmet in these matters, can I convey to your more ascetic taste the desire one has for the occasional, more astringent dish?'

The finer points of the irony may have slipped past Baldwin, but he knew he was being toyed with. He knew too that, however hard he tried to hide it, it was agony for him, and it was beginning to show. And he knew that Fulk knew.

In a gallant attempt to sound careless, he said, 'I suppose you

can claim two more murders as well as two more conquests?'
Uttering the mere words was pain.

Fulk simulated surprise again. 'Murder? Oh, precious saints,
no! The mill is on one of your duke's famous avenues, I believe.
"Nothing is to be taken."' He bowed. 'Have no fear, Sir Baldwin.
You can report to your duke that all I took was a – a liberty or
two. Everyone was very much alive when I left.'

He threw a last pebble, and leaned close to Baldwin's ear. The
scar crinkled as his face creased into a parody of a smile.

'Very much alive – and kicking.'

He strolled away, whistling.

Driven beyond endurance, Baldwin hurled an insult that he
would not have contemplated before.

'Delighted to hear of your success. No passing out on the job
this time, then?'

Fulk stopped dead.

Baldwin and Crispin saw his shoulders go taut. He whirled
round. The face was suffused with blood. Lips had been drawn
back from set teeth. He breathed deeply as if trying to keep control. His fingers made clawing movements close to his thighs.

Baldwin's hand stole towards the hilt of his dagger.

Slowly Fulk mastered himself. The symptoms of rage faded
and the insolent air returned. He bowed again, his right hand on
his hip.

'Truly, Sir Baldwin, you are becoming our master in the art of
repartee. What the philosopher said was true: "There is naught
surpasses passion for the filing of the tongue."'

He sauntered off.

'Bastard!' muttered Baldwin after him.

He stooped, picked up a stone, and threw it hard into the
water almost at his feet.

Crispin shivered with reaction, and crossed himself. Was Fulk
evil because he was left-handed, or left-handed because he was evil?

*

Gilbert knew he was getting closer. The freshness of a pile of droppings told him that.

He had no real idea of what he was going to do when he found Edwin; his nervous excitement was impairing his capacity for clear thinking. One or two shivers ran down his back. He could not explain it, but it seemed the very air was telling him that he was nearing the end of his chase. He shook his head to clear the confused murmuring in his brain.

Suddenly the trail disappeared.

He gazed in disbelief. It was impossible.

He dismounted and walked forward a few paces. There was no sign.

As always, he fell back on Ralph.

'Trails do not disappear,' Ralph would say. 'It simply means that you did not see them go.'

He retraced his steps until he picked it up again, then paused and looked round. He was thinking like a scout again and not like a jealous husband.

To the right of the trail rose some steep downland criss-crossed with broken sheep runs.

'Look up as well as down,' Ralph said.

Halfway up was a line of gorse and bracken. Somewhere about its middle was a gap. The lighter colours told him that under-growth had been pushed down and pushed aside. Taking a line from where he stood, he advanced slowly along the nearest run, and exclaimed in satisfaction when he saw a shoe mark in some sheep droppings.

Pulling his horse after him, he advanced across and up the slope, his confidence and excitement returning with every stride. Again those shivers, and again that odd murmuring in his head. It grew as he neared the top.

'Great Jesus!'

The whole army sat before him. A million guttural Saxon words rose to his ears like the rumble of the distant sea.

Plunging back over the brow again, he looked for somewhere to tether his horse. The crest was bare.

He cursed himself for his carelessness.

He careered back towards the line of briar, and tied the reins as best he could. He took off his helmet and hung it on his belt. He was about to return, when he thought of the hauberk. If the sun showed again, it could reflect off that as well; after all, he had been oiling and polishing it enough. He paused in indecision. Was it wise to take it off in the presence of the enemy?

He unstrapped the bundle behind his saddle, shook out his blanket, and draped it round his shoulders. He checked that his sword was loose in the scabbard, and returned to the summit.

Holy Virgin, there must be twenty, thirty thousand of them! They were strung out as far as he could see both ways, from the shoulder of the hill on the left to where the track disappeared into forest on the right. Or rather sprawled out. It was the midday rest period. Men were eating, drinking, dozing, examining sore feet, relieving themselves. An orchard was being picked clean. A couple of squawks came from a cluster of cottars' huts near the bottom of the hill; one prudent group of fyrdmen would eat well that night.

The very fact that the huts were still standing showed that they had been spared by the wasting parties. So, the plan of the avenues was working; Harold was going where the food was easiest to obtain. At the very least he was taking the line of least resistance.

Gilbert glanced up at the sun. It was almost due south. His sense of direction told him that in his pursuit of Edwin from the mill he had taken a wide swing from the north to the north-east. Thanks to Ralph's training, he had kept a check on landmarks that he passed, and had constantly verified his position by looking back at them.

His route therefore had brought him on a course to cut

directly across the English line of march. At this rate they were exactly on course for Hastings, and would probably get within striking distance by nightfall. The chances were that they would come out of the woods not far from the hill with the apple tree on it.

Senlac Hill!

Gilbert tightened his jaw. There would be no more jokes about 'Young Master Senlac' when he returned with this priceless jewel of military intelligence. What praise from Ralph! Bishop Odo's face ludicrous in its amazement! A slap on the shoulder from Fitzosbern! A compliment from Sir Walter Giffard! Congratulations from the Bastard himself! He tore his mind away from the dizzy dream, and concentrated fiercely on the scene below him, trying to force every detail of it into his memory.

He could make out the housecarls easily enough. They were marching in mail, and it looked as if each man carried shield, axe, and sword as well as food and protective gear. Gilbert shook his head in silent wonder ... All the way from Stamford – those men must be made of iron.

Clustered around one of the larger cabins were soldiers even better dressed. One or two brightly coloured cloaks stood out against the regular greys, greens, and browns. Horses were tethered in orderly lines. Two banners fluttered from lofty standards. It had to be the King and his headquarters.

Strung out along the route were sizeable detachments, visibly separate from each other despite the disorder and straggling that occurred in rest periods. Probably the county fyrdmen. Gilbert had heard talk of 'the Surrey contingent' and 'the men of Essex'. There were other shires whose names he could not remember. Like the different *pays* in Normandy, he thought. These shire fyrdmen kept themselves to themselves, just as men of the Pays de Caux did not drink with men of the Pays d'Auge, as dwellers in the Bessin were wary of folk from the Bocage.

All around these groups were countless small knots of men, with hardly a scrap of proper protection between them. Their weapons were not up to much either. He could swear that he saw scythes and pitchforks, even plain staves.

All told, it looked a vast host – perhaps forty thousand, on second thoughts. Would the Duke be well advised to wait behind the protection of his castle walls? Or would these scruffy peasants break before the thunder of a charge of knights? Gilbert rested his chin on his hands. If he were the Duke—

His horse fell on him, winding him completely. He struggled frantically to twist round and away, the helmet at his belt digging agonisingly into his side. Then he saw that it was not his horse, but an enormous Saxon, who was now astride his chest and pinning his arms to the ground with his knees. A second one pointed a sword at his throat, while a third was hobbling his ankles.

Still gasping for air, he was hoisted to his feet by the scruff of the neck, disarmed, and made to march down the hill. The big man tied his wrists and led him like a donkey; the second walked behind, still with naked sword; the third brought his horse.

Each group of men looked up and fell silent as they approached. Heads came together again when they had passed, and the mutterings began, with final glances over watchful shoulders.

By the time they reached Harold's headquarters, Gilbert had accepted that he was as good as dead. He was so consumed with self-reproach that he now welcomed the prospect. He had failed to find Edwin and therefore failed to redeem his honour. He had failed to get vital news back to the Duke, and so had nothing to justify his breaking of Sir William Fitzosbern's strict orders. Worst of all, he had proved once again his incompetence as a scout; he had neglected the most basic points of Ralph's training, and had allowed himself to be surprised and caught like a stupid farm boy stealing eggs. He had betrayed his family, his honour, his friend, his comrades, and his duke. What would Adele say? What would Ralph think of him when he heard that he had tamely allowed a Saxon fyrdman to pull from him the precious hauberk? What shame would his poor father feel!

By the time he stood before the King, he was looking forward to the royal gesture of dismissal and the axe-blow that would release him.

At first the questions were put in English. The King lowered his head and watched him carefully as he waited for an answer.

Gilbert shrugged.

A priest was brought who spoke French.

'I have nothing to say.' Gilbert decided that he would at least not add cowardice to his other crimes.

Again that watchful look with lowered head. Gilbert stood and awaited the inevitable.

The King walked away to another group sitting by a wagon. There was a murmured conversation. The King returned with another man.

Gilbert gaped. They were almost identical.

The two men looked at each other and laughed. Then one of them stepped forward and took out a knife.

Gilbert braced himself and shut his eyes. He heard a second laugh, and felt the rope fall from his wrists. When he opened his eyes, he received another shock. Standing between the two 'kings' was a third, taller and fairer. He put an arm round the shoulders of each of them.

'This is my brother, Gyrth, and this is my brother, Leofwine.' He grinned. 'Baffling, eh?'

Gilbert found some memory of 'sixty-four coming back. During Harold's visit to Normandy, he had seen the Earl, as he then was; but he would not have been able to distinguish him now from his two brothers.

Harold's French accent was good. Gilbert was also taken

aback by the charm and the frankness. The man in the middle was watching him.

'Surprised at my French?' he said. 'We had plenty of Normans here in the Confessor's day. Court was crawling with them. And I got a lot better when I was in Normandy in 'sixty-four – visiting your duke. You will know therefore who I am. Now, who are you?'

'Gilbert of Avranches, sir.' Gilbert amazed himself at how easily the 'sir' came out.

The King looked him up and down.

'Well, Gilbert of Avranches,' he said at last, 'it was careless of you to get captured, was it not?'

The question was so direct that Gilbert found himself answering with total honesty.

'Yes, sir.'

The King began munching an apple.

'And now that you have discovered us, what are you going to tell your duke?'

Gilbert began to resent the bantering tone.

'Why play with me, sir? I was stupid. You have caught me. Why not kill me and have done with it?'

Harold paused with the apple in front of his lips. 'If for no other reason, because it seems to be the one thing you want me to do. Why does a young soldier with everything to live for wish to die?'

Gilbert lowered his head. 'I have nothing to live for, sir.'

'Hate yourself that much, eh?'

Gilbert looked up again. Harold chewed thoughtfully.

'Well, I am going to give you someone to hate even more – me. That should keep you going – till you get back, anyway. Tell me,' he continued, 'did you ever hear the story of the torturer and the martyr?'

Gilbert looked blank.

'No? Well, it went like this: the martyr said to the torturer,

"Torture me and kill me." And the torturer thought, and said, "No."'

The King beamed at him. Gyrth and Leofwine chuckled.

'Well?'

Gilbert still looked blank.

'Never mind,' said Harold. 'Just understand – I shall not oblige you by killing you. If one Norman scout has seen us, I am sure a dozen have, and they did not get captured.'

Gilbert grimaced in bitter shame.

'So,' continued the King, 'if we can not arrive quietly, we shall arrive with a banging of drums. It is all one in the end. You will return from here and you will tell your duke from me that he can squat in his castle and wait for me. He has a castle, of course?'

'No,' said Gilbert feebly.

Harold roared with laughter.

'Boy, you are an even worse liar than you are a scout. A Norman duke goes campaigning without building castles? Perhaps you should be a jester. I fought beside him in Brittany – remember? And anyway, do you think I have been awaiting this fight for nearly a year without studying my enemy?'

He threw away the apple, walked up to Gilbert, and prodded him in the chest with his finger.

'You tell your duke – Duke William the Bastard, the son of the tanner's daughter – tell him that he can cower behind his castle walls and shiver beneath the shelter of his precious Papal banner, but Harold the King is coming, and coming very soon. He has already thrown one load of waterborne vermin back into the North Sea, and he is about to throw another into the Channel.

'If Duke William sees sense and wishes to change his mind at the last minute, then he can leave under my flag of truce and I shall hold the door open for him. If he does not . . .'

Harold looked hard at Gilbert.

'I could kill you now, but it will be easier, and tidier, to kill you all together at Hastings. You are a fine young fellow; it would be a pity if you were to die for an act of foolish presumption by an illegitimate adventurer.'

'I follow my duke,' said Gilbert, finding his voice. He sensed that Harold was a man who respected honesty.

The King smiled. 'Well spoken, son. Nevertheless, go tell your duke what I have said. Follow him by all means. Follow him to Normandy, or follow him to the grave.'

Harold turned to Leofwine and took the apple that his brother was holding. He tossed it to Gilbert, who was so surprised that he nearly dropped it.

'Here! Not as good as Norman apples, perhaps, but we do our best. While you eat that, you can wander round and see a real army. And it is all army too – no excess weight or surplus fat, lumbering wagons or screeching whores. You will have my safe conduct, and I give you my housecarl Wilfrid here. He will accompany you until you decide to leave. You will take with you everything with which you came.'

'Including my horse, sir?' said Gilbert in surprise.

'Well, of course. We want you to get there ahead of us, you idiot. Is there anything else?'

'Yes, sir.' Gilbert pointed at the large fyrdman standing behind him. 'My hauberk. He has it.'

'Take it off,' said the King.

'But, sir,' protested the fyrdman.

Harold nodded to Wilfrid, who at once began to bear down on the dismayed Saxon.

'Oh, all right, all right.'

He wrenched it off with a bad grace and flung it at Gilbert.

The King ordered Gilbert's remaining bonds to be cut, and himself put his sword and dagger back in place. For all that, he was the enemy, Gilbert could not help experiencing a thrill of excitement at such proximity to this remarkable man.

'There!' said Harold. 'Now you are all in one piece again. Soon we start afresh on the march. See what you want. Ask what you want. Then go. You can rely on Wilfrid. We do not want any of my wild fyrdmen slicing you up, do we? And I have an interpreter for you. Goodbye.'

'Goodbye, sir.'

The King smiled, and his moustache twitched. Then he turned away, beckoning his brothers after him. As the three moved away, he shouted over his shoulder.

'Edwin! See to him.'

Edwin and Gilbert stared at each other, then went off in awkward silence.

Gyrth said to Harold, 'That was a fine performance.'

Harold sighed wearily, and flopped onto a fallen tree.

'You take any luck that presents itself. We have lost the element of surprise. So let us try to overawe them. We can be no worse off.'

'You will not quicken William.'

'No. But I quickened that boy. And he will talk. And the stories will get bigger every time.'

'So you show him the army? We are hardly at our best. Look at us.'

Gyrth gestured at the bent backs and sagging shoulders all round them.

Harold shook his head. 'It is numbers, not faces, that the boy will take away with him. We must be strung out for over two miles. How can he count? By the time he gets back to the Bastard, we shall be fifty thousand strong.'

'That will not fool William either,' said Leofwine.

'Of course not,' said Harold.

'Well?'

'My brother, everyone will know the boy is wrong, but they will not know *how* wrong. We have sown doubt – and that is the most fruitful seed of all in an enemy camp. Come. We now have a meeting to keep.'

'Where?'

'In the hall of the Bastard's castle at Hastings. The one he has not built.'

When Godric caught sight of the thin column of smoke, he feared the worst. Gritting his teeth against the pain, he tried to hobble faster to the top of the hill.

Thank God! It was not the mill that was burning. The smoke was coming from further down the valley, where two or three cottars' huts were in ruins. A burning wagon was slewed across the track between them.

There was no sign of life anywhere.

Godric made what jerky speed he could, fresh sweat running down his neck and back. No figure emerged when he splashed noisily across the stream.

Then he heard it. A moaning. Not a sound of physical pain. More a lament.

Turning a corner, he nearly fell over Gorm. The miller was sitting propped against the wall. Across his lap lay Sweyn, his neck loose, like a broken doll. Hideous red-ringed holes gaped in the boy's clothes. Gorm cradled the body in bloodstained hands and gently rocked it. He gazed into the distance and intoned a tuneless dirge in his native Danish.

Godric spoke, then shouted. Gorm took no notice until Godric flopped to his knees and shook him.

'Where is Rowena? Where is Aud? Edith?'

Gorm paused briefly at the sound of the names, then continued moaning.

Godric hit him across the face.

'Rowena! Where is she?'

The shock brought awareness, then recognition. Gorm reached into his jerkin, pulled out a rag, and began wiping his brow. His eyes narrowed in hatred.

'You!'

'Where is Rowena?' shouted Godric, his voice almost breaking.

'You! You dare to lust after my daughter.'

Godric shook him again. 'Is she alive?'

Gorm's tiny eyes gleamed at the frantic appeal in Godric's face. At last, after all these years, he had seen Godric truly moved.

'You want her. Admit it – you want her.'

Godric clenched a fist under Gorm's nose.

'Do not play with me, old man. Your son lies dead in your lap. It is no time for riddles. Where – is – Rowena?'

Gorm wiped his face again. His eyes caught sight of the piece of cloth in his hand, now stained with blood as well as with sweat. He gazed at it for a moment, seeming to draw inspiration from it.

'They were taken, all of them. Dragged away. I tried to stop it. See? A piece of her dress came away in my hand.'

Godric cried aloud.

Gorm leaned forward, his eyes alight. 'You know what that means? One man after another, passed from hand to hand, and the remains spitted on a sword. Look at my Sweyn.'

Still groaning in pain, Godric struggled to his feet, and began to move towards the door of the house.

Gorm, sensing triumph, called after him, 'If she died after one or two, she would be lucky.'

Godric disappeared. Gorm eased Sweyn's body off his lap and stumbled after him.

Godric was putting food into a satchel.

Gorm came close and shouted in his ear, 'Now you will never have her. Never!'

Godric turned in fury. Gorm reeled backwards at the awful sight of him. One blow from those huge hands could half kill a man.

Gorm flopped on to a stool, leaned his elbows on the table, and put his head in his hands. Godric moved to and fro, adding to the pile on the table. The limp somehow added to his deliberation. Last of all, he went out and came back with his great axe. Gorm had retrieved it after the Normans' previous visit.

Godric rummaged in Rowena's kitchen corner and pulled out a knife. He sat down at the table, and started to fashion a proper crutch out of a stave he had brought in from the barn. When he had finished, he picked up a whetstone and began sharpening the edge of the axe. The slow, regular rasping grated on Gorm's nerves.

'What are you going to do?'

Godric ignored him.

'Where are you going?'

Godric behaved as if he were simply not there. He packed the satchel and slung it over his shoulder, along with a rolled blanket and a sheepskin. Fixing a thong near the head of the axe, he hung it from his belt, and put the knife in a scabbard on the other side. The whetstone went into a pocket. He tied some material round the crosspiece at the top of the crutch, and tested it under his armpit.

Satisfied, he moved towards the door without a glance in Gorm's direction. Gorm looked up in alarm.

'Where are you going?'

Godric paused, but not because of the question. It was as if something had just occurred to him. He turned and looked very hard at the miller. Gorm swallowed nervously. His lower lip hung loose.

'Why are you not dead?' said Godric at last.

'What?' Gorm played feebly for time.

'Your son is dead. Your daughters are dead. Yet you are alive. You are not even hurt; the blood on your hands is Sweyn's.'

Gorm's whole body seemed to sag.

'I – I was only one. There were many.'

'Did you not try, man?'

357

Gorm grimaced piteously. 'I – we needed help. Yes. I tried to get help.'

Godric stared. 'You ran?'

Gorm slid off the stool and onto his knees. Godric hobbled across the floor.

'Look at me!' he roared.

Gorm raised his head by inches. Godric spaced the words with terrible clarity.

'You – ran – away?'

Gorm put up his arm as if to ward off a blow. Instead, he heard Godric kneeling down. Huge hands grasped his shoulders. He found himself looking into the dark eyes that had baffled him so many times over the years. Now they no longer glowed or smouldered; they blazed. Gorm was struck with fear to his very soul.

'Old man, you have befouled your name, broken trust with your kin, blotted out your flesh and blood. You had no wife. Now you have no son, no daughters, no reason for living. What is left to you is the memory of how you helped to lose it all.'

Gorm's face practically crumbled. The chins hung like half-filled bags on a hook. What made it more terrible was that Godric did not raise his voice. It was not temper but truth that Gorm was hearing.

'You do not need my curse upon you,' said Godric. 'You could fly from it. But the great burden you have fashioned for yourself – your own memory – you will never fly from that. Never.'

Godric fought his way to his feet and readjusted the crutch.

Gorm collapsed to all fours, grovelling and whimpering.

Godric paused at the door.

'I have no life now, only strength. Enough to fight, and maybe find the man who did this. You are the only father I remember. I am the only child you have left. Yet I tell you this: I strike you from my memory, I strike you from my mind, I strike you from my heart. Gorm Haraldsson, you do not exist! You are a *nithing*!'

Gorm cried aloud in torment, but Godric did not hear him ...

When the tears would no longer flow, Gorm sat up. He picked bits of straw off the front of his shirt. Then he looked around the house. Nothing moved. Outside, the only sounds were the rippling of the stream and the steady creaking of the wheel. No animal made a noise, no chicken scratched at the straw, no gate rattled.

Gorm clawed his way to a sitting position on the stool. The pot of beer lay smashed in front of him, but for once it did not matter.

He gazed for a long while into nothing, his chest still heaving with emotion, his eyes wide ... What did it matter whether it was deceit or cowardice that had brought him to this?

At last, levering himself to his feet, he went searching. Tools, pots, bags, clothes were swept or kicked aside. He paused when he pulled out an old leather strap that looked as if might serve his purpose. It was grey with dirt and stiff with age, but he recognised it. How often had he used it on Godric's young back! How suitable, therefore. He continued searching, and found what else he wanted in the end.

He knotted together the few scraps of frayed rope, and attached one end to the leather strap, which he fashioned into a noose. He could not control the trembling of his hands.

He looked up at the beam in the house, and placed a stool underneath it. There was not enough space.

Lumbering into the mill, he found a beam high enough, but could not get the rope over it. Every time he swung it up, he overbalanced. He tried putting the noose round his neck first and then throwing up the other end, but he fell, and grazed his chin painfully.

He crawled to the doorway, trailing the rope from the noose still round his neck. Using the door jamb for support, he struggled once more to an upright stance, and tottered back to the house.

He took the table apart, and began lugging it, plank by plank, to a position under the beam in the mill. He could think of no other way except to hold one end of each plank and drag it backwards. Several times he caught his heel and fell down. By the time he had dragged the two trestles as well, there was a large patch of mud over the seat of his sacking breeches.

He reassembled the table under the beam, then tried several times to climb on to it. He simply could not get his knee high enough to provide leverage for his body. Sweating and whimpering, he went to get the stool.

He placed it beside the table, put one foot on it, and paused. There was no going back now. He was shaking all over. He looked up at the beam, gathering the rope over one arm.

Grunting with the effort, he got onto the stool, then, very carefully, onto the table. He waved his arms to keep his balance. The mill wheel swished and creaked.

He would make absolutely sure the first time – no half-hearted efforts. He coiled the rope in loops in his right hand, and looked up once more at the beam above him. Sweat poured down his face. He blinked as it ran into his eyes.

He swallowed, licked his lips, took a huge breath, swung his right arm, and heaved. The effort took him off balance. As he saw the rope flop over the beam, he knew he was falling. The rope slipped back. He crashed on to the table, the planks broke, and the trestles collapsed. The old leather noose grazed his neck again.

Sprawled in the ruins, weeping and panting, he thumped with his fist on the ground.

Once more he crawled to the doorway. The sound of the stream came more clearly to his ears.

Still on hands and knees, still with the rope trailing behind him, he set out towards the water. When he reached the gravel at the edge, he stopped. It was not very deep here. The mill pool was really the best place.

He struggled up, turned, and caught sight of Sweyn's body.

With damp patches now on his knees as well as on his buttocks, he came back to look on his son. Already the flies were clustering round the edges of the wounds.

A frown appeared on Gorm's face. He pulled off the noose and went to get a spade . . .

He stuck the rough wooden cross into the earth and stood up. His wife would have liked the cross. At least he had done something right.

Only Godric was left now.

Aud was taken. He could do nothing for her. If she were not dead already, she soon would be, and he had no idea where she was.

Rowena and Edith were away, and there was nothing he could do about that either.

Only Godric remained. He must tell Godric. Godric must come back and they must carry on with the mill – together. He always had Godric. And a freeman always had his land.

All he had to do was to stop Godric fighting in that stupid battle. What use was a dead miller? Even if the Normans won, they would need millers just like everyone else. He and Godric had dealt with Saxons; they could deal with Normans. It was only exchanging one set of foreigners for another.

Godric was no soldier; he would be cut down in the first charge. He had to be made to see sense. It was unlike him to go charging off like that.

Gorm looked for his travelling stick. It was gone. A curse formed on his lips, but he remembered the wooden cross.

He rescued a leather jerkin from the tumbled pile on the floor of the house, and stuffed some food into a bag. He undid his clothes, rearranged his shirt and breeches, and refastened his belt. Outside, he went to the stream and threw some water into his face. He filled a leather flask and fixed it to a strap over his shoulder. He cut a makeshift walking stick and stuck the knife into his belt.

Godric would not get far on his crutch. Catching him up would not take long. And then he would tell him everything. Everything. Godric would understand. Godric always did.

'How much further, Sir Baldwin?'

'Not far now. Just the other side of this hill.'

'Praise be,' muttered Brother Crispin.

'I found you an easier horse,' said Baldwin. 'I thought you would be grateful.'

'As the martyr is whose scourge of nails is exchanged for a scourge of thorns.'

They came up over the crest.

Baldwin pointed. 'There it is. No sign of fire.'

'There is down there,' said Crispin, pointing down the valley, where the wagon still smouldered.

Baldwin had not heard him. He was urging his horse impatiently down the track towards the mill.

Crispin made his best possible speed. His master's ways were becoming as inscrutable as those of the Almighty. There was clearly something pulling Sir Baldwin to this mill, and it was connected with the conversation he had witnessed with Fulk Bloodeye that morning. Sir Baldwin had been agitated ever since, alternating between fits of savage swearing and moods of total abstraction.

When the last supplies had been checked, moved, and put under lock and key, Baldwin started to make excuses as to why it would be a good idea to come on this journey. It started with the expressed desire to 'get away for once from camp smells', to be followed with the need for 'checking the avenues of clear ground'. Out of the blue, he said he thought it would be a change to 'do a turn of scouting', which he had 'not done for years'. Finally he declared that as everything possible had been done and Harold had still not shown himself, he had time on his hands, and he had to do something. Crispin knew better than to ask questions.

The real surprise came when Sir Baldwin ordered Crispin to accompany him. Again, Crispin kept silent. He noticed that they took no outriders with them, and that they left camp by way of the archers' lines, well away from any knight's quarters or senior commander's establishments. On the journey, Baldwin made no comment except bad-tempered remarks when Crispin failed to maintain the required smart pace.

Now that they had arrived, Crispin was none the wiser. He kept as close behind Sir Baldwin as he could.

By the time he crossed the stream, Baldwin had been through all the buildings, and was kneeling by a freshly dug grave.

He scrambled to his feet and beckoned Crispin over to him.

'There is no one else here. Only this. I have to find out. Use this spade. Tell me who it is.'

Crispin dismounted painfully, and stared at the grave and its humble little cross. Then he stared at Baldwin.

'Open a grave marked with the cross of Our Lord? Disturb a soul at peace?'

Baldwin burst out. 'Jesus of Nazareth, man. I have to know, or *my* soul can never be at peace.'

'You may find it – not pleasant,' said Crispin.

Baldwin flung the spade.

'Damn you – dig!'

It did not take Crispin long.

'It is a boy, sir.'

Baldwin ceased his frenzied pacing.

'You are sure?'

'The face is unmarked. Would you like to see?'

Baldwin came and peered.

'So – he kills boys too.'

'The Devil and his minions know no mercy,' said Crispin.

Baldwin stormed off.

Crispin remade the grave and gently replaced the cross. He kneeled and said a prayer, crossed himself, and rose to follow Baldwin, who was halfway towards the smoking ruins of the wagon and the cottars' huts.

Crispin saw him suddenly tense, and stop. Then he burst into a run. He dashed past the wagon and kneeled beside a figure sprawled on the track. Crispin hitched up his skirts and ran too.

When he arrived, Baldwin was wringing his hands.

'Look at her back. See what they have done to her back.'

Crispin crouched. 'These marks were not made by the whip; they are burn marks. They tied her to the wagon, set fire to it, and let it run down the slope. She must have freed herself. Look at the blood on her wrists. She must have had great strength. Then she flung herself down from—' Crispin stopped, bent low, and examined her more closely.

'She lives!'

'What?'

'She lives. She is warm. She breathes.' Crispin ran a hand over her. 'There do not appear to be any broken bones. Nor any wounds.'

Dear God!

Baldwin cleared his throat.

'Is she – did they . . .?'

Crispin glanced uneasily. 'The clothing does not appear disordered.'

'Is there not a better way of making sure?'

'I am not a doctor, sir.'

'You come from Bec; my house is famous for its learning.'

'We can not all aspire to Lanfranc's eminence, sir.'

'You must have taken your turn in the infirmary. You picked up enough to – well – you know. ' Baldwin gestured vaguely.

Crispin looked troubled. 'Our vow of chastity, sir.'

Baldwin lost his temper.

'To the midden with your vow of chastity. What about your vows of mercy and charity? Find out.'

Crispin lifted the material. Baldwin turned away and waited, drumming with a fist on the pommel of his sword.

Crispin gently replaced the skirt.

'I should say that she has not been dishonoured.'

Baldwin raised his eyes and sighed hugely. 'We must get her to shelter and safety.'

Crispin stared. 'Sir Baldwin, you know the wasting parties. There must be a hundred women in this condition, spread all over Sussex.'

'Not like this one. I want her ... saved.'

Crispin noticed the odd spacing of the words. He tried to choose his own words carefully.

'You have ... a special reason?'

'You could call it that. We met once before, when I came here on patrol.'

Crispin said nothing.

Baldwin gestured in annoyance. 'Damn it, man, I can not properly explain it to myself, much less to you. All I know is that I shall not be at rest until I have done what can be done.'

'You mean until *I* have done what can be done,' said Crispin.

'Of course. That is why I brought you. I was afraid we should find something like this. You heard Fulk. God knows what he did to the others.'

'We must make a litter,' said Crispin.

Baldwin stood up and looked all round the valley, partly to ensure that no Saxon soldiers surprised them, partly too – if he were honest – to make sure that no Norman man-at-arms was a witness to his doing manual labour.

Under Crispin's directions, Baldwin fetched and carried, casting furtive glances at Aud's white flesh, which had to be laid bare. While Crispin bathed and bandaged, Baldwin revived the fire and searched for something to drink.

When she was as comfortable as they could make her, clerk and quartermaster sat in front of the fire and sipped beer.

'Do you think you can manage?' said Baldwin.

Crispin nodded. 'I think so, sir. I have my horse. It will not take long to find a wagon lower down the valley.' He smiled wanly. 'It will be a relief not to have to ride any more.'

'You should be safe,' said Baldwin. 'That animal Fulk will not come again; there is nobody left to destroy. The battle will be tomorrow or Sunday; there will be no more patrols out this far.'

'I shall get her to the coast. Some ship or other will be sailing to Normandy if we are patient. A few days of waiting at most, I should say.'

Baldwin gave him some coins.

'Will that be enough? Do you want an escort? I can arrange it.'

Crispin considered.

'I take it you wish this mission to be as – discreet as possible?'

Baldwin blushed. 'Yes.'

'I assume too that you wish me to get her there, win or lose?'

'Win or lose,' said Baldwin. 'Besides, she has no family here now.'

'Then I think we shall manage better alone. A monk and a sick woman will attract less notice than two foreign soldiers. In England, I can speak Latin if necessary; in Normandy, there will be no problem if she stays silent.'

'You will go to Bec, I should not wonder?'

As soon as he said it, Baldwin knew it was a mistake. True, Bec was in his demesne, and he was its chief benefactor, patron, and protector. It was also Crispin's parent house. For all that, it was also the last place to use as a refuge for a woman with whom he could claim no legitimate connection. It was too close to the family seat at Brionne. The lady Albreda would certainly hear of it sooner or later.

Baldwin made a face. Knowing Albreda, sooner. It was asking

for trouble. Never mind Albreda's tongue; think of the scandal, the Duke, Lanfranc – there would be no end to it.

Crispin read his thoughts.

'There is the lady Matilda's new house at Caen,' he ventured.

Holy Trinity. Baldwin remembered all too clearly. Everyone had been there for the consecration in June. Matilda might understand; she was a friend. On the other hand, she was also the Duke's wife. It was not fair to her.

Baldwin thought again.

Geoffrey! He would help. His lady Sybil. Since Fitzosbern's mother, the lady Emma, had been in indifferent health, Sybil was practically in charge at St Amand. If anybody should understood how he felt, and appreciated the need for discretion, she should. So should Geoffrey. A word with Geoffrey here as soon as possible, and a message sent to Sybil by Geoffrey's man, Thierry – if he had not already gone. Yes, that was the answer. Time enough to attend to the details after the battle. If they were not still here, the problem would not arise ...

'Go to St Amand at Rouen,' he said. 'Use my name, and that of my lord Geoffrey de Montbrai, Bishop of Coutances, and ask to see the lady Sybil of Hauteville.'

Crispin made no comment.

Baldwin held out his hand. 'Goodbye, Crispin. I am in your debt.'

Crispin took it. 'Goodbye, Sir Baldwin. Have no fear. I respect your trust in me, and I shall therefore respect your confidence. She will be well cared for.'

Baldwin hesitated before going.

'If I do not – I mean, if the battle – go quietly to my head bailiff at Brionne. He will give you money for – you know.'

Crispin nodded. 'I understand, Sir Baldwin.' He allowed himself one of his rare dry smiles. 'We shall make a good Norman of her. God go with you and God preserve you.'

*

If Gilbert expected his information to come as a thunderbolt, he was to be disappointed. He was able to enjoy the thrill of a dramatic arrival at the gallop. He leaped from the saddle, flung the reins at Ralph, and dashed off towards the Duke's hall.

'Take me to the Duke,' he demanded of a bodyguard.

Instead Sir William Fitzosbern came out.

'I am the one you tell.'

Gilbert blurted his news, though he was careful to omit Harold's sharp references to the Duke's parentage.

Sir William questioned him closely about direction and distance and speed. Gilbert answered as best he could, a little breathlessly, then stood with his hands on his hips awaiting the dramatic reaction and the congratulations.

Sir William grunted. 'Well, that makes sense. It confirms that they are coming through the forest towards Senlac and Telham.'

'You mean you knew?' said Gilbert, forgetting his manners in his surprise.

'You are not the only scout in the army, boy.'

Gilbert's world of triumph began to crumble.

'Others found the English first?'

'We have had news of reliable sightings for the last two or three hours.'

Damn Ralph! Damn Bruno! Damn everyone!

'It seems,' continued Fitzosbern, almost to himself, 'that many of our complicated precautions may not have been needed. Harold is coming the simplest and most direct way after all. Hm!' He seemed to find it faintly amusing.

Gilbert's face fell. 'So you are not surprised?'

'God's Face, of course not. Relieved, I should say. Now we know. Now we can react.'

Fitzosbern rubbed his chin, gazed away abstractedly, and seemed to have forgotten Gilbert. Gilbert fidgeted, not knowing what to do. He coughed politely. Fitzosbern looked up.

'Go on. Go and eat. You have done your job.'

'Sir!'

Gilbert trudged away, thoroughly crestfallen. The only crumb of comfort was that he had not been reprimanded for breaking orders. Thank the saints Sir William had a lot on his mind.

'Hey! You!'

Gilbert stopped and turned.

'Yes, Sir William?'

'You are late!'

'Yes, Sir William.'

Fitzosbern glared, then retired into the hall.

Gilbert did not escape Ralph's wrath so easily.

'And all because of your thrice-damned honour.'

Gilbert – tired, disappointed, ashamed, frustrated – blazed back at him.

'And I suppose you have all had a good laugh about it, thanks to that senile sot, Taillefer.'

'I have told Taillefer exactly what I think of him,' said Ralph. 'Telling you all that nonsense. He might have known you would do something st— Well, no matter. You are back.'

What was the point? The battle was coming tomorrow. Far better to talk about friendship, and loyalty, and duty, and pride in work, and a hundred other things. And no Bruno to raise his eyebrows.

When he had finished, Gilbert drooped.

'I am sorry, Ralph.'

He raised his head. He looked so contrite and lost that Ralph could have put his arms round him. Instead he growled. 'I should think so too.' He swallowed awkwardly. If only for something to say, he asked, 'Did you find him?'

Gilbert blinked. 'What?'

'After all that, did you find him – the Saxon?'

'Yes.'

'And?'

Gilbert waved his hands helplessly. How could he possibly

put it into words? His shock at seeing Edwin at the King's head-quarters. The stilted formalities they exchanged in the company of the stolid Wilfrid. The aching time spent wandering among the clusters of tired fyrdmen, Edwin offering trite comments, himself pretending to be interested, and all the time trying to think of a way to bring up an impossible subject. Taking gloomy bites at the apple every time he came close to forming actual words. Knowing about Adele, and – even more ridiculous – knowing that Edwin did not know that he knew. Unless Sandor had told him – which, come to think of it, was not altogether too fanciful. After all, he had told Taillefer. All of which only added yet another crazy dimension to the situation.

Beyond that, the shame of stupidity, incompetence, and capture, the greater disgrace that he was not worth killing at that time. Above all, the need to get back with what he thought was vital news. Vital! That was a laugh. Finally, the parting, and, just when he was screwing up courage to broach the matter, Wilfrid had given his horse a great wallop on the rump and sent him on his way.

'I do not wish to talk about it. It is a private matter.'

Ralph grimaced to hide a smile.

'So be it. Now, come and eat. You have had a full day. And tomorrow will be yet fuller.'

He put an arm round Gilbert's shoulder. 'Do not carry your anger to sleep with you tonight. When you meet Sandor and Taillefer, remember they are your friends, the best friends you have in this army. If you are wise, you will make the most of them this evening.'

As he would make the most of Gilbert.

Harold patted the trunk of the tree, and looked around.

'This will do.'

'Not much of a tree,' observed Gyrth.

'Apple tree, pear tree, oak tree – who cares?'

'It is half dead, too.'

'I care not if it is black with lightning blast and split from top to bottom. It is the only tree, my brother; that is what matters. A fine rallying point. If the standards fall, the tree will not.'

He gazed up at the gnarled, grey-green branches.

'Think of the magic I can make out of a lonely tree reaching up to God from the summit of a bare hill. I wish I could talk to the Normans as well. I should have them shaking with dumb fear in an hour.'

Gyrth looked at Leofwine and grinned as he shook his head. After a lifetime of regular companionship, his elder brother still had the capacity to take the breath away with his superb self-confidence.

Harold saw them smiling and smiled too, then became more practical.

'Look around you. We overlook the land in front. Good sharp slopes either side, especially on the left. Woodland either side too, and plenty of it behind. We can not be outflanked. Cover for retreat, if necessary – which it will not be. But just in case, there in that ravine behind us, which they will not know is there because of the undergrowth.'

'What about the causeway crossing it?'

'It is centuries old – falling to pieces,' said Harold. 'It will not stand armed men marching on it, much less galloping. If the worst happens and we lose, they will get a shock when they chase us.'

'You are sure, I take it, that William will beset us here?' said Leofwine.

'He has to,' said Harold. 'Our scouts tell us that he has his castle just in from Hastings, between two rivers. We stand on the neck of land between those rivers. We are also astride his route to London. He has no choice.'

371

Gyrth slapped his thigh. 'And if he tries to go past us, we fall on his camp and destroy his ships.'

'He can not leave us to threaten his lines of supply,' said Harold.

'Ha!' said Gyrth. 'Then we have him.'

Leofwine looked searchingly at Harold. 'I take it,' he said, 'you have now given up all idea of an assault on his camp, with his army still in it? You know, speed and surprise, as we have always said.'

'I tell you now,' said Harold, 'I have never thought it was a serious option.'

Gyrth stared. 'What?'

'William is a good general, and not easy to catch napping.'

'You caught Hardrada.'

'Hardrada was resting and celebrating after victory. The last thing he was expecting was me. William is searching for a victory; the *only* thing he is expecting is me. Of course he has had his scouts out. When we caught that boy today it only confirmed what I had suspected all the time.'

'Then why let everyone think we were rushing headlong to fling ourselves on the Normans and throw them into the Channel?'

Harold stroked his moustache. 'It got us here.'

Gyrth looked at Leofwine, who shrugged. Harold tapped him on the shoulder.

'I tell you something else it did too. It kept the Bastard busy building castles. He must know about Stamford by now, and he must know how we won. He would not be human if he did not expect me to try the same thing on him. If an enemy uses a method once, you naturally expect him to use it again, the more so if it is successful.'

'Why are you so sure of William?'

'Because I have seen him fight. There I have the advantage over him; he has never seen me, or at any rate not in the lead. I know how thorough he is. I have said it before: the Normans make war with a spare saddle on every horse. William makes plans to deal with every mishap; I make plans only to deal with the next one. It gives me the advantage; I can bend and turn and catch him on one foot. He thinks we can fight only one way. He is wrong.'

'So you will not strike at his castle simply because he is expecting it,' said Leofwine.

'Not so,' said Harold. 'That would show only scorn for my foe. I shall not strike because of my wariness of him. I have seen Norman castles. Believe me, they are very good.'

He waved an arm to the woods where the army was resting. 'What strength, what gear do we have for a siege? What do we have to get us over fortified walls? How many shire levics and farmers' boys will camp in the open for weeks and watch the Normans feasting in the warm inside? Because, be sure, they will be well stocked and furnished. Thorough, see?'

Harold shook his head. 'No, my brother, we must prise the Bastard away from his cosy castle and his beloved ships. Far enough away to get his feet tired reaching us, and close enough to tempt him to cut and run if the fighting gets too hot.

'And the way to get the best out of our surly yokels and puffing fyrdmen is to tell them there is to be a fight – a big one, once and for all, and that it is tomorrow – before they can change their minds or get their breath back. Exhaustion and curiosity will keep them here tonight.'

Gyrth waved an arm about them. 'And we have it here?'

'It is as good a spot as any.'

Leofwine squinted into the dusk towards Telham Hill. He pointed. 'What about that one?'

Harold shook his head. 'No cover this side of it for approach and retreat. One side too shallow. Field of vision not so good. For the sake of an extra mile or two, not worth considering. William knows we are near. He could start early tomorrow and get there first, and we do not want to be caught down there, halfway, in the open. But we can get here first. Once here, we are astride his way to London, as I said. He dare not go round us.

'So we can watch him getting here second. He has to come to us. We have the high ground. Down there it is full of sandy streams, marsh, soft ground at best – bad going for horses. Woods on our flanks and rear. If we dig our heels in on top here, and bristle with enough spikes and spears, they will never shift us. They will be puffing like old men before they even reach us. Our yokels are used to hoiking bales of hay off carts; all they will have to do instead is poke a few knights off their frightened horses.'

Gyrth lowered his head and looked at him. 'You make it sound easy.'

'No. Simple. Not easy, I agree, but simple. The best plans are the simplest ones. The dullest clod in the whole army will understand that all he has to do is stand fast and poke away all day. I can not in fairness call upon them to do much else.'

'Will they hold? Against heavy cavalry?'

Harold considered.

'If they are still there after the first onset, I should say, yes. If they can turn back the Normans once, it will lift their hearts, and they can turn back the Normans again. We can stiffen them by sprinkling a few housecarls among them if you like.'

'Might be a good idea,' said Gyrth.

'Do you have any plans for counterattack, for pursuit?' said Leofwine.

'Ideas,' said Harold readily, 'but no plans. Have you ever seen a fyrdman capable of bearing more than one thought at a time in his head?'

Leofwine grinned.

'No, my brother,' said Harold. 'First things first. If God shines on us the light of victory, He will also light up for me the way to exploit it. If the Bastard dies, his army will melt away. If not, we besiege him at leisure in his castle and wait for him to run out of salted ox and stacked-up fuel, to starve and to freeze in our winter rains. If the storms are not too bad we can call out our ships to blockade his harbour. If they are too bad, no Norman ships will get through anyway.'

Leofwine gaped.

'No,' said Harold. 'If we are still here at dusk tomorrow, the rest will be easy.'

He clapped his hands and called up the groom with the horses.

'Let us go back and pass on all the good news.'

'Tell me, brother,' said Leofwine, 'are you really so light-hearted? Is there nothing that weighs you down?'

Harold looked hard at him, then at Gyrth.

'Because you are my brothers, I speak openly to you. But remember, only to you.'

He made a signal to keep the groom at a distance.

'It does not fall to the lot of many kings to have to ward off threats to their country's life twice in one year. It is the burden I bear, but it is a burden that becomes light. Why? Because it is for this that kings exist – to guard and to save their people. Because of this I can feel almost glad that God has seen fit to let me justify my kingship – and not once, but twice. If our Father in Heaven sees fit moreover to reward my efforts with victory, so be it. That is over and above. If not, His will be done. My sense of fulfilment is no whit the less.

'I am also easy in my mind because I feel that, in all honesty, I am the only man in England who could do what I am doing now. I may not be of the blood royal, and I know that the boy Edgar still lives, and he has the blood of Cerdic in his body.

'But I am at least English and I am legitimate, which is more than can be said for the son of the tanner's daughter. Above all, I am King. William may talk of broken oaths and perjury and holy relics and Papal banners, but I know exactly what I pledged

in that oath and what I did not, and so does he. All this panoply
of righteous display is only to hide the weakness of his case; he
is a foreign, base-born, invading usurper, and I am legally des-
ignated, elected and proclaimed; I am a crowned and anointed
King – by the Grace of God!'

He paused, then smiled softly.

'I am easy too, because of much love – from my mother, from
my dear Edith, from my children, and from you, my brothers. I
weep only for dead Sweyn and Tostig, and for absent Wulfnoth.'

Gyrth spoke with a catch in his voice. 'Harold, when you talk
like that, I could fight them with my bare hands.'

Each brother flung himself into the arms of the other two. The
mystified groom looked the other way.

'Now,' said Harold, sniffing and wiping his nose. 'Let us go and
tell them all about Caldbec Hill.'

As they mounted, Leofwine frowned. 'How did you know the
name of this place?'

Harold shrugged. 'I often stay in Sussex. I have many manors
here; you know that.'

Gyrth edged beside Leofwine. 'What he means, brother, is that
he has known about this place all the time.'

Leofwine gaped. 'Do you mean you were always going to fight
here, right from the start?'

Harold laughed. 'Not exactly that. But I did know about it, and
I did think it might come in handy.'

Gyrth threw back his head. 'Handy!'

'*Ego te absolvo, in nomine Patris et Filii et Spiritus Sancti.*'

From there to the fire. But not the fire of Hell; only the fire of
warmth and companionship. And of cooking.

Everyone ate well. Carefully hoarded titbits were tossed prodi-
gally into the pot. Even those languishing with nausea or the flux
struggled to a place round the flames and forced something

down. It was better than retching on an empty stomach in a chill Saxon dawn. Only the young and foolish talked loud and long. Those with any imagination asked questions of the men who had fought before. Those with any knowledge thought little and said less; it was safer. Those with long ears, as they returned from confession, hung around the door of the Duke's hall, hoping to pick up fresh gossip to take back to the fireside. They were seen off by short-tempered sentries, who, for once, were not anxious for company.

Inside, the Duke's senior commanders and contingent leaders stretched out hands for a dozen attractive dishes. William was famed for his frugality, and a summons to dine was rarely met with more than mere obedience. This time, though, as even the most fastidious admitted, he had done them proud. It was certainly a delight to eat meat that was not high. God alone knew where the kitchen staff had been hiding that sheep all the time. And the beer was actually drinkable.

William sat and sipped, and watched his vassals making free with his meat and drink. These were the men who were going to make his fortune, and their own, on the morrow – his brothers, Odo and Robert; Fitzosbern, his right hand, who always knew what he was going to decide almost before he did himself; Baldwin, gruff and stuffy, but totally loyal and totally dependable. Were Fitz and Baldwin thinking of their boys' frightened oath to each other, all those years ago in the chapel at Vaudreuil? They had followed a long and choppy path since then, and now they were about to share in the greatest prize of all. Walter Giffard, quick to anger but brave and honourable; Robert of Beaumont, full of promise, but as yet untried in battle command. Giffard sat well away from him. Roger of Montgomery, stolid and patient, pulled meat off the bone and chewed as deliberately as he soldiered. Count Eustace of Boulogne, the hothead, thirsting for honour, like Beaumont. Count Alan of Brittany, excitable, not a Norman, and not popular with the others, but a dashing leader of men – his swordsmen were vital to the general plan.

Further down the table, de Tosny, de Montfort, de Warenne, de Grandmesnil ... Hard men, all of them, but William knew he was their master, at any rate until or unless the battle were lost ...

A pity Coutances was not here. Still, fortunes of war. The training scheme and tactical plan were still sound. He owed a lot to the military prowess of the Bishop of Coutances.

Coutances would also help him to rule the new kingdom. The men round the table would suffice to help him win it.

And Lanfranc! He had to have the moral support and advice of Lanfranc. That obstinate Italian cleric preferred the cloisters at Caen, and had said so many times. Time enough to persuade him afterwards. Present him with the challenge of an entire country-ful of run-down sees and corrupt clerics to reform, and maybe even Lanfranc would succumb to temptation ...

Matilda? Ah ... Soon, perhaps – God willing ...

William set down his cup, clapped his hands, and called for the table to be cleared. Those who were still hungry grabbed what they could and stuffed it into their mouths, while the Duke went over details that had long since been arranged.

They were chiefly concerned with plans for the regency of the lady Matilda on behalf of the boy Robert, in the event, God forbid, of his Grace not surviving the morrow.

Here William spoke with great deliberation.

'May I remind you that you have all sworn a sacred oath – on holy relics – to support my lady and the prince Robert. May I remind you too that we are all here because Harold broke *his* oath, and will fully merit the divine punishment that awaits him.

'He too swore on holy relics,' said the Duke. 'Tomorrow, I shall have some of those relics round my neck.' He looked sternly round the table. 'God will always search out and punish the false perjurer.'

Everyone kept his eyes discreetly down.

The Duke went on to give an account of the progress that his chancellor and clerks had already made in drawing up a full list of the estates owned by most of the leading Saxon earls and thegns. It was nowhere near complete, and Fitzosbern and the senior commanders knew it was not complete, but it was an obvious carrot to dangle at this time.

'In other words,' Sir Walter Giffard whispered to Montgomery, 'the more Saxons you kill, the better off you will be.'

Sir Roger of Montgomery frowned. He knew he was not a man of great intelligence, but there were some things that were so obvious that even he did not want them spelled out to him. Like everyone else round the table, he was looking forward to a mighty enhancement of his personal fortune after the victory. Being the master of a border fief in southern Normandy called for more expenses on security than the average. And Mabel spent money like water, much of it for the wrong reasons. Besides being a shrew, she was a snob, and riven with jealousy of any other man's wife who lived in what she saw as greater state than herself. Her extravagance was embarrassing and infuriating as well as worrying. Montgomery often did not know where the next penny was coming from.

However, his friend Walter kept silence while the Duke rehearsed plans for the defence of the castle, the rearguard action in case of withdrawal, and embarkation in case of total defeat. Sir Walter did wonder whether, in the event of defeat, there would be any ships needed for evacuation. The news from Stamford appeared to indicate that Hardrada's army had been virtually annihilated. One account spoke of three hundred ships arriving and only twenty-odd required to carry off the survivors.

Giffard shook his head. It was all very well for Fitzosbern to trot out one of his favourite sayings: 'There is always something to be saved from any situation.' But that always depended upon the saviour, whoever he was, being still alive. He looked round the table. Everyone here – the Duke included – knew perfectly well that this was a life-or-death gamble. Hardrada had known it too, and look what had happened to him.

Everyone had known it from the moment the Duke had unveiled his plans for conquest and sought their support, way back at the Council of Lillebonne, and at every other council too. They had rubbed their chins at Lillebonne, and they had scratched their heads at Bonneville, and they had made long faces at Caen. It was not faint-heartedness nor fear that had held them back; it was a careful calculation of the odds, and they looked impracticably long. Until wily Fitzosbern argued them round, as he always did.

Giffard listened to Fitzosbern and the Duke going patiently through the order of march and order of battle. He had heard it so many times before that he found himself mouthing the words with them . . . 'Archers first, then infantry, then the knights.' It was the usual method – arrows and crossbow bolts to soften them up; heavy infantry to shake them up; and cavalry to break them up, carve them up, and, with luck, chase them up. Nothing had changed, substantially, since the days of Charlemagne and the arrival of the mailed knight on the battlefield. God knows how the Romans had managed to conquer the world with little more than the legions.

Giffard yawned. Fitzosbern continued imperturbably. 'Count Alan of Brittany will lead the left; Sir Walter Giffard the centre; Sir Roger of Montgomery the right. Count Alan will have, besides his own swordsmen, the knights of Maine and Poitou, and the Angevins. Sir Roger will have the knights from the Ile de France, Champagne, and Vermandois, and the Flemings. He will be attended by Robert of Beaumont, who has distinguised himself in the summer campaign in Normandy and the training since we landed.'

Giffard sniffed. Summer campaign? Little more than armed reconnaissances and recruiting drives. Call that fighting? And as for the parades and drills that Geoffrey was pleased to call advanced training ... Giffard had said it before and he would say it again: there was no substitute for battle experience. There was no substitute for the tried and tested methods. And there was no substitute for a man's knightly honour if you wanted to get the best out of him.

He felt a distinct thrill pass through his fighting arm as he contemplated the coming conflict. Eyesight going? Running out of puff? Muscles turning to flab? Living in the past? We should see, we should see. When that puppy had survived half as many clashes as he had, then, perhaps, he could claim that he had done some service.

Baldwin de Clair ploughed through endless details about wagons and spare arrows and spears, lanes of withdrawal, buckets and water-bearers, grooms and extra mounts, concentration of reserves, until Sir Walter could barely sit still for impatience.

What was all the fuss about? The Bastard had the finest body of experienced, battle-hardened, heavy cavalry in Christendom. All he had to do was find some open ground and turn it loose against these stolid, plodding fyrdmen. If that failed, well, it would be just too bad, and the planning for patterns of withdrawal and priorities of embarkation and all the rest would prove a complete waste of time. A defeat was a shambles and that was all there was to it. If it was not a shambles, it was not a defeat, and it could be turned round to a victory. And God knows, victories were chaotic enough.

The time for debate and council and planning was over. The only thing to do now was to move fast on to the enemy and get the battle over and done with, and the sooner they did it the better.

As for God's Will and the holy relics, Sir Walter could not help thinking that a good night's sleep, an early breakfast, and a brisk march to set the blood tingling would prove a great deal more use than a neckful of holy relics and a forest of Papal banners.

God, he had noticed in a long and eventful life, was distinctly inclined to help those who showed willingness to help themselves.

That reminded him: as soon as this infernal meeting was over, he must find a priest and—

He jumped. The Duke was on his feet. The meeting was breaking up. Limbs were stretched; yawns were stifled.

'Now,' said William, 'we visit the army.'

There was a noise that sounded dangerously like a grumble. One man spoke up, however.

'All of us, sir?' said Fulk Bloodeye.

'All of us,' said the Duke, not even looking at him as he gathered his gloves. Nobody else met Fulk's eye.

Fulk, deprived of an audience, shrugged and made ready.

Everyone stood back as the Duke strode towards the door. He paused in the open space of the threshold, with the evening sky behind him. There was just enough light to pick out gleams on the rings of mail at his shoulders.

Nobody could see his eyes in the shadow, but no man doubted that they were darting from one face to the next as he spoke. The voice shed a little of its customary harshness and speed of delivery.

'My lords,' he said, 'tomorrow, if God wills it, we commit ourselves to the greatest quest that could be offered to any knight in Christendom – to fight under the sacred banner of His Holiness the Pope to secure a whole apostate kingdom. A whole kingdom. Surely no man can reasonably expect such a moment to come twice in a lifetime.

'Each of us, therefore, must make sure that nothing has been overlooked that may prevent us from acquitting ourselves to the very limit that our honour, our courage, and our ambition demand.'

Saints and angels! thought Montgomery. Never before had he heard the Bastard string together half so many words.

The Duke looked out towards the tents and shacks and wagons and fires, then back at his silent vassals.

'Out there is an army. I say that word with due consideration and pride. A whole army. Not a motley of faint-hearts, drained by a daily dribble of desertion; not a pack of caged animals, awaiting only the key of the keeper to be able to roam at will in selfish lust of blood and private profit. I have taken all that Christendom has to offer, and I have forged it and tempered it until it is a single weapon to do my will. My will!'

Somebody coughed.

William glanced in his direction.

'I know their motives, true. But they also know mine, and they know my will. We shall all achieve our desires – God willing – because I have built a force that is capable of it. All through spring and summer I have trained it and held it, with not one mutiny, not one revolt, not one false dissipation of strength. Every tremor of energy has been turned inward to tense the spirit. Week after week I have strung the bow tighter and tighter. Only I, Duke William of Normandy, could have held such a bowstring.

'And now – we are ready to release it, to deliver at the perjured Saxon such a shaft of concentrated force that even the conqueror of Hardrada himself, the man who mastered the greatest Viking of all, will be unable to stand against it. Splendour of God – how great will be our victory!'

He paused. The gleams on his hauberk grew fewer; his silhouette darkened against the fading light.

'But first, we visit my army. All of us,' he added meaningly. 'Avarice draws men to the field, but only leaders take them into battle. Tomorrow we shall expect many of these men to die. They have a right to see the faces of the men who will lead them to that death, or, worse, send them.'

William fastened his short cloak. 'Follow me, and be seen.'

He went off, humming tonelessly to himself.

As they filed out, Walter Giffard looked at Roger of Montgomery, and smiled. How could they possibly lose?

Sir Walter Giffard found further reason to admire his duke as they progressed round the camp.

William was not a man who was normally good at company. He did not charm men as Harold did (even Normans testified to the Saxon's personal magic on his visit in 'sixty-four). He did not coin jokes or clap soldiers on the shoulder. He did not make memorable remarks or grand gestures. His eye was cold and restless, his tongue was harsh, his hand was hard, and his lash was savage.

Yet he had made his authority total and his will spring-clear to each and every man.

Giffard marvelled at the effect of William's presence. Everywhere men leaped to their feet, their expressions a mixture of gratification, eagerness, and apprehension. A man as tense as that, they felt, would miss nothing. They fell over themselves to answer his questions, partly, Giffard realised, because they were such practical, understanding questions. They dived to show a piece of equipment; they fumbled in their excitement to demonstrate it. They agreed fulsomely with his predictions for the coming day. As he turned away to move on, they exchanged delighted glances with each other behind his back, their eyes glowing in the dancing firelight. When he had gone they fell back to their sacks and sheepskins, put their heads together, and relived the previous few minutes a dozen times over.

For a man who habitually said little, William made Giffard's jaw drop at his uncanny skill in communicating. Understandably the men of Normandy responded easily enough – soldiers from the Bessin, Perche, the Pays de Bray, the Cotentin, the Pays de Caux, the Bocage, the Vexin, the Pays d'Ouche – though it was something of a feat to get these men of often rival regions to work together. But men from the surrounding lands responded too; Giffard recognised details of dress or heard idioms and accents from Ponthieu, Artois, Picardy, Vermandois; from Champagne, Nevers, the Auvergne; from Maine, Poitou, Anjou, Touraine, Brittany. There were men from as far south as Guienne, Périgord, Gascony and Toulouse. The stolid mercenaries and shifty soldiers of fortune – from Hainault, Brabant, Lotharingia, Franconia; from Swabia, Bavaria, Lombardy; from Apulia, Calabria, Sicily – many with feeble French – took strength from the resolution in his voice. Small stray groups from distant lands on the outermost frontiers of Christendom and Moorish legend – Navarre, Béarn, Leon, Barcelona, Castile, Roussillon and Foix – felt a surge of confidence at the sight of the tall, vigorous, commanding figure.

The Duke gave much attention to the archers and the few crossbowmen. Giffard was again surprised at the extent of the Duke's knowledge. Surprised too that the Bastard should bother so much with such troops – mere skirmishers, optional extras, expendable material. They were fringe men, base-born, poorly paid and easily lost. They had little discipline, less tradition, and no code of honour. They were notoriously difficult to organise, and tried to surround their simple craft with a cloud of false mystery. Archers were bad enough, but crossbowmen delighted in baffling you with deep talk of ratchets and lubrication and tension and trajectory. Moreover, they seemed to be under the impression that there was nobody else on the battlefield except themselves.

All bowmen were gloomy by nature too; everything was wrong. They were forever gazing bleakly at the clouds and muttering about bowstrings, or testing the wind with a damp finger and shaking their heads.

'Why does he concern himself with them?' Giffard asked sourly, as they plodded through sticky mud between wagons and fletchers' fires.

'Because they are first in,' said Montgomery. 'If they falter, what will the rest do? Especially the paid infantry.'

'Damned mercenaries!'

'Damned they may be, especially with Bloodeye in charge of them. But necessary, Walter, necessary.'

Giffard growled. He stood apart in stiff silence while William and Fulk talked to Florens of Arras and the tall Rainald and one or two others. Even so, his soldier's eye told him that Fulk's men were well equipped, purposeful, and in fine shape. The workmanship on their padded and studded jerkins was of high quality. Many had steel-banded helmets with nasal guards. A few possessèd mail. All were well shod. Fulk maintained, among other things, a full-time shoemaker who went everywhere with them. They had their own armourer too.

'You have to hand it to him,' said Montgomery quietly. 'They are beautifully turned out. He may be a devil, but he knows how to lead men and he is a fine soldier.'

'Until he gets paid,' said Giffard. 'Then watch out.'

Montgomery smiled. 'Walter, we are all here in hope of reward.'

Giffard glared at him, but said nothing.

He became better tempered when they reached the knights' area. After a few words with his own contingent from Longueville, he felt more disposed to follow the Duke around the rest. He was also familiar with the talk – of saddles and gauntlets and shield-straps, above all, of stirrups. A wise knight checked his stirrups time and time again. Even when he was ready in the saddle, it was the last thing his groom looked at before he rode off. And before the charge, secure the wrist-thong of the sword, tighten the shield-strap on the arm, ease out awkward folds in the mail, fasten the chin-strap of the helmet, flex fingers in the gauntlets – all these things. But finally, brace the feet in the stirrups: a man's life depended on their strength and sure fastening.

Giffard felt at home. Here were men he understood. They lived and thought and fought the same way that he did. Some, perhaps, were roughly born, but their career and training gave them all the same outlook. You had to pass through the long years of practice and apprenticeship before you could appreciate the full meaning of the word 'knight'. No wide-eyed beginner, no envious clerk, no gawping ploughboy, no fat tradesman, no clever book-reader – nobody could understand the many skills that were necessary to the mastery of the knightly craft.

The sword, the dagger, the mace, the spear, the lance – all had to be studied, weighed, handled. All made their own demands of strength, dexterity and finesse. The horse too: not your plodding pack pony, but a huge animal of great strength and spirit, which had to be mastered, understood, handled, and taught to obey a hundred commands of gait, speed and manoeuvre, to tolerate violence and clash and the most terrible noise. There were a thousand details of gear and equipment that had to be learned, if a knight was to be reliably prepared for battle, and moreover if he was not to be deceived by wily grooms and slovenly craftsmen.

When you were on the animal's back at last and ready for action, the most difficult trick of all – that of coordination, the putting together of all the skills so smoothly that horse and rider and weapons moved as one, each an extension merely of the others.

Men who had triumphed over all these obstacles shared a past and a commitment and a professional pride that needed no words of expression or communication. It was obvious – or if it was not it ought to be – that any other soldiers were second-rate by comparison. Man for man, there really was no question of their superiority. All they had to do tomorrow was prove it.

Proving his own capacity was another matter, but Beaumont would get a surprise that would blow the fluff off his face ...

Giffard was dismayed, and furious, when the Duke moved on yet again.

There was a tour of the new castle. They all had to put up with the company of the gloomy cripple, Ranulf of Dreux, as he moaned about imperfections and deplored poor fields of fire. Giffard noticed, however, that some timbers had decorative carvings and protective paint on them. If workmen had found time for that, Ranulf's preparations must indeed be well advanced.

Still the Duke was not finished. Interminably the tour went on, through what Fitzosbern called the 'hidden army'. When Giffard and the others tried to hang back, William looked sharply and said simply, 'Talk to them.'

So Giffard and his fellows swallowed hard and tried to think of things to say to servants and grooms and water-boys; to wagoners and carters and carriers; to armourers and saddlers and smiths; to the teeming host of men whose work would put the Duke's army in the field the next day.

'Why? Why, for God's sake?' said Giffard to Fitzosbern during another weary trudge. 'All they react to is a sharp command and a cheap reward. They will not respect us for all this friends-and-comrades nonsense. Do it with soldiers – yes, I can accept that, up to a point. But not this riff-raff. We are like travelling preachers, calling sinners to repentance.'

'It is not sin we are fighting, Walter,' said Fitzosbern.

'What then?'

'Fear,' said Fitzosbern.

'What?'

'Fear, Walter. No man is proof against it. If a man told me he was, I should fear him more than I fear the enemy.'

He waved a hand at two dark, cowled figures flitting past. 'Have you ever seen so many priests so busy before? Geoffrey will have penitents lining up at his bedside, broken leg or no broken leg. Even Odo will be doing God's work tonight for once instead of his own.' He poked Giffard familiarly in the chest. 'And if you are honest, Walter, you will admit that you will seek to cleanse the soul before dawn comes. I know I shall.'

Giffard made a vague noise in the back of his throat.

'The Duke is a wise man, Walter,' continued Fitzosbern. 'He

is also a professional. He leaves nothing to chance. He does not talk to cooks and pot-boys because he is a kind shepherd. He does not squat round fires with rude bowmen because he is a saint. He knows that the greatest enemy, next to Harold – perhaps greater than Harold – is fear. Fear is a disease that can break out anywhere, and can spread with terrible speed. It can eat into a man's mind and paralyse a sword arm without his knowing whence it comes. The only way to stop it is to throw a blanket of reassurance around the shoulders of every man here, so that none will suffer the chill of dread, and none therefore will infect his companion.'

Fitzosbern stopped outside his tent. He scuffed some mud off his boots.

'There is maybe something else too. Tomorrow will be a special day. William wants them to realise that.'

Giffard grunted. 'They surely realise they might die. Is that not special enough?'

Fitzosbern shook his head vigorously. 'No. I mean really special. Besides, a man might die any day. Just think, Walter. Hardrada, Harold, and William. The three greatest commanders in the whole of Christendom. Striving for supremacy, each against the other. And all within three weeks. For an entire kingdom. We are not talking about petty border forays and a scuffle of sieges at frontier castles. An entire kingdom! And only one of those three champions will be alive at the end of it. One has already gone. What a challenge for the other two! What a moment!'

Giffard had never seen Fitz so carried away. Fitzosbern realised it, and made an effort to resume his usual flat style. He shrugged.

'Well. I think William is trying to convey to them the sense of the occasion, that is all. This will be no ordinary battle, and they must rise to it. Victory will go – God willing – to the man who plans for everything. Everything.'

Giffard did not look entirely convinced. 'Well . . . all I can say is, I should never have done all that.'

Fitzosbern grinned. 'Just so. And that, Walter, explains why you are a vassal and he is a duke. Soon, we hope, a king.'

Wilfrid the housecarl stopped by a group of Berkshire fyrdmen.

'Everything all right?'

A voice came out from under a fresh shelter of sticks, fern, and leafmould.

'Marvellous. Just send up another cask of ale and a couple of shoulders of roast pork, will you? And see that the crackling is properly done this time.'

Wilfrid smiled wryly as he looked around. They had made several small coverts and windbreaks. The fire burned confidently. The remains of some animal were still spitted over the flames. One man was darning a hole in his breeches. Another was combing his beard. From the shadows of a wattle refuge came the noise of a blade being sharpened. Spread all over the ground were a score of bits and pieces. Wilfrid never ceased to be amazed at how quickly these men could turn a tiny patch of open countryside into a scene of domesticity.

'You seem to be settled enough,' he said.

'Our work is sheep, mate. We spend half our time doing this.'

A stocky, youngish man, prematurely balding, made himself the spokesman.

Wilfrid used his toe to push a stray log back into the flames.

'Your work tomorrow is Normans.'

The sheepman shrugged. 'Sheep or Normans – we trim them both to size. All the same really.'

'Just so long as you stay put and do not go running all over the hill after them.'

'We do not chase our sheep.'

'Good,' said Wilfrid. 'Make sure you do not break the line and chase Normans.'

'Not even if they run?'

'Not even if they run.'

'Seems daft to me.'

'Nobody asked you to think about it.'

'Just die for it, eh?'

'If need be, yes. Now, is there anything else? Before I send up the ale and the roast pork.'

The sheepman allowed himself a smile, then became serious again. He stood up and came close to Wilfrid.

'There is one thing,' he said quietly. 'Who is that?'

He jerked his head towards a big, dark man who sat a few yards away. He too had made a shelter and a fire, but shared it with no one.

'No idea,' said Wilfrid. 'Try asking him.'

'No fear,' said the sheepman. 'Look at his face. Who would want to go near him?'

'Has he spoken to you?' said Wilfrid.

'No. He just came from nowhere, made himself a spot, and there he is.' He shuddered. 'Makes my flesh creep.'

'Why?'

'He is a cripple, for a start. See his crutch? What are cripples doing here?'

Wilfrid peered. 'Is that all?'

The sheepman grimaced in bafflement. 'And he seems to be – well, the best way I can say it is – he is in a sort of shock. He moves as if he is in his sleep. Crazed, you might say. If you ask me—'

'Is he armed?' said Wilfrid.

'I should say so. Christ! You should see his axe. Apart from eat, he has done nothing since he got here but sharpen it. Gets on your nerves. Oh, yes – talking of eating – another funny thing.'

'What is that?'

'Mushrooms. He has a pocketful of mushrooms.'

'How do you know?'

'Seen them.'

'So? We all eat mushrooms.'

'Not the ones he has. Besides –' he dropped his voice to a whisper – 'he has not eaten them. Takes them out, looks at them. As if he is making sure they are there.'

Wilfrid looked towards the new arrival. He could make out only vaguely dark features and a few locks of dark hair under the blanket hood. He seemed quiet enough – hardly the raving madman or the Devil-gripped invalid.

'Leave him alone, I should. He is not bothering you.'

'But the size of him!'

'He is on our side. Why else would he be here?'

'Makes my flesh creep,' muttered the sheepman again, as he returned to his fire.

Wilfrid spared a few thoughts for the matter as he walked back to headquarters.

Mushrooms before a battle? He had heard stories. They were common enough in the Danelaw. The man did not look Danish. Then Wilfrid had not been able to see much of his face. Not all Danes were blond; there had to be some dark ones, he supposed. Would they really keep up such practices so long after Alfred and the wars against the Great Army of Guthrum? He had seen no sign of it at Stamford. Then he had hardly had much time, under the circumstances, to look for it.

Wilfrid kicked some dead leaves.

Ah, well, mad or sane, he was a big fellow, able to look after himself. If his axe was as big as they said, he might topple a Norman or two before they ran him through with a spear.

'*Ego te absolvo, in nomine Patris et Filii et Spiritus Sancti.*'

Geoffrey had said it so many times that he was listening to his own voice as if it were that of somebody else. He had given up listening to the muttered confessions of the endless line of penitents. What did it matter? Absolution was what they wanted, not a shoulder to cry on. Not at a time like this.

They got penance first, of course, and, did they but know it, they owed the heaviness of it to my lord bishop's broken leg. Their prayers to the Holy Virgin to shepherd their souls into Heaven were curiously punctuated by muttered, and equally fervent, desires that the Devil would pilot that of my lord bishop into Hell. My lord bishop's clerks were filling a sizeable box with physical, and metallic, proof of the army's true sorrow for its sins. Geoffrey remained gruff and grumpy and unashamed. The chances were that my lord bishop of Bayeux was charging them for hearing confession in the first place.

'Bless me, father, for I have sinned . . .'

Thierry should be well on his way by now, his head as full of messages as his stomach was full of stew from my lord duke's kitchens.

'Never miss the opportunity, my lord, of a good meal. You never know where the next one is coming from. If God puts a full plate before me, who am I to go against the Will of the Almighty?'

You could never shame Thierry. Nor could you ever teach him; most of that last meal would finish on the foam lined waves of the Channel.

But he would deliver all his messages, and reliably too. My lady Matilda, now waiting and swearing at her serving women in St Valéry, would have word of the Duke. At St Amand in Rouen, my lady Emma would have news of her son Fitzosbern, and her sub-prioress, the lady Sybil, would receive the curious request of Baldwin about some Saxon woman or other.

Most unlike Baldwin. Difficult to understand it properly. Baldwin had been embarrassed, and had not given a very clear account of it. Still, if that was what he wanted. What criticism could a bishop offer, a bishop whose own ex-paramour was the sub-prioress in question?

And what could he say to Sybil on his own account? What words could be put in Thierry's mouth that would be a substitute for the look in his eyes or the feelings in his heart? He was not sure of them himself.

That he loved her? Did he still? After all these years? Could any unrequited passion, however strong, remain constant all that time? Was it then no more than friendship? Surely not. A true spiritual fusion of like souls? Hardly! Sybil may have been true to her veil, but my lord bishop of Coutances had had occasion to let the vow of chastity slip *his* mind.

And yet, at a time such as this, it was Sybil whose image came to him – nobody else's. Except, naturally, his family – Mother, Father, brother Mauger, and Ivo, who had taught him nearly everything he knew. Certainly no other woman.

So what was he to say?

Thierry cleared his throat. 'Beg pardon, my lord.'

'Yes?'

'There is no need to concern yourself.'

'What do you mean?'

Thierry burped.

'I have been taking messages to the lady Sybil for many years. I have been passing on the spirit of them all that time. Believe me, my lord, you do not have to think of anything special. The lady Sybil will understand. And, if your Grace will pardon the liberty, so do I.'

Geoffrey opened his mouth to chastise him, but, to his surprise, Thierry went down on his knees.

'You have been a good lord to me, sir. I could have hoped for none better. If Ivo were here, he would have said the same. If anything – I mean if – well, I just wanted you to know.'

Geoffrey again opened his mouth, but lumps formed instead of words.

Thierry prompted him. 'If you could bless me, my lord. Please. It would mean a great deal.'

So Thierry had gone, and Fitzosbern had come in, and Giffard, and Montgomery, and Count Alan. Together they had gone over the plan of battle yet again. If Giffard had any reservations about it, he kept them to himself. Now was not the time. If that was the way the Duke and Geoffrey wanted to do it, he and the others would give it their very best effort. If it did not work, thought Giffard, the chances were that he would not get the opportunity to say, 'I told you so,' so the argument was one only for scholars.

Geoffrey had been full of last-minute thoughts, final recommendations, late suggestions.

Fitzosbern grinned. 'Trust us, Geoffrey. We do know. We have all been here as long as you.'

'It is all right for you,' Geoffrey grumbled. 'You will not have to lie here all day tomorrow, wondering.'

Montgomery laughed. 'You will find out soon enough, Geoffrey, if it is a Saxon hand that pulls back your tent flap in the evening.'

After they had gone, Geoffrey turned again to the line of penitents.

'Bless me, father, for I have sinned . . .'

Could it be done? To control a line of knights once committed to the charge. To wind back its strength as one would the ratchet of a crossbow, and release it again at will.

Ever since he had first commanded cavalry in battle, he had dreamed of putting the might of the mailed knight to better use. Tighter formations, straighter lines, stronger impact, greater numbers – always greater numbers. Planned withdrawal, swift re-grouping, fresh assault. Unstoppable hammer blows that no enemy could withstand.

Years of trial and error, of plan and mishap, of hope and frustration; of stupid knights and stuffy commanders; of bad timing and poor execution. Now – at last – here in England. A duke committed to the value of the idea; time to practise and to convince squadron commanders; excellent strategic planning and logistic backup; spare mounts by the hundred; and the greatest number of knights seen in the whole century. There would never be such a chance again.

True, the Duke relied also on his archers and his infantry, but they would only start the battle; it would be the heavy cavalry that would press it home and finish it. What a victory it could be! An entire kingdom. If Harold died, there would be little effective resistance. If the boy Edgar had had any appreciable following, they would have chosen him King in the first place.

What a chance then. And what a prize!

Against them? One of the three greatest commanders in Christendom. Since the defeat of Hardrada, one of the two greatest. Backed up by a core of the finest heavy infantry since the legions. They were the ones who had to be broken. If they went, the fyrd and the ragtag would melt away.

But how to move them? If the hammer blows did not do it, dare they try the most ambitious idea of all? Could the English be duped by a feigned retreat? It was the greatest test of his plans. Could the knights really be held together through an assault, a timed withdrawal, a planned full wheel and re-form, and a second charge?

He hoped it would not be necessary, but, if it were, would Fitzosbern do it? Would the Duke back him when it really came to it? Or would the old ideas of Giffard prevail? But – if they tried, and succeeded, what a vindication!

Ivo had always said that Geoffrey's father was a greater warrior than his son, but to be proved the greater tactician was a worthy consolation.

Geoffrey sighed. If only Ivo were alive to see. Dear Ivo – that gruff, thick-handed barrel of a man who had been his guardian and friend while Father was away; who had set him on his first destrier; who had taught him the profession of knightly arms; who had been at his side through a score of battles and sieges and a hundred skirmishes and a thousand rides; who, alone of the household, still called him, though admittedly only under great stress, 'Master Geoffrey'.

Would Ivo be proud of his work tomorrow? Geoffrey grimaced. Not if it was a Saxon hand that pulled back his tent-flap in the evening.

'Bless me, father, for I have sinned . . .'

'I am sorry to hear about Berry,' said the King.

Edwin grimaced. Harold put an arm round his shoulders.

'There will be others to love. You have my word. We shall have good times again, eh?'

'Yes, sir. I shall get the swine, sir.'

Harold smiled. 'Do not try too hard. We shall win this fight by staying put, not by rushing about to settle personal scores.'

Edwin looked unconvinced.

Harold finished his meal and stood up.

'You are not fighting for revenge.'

'It was not your dog, sir.'

'No, but it is my kingdom, and I know best how to save it. You will do as I say.'

'What about my honour?'

'To Hell with your honour. If you wish to serve me in this battle, any "honour" you have will be to stand in my line with my housecarls and my fyrdmen. Think yourself lucky to be there tomorrow morning. Think yourself even luckier to be there tomorrow evening. In between, you obey my orders. Do I have your word?'

Edwin gulped. 'Yes, sir. You have my word.'

'Good.' Harold fastened a big cloak round his shoulders. 'I think you had better come with me. I shall show you many men of "honour" who do not wear their private misery like a beggar's sores. Follow.'

Waving to a few housecarls to accompany him, Harold strode off without glancing back. Edwin, after a moment of hesitation, hurried unwillingly after him.

What he saw in the next hour or so drove all grief and injured pride from his mind. He had seen Harold charm men before, but never had he witnessed such miracles as his king performed that evening.

Whenever Harold reached a group round a fire – proud housecarls, lofty thegns, dour fyrdmen, grumbling ploughmen – he had the trick of becoming one of them without diminishing his royalty in any way. An uncanny instinct told him exactly what action to perform. Edwin was never conscious of Harold working his way in from the outside. He picked a piece of meat off a spit, or peered at the sharpness of a spearhead, or simply squatted and warmed his hands at the blaze, and instantly he was a full member of the group. He did not make speeches to them; he gossiped with them, asked about their families, moaned about blisters. They accepted him at once and spoke without fear or affectation.

Edwin observed, however, that Harold usually managed to slide the occasional piece of military intelligence or general encouragement into the conversation without anyone noticing. It was as if he were an ordinary soldier discussing the King's plans.

'The top of a hill is as good a spot as any ... there are earth spirits up there, you know, round the only tree. Very bare hilltop. Especially unkind to outsiders or intruders. Very strong local tradition. Of course, I know you lads are not superstitious and neither am I. All the same, I do not think I should like to be in the Normans' shoes – if only to be on the safe side, eh? ... high ground – they will have to come to us, and we can watch them struggling in the mud ... a Viking bandit or a Norman bandit – what is the difference? The owner always fights better than the thief ... William is unfit and overweight; needs a big

box, I hear, to help him mount a horse. God help the horse,
eh? . . . he knows he has bitten off more than he can chew this
time . . . we have a victory under our belts. What do they have?
Seasickness . . . we have done it once; we can do it again – stands
to reason . . . he has mercenaries, foreigners, all sorts of riff-raff.
How well do such men fight in a bad cause? Can they stand with
the men of Anglia, or the lions of Wessex, or the heroes of
Stamford, in defence of their own land? . . . horses will not jump
at spears; it is a well-known fact . . . you will have an easy time
tomorrow; you can fight all day sitting on your arse. It is up to
the Bastard to get us off it. Those of you with fat arses are laughing . . . we are up here; he is down there. It is as simple as that.
And that is how we keep it. And we keep it by doing nothing . . .
how much easier can you have it? Stay put all day and win a great
victory . . . if you think you will bore your children with talk of
Stamford and the bridge, just wait till they hear about the
Bastard and Caldbec Hill . . . William is the gambler; we are on
to a sure thing . . . the son of the tanner's daughter? Bah! We shall
skin him alive!'

Time and again great gales of laughter rose into the night air.
When Harold arrived, men could hardly wait for sleep; when he
left, they could not wait for the dawn.

Edwin knew, with every sense, brain, and instinct at his command, and beyond any shadow of a doubt, that he was close to
a man who could make history. What did Berry matter? What
did revenge matter? Aud and her clawing desire? Gorm, Godric,
the mill, even a lost love in Normandy? Destiny dawned on the
morrow, and Edwin was conscious of a fullness of existence that
he had never known before. It came with the knowledge that he
was going to be part of that destiny. He knew in his bones that
tomorrow, Saturday, the fourteenth of October, in the year of
Our Lord one thousand and sixty-six, would be a day like no
other. He knew that it would be the longest day – and the greatest day – of his entire existence. He knew that, if he survived, and

whatever the outcome of the battle, he would look back on that day as a turning-point in his life.

Long after stand-down, the candles continued to burn in Baldwin's tent.

He sipped some hot broth; beer at this hour of the night only made him colder than he already was. He hitched a blanket tighter round his shoulders. It would get colder still before the dawn.

However, he was ready. The wagons had been checked and double-checked. He had inspected the guards on them nearly every hour. If the Flemings were to steal from them tonight they would have to be invisible. Spare wheels and axles, extra draught animals, drivers, baggage guards, miles of rope, great buckets of grease – he did not see how he could have forgotten anything. Food, drink, rough bandages, leather for emergency tack – the baggage train was bursting with readiness, almost literally. It was ready to move at an hour's notice.

Baldwin sniffed like Crispin. If something were to go wrong from now on, he did not see how the blame for it could be laid at his door.

The Duke had kept them at stand-to since clear sightings of the English arrival had been confirmed. As long as an evening or even a night assault had seemed remotely possible, he had maintained full readiness. Now the latest relays of scouts had brought detailed reports of a definite slowing down of the English army, and, later, of hosts of campfires over seven miles away.

Surely there was no danger now, not tonight. Harold had marched his men from Yorkshire. Yorkshire! That had to be over two hundred miles. If they were sighted only today and were out of normal scouting range yesterday, that meant they must have covered well over twenty miles since dawn. They could not possibly manage another seven miles on top of that in order to fling themselves, in the dark, on a heavily fortified position that had not been reconnoitred. Not even an army of Nordic gods would contemplate such a manoeuvre.

Nevertheless, William had waited until he was quite sure, until his best scouts told him that the campfires were genuine. There were old stories of clever generals who had fooled their enemies as to their whereabouts by getting their men to light hundreds of bare fires while the army left the camp empty. One was forced to admire William's thoroughness, but his refusal to take the slightest avoidable risk could be tiresome.

So William at last gave the word, and everyone had a few hours to himself. For what? For sleep? Baldwin grunted and shivered. Hardly.

For confession? He had done that.

For talk? Crispin was not there. Baldwin had never thought he would miss Crispin's hatchet fact and his disdainful sniff. The other commanders – Giffard, Montgomery, Alan of Brittany and the rest – had their own worries and their own preoccupations. Fitzosbern was still closeted with William, but the time would come when even Fitz would be sent away. Their threefold bond of mutual loyalty was no whit less valid now than it had ever been, but at a moment like this, only William carried the ultimate burden, and, without Matilda, the only company he could tolerate would be his own.

Baldwin wound his blanket closer and wandered to the door of his tent. His fire was blazing well – of course. Yet, from force of habit, he stooped and picked up another log to toss into the flames. There was still a big pile. And why not? He was the quartermaster; if he could not have a good supply, he would like to know who could.

For once, he did not wave away the young soldiers who sat around.

He looked up at the night sky. Plenty of stars were coming out.

It was going to get colder before the morning. No wind. Probably sunny tomorrow. Good for moving an army – the less mud the better.

Someone had dragged a plank from the Duke's kitchen and propped it across two water barrels. Baldwin came and sat on one end. Without saying a word, the young man next to him edged up to give him more room.

He was peeling a carrot.

He glanced up at Baldwin, recognised his rank, and kept silent. He had been brought up by a stern father to speak to his betters only when he was spoken to, and the faraway expression on this officer's face warned him against interrupting a private line of thought.

Baldwin sighed. It was a funny thing in life, he had noticed, that a man never really knew himself. If anyone had told him a week ago that he would feel easy with a woman, he would have laughed, albeit somewhat bitterly, and no doubt only inwardly. If they had told him that the woman would be English, he would probably have struck them.

For the life of him, he could not understand what had made him do what he had done for Aud. Aud ... thank God it was a Danish name; getting his tongue round some of the Saxon ones would have been the very Devil. Thank God too for Crispin. He could be trusted to care for her. Trusted too not to blurt the name of Sir Baldwin de Clair all over Sussex.

He did not relish the idea of the story being passed round the camp. With Crispin and Aud out of the way, it would not be. He flushed at the thought of the insolence he had already been forced to tolerate from William Capra and Ralph Pomeroy. Well, he had seen to them; their sore backs would make them think twice before they did it again. They had disobeyed orders by not reporting to him that morning, but he would catch up with them after the battle – assuming that some Saxon housecarl had not obliged in the meantime by cutting them in half.

Baldwin raised his head suddenly.

Fulk!

Bloodeye! That monster. *He* knew. He knew about Aud. He had seen them together. That was why he had done it.

Baldwin knew he often became annoyed. He shouted and he swore at men. He had been furious with Capra and Pomeroy. Fulk Bloodeye he now hated. Not only for his outrage on Aud, but for his taunts about it beforehand. Yet more, because Baldwin suspected that Fulk enjoyed the taunting more than he had enjoyed the outrage; that he enjoyed creating badness for its own sake. With Baldwin's hatred was mingled revulsion and fear.

He, Sir Baldwin de Clair, was no saint, God knew! He was an ordinary, human, fallible man, no better and no worse than most others of his class. He looked after himself and his own. Naturally. Why else would God have placed him here? What else would God expect him to do with the resources with which He had endowed him? What self-respecting Norman knight would not avail himself of every chance that presented itself? How else had they survived and prospered since the days of Rollo and his band of adventurers? How else were the Hautevilles surviving in Italy and Sicily? Why else was he here now, shivering by a campfire in a foreign land, committed – to the death – to a gamble so colossal that Robert Guiscard himself might have thought twice?

He, Baldwin de Clair, had made a good marriage, fathered sons, guaranteed his line. If Albreda's tongue was the price, so be it. There were higher prices; look at Mabel of Montgomery. He respected the proprieties – the Truce of God, the knightly code, the concept of honour. He was not a blasphemer, aside from normal campfire swearing; he heard Mass; he went to confession; he gave alms; he endowed, and was proud of, his local monastery. Perfunctory, maybe, but he could never imagine himself *not* doing any of those things. They were all part of life, like camping or riding a horse.

There must be a worthwhile reason for it all; there must be something pushing him to do it. For want of a better word, you could call it goodness.

Certainly, the recent impact of Fulk Bloodeye on his life was causing him to suspect the existence of the presence and power of evil. He was enough of a philosopher to see that if you believed in the one you had to believe in the other.

It was not Fulk's size or appearance; he had seen big and ugly men before. It was not Fulk's profession; Baldwin understood the mercenary mentality. Nor was it the misshapen little Turk who fawned and purred at his elbow – though, God's Teeth, there was something unnatural in that too. It was not the violence, the insolence, the cruelty. One saw only too much of that in life.

Perhaps it was all of those things, the sum total that by its very agglomeration created a fresh element, a new dimension that Baldwin could not put into words, could barely conceive in his own mind.

Perhaps it was simpler. Perhaps it was Fulk's ease, not his effort; his casual strength, his lazy talent, his obvious education, his lack of interest in so many things that his betters thought important; the fear that, should Fulk ever put out all his force and all his powers, very little could stand in his way. Only William showed no wariness of him.

Baldwin, in short, felt threatened. This caused him, for the first time in his life, to bend his mind to, to concentrate on, the means of destruction of a single human being . . .

The sound of crunching broke into his thoughts. He looked at the young soldier, now halfway through his carrot.

'What is your name, son?'

The young man swallowed quickly.

'Brian, sir.'

'Breton, eh?'

'Yes, sir, from Dol. In the north it is, not far from the River Couesnon, just where—'

'I know where it is.'

'Sorry, sir.'

He fell silent. Baldwin, having found a friendly spirit to take his mind off disturbing matters, did not wish to kill the conversation through a misunderstanding.

'In action tomorrow, then?'

'Yes, sir. Swordsman, me. We go in after the archers.'

'On the left?'

'Yes, sir. Count Alan commanding. We have the Angevins with us, and the Poitou lot. Some Manceaux as well.' He laughed nervously. 'So we shall not be lonely.'

In the firelight his face looked pinched and tight.

'First time, is it?' said Baldwin.

'Beg pardon, sir?'

'This is your first major enga— your first big battle?'

'Yes, sir.' He pulled a face. 'Always a first time, eh, sir?'

For some odd reason, a phrase from two or three days ago drifted into Baldwin's mind: 'All right for learning on.' He pushed it away, forcing himself to concentrate on the youth beside him.

'Going to kill plenty of Saxons then?'

Brian fished another carrot out of his pocket and began peeling it.

'Hard to say, sir. One at a time, I dare say. To be honest, all I have thought about so far is staying alive.'

Baldwin harrumphed. 'Not a bad idea at that.'

Brian took another bite and chewed thoughtfully.

'Well, you see, sir, a lot of these men here have nothing on their minds except victory and loot and honour and glory and trampling the faces of the dead. Me, I want more than that.' He waved the stub of carrot. 'Oh, I want to win, of course. And I want to – well, I do not want to let down the men beside me. But I have someone waiting for me at home. Most of this lot –' again the carrot stub waved airily '– most of them think of nothing but killing and winning. I think about afterwards. It is good to have something to think about afterwards. Do you not agree, sir?'

Baldwin found himself smiling. 'Yes. I do.'

He stood up. Perhaps he would have that doze after all.

'Good night, sir,' said Brian. 'And good luck tomorrow.'

Baldwin patted him on the shoulder, a familiarity that he rarely had the confidence to display.

On an impulse, he turned away from his tent door and went to a store shed near the castle kitchens.

'Open up,' he said to a startled guard.

It took him a few minutes of groping in the dark before he found the sack he wanted. He ordered the mystified guard to lock up again.

As he passed the fire on the way back to the tent, he tossed the carrots into Brian's lap.

'For tomorrow,' he said. 'One at a time, eh?'

Brian gaped for a moment, then exclaimed in delight.

'Thank you very much, sir. Good night, sir, God bless.'

'Have you seen a big man, a big man with a crutch?'

If Gorm asked the question once, he asked it a hundred times.

For a mile or two he had tried to follow Godric's trail, but lost it in leaf-strewn woods. He knew that if he kept in a rough north-easterly direction he would cross the track of the army, though before or after they passed he could not be sure.

When he had been travelling for two hours, he began to realise how many years it had been since he had settled down after his journeyings. He was bathed in sweat; his legs ached; his breath was short and laboured. One or two steep hills brought him almost to his knees.

Driven as he was, he would take no rest.

Find Godric. Find Godric and tell him. Then rest. Find Godric before it was too late.

By dusk, he was reeling with fatigue, when he came upon the marks left by the army. A few stragglers littered the sides of the churned track.

'Have you seen a big man, a big man with a crutch?'

Tired beyond words, they shook their lowered heads without even looking at him, as if the mere sound of his voice added to their misery.

Stumbling and slipping on the broken ground, Gorm struggled on, pausing before each broken fyrdman and fighting for breath before he could gasp out his question.

'Have you seen a big man ...'

Now and then, he was forced to pause when nausea swept over him. He leaned on his stick, swallowed, and licked his lips, fighting to overcome the fullness in his throat and the tightness in his chest.

The only comfort was that it was now impossible to lose the trail. He knew he was getting nearer because the number of stragglers grew. Wiping the sweat from his stinging eyes, he accosted each one.

'Have you seen ...'

By nightfall, he knew that he had to stop. He was barely moving at all with each pace. Peering into the growing darkness, he made out a tiny, half-derelict hut on the edge of a copse – some makeshift shepherd's windbreak or other.

With his breath rasping and his temples throbbing, he staggered the last few yards and crawled inside.

Weary swearwords met him. For once his extra weight told in his favour. He squeezed further in, and pushed aside the two mud-strewn fyrdmen by the sheer bulk of his body. They swore again, eased arms and legs into a better position, and went back to sleep.

Gorm had just enough presence of mind to wipe off as much sweat as possible and put on his jerkin, which had been dangling from his shoulder.

In the morning he would be less tired. He would be up early. A quick drink and a bite, then off. It would be easier to find Godric in daylight. With his height, you could pick him out anywhere, even among the housecarls. Then a few words of explanation and Godric would see.

Funny how you thought more clearly when you were resting. Silly not to have done it before. God's Face – they smelled, these fyrdmen. But at least they kept you warm.

Robert of Beaumont stared up into the shadows at the top of his tall tent. Grand it all looked during the day. Now that he had dismissed his servants and valets, it was empty, vast, cold – like the vault of a great cathedral. He had had them take away his favourite dog.

He put his hands behind his head. His thoughts were more than company enough for this night . . .

It was not death he feared on the morrow; it was failure. No success meant no glory; no glory meant no reward; no reward meant no Judith. Waiting for his inheritance was out of the question; his father was in sound health. The very idea was base, not worthy of a knight. In the chill dark he blushed that the thought had even occurred to him.

To go to Judith's guardian as a landless suitor – an adventurer – was worse. To have the world think that he did not love her. That he lusted after the fortune and the body of an underage girl. He took hold of the crucifix she had given him – the crucifix that had once been warm with the clasp of her soft hands.

He would never dishonour her, never! He would go back after the battle, loaded with favours and rewards from the Duke. The King! And he would marry her, make her his lady. No true guardian could refuse such an offer.

He almost moaned at the memory of their last meeting. Her

shining eyes. Her merry, skipping step. Carrying her piggyback, feeling the caress of her forearms under his chin, the glow of her body against him, the vibration of her laughter.

Please God, on this one day of all days, let him do well!

Five blanketed figures lay in the straw at the bottom of the wagon.

Flat on his back, his long legs stretched out and his toes pointing straight up, Taillefer looked up into the blackness under the awning.

He had yet again played the role that the world demanded of him. He had lounged and slept and snored. He had returned joke for joke. He had drunk more than his share and played the coward and the sot and the false scholar.

'Tell us a story, Taillefer.'

'Blind us with knowledge, Taillefer.'

'Wake up, Taillefer, you old trembler.'

'Taillefer is at it again.'

'Taillefer the "Cleaver of Steel"? Taillefer the "Cutter of Iron"? Ha! More like Taillebeurre, the "Cutter of Butter". "Butter-Cutter"!'

They had all roared at that one.

How they had laughed too when they saw him sharpening his sword.

'Not much butter in the English army, Taillefer.'

'What is it for, Taillefer? Cutting a dash?'

The weariness of habit with which he replied was taken for the habit of weariness with which they liked to identify him.

Was he really somebody else, or had he become the person they expected him to be? Had the mask become the man?

Suppose they could have seen him as he was.

If they could have gone back thirty-odd years and seen him as a lusty young shepherd, as a lover, as a mourner, as a bitter, failed novice, as a soldier of fortune, as a pilgrim. Such stories could he tell them! Real stories!

He raised his eyebrows and pulled down the corners of his mouth. They would not believe those either. It was hard to believe them himself. Now.

Did his heart really leap with such love in those brilliant mountain dawns? Were the reds and blues and greens so vivid that no artist would dare to paint them for fear of being called a liar? In the agony of his loss, did the colour really drain from the world? Was he dead to everything save to the bleating of a new-born lamb? Did he really perform such prodigies of piety and self-denial in his search for purpose and peace? Did he really commit the whole range of deeds, from the heroic to the obscene, that all soldiers do in time of war? Did he really weep and tremble, at the end of his long journey, and feel such fullness that he expected his heart to burst?

He sighed.

The past existed only in the minds of those who remembered. It began to trickle away the minute it had happened, and, no matter how hard you tried, it continued to drain away from the vessel of the memory until nothing was left but a scum round the edge and a stain on the bottom. That was all you had to remind you of the richness and depth of it.

All he did nowadays was to make up a false brew to put in its place.

His hand felt the pommel of Edwin's dagger. He wished now that he had not stolen it; it was a smallness that he regretted. He should have given it back when they parted yesterday. But then he had been in no fit state to remember such things.

He hoped the two prisoners got back to their home, that the big one was able to save his woman. It would be only just; they were good folk, whose only crime was to be in the way of war.

How many times had he seen innocent people – struggling to

be happy with their life in the tiny world in which God had imprisoned them, the tiny world that they had made rich with their love and their work – turned into shocked cripples or baffled scarecrows by the blind irruption of war? Small wonder they hoped for mercy from God; they rarely received it from the men who broke in.

And many of the men who broke in were just as lost in their way – lonely, far from their own tiny world, frightened of dying, afraid of fear itself. Taillefer knew; he had seen their faces gazing up at his in the light of a thousand fires. His own craft existed to try to take away some of that fear and loneliness. When they teased him with cowardice they were only hiding the fear of showing their own.

When they drank and talked to each other, they boasted of past exploits. They relived the glory. If it did not exist, they created it. When they listened to Taillefer in the firelight, their faces told a different story – silent, intent, wistful, eager, sad, exultant by turns. They became what they really were – worried, diffident, homesick young men.

Perhaps this truth was the mainspring of Taillefer's devotion to his craft. Men teased him with being a word-wizard, a teller of tall tales, a spinner of stories. Such a man, who could never say a straight sentence – how could he be relied upon? What did he know of real life, of the world of truth?

Taillefer smiled sadly to himself. He knew the truth. He saw it every time he told a story. God had given him this gift of word magic. He poured fable into men's ears, but he saw truth come out of men's eyes.

No written book could ever reproduce such a spell as he wove. No wonder Jesus had been a talker, not a writer.

Taillefer's eyes gleamed – to share with Our Lord such a gift for moving men.

He sighed. How awful then that such men should, on the morrow, be turned by war into paralysed, self-soiled cowards, or screaming lumps of writhing flesh, or slavering monsters of demonic energy.

It would be his fate to witness it yet again. Later he would have to spin his story about *this* battle, and tell it before the next battle. He would have to grovel in the mud of reality to find brightly coloured threads to weave into a tapestry of epic and glory. And why? To induce men to leap with joy into the mud of reality once more when the trumpets blared again.

He coughed, wiped his mouth, and replaced his damp kerchief.

Or perhaps not.

Further along the wagon, curled tensely in his blanket, and trying to command sleep, Gilbert resolved that tomorrow – tomorrow of all days – he would be a model of caution and correctness. He would be sensible, he would follow orders, he would remember all that Ralph had taught him. He would push his private miseries to the back of his mind; only the most observant would notice the occasional flicker of pain that would pass across his impassive face.

Not that he intended to go unnoticed – far from it. He would distinguish himself, though, not by rash indiscretion but by his superb example of duty and obedient service. His serene courage would shine as a beacon to frightened archers and unsteady infantry, as an example to hesitant horsemen. Not only would Ralph commend him; Fitzosbern could not but notice him, even perhaps the Duke ...

'Arise, Sir Gilbert of Avranches.'

A battlefield investiture. It did happen sometimes, so they said.

There would be no more 'Master Senlac' jibes then, no more sniggers about his capture. And if anyone dared to refer to Adele in a disrespectul way, he would call them out to single combat – assuming of course that they were of similar knightly standing to himself.

How proud his father amd mother would be. How Mahaut

would cry! No more back-breaking toil for them. Land and an inheritance for baby Hugh. And for the new son. Time enough to see to Edwin the ravisher after the battle – assuming he had survived (being a cowardly seducer, he probably would). Much more dignifed too. One might even take him through the courts, as befitted the new status. It would display to the Saxons that their new Norman masters had proper respect for the law. It would make Adele respect him more.

His hand went to his neck for the crucifix she had given him. It was not there. He groped feverishly.

When had he lost it? In the ravine? When he was knocked off his horse by the tree? At the mill when they stripped and washed him? He grimaced, and almost whimpered in his mortification.

He felt in the straw around his blanket, more in the need to do something than in any real hope of finding it . . .

Of course! When he lay in the grass, waiting to die. It must be still there. He cursed.

Sandor heard him, and was instantly awake.

'You have a thing wrong?' he whispered.

Gilbert told him.

Sandor reached out and held his hand. 'Have no fear. You have the love of friends, and God is love.'

Gilbert swallowed a lump in his throat. 'Thank you, Sandor. All the same . . .'

Sandor nudged the blanket under which Gilbert's hauberk nestled, away from damp night air.

'You have this too.'

Gilbert put his hand on it, and heard the slight, muffled jingle. 'I know, but—'

'One moment.'

He heard Sandor moving. Then something was pressed into his hand.

'Sandor, it is a cross.'

413

'Is what you want, yes?'

'But I could not take yours.'

'No worry. I have two.'

'Sandor?'

'Yes?'

'You are a liar.'

'Devilish good liar too. Better than you think. But do not worry for me. I have many old Magyar gods for my company. They follow me across the plains from far, far east.'

'Then why do you have this cross?'

'Many gods better than few. Some could forget a man. Gods are only human.'

'But a crucifix?'

'A man collects many things to help through his life – or his death.'

There was a pause.

'Sandor?'

'Yes?'

'That ivory horn of yours. Where did it come from?'

'Long story. Sleepy wagon before battle is not a good time. Some day I play it for thee.'

'You mean it sounds too?'

'Is first use. Drinking is only good idea after.'

'But how—'

A hand closed over Gilbert's mouth.

'My friend, you put a stopper in a hole to stop things running out when not needed. Now, sleep!'

'Yes. Sorry. Good night, Sandor.'

'Good night, my friend.'

Gilbert wriggled into a more comfortable position.

Great Jesus! If only Sandor did not smell so much.

The dried vomit odour still clung to his clothes. The greedy little goblin had deliberately made himself sick twice that evening. It was revolting.

'The food is there, my friend,' Sandor had said, waving a greasy bone in the air. 'We must not waste it. When shall we eat like this again?'

So Sandor had eaten and eaten as if his life depended on it. The blood from half-cooked meat ran down his chin.

Gilbert saw him staggering from the fire to the wagon, and suddenly realised that he was drunk with food.

Gilbert shut his eyes, and screwed up his face again as Sandor tensed himself and broke wind ...

Sandor grimaced. Tomorrow, all his babies, his beloved horses, went to war.

What protection were they going to get from the Christian god – that humble, dead carpenter? Sandor fingered the jade talisman that hung on a horsehair lanyard round his neck. It was smooth after many fondlings from many generations during many journeys over many miles across the great plains and steppes to the very edge of the world.

On the other hand, Taillefer seemed to think highly of that carpenter, and Taillefer was a man of much wisdom, a man who understood men's hearts.

Sandor put a hand into his pocket, and found his little wooden crucifix, given him by Alexius, his horse-teacher.

No harm in being on the safe side. Whichever god was stronger would know that the other was weaker, and so would not be angry or jealous.

Even so, fighting in battle protected by a god of love? Risky. And struggling to seize from its guardians the top of a hill where a lonely tree might harbour angry spirits? Risky too ...

Ralph lay on his side and listened to Bruno's snoring. How annoying and reassuring that noise was, all at the same time. Bruno could be dull; he was taciturn and inclined to shortness of temper. The great slab of a face rarely creased into a full smile.

He could be clumsy and awkward, the common fault of the tall, gangling man. When he was off horseback, there seemed to be simply too much of him.

Ralph smiled wryly. In over ten years of close associaton, Bruno had hardly uttered a score of words about himself. He had not referred to father, mother, wife, or family. He had betrayed no worries, confessed to no sins or regrets, admitted no aspirations. His friendship was undemanding and undemonstrative. Ralph could count on one hand the number of times Bruno had shown anything approaching depth of feeling in his direction. After ten full seasons of campaigning, Ralph knew no more about Bruno than he had at the outset.

The only thing he had seen him show affection for was his horse, Sorrel. The swelling on the leg had not completely disappeared, despite Sandor's best attention. Bruno would have a difficult decision to make in the morning. He would make it on his own, without fuss. Ralph had long since learned not to feel excluded. Bruno would not have seen it like that; he would simply decide that Sorrel was his worry, not to be inflicted on others, certainly not on those close to him. Being excluded, in fact, was a sort of compliment.

However, Bruno had one priceless gift: he was totally dependable. Ralph could trust him with his life – indeed had done so more than once. Bruno had placed the same confidence in him, as if it were the most natural thing in the world, with a readiness and lack of fuss that were almost unnerving. Ralph could think of no man he would rather have at his side tomorrow than the man who was snoring beside him tonight.

Gilbert? Ah, that was different. You saw nothing of Bruno's heart; you saw all of Gilbert's. He wore it on his face as if someone had painted it there. It was both touching and flattering to have a lad who was so keen to learn, so bitter about his mistakes, so desperate to improve. Loyalty shone out of his eyes. He watched as a dog watches his master, rejoicing at his pleasure,

crushed at his censure, glancing warily for signs of returning favour. Being close to Gilbert was like carrying a mirror round with you.

'He wants to see admiration in your eyes.' Taillefer.

'The boy is a loser.' Bruno.

Ralph grimaced.

Taillefer said he was too hard; Bruno said he was too soft.

'He could become a winner.' Taillefer.

'Michael is dead.' Bruno.

Ralph sighed.

They were both right. If he, Ralph, did not show some favour, however small, the boy's heart would break, and Ralph would lose him. If he did not put some iron into him, he would make one mistake too many. Only a matter of time. And Ralph would lose him again.

If he confounded Taillefer and Bruno, and made a man of Gilbert, that would kill the part of him that was Michael, and Ralph would lose him a third time.

Ralph turned over and tried to command sleep. He was looking all round a problem again. Seeing too much.

It would be the same with the battle tomorrow. The Duke would keep them free from the fighting, for courier work and for maintaining contact with a retreating enemy. So he and Bruno could watch every move from a safe distance, like a third party watching a game of chess. He could study and appraise like ... like God Himself. With little or no involvement. As always.

Nor could he get excited about the prospect of spoils in England. He had never joined in the eager campfire conversations, when men were drooling over the rumours of loot and land beyond flash-eyed greed. England did not attract him as a country. Neither did its weather. Neither did the picture of himself as a settled man.

So he would probably do what he usually did – move. So much for the future.

The morrow? There seemed little cause for nerves, at any rate not on his own account. Perhaps not on Gilbert's either, if God could be relied upon to toss a tiny piece of His much-prayed-for Divine favour in their direction.

As scouts they would be out of the way, so Gilbert would not be allowed to fling himself dramatically at the English host in the first onset. A host of – what was it? – 'fifty thousand men'?

Where did the boy get his figures from? There were probably not that many able-bodied men in the whole of Normandy.

However, the battle would take his mind off his precious honour for a few hours. If he survived, it would be ten to one that the Saxon who had got in first with his wife would be dead, so the sooner he went home and forgot about the whole business, the happier he would be. Pretty, plump little thing she was, too. A lusty son and another on the way. He should think himself lucky. Perhaps it would be that which would really make a man of him.

And if it meant that Michael was dead and buried, once and for all? Well, perhaps he, Ralph of Gisors, should think *himself* lucky too.

So all Gilbert had to do was get through the day without doing anything stupid . . .

Ralph crossed himself and shut his eyes.

14 October

'The gleam of Durendal'

'God's Face, what an hour to move an army!'

A Norman knight spat.

Sir Roger of Montgomery grinned to himself in the dark. The men were grumbling well this morning – a good sign. All the grooms, valets and servants had turned out of sleep at the first order and worked with a will – another good sign.

Sir Roger looked towards a faint glow announcing the coming dawn. Where would he be this time tomorrow, he wondered.

He crossed himself, took the reins from his chief groom, and mounted. It was time to bring his contingent to the assembly point. Scouts had been out yet again since midnight. The bowmen were already on the march, and the infantry would be starting about now.

He looked at the huge dark shadow that he knew represented the armed knights he had brought to the Duke's army. This was his personal contribution, paid for out of his own pocket – already half-drained by Mabel's extravagances. He would command many more than this in the coming battle, but these men stood for his own fief, his most intimate pride and honour. With them, he was fulfilling his promises made at the councils of Lillebonne and Bonneville and Caen. If his men did what they were trained for; if they received the Divine Grace they had been praying for; if they came through the dangers of the day they had been waiting for – the rewards were going to be enormous, greater than a man's slit-eyed visions of greed.

He heard the reassuring chink of mail and the jingle of harness and the slap of leather.

'Let us be on our way.'

A man bit into an apple. The chopping noise sounded unnaturally loud.

'Ready when you are, Sir Roger.'

On their way to the assembly point, they passed Baldwin's baggage wagons. A veritable herd of spare draught oxen stood patiently tethered, while a small army of drivers, stable lads, potboys, and carriers rushed about under the orders of Baldwin's staff.

Montgomery paid Baldwin a silent compliment. Baldwin was a terrible old woman, but his wagons would reach the field, which was more than happened in some armies. The fighting men would not be gasping with thirst and forced to break off the engagement, or driven to forage for food after the battle. Nor would they go short of spare arrows or spears.

A storm of neighing told Montgomery that the column of war mounts was also nearby. The bandy little Hungarian knew his job too. Hardly a single broken leg on the crossing. And nearly all mounts kept in fine fettle since. Plenty of fodder too – thanks once more to Baldwin. The thought occurred that, victory or no victory, breeders like Sir Walter Giffard had already made a fortune out of the expedition.

Near the castle, more wagons were being loaded with the Duke's tent and personal gear. One had to admire the man for his supreme confidence. Heaven help the steward who did not have his Grace's frugal comforts immediately on hand when he had won the battle.

Montgomery remembered the story that was already common talk in the army about the Channel crossing. According to the usual version, the Duke's own ship had sailed out of sight of the others, despite its warning lantern at the mast-head. Early dawn had found it alone off the English coast with not a friendly sail in sight. The Duke told his staff to stop fussing and to get on with serving his breakfast. The other ships duly caught up. It was easy to make light of it afterwards, but it had been a nasty moment, and the Duke had not turned a hair.

Sir Roger could think of no man he would rather have leading him on the day – not Harold, not Hardrada, not the fabled Guiscard. He remembered the glance of smug confidence that Walter Giffard had flashed to him the night before.

At that moment Sir Walter himself loomed out of the shadows and greeted him.

'Clear night. Should be a good day.'

'I hope so, Walter. Where is the Duke?'

'Mass, would you believe it.'

'How do you know?'

'I was there. Odo was officiating – of course. Full pontificals. At this hour!'

Montgomery smiled. 'So you did go to confession after all.'

Giffard pretended he had not heard.

'And do you know – the reprobate was wearing mail under his bishop's robes. You could hear it. Truly the most convenient consciences of all reside with the princes of the Church.'

'Just so long as they use a mace and not a sword. You know what it says.'

Giffard grunted. 'Yes. Smash a man's head in; that is God's holy work. Cut him down or run him through, and you have committed mortal sin. If that is theology, I am glad I am a soldier.'

Montgomery leaned over and patted him on the shoulder. 'Come, Walter. Leave Odo to his capacious conscience. Let us do a day of simple soldiering.'

'Enjoy the roast pork?'

Wilfrid edged up beside the sheepman and his friends.

Although the morning was clear and sharp, they were stumbling along with their hoods thrown back.

'If we had, we could bear these stakes without sweating like horses.'

'You will be glad of them when you get there.'

'Where is "there"?'

'There.'

Wilfrid pointed to the bare hilltop where a solitary tree stood black against the light morning sky. A scrap of moon was fading.

The sheepman squinted. 'There is no cover there at all.'

'That is why you will be glad of the stakes.'

The sheepman spat. 'What do we do? Hide behind this bough of a tree when they fire the arrows?'

'No. You stick it in the ground and point it towards the Norman knights. Their archers will not trouble you; it is the cavalry who will be the threat.'

'All right for you. Those great shields.'

'Just as heavy as your stakes.'

The sheepman lifted his load from one shoulder to the other. 'Here – did you really walk all the way from York in a week?'

Wilfrid glanced down at him with fierce pride.

'All the way.'

'In a week?'

'We had a break in London,' Wilfrid admitted.

They walked on in silence for a while, the sheepman glancing occasionally at Wilfrid's gleaming mail and beautifully decorated scabbard. But they were not what he looked at most.

'Can I have a look at your axe?'

It was the best way he could think of to get a rest; they had been rushed off their feet since they rose.

Wilfrid stopped, unhooked the thong, and held it out to him. The sheepman unloaded the stake and leaned it against himself. He took the axe reverently in both hands.

The madman with the mushrooms had a large axe, but nothing like this. The handle was much longer than the farm tool the sheepman was used to, and the head was gigantic. The edge was deeply curved too, more than that of the farm axe.

It was of course heavy, but not as heavy as he would have expected, because it was so beautifully balanced. The handle was darkly polished and smooth, except for an area of grooves and chafing around the hand-grip. The sheepman paused with his fingers over the leather sleeve covering the blade.

'May I?'

Wilfrid unloosed the laces and slipped it off.

The others gathered round the sheepman and stared in amazement and admiration. Never before had they seen such workmanship, such harmony of line, such dazzling brightness. The patterns and decorations on the two faces and the back of the head had been done with as much loving attention to detail as could have been bestowed upon an altar cross. Its very beauty gave them a thrill of horror as they remembered its awful purpose. Somehow it would not have been so awful if it had looked ugly, or even plain.

Inevitably one of them tried the edge with his thumb.

'Christ!'

The sheepman carefully replaced the leather sleeve and handed it back for Wilfrid to do up the laces.

'Who would be a Norman, eh?'

Wilfrid rehung the axe. 'Who indeed?'

'What do all the patterns mean?'

Wilfrid smiled. 'Enough questions. Move.'

As they humped their loads once again, the sheepman asked, 'What is the great hurry? There are no Normans up there.'

'Nor do we want them. But they are coming soon. The King's scouts have made contact. We have dug the Bastard out of his castle. He will now fight on our ground, but we must be there first. And we are late already. Everyone was tired yesterday and slept too long.'

'It is all right for you; you march hundreds of miles every day.'

'You bear your loads badly,' said Wilfrid. 'Look at those things there. Bouncing like udders on a frightened cow.'

'Only made them last night,' said the sheepman.

'Looks like it.'

The sheepman fished one out and tapped it on his palm. It consisted only of a stick with a sharp stone bound to one end.

'We used to make these when we were boys, to throw at birds. Never thought we would be throwing them at men. Just made them a bit bigger.'

Wilfrid grunted. 'Any more secret weapons?'

The sheepman indicated his crook and his knife.

'You can get hold of anything with this. Fetch anything down. And with this – a tumbled Norman on his back is like a sheep on its back.'

Wilfrid laughed. 'I hope so, for your sake. Now – go to the right of that old apple tree. Make for the right-hand end of the hill, the western end, the end away from the sun. When you get there, you will be put into line by Earl Gyrth. Make your position as strong as possible and stay put.'

'Where are you going?'

'To say the same thing to other groups like yours. I have lingered here long enough.'

'Here – before you go ...'

'Yes? Be quick.'

'That madman – the one with the mushrooms. Have you seen him today?'

'No. Too many other things to see to.'

'Well, we do not want him round us. Staring into air like that. Upsets a man.'

Wilfrid sighed. 'Throw one of your bird-sticks at him. Perhaps you will frighten him off.'

Wilfrid moved away.

'Oh – one other thing,' said the sheepman.

'What now?'

'What is it called?'

'What is what called?'

'This place. Where we are now. What is it called?'

'Caldbec Hill. Why?'

The sheepman shrugged. 'Just thought I should like to know the name. Considering.'

'Well?'

Ralph and Bruno dismounted.

'They are on Senlac, sir. As we suspected.'

Bruno glanced at Ralph. The word 'we', implying that they shared in the Duke's private thoughts, was only part of Ralph's swagger, but it could have been taken as insubordination by a lesser man. The Duke ignored it.

'What short of shape are they in?'

'Confused, I should say, sir, though a line of battle is being formed.'

William glanced at the bright eastern sky. If they moved fast, they might get in one attack with the sun directly behind them. On the other hand, he had no intention of spoiling things at this stage by unseemly rush. Let the English do the hurrying.

He turned to Fitzosbern and asked a question with his eyebrows. As usual, Fitzosbern's answer was an echo of his own thoughts.

'I suggest, sir, we move with all haste to concentrate behind Telham.'

'I agree. Haste, but no rush. And we wait this side until all main contingents have arrived. We do not show our hand until we are ready to show our whole body.'

'We could commence deployment, sir,' suggested Fitzosbern. 'It would ease congestion behind Telham as all units arrive.'

'No! We march as an army over the brow of Telham. I do not want the English sneering at parts of us; I want them trembling at all of us. We concentrate behind Telham.'

'Just so, my lord,' said Fitzosbern formally. He stood to attention. 'Permit me to congratulate you on bringing the Saxon to battle.'

William grunted. 'Pass the word, Fitz. Not a man over the brow until I say. And get my grooms to me. You?' He turned to Ralph and Bruno. 'Go and have another look. I want a clear picture of their battle array.'

He began his familiar tuneless humming, and walked off to see his brothers. Odo was seen to pray and bless him.

Ralph looked at Bruno, who was crouching to examine Sorrel's leg.

'How is it?'

'So far, so good. Sandor has done marvels, but I do not wish to strain it more than I have to. I would have wished not to make a second trip to Senlac.'

'Stay and rest her,' said Ralph. 'I shall take Gilbert. The boy is burning to do something.'

Bruno looked up. 'And you can keep an eye on him.'

'Go to Hell,' said Ralph, and cantered off.

*

When Gorm woke, he was alone. He was also hungry and shaking with cold.

He crawled backwards out of his shelter and stood up with difficulty. Dusting the dead leaves from his clothes, he looked about him.

The countryside seemed empty. There was no trace of the army. No stragglers either.

He looked up at the sun. Great God, he had slept a long time! No wonder the fyrdmen had gone.

Speed! Haste! It would be hard enough to find Godric in the battle array; it would be impossible once the battle started.

He paused only for the needs of nature, and a few wolfed mouthfuls of bread and cheese. He crawled back into the shelter to retrieve his stick, took a gulp from his leather flask, and stumbled back to the main track.

Before very long he had ceased shivering and started sweating again. His legs were stiff. His sore feet reminded him of the blisters they had gathered the day before. There was a dull ache across his shoulders.

As his fatigue grew, his judgement dimmed. His thoughts faded and blurred into only one theme – find Godric and tell him. And, please God, find him before he did something stupid in the battle.

'Never mind the point. Get them in first.'

A ploughman stopped his whittling and paused with his knife in mid-air.

Earl Leofwine gestured impatiently from his horse. 'Get the foot of the stake firmly set.'

'How?'

'Think of something!' blazed Leofwine. He turned to a housecarl. 'Tell him, for God's sake,' he said, and trotted off down the line.

Some clods were still putting them in upright.

'They are not for hiding behind,' roared Leofwine. 'They are for fighting behind. We want a hedgehog, not a wall. And sharpen them afterwards, if you have time.'

He had never seen such a crowd of fussing old women in his life. They might be milling round a stall in a market. You had to say the same thing time and time again, and the minute you turned your back they were doing it wrong once more.

They still thought a battle was some kind of exciting duel, with the victor chasing gloriously across the field after the flee-ing, eye-popped enemy. They had no idea – yet – that it meant a lot of crouching and watching and waiting and sweating; of pushing and shoving and bleeding and dying; of fluke and chance and coincidence and rank bad luck – with the victor grateful, if he was able, to limp away to camp for a drink and a rest, too tired to cheer or weep.

Harold had told him, and Gyrth, and the other thegns, over and over: 'Get it into their heads: whatever happens, they stay. Win or lose, they stay. If the sky falls in, they stay where they are. It is a chance they may die where they stand, but if they run down into that low ground, without flank support, it is not a chance; it is a certainty.'

'What if the whole Norman line breaks?' said Gyrth.

'I do not care if it shatters,' said Harold. 'So long as there are Norman knights down there, it is dangerous. We do not go for-ward until there is a field of Norman dead under our feet, and I appear as the Angel of the Lord to lead them by the hand. Is that clear?'

Leofwine repeated it and repeated it, up and down his end of the line. Over on the right, Gyrth did the same.

Some of them clearly understood, but others merely looked at him, muttered 'Surr!' in their thick accents, and carried on with what they were doing.

The fyrdmen were somewhat better. They at least had some

experience of campaigning, though Gyrth wondered, as he counted the grey hairs, how long it was since many of them had been in the field.

Gyrth felt a sudden sinking of the heart; one third of the army stiff in the joints and another third stiff in the head. Oh, for two hundred of the heroes who died at Stamford! A hundred!

He heard a shout from behind the stepped ranks of house-carls. Every man turned his head. There, up above, by the grey apple tree, was a small knot of men. Gyrth recognised Harold among them; it was probably Harold's voice he had heard.

As he looked, two tall standards were raised aloft. First to be unfurled was the great Dragon of Wessex. A cheer went up from the housecarls and rippled along to each end of the line.

Then the King's personal banner fluttered proudly into its fullest length – the Fighting Man, its golden threads glittering in the morning sun.

The roar that went up was deafening. Harold, sensing the moment, mounted a horse and rode to and fro in front of the apple tree, turning and waving to every part of the line.

The chant arose on the left – 'Harold the King! Harold the King!' – and was taken up throughout the whole army's length. 'Harold the King! Harold the King!'

Gyrth's heart, which had been sinking only a moment before, took such a leap that he almost choked. He looked over towards Leolwine, who returned his look with a vigorous wave of the arm. Each brother was grimacing to fight back the tears. How could they possibly lose?

Heralds and marshals cleared a way. The Duke trotted from the rear to the front of his whole army. Apart from his helmet and shield, he was now fully dressed for battle. He sat astride his famous Spanish white destrier. As the army was still roughly in column of march, it was a ride of some duration.

William intended it to be. He was taller than most. Like all men with a commanding eye, he knew when to use it, and could employ it at will. The white horse made a stark contrast to the dark colours around him. His was a striking figure, and he understood exactly what sort of an impression he was making.

With him rode his two half-brothers, Bishop Odo of Bayeux and Count Robert of Mortain. Odo still wore his episcopal robes. Immediately behind rode Sir William Fitzosbern, the Duke's deputy, his second brain, his other self. At his shoulder were the three senior battle commanders – Count Alan of Brittany of the left, Sir Walter Giffard of the centre, and Sir Roger of Montgomery of the right.

Behind again, but close, came Robert of Beaumont, flushed and excited, followed by the pride of Norman vassalage – de Tosny, de Grandmesnil, de Warenne, de Montfort, de Mortagne, Malet.

'Look around you. Be seen!' the Duke had commanded.

As they rode, they looked hard at the horsemen in the rear – vassals and knights and soldiers of fortune; in the centre, at the infantry – the Flemings and Bretons and Angevins and Manceaux; finally, as they neared the front of the huge column, at the archers and crossbowmen and scouts.

Ragged cheering rippled along the lines as they passed. It changed to reverent silence as men saw what came behind – the holy gift of Rome, borne aloft by Count Eustace of Boulogne and his aide, young Turstin of Bec. This was the Papal banner, the present of Cardinal Hildebrand himself. This was the Duke's sign to all men that their mission – to punish the perjurer Harold and depose the false archbishop, Stigand of Canterbury – was favoured by His Holiness and blessed by God. Those who died shriven this day would go straight to Heaven. Men muttered a prayer and crossed themselves.

'A saintly mission indeed!' said Fulk Bloodeye when the command party had passed and men began replacing headgear.

'Fight hard, murder the enemy and die full of Divine Grace, and you will go to Heaven, and do the world a favour by leaving more to be shared among the rest of us . . .'

Florens of Arras chuckled, and took up the refrain.

'. . . and we who remain will live a life of comfort, and riches, and send ourselves to Hell with our avarice and sloth.'

They heard the Duke's marshals calling for closer order and silence. The foot soldiers near the front crowded forward. The cavalry behind, out of earshot, waited patiently and began to give orders to grooms.

Fulk eased himself on to the tailboard of a supply wagon.

'Time for a bite,' he said.

He stretched behind him and pulled out a package of food and two leather flasks. He offered some ham, cheese and biscuit to Florens, who took it without a word. Matthew took only cheese and biscuit. Fulk drank from one flask and passed it to Matthew. He tossed the other to Florens, who held it up and took a long swig. He wiped the spout with his palm, fastened it and passed it back.

'Good stuff,' he said.

Fulk grunted with his mouth full, and stowed it away again.

Odd, thought Florens – you would think a man would be tempted to a drink just before a battle. He never was. It added to the uniqueness of him; his self-denials could be as disturbing as his self-indulgences.

They all munched in silence.

'What do you reckon?' said Florens after a while.

Fulk shrugged. 'Quite good.'

'And if not?'

Fulk looked about him. 'Here is as good a place as any.' He turned to the cook. 'Tether them in that copse over there. Get the wagon in there too, as soon as we deploy. Matthew will help.'

The cook nodded.

Florens got up and brushed off the crumbs.

'This could be the big one.'

'Could be. Want to retire, do you?'

Florens looked doubtful. 'Hard to break habits.'

Dietrich and some of the others came running back.

'Any time now,' Dietrich said breathlessly.

'Probably,' Florens replied.

'Well, you heard what he said.'

'No,' said Florens, 'but I can guess. He told you that we are all going into battle soon against a perjurer, and that God and the Pope and all the saints and angels are on our side. We shall hardly need an army. He said he would share our dangers and conduct us to victory and riches and fame, and that if a man did not fight well he could expect only capture or disgrace or death. He said we are trapped between the enemy in front and the sea behind, but he was sure we would all do well, because we are the greatest army in the whole wide world. Praise God, damn the enemy, and down with that swine Harold.'

Dietrich gaped. 'How did you know?'

Florens and Fulk looked at each other and laughed.

'Just a little secret we share,' said Fulk, with that gentle growl in his throat that made Dietrich shiver.

'Now,' he said, clapping his hands, 'to your positions.' He raised his voice. 'Do as I tell you this day, lads, and I shall make you all rich men.'

'Or lonely ones,' muttered Florens to himself.

Wilfrid watched their own scouts labouring back up the slope towards them.

'See that mud fly?' he said to Edwin. 'Heavy going. Damn good thing too.'

'It will be wetter still either side of the stream,' said Edwin. 'All those rushes.'

Wilfrid sniffed hugely. 'Aye. So they will get wet feet first, and when they get here, we shall give them a dose of cold feet too.'

Edwin looked up at the fierce eyebrows, the beak of a nose, the magnificent moustache, and felt a surge of confidence. It was surely no mere chance that his king had put him to fight beside a champion such as this.

To his left stood the stolid rows of fyrdmen, balancing spears, flexing fingers, digging with heels to make firmer footholds. Further left again were ranged the extra shire levies, and all the other rag and tag who had been scooped up by the army on its rush south from London. In front of them had been placed many of the shields of housecarls who stood in the third and fourth ranks and further back. Between and in front of the shields were scattered whatever stakes they had been able to bring with them from the woods behind, some firmly rooted, others already lolling badly – all in a crazy variety of angles and intervals. Some were still being sharpened at the last minute.

These yokels talked loudly, and swung a wild assortment of weapons. As they watched the housecarls prepare, they too decided it was a good idea to jab and poke at imaginary enemies to their front. Even to Edwin's unpractised eye it was faintly laughable, especially when he turned to his right and saw the real thing.

If the earth allowed it, the housecarls rammed the butts of spears upright into the ground beside them. Edwin bravely did the same, gazing in awe as Wilfrid and his fellows uncovered their fabled axes. Up and down the line, these mailed giants walked and squatted and stretched, and flexed shoulders and swung arms. Then came the practice swings with the axe – forward and back and cross and down – faces vacant with concentration until they were satisfied with tension and response and performance. Whetstones were stuffed into pockets. Blades were caressed and breathed upon.

Gradually the line settled down.

Earl Leofwine rode the length of the left wing once more, making final adjustments of concentration and strength. Edwin noticed that a solitary archer had appeared from nowhere, and now crouched furtively behind a shield at his side.

He felt a nudge from Wilfrid, who leaned down and whispered throatily in his ear, 'One thing – he will not be short of arrows when the Normans get going.'

'Do you think it will be long now?' said Edwin.

Wilfrid glanced over his shoulder, past the stepped ranks of housecarls behind him, up to the top of the hill, where the scouts were making their last report. They pointed to Telham Hill, and Edwin saw Harold shield his eyes against the sun to look in the direction they showed. The banner of the Fighting Man gleamed above him.

The King made a sign to his groom, who led his horse away to the rear.

'Not long, I should say,' said Wilfrid.

Edwin turned back to the front, straining his eyes to the top of Telham Hill. He found himself yawning, of all things.

Wilfrid glanced at him, and smiled.

'Ever used these things before?' he said, indicating the sheaves of spears.

Edwin thought of a score of boastful answers, but looked at Wilfrid's sharp blue eyes and said, 'Yes – a bit.'

'Make every one tell,' said Wilfrid. 'If you miss, you can not run out and get them back. If you hit something, you will not have time to go and dig it out.'

'I – I shall do my best,' said Edwin.

Wilfrid patted him on the shoulder. 'I dare say you will, son.'

Edwin's face twitched in thanks.

'Frightened?' said Wilfrid.

Edwin swallowed. 'Yes.'

'Good. I like to fight beside a truthful man.'

All the same, Wilfrid would have preferred his cousin Oswy,

now lying with a split skull in two feet of water under the bridge at Stamford.

Gilbert ground his teeth.

'Did you hear what he called me?'

'Keep your temper,' said Ralph.

'At a time like this, he can still manage to be sarcastic.'

Ralph pointed. 'There is Senlac Hill. We have just reported the enemy's dispositions on Senlac Hill. Odo would not be human if he did not recall the joke.'

'It is not a joke!'

'All right, all right, it is not a joke. But keep your temper. Lives will be saved today by cool heads, not hot ones.'

'A fat chance we have, up here all day.'

Ralph was not listening; he was watching the deployment. Bowmen were already fanning out on the front slopes of Telham this side of the stream. Ralph smiled – Sandor's 'Sandlake'. Blocks of infantry were forming up on the brow, waiting for the word to follow. Behind them, the knights and senior commanders were changing mounts, and checking gear on their war destriers. At the rear, baggage wagons and their drivers were looking for dry patches of level ground; marshals and other harassed staff were yelling at them to keep away from the horse lines and other con centration areas.

The Duke had listened to Ralph's report in his usual tense way.

'Roughly what we expected, sir. Housecarls in the middle, several ranks deep. Fyrdmen either side and country riff-raff at each end. I think he has his headquarters round the tree on the top.'

'Any defence works?'

'Shields, mostly. They have made a sort of wall out of them. Difficult to see anything at this range.'

'It can not be very strong,' said Odo. 'They have not had the time.'

He rode resplendent now in mail. Not a stitch of clerical cloth on him.

'It will provide protection rather than strength, sir,' said Ralph. 'Against the archers.'

'Nevertheless,' said the Duke, 'I see no reason to depart from our general design. They can not have a shield for every man there. Those without will suffer.'

Ralph looked across once more at the English army, then down at the bowmen and infantry arranging themselves before him. The English would not look so ragged when you looked up at them from down there. Already men's eyes were being caught by a thousand gleams from spearheads and axes.

'I said, "A fat chance we have,"' repeated Gilbert.

Ralph came out of his reverie. 'Your time will come. Many men down there at this moment would gladly change places with us.'

'Then let them come and change,' said Gilbert.

'Be patient,' said Ralph. 'You wanted to be a scout. Now be one.'

Gilbert moved his horse restlessly. 'So we remain here all day?'

'If necessary – yes.'

'And what do we do, pray? Get blisters on our—'

'We learn, that is what we do. We watch, and we learn. If you ever stop learning in our trade, you stop living very soon.' Ralph pointed. 'Out there, today, you will see in action two of the finest commanders alive. If you do not find something to learn from them, you are either blind or stupid.'

Gilbert grimaced. 'But – all day?'

Ralph softened a fraction. 'Have no fear; a lot can happen in a battle, and very quickly. When the first blow is struck it is like a stone tossed into a pond. The ripples will reach us all on the edges – in time. And when they do, you will wish otherwise, I promise you. You will not have time even to offer a prayer for Adele.'

Gilbert winced with remorse; he had barely given her a thought.

Ralph stretched a hand and waved it to and fro in front of them.

'Look before you. What do you see? Tell me honestly – what are you thinking?'

'How quiet it is.'

'Exactly. And perhaps slow?'

'Yes – yes!'

Ralph nodded. 'Just like laying out the pieces on a chessboard. Well, by the end of this day those pieces will be all over the place and the board itself may be overturned. You will see and hear such confusion that you may be forgiven for thinking that the last day of the world has come. We shall become involved – that is almost certain. But it is the time and manner of our involvement that is hidden from us. All I can tell you is, it will be a surprise. You must prepare for a surprise, and you must react as if you were expecting it.'

Gilbert stared. 'You mean – we might lose?'

'Oh, that? Yes, that is possible too.'

'That is treason,' spluttered Gilbert.

'Not treason – common sense. Our two commanders are very evenly matched, I should say. If I were a Saxon, I should cheerfully follow Harold, and I should be standing up there now, sneering at the Normans.'

'How can you say that?'

'Easily. Look at them. Now imagine yourself down there. Would you like to slosh through that stream, plod up that hill with mud weighing you down, and throw yourself against axes that can cut a man in half?'

'But – but they are the enemy.'

Ralph laughed. 'They are not "the enemy"; we are. It is their land.'

Gilbert sighed. 'Now you have thoroughly confused me. Why are we here then? How do we ever get started?'

'Because all war is a form of madness. No battle can start without it. There comes an instant when men stop thinking of common sense and reason, and think only of killing and surviving – sometimes not even of surviving.'

'If that is all it is, how can you get a decision between equal commanders when everyone is going mad?'

'Because there will come a moment – a hesitation, a gap, a weakness, a tension – *something*. Victory will go to the man who sees it and pounces.'

'Suppose the English break at the first charge?'

Ralph grinned. 'That will be the surprise I was talking about. Come. Let us find Bruno.'

As they cantered off, Ralph sighed at the irony. Gilbert was depressed because he did not understand everything clearly; he, Ralph of Gisors, the great scout, the great observer, was depressed because he did.

A cloud moved across the sun.

The Norman archers looked faintly ridiculous as they skipped across the tussocks of grass, their quivers bouncing on their buttocks. In the stillness Edwin could hear the ratchets of the crossbows being tightened.

A small group of horsemen cantered down from Telham Hill. Slightly ahead was a magnificent white charger.

'There he is,' said Wilfrid in Edwin's ear.

A murmur of recognition ran along the line.

'Steady, lads.'

Single housecarls stood at intervals behind the line on either wing.

The bowmen were across the stream now. Behind them, the blocks of French infantry edged towards the far bank.

Every eye on the field was now held by the figure on the white horse.

William turned to his groom and took his helmet. He looked to left and right as he fastened the chinstrap. Two heralds moved up, one on either side of him. He glanced up at the banner with the embroidered cross, then took a lance that trailed a long pennon from behind its head.

'Ready!' said the archer sergeants.

Fingers curled round bowstrings.

William looked over his right shoulder. The straggling cloud moved away, and sunlight flooded the field. Right into the English eyes.

'Now.'

He raised his lance, and his heralds put their trumpets to their lips. The thin, brassy braying floated towards the stream.

The lance dropped.

'Fire!'

The volleys went humming and whistling up the hill.

'Down!' roared Wilfrid and a hundred others.

Every head in the English army vanished.

As he crouched and shivered, Edwin could hear the whizzing in the air and the thudding on the shields. Commands in French floated up the hill. A scattering of screams and curses broke out behind him. The lonely archer trembled and muttered prayers.

Wilfrid nudged him. 'Do you fancy the odds?'

The archer managed a sickly smile.

'How long?' said Edwin.

'Till they run out,' said Wilfrid.

A few foolish yokels put up their heads to have a look after the first volley, and died without striking a blow. Friends dragged them away, and broke off shafts that stuck from eyes and mouths and windpipes.

On the right of the line, Gyrth peered through a slit between the shields.

'Not long now, lads; then you can stretch.'

The sheepman found himself gazing into the face of his

madman. True, the fellow had crouched when everyone else did, but he had done nothing to show that he was aware of the slightest danger. He had taken up a place in the line – would that it had been any other – and had not uttered a word. Now he squatted with his face a few inches away, and gazed emptily at nothing. And, great God! He was eating. Eating! Huge hands caressed the shaft of the axe.

It would drive a man off his head just watching him. The sheepman struggled to turn the other way. He put out his left foot to brace himself, and bellowed in pain. An arrow had found the small gap between the narrow, tapering feet of two shields. It had not transfixed the flesh, but it had made a nasty cut in passing.

The sheepman tied up the wound as best he could, and stared at the vacant face before him. The man had not shown a flicker of emotion.

When the quivers were empty, the bowmen withdrew.

'Steady, steady,' warned the housecarls. One or two stepped out in front of the restless wings and held up axe-handles.

'Quick,' said Wilfrid to the archer. 'Now is your chance.'

The man scrambled to his feet. Wilfrid eased back two shields.

'Let them have it!'

With each arrow that flew after the retreating Normans the English cheered. When one stuck in the buttock of a burly Picard and made him fall in the stream, men roared with laughter. Ribald advice was bawled down the hill at the two comrades struggling to fish him out.

Gyrth scanned the field. 'A good start,' he said.

'They will be back,' said Harold. 'If I know William, he has wagons bursting with fresh arrows behind the brow. But we have respite, at least.'

'So far, so good,' said Leofwine.

Harold looked up at the two standards, and nodded at the two eager young bearers.

'Give them a wave,' he said.

When they saw the standards fluttering defiantly, the line cheered like thunder. They were mightily pleased with themselves. For a few heady minutes the bewildered, back-slapped archer was a hero.

'It does not seem to have done much,' said Gilbert.

'Pricking and probing,' said Bruno flatly.

'Every little counts,' said Ralph. 'As a mouse gnaws at a tree.'

While the archers replenished their quivers, it would be the turn of the infantry to probe with sword and spear. On the wings, where the enemy was weakest. It was sufficient to present only a show of force in the centre just to keep the housecarls occupied – for the time being.

Behind the heavy contingents in the centre, Sir Walter Giffard flexed his toes in the stirrups and waited. He looked towards Fitzosbern and the Duke. Not that he expected an order yet to advance in strength. Please God, the infantry must not do it at the first attempt, on their own!

"There go the Flemings,' said Gilbert, pointing to the right. 'Look at them. Great Jesus, you have to hand it to Bloodeye.'

Bruno pointed to the Bretons on the left, who were stirring towards the stream. 'Count Alan's pride and joy.'

Ralph tensed in the saddle. 'Who is that?'

The Breton line had halted on the very edge of the reeds and sandy patches. Sergeants were running about urgently. To the left again a man had appeared on a thin, rangy horse. He wore no mail.

Gilbert gasped. 'Taillefer!'

A small rider emerged on a light pony.

'He has Sandor with him.'

'I hope you are pleased now,' grumbled Sandor. 'To be close to the enemy like this.'

'Not pleased,' said Taillefer, 'but content.'

He took an onion from his pocket and ate it.

A young soldier near the end of the line looked up at him. His face seemed familiar, though Taillefer could not place him at first. He knew he had not seen him strained like this.

'I know you,' he said.

'That night in the hall, sir,' said Brian. 'The one with the carrot.'

'Ah!'

The boy's colour was awful. All down the line it was the same. Fear was spreading like spilled wine on a sloping table.

'Prepare!' bawled the sergeants.

Swords came out; thongs were fixed over wrists. Spears were couched.

'At the walk – advance!'

Not a foot moved.

The sergeants, uneasy, gave the command again.

'At the walk – advance!'

Another sickening pause.

Taillefer urged his horse forward. Sandor, alarmed, followed.

Taillefer dismounted in front of the Breton line.

'So, my babies, today we walk to glory! 'Tis I, Taillefer, the Cleaver of Iron, who will be your guide. Behold the brand that will be your standard!'

He took out his sword and waved it above his head, well knowing how the sun would catch it.

The slightest of sighs ran along the line.

One of the sergeants swore, and moved to stop him, but another held him back.

'No. Wait. You may witness a miracle.'

Taillefer flung his sword in the air and caught it. Then he flung it again, making it twist and turn and flash. He made it leap and somersault from hand to hand, and all the time he was chanting names of heroes. 'This sword has seen – the feats of – Rollo –

and Richard the – Fearless – our first duke – of that name – and Charlemagne – and Roland – and Oliver – and Arthur – and now …'. He caught it for the last time. 'My sons – it leads you to glory eternal.'

He mounted again and whispered in Sandor's ear, 'Come, and do as I say.'

He edged his horse into the stream. 'Who is with me, my dears?'

The Breton line moved. The sergeants blinked in disbelief. Across the stream, the line slowed again.

Taillefer swung and twirled his sword once more. It caught the sun again and held it. Men gasped and were dazzled. Taillefer's wrist was the blurred centre of a circle of blinding light. Then they heard his voice again, strong and sonorous.

> Look hard, my sons, and there, before the van,
> You shall behold the gleam of Durendal.
> And hearken always, those of you who can –
> The horn of Roland sounds in Roncesvalles!

Taillefer looked quickly at Sandor.

'Blow! Blow!'

Sandor fumbled with the ivory horn at his belt.

'Now!'

Sandor took a huge breath, which nearly lifted him off the saddle.

The hollow boom echoed eerily across the Breton line.

Brian, his face now suffused with blood, leaned forward, licking his lips. His chest was heaving.

'Again!' muttered Taillefer, watching him.

It was like touching a spring.

His eyes blazing, Brian leaped forward.

'Rol - a - a - a - a - nd!'

The whole Breton line answered him.

'Rol - a - a - a - a - nd!'

Taillefer was swept forward in the rush. Sandor was brushed aside. A human wave of screaming energy surged up the hill.

'ROL - A - A - A - A - ND!'

When it seemed that nothing could stop the onslaught, the English line erupted into activity.

There was a mighty roar of, 'Out! Out!'

The sky darkened with missiles – spears, sticks, maces, clubs. A man beside Brian was felled by a flying axe.

There was a great tramping and shouting and cursing, but Brian heard only the sound of his own voice.

Taillefer could not control his terrified horse. Only the press of bodies on either side prevented its breaking away. With frantic neighing and staring eyes, it bore him, helpless, forward. His sword was knocked out of his hand.

He had a vision of a rampart surmounted by tousled heads and whites of eyes. He tried vainly to draw a knife. A sharp stone on the end of a stick struck him on the temple and flung him backwards. His horse reared as it came up to some large stakes projecting from the ground. He fell out of the saddle, but was held dangling by one stirrup.

Brian, his arm upraised, his lungs bursting, reached the English line. Mad with excitement, he began hacking blindly at a shield. As he raised his arm for the third or fourth time, a stocky peasant jabbed at his armpit with a pitchfork. The two prongs went either side of his flesh, but caught in the mail.

He jerked to get away and the Saxon pulled to get his fork back. Almost weeping with frustration, Brian grabbed his end of the handle and gave a huge tug. The Saxon was dragged between two shields, pushing them aside, but would not leave go.

Suddenly a sword swung past Brian's face and severed the Saxon's left arm. It was his cousin Geoffrey. Brian opened his mouth to say something, when Geoffrey collapsed under a hammer-blow to his helmet.

Brian fell back, and saw to his horror that the bleeding hand and half its arm were still dangling from the fork handle. He flung it off with loathing, and at last dragged the fork free.

In front of him the two shields lolled drunkenly. The earth was dark with the Saxon's blood. Behind the wounded man another English face appeared. It was a round, well-filled face. The head above it was balding.

Brian swung his sword again, but the distance was too great. As he braced himself to pull back, he felt something else curl round his arm. When he jumped back it slid down to his wrist and caught in the thong of his sword.

A shepherd's crook! Gasping with surprise and disbelief, he wriggled to dislodge it. Dear God – to die by a shepherd's crook! The leather thong of the hilt snapped, and his sword clattered down inside the shields.

Disarmed and unnerved, he sprang back, tripped over Geoffrey's body, and fell.

The fall saved his life.

As he put up his arms to protect his face from the milling feet, he heard a roaring, followed by great noises – ringing blows of metal, hideous crunches, screams of mortal agony.

Two Breton bodies fell on top of him; boots trod on his legs and passed over. The roaring went on.

Brian squirmed out. He recoiled from contact with Geoffrey's blood-soaked face, but instinct for survival made him prise open Geoffrey's fingers and ease the sword-thong off his wrist.

He struggled up to hands and knees, and saw that he was one of the few Bretons still alive near the English line.

Just in front of him, a giant Saxon was swinging a huge farm axe. Swords and spears were swept aside by sheer animal strength; limbs were split and severed. On the return swing he used the back of it as a hammer to smash heads and ribs. Stupefied by terror and disbelief, men were falling like corn before the sickle.

The survivors hung back out of range, while the giant, ringed by a rampart of writhing bodies, paused, for a moment baffled. He seemed as if he was looking for something.

Brian dropped flat, and feigned dead. His cheek, he found, was against mail, through which blood had oozed. He fought down the nausea, and prayed that the giant did not turn and see him breathing.

As he lay rigid, he fancied he heard a new sound. At first, he thought it was his own heartbeat.

Gorm could not remember seeing the woman approach.

He rested on his stick, wiped his face, lifted his eyes, and there she was.

She looked neither tired nor fresh; neither hurried nor leisurely. Although she had drawn level with him, she offered no greeting, asked no question. She did not even turn her eyes towards him. He might as well not have been there.

She wore only a shawl as a protection against outdoor conditions. She carried no load, yet she put one foot in front of the other as if pressed down with a great weight. For all that, there was a deliberation in her gait that told of total resolve; nothing would divert her from her destination.

Gorm opened his mouth to ask his question – 'Have you seen a big man, a man with a crutch?' – when, out of the corner of his eye, he saw another woman, then another, and another.

He turned round, and gasped. There were hundreds of them, scattered along the track the army had made. Some carried blankets, others baskets under white cloths. Many simply held their arms tight across their bodies, palms pressed to elbows. All moved as if sleep-walking, like spirits of the dead on clouds of Heaven.

Despite his sweat, Gorm felt a chill to see this silent, floating pilgrimage of bereavement.

Facing the trail again, he quickened his step, anxious to get away from them. Their deadness of countenance made him more fearful of what he might find. He became oblivious of the drummings in his head and the poundings in his chest.

He heard something ahead that made him hesitate. Twice he paused, but the breeze seemed to have carried it away.

Again he thought he heard it, and cocked his head in its direction – a vague, braying mixture of a sound – but perhaps his fatigue was playing him tricks.

Then he saw a flicker of feeling on a woman's face. He had not imagined it!

Now he stopped completely, dropped his head, and strained his ears, grimacing with the effort of concentration.

This time it reached him in fullest flood, and there could be no mistake. He had never heard a sound like it before, but he knew beyond any doubt what it was.

He pressed forward to the next stretch of woodland, leaving the women behind. Sweat poured down his sagging cheeks.

Dear God – Woden, Thor, Christ, Heaven, Valhalla, anybody – please let Godric be alive, alive to hear him and see him. Alive to recognise his existence.

The Duke and his bodyguard knights splashed across the stream behind the Bretons.

From the centre, Fitzosbern watched. Behind him, Eustace of Boulogne fidgeted with the Papal standard at his knee.

'Is there danger, do you think?'

'Yes,' said Fitzosbern. 'That is why the Duke rides to quell it.'

Eustace was not the first to feel annoyance at Fitzosbern's refusal to show emotion. He looked up at the embroidered cross.

'I should be where the Duke is.'

'You should be where you are told to be,' said Fitzosbern.

Eustace pointed. 'Even if the Duke changes his plans?'

'Not a change; merely an adjustment. He leaves us here, and the banner, to show the army that all is well. Stillness at the centre is a great thing.'

'I should be with him.'

'Save your energy for obeying orders when they come.'

Fitzosbern screwed up his eyes to make out what was happening on the left. Orders would come soon enough if Count Alan had fallen in the first attack.

William looked up the slope at the confusion above the stream. The first impetus had gone, and too many sergeants had been lost. There was not enough leadership near the English line to create a second onset.

Count Alan was yelling himself hoarse, but the fighting had degenerated into scrappy dog-fights.

William swore at the count, who had allowed himself to be drawn too far into the battle in his attempt to save the honour of his own countrymen. He should now be back with the reserve cavalry, waiting to time the second attack.

Alan saw the error at once, and galloped back with William, furious at the failure and at his own mistake. He careered towards the waiting cavalry, their reins tight with suspense, and came to a halt in a flurry of foam and flying mud.

'The cavalry will advance upon the English positions – now!'

From behind Count Alan came William's harsh voice.

'Take them up, my brothers, and good grace attend you. I shall be watching from the standard. Hard now!'

Odo gazed up at the shield wall. It was broken in only one or two places. Near one breach was a sickening pile of Breton dead. A huge Saxon was standing over them and waving an axe; he was shouting at the top of his voice and trying to get at those retreating, but appeared to be wounded in the leg. A group of frenzied English were trying to drag him back to the line.

Odo glanced at his brother, Robert of Mortain, and raised his mace.

'Right, my lads – for God and the Bastard! God help us! *Diex aie!*'

The trumpets blared. Spurs dug in.

'*Diex a - a - i - i - i - e - e - e!*'

The Bretons rallied, waited for the horses to come level, and ran in again at their tails. Count Alan, still smarting from the Duke's tongue, watched from behind, near the reserve squadrons. It was agony for him.

William Capra and Ralph Pomeroy found their new mounts difficult to control. The noise, the confusion on the slope, the mixture of infantry with cavalry, were too much for them. They began to go faster.

On the slope below the English line, Taillefer's horse was at last free from the press of the first attack. It galloped wildly downhill. Taillefer's body, still held by the stirrup, bounced along like a broken doll. The horse did not pause till it reached the Norman side of the stream.

'Look!' shouted Gilbert from Telham. 'Sandor has seen him.'

Capra and Pomeroy, to their alarm, found that their horses were taking them out into the lead. They reached the Saxon line first, and were appalled at the forest of spears, clubs, and staves above the surging ranks in front of them. They hurled their spears blindly and turned away to find space to draw a sword.

Bretons rushed past them, and were flung back again by a hail of missiles.

Capra's horse took a spear in its neck, and rolled to the ground. Capra wriggled out from under it, and looked for his brother.

He heard a roar, and saw the shield wall part to let out a large Saxon with an axe. Capra stared. God! It was the giant from the mill. Capra's mouth went dry. The man was limping! It made the whole scene devilish. This wild cripple broke swords, smashed horses' legs, split skulls, and created a humming ring of death within the circle of his arms.

Capra felt naked without a saddle beneath him. He got up, and ran. He heard brother Ralph call after him, but did not stop.

Breton and Angevin footsoldiers were now running too. He passed one man, staggering drunkenly down the hill, still clutching the broken haft of a spear sticking out of his midriff.

William turned to Fitzosbern. 'Stay here. I am taking Montfort's men. Contain it here – just contain it.'

Fitzosbern did not have to answer. From their central position the situation was all too obvious. The shock of impact had caused recoil. The slope was also making men run. The left was peeling away from the shield wall. It was like a piece of cloth being torn in two. Unchecked, the rent would go along the entire line, and the disengagement would become a rout.

William galloped to the left for a second time. He bawled orders over his shoulder at de Montfort and his men.

'Round them up. Get them back. Hold them.'

William himself rode right into the fleeing infantry. He shouted and swore at them. They barely heard him. From his rear position, Count Alan of Brittany looked at his broken countrymen and wept with impotent rage and frustration.

William snatched a broken spear from the hand of a frightened Poitevin and began belabouring the fugitives.

'Get back, you swine. Get back!'

A great cheering broke out above him. He looked up and saw that his impetus had taken him through his own retreating troops, and he was now approaching spear range of the English line. Worse, the shield wall had opened, and men were pouring in pursuit down the hill.

Wrenching at the bridle, William turned to escape. He had hardly gone a few steps when he felt his mount struck.

Almost before he hit the ground a group of Maine and Bessin knights had placed themselves round him. Two of them dismounted and helped him to his feet.

Without pausing for thanks, William demanded a horse from

one of the Manceaux. The man hesitated. William struck him
with his gloved hand and seized the bridle.

Already the word was spreading – 'The Duke's horse is
down!'

It surged like fire in dry thatch.

'The Duke is down!'

'The Duke has fallen!'

William rode frantically to and fro, yelling at the top of his
voice. 'I am here! I am here!'

Away in the centre rear, Fitzosbern stood intently in his stirrups. He had seen the white charger disappear in a sea of flailing
bodies. He sighed with relief when he saw the familiar tall figure
reappear, waving to stem the tide of retreat. Men still spewed
downhill from the gap in the shield wall.

From where he was placed, Fitzosbern could see that William
would, with luck, contain the trouble on the left, but he would
need help. The centre and the right were holding.

'Warenne – take your men and get down there. Round them
up. If any Breton tries to get past you, kill him.'

'With the greatest of pleasure,' said Warenne, glancing at
Walter Giffard, who was already glaring in disgust at the cowardice of infantry.

Fitzosbern turned to Eustace of Boulogne and gestured at the
banner. 'Take that to the Duke.'

Eustace stared. 'But you told me to keep it here. So did the
Duke.'

'Now it has changed. He needs you down there. Move!'

Fitzosbern watched them go. He could feel Giffard fuming
beside him.

'If you say "I told you so", Walter, I shall strike you.'

Giffard held his tongue, just. If they had put the knights at
them in the first place . . .

As soon as Warenne and his contingent arrived, William
bawled at them. 'Tell them I live. Tell them!'

They galloped everywhere, feeling like untrained shepherd boys after wayward sheep.

William, furious and red in the face, cursed men, struck them, ran them down – anything to stop the panic. One man grabbled his ankle, looked up at him, and yelled, 'The Duke is dead!'

By this time, they were back across the stream, away from the English. William spurred ahead of the leading fugitives, and turned in front of them, so that they could get a good view of him in the open. He pushed back his helmet, straining the strap under his neck. Wrenching at his mail coif, he stood bareheaded in the stirrups.

'Look at me. I am alive. I live! We shall win!'

Between them Montfort and Warenne and their men rounded up enough fugitives to halt the full retreat. Odo and Mortain rallied the shreds of the first cavalry assault group. Eustace of Boulogne brought the holy banner.

Many Bretons and Angevins now stood round William's horse, looking sheepishly at each other. Count Alan rode up, his face stained with tears of shame.

William looked over their heads at where the English pursuers had reached the bottom of the hill. Their impetus had taken them up a small grassy knoll near the stream. There they stood, puffed and uncertain, deprived for the moment of an adversary. A few random flurries of fighting continued, but the initiative seemed to have eluded both sides.

William seized it.

He gestured to Montfort. 'Get your men between the knoll and the hill – now!'

'Sir.'

'You?' William looked at Eustace and nodded at the standard. 'Keep that with me.'

He turned back to the growing crowd of foot soldiers. Odo brought back the remains of his group. Ralph Pomeroy looked desperately for his brother.

William gazed at the upturned faces around him.

'You infants. You squealing, frightened dogs. You – you *women!*' They wilted.

'Look to the centre,' bawled William. 'Do you see it out of formation? Look to the right? Do you see Montgomery's men running? Or Sir Robert of Beaumont's?'

Heads hung. William flung a hand towards the knoll where the English were being cut off by Montfort's knights.

'Well, we have a chance for you to redeem yourselves. Because you can not climb a proper hill, we have found a special small one for you, designed for children. Look at it.'

They did.

'Do you think you can manage that one? Get the English off there and I may – I may just – look at you again. Meantime, I go to lead some *men!*'

Brian felt his cheeks burn, and longed to avenge his dead cousin. Count Alan wept and swore.

'Get that gap mended,' said Gyrth.

'But, sir,' said the sheepman, 'we must leave somewhere for them to get back.'

'They will not be back. Look there, man. What chance do they have? Out in the open, no shields, and charging cavalry. And what their cavalry miss their infantry will get.'

The sheepman looked down the hill. On the top of the knoll, his comrades were clustering closer together, watching the returning Breton infantry. Further out and all around, Norman knights stalked like cats.

'But can we not go down and help them?'

Gyrth spat. 'Throwing live men after dead ones.'

'They are not dead yet.'

Gyrth glared at him. 'No? Watch!'

He strode away, hectoring the rest of the line. 'Look and learn.

Stay! Whatever happens, stay. We are up here and they are down there. Keep it like that and we win. Change it and you die, like those dolts.'

The sheepman leaned on his crook to ease the pain in his foot. The Normans began silently to close in on the knoll. He wondered how long it would take.

The only consolation was that he would not have to fight beside the limping madman any more. He was down there somewhere, though God alone knew how he had got there.

'*Diex aie!*'

They heard the Norman battle cry and watched. All along the right of the English line, men wanted to turn their eyes away but were unable to. To see their comrades die was the only loyalty they could now give them. Eyes blinked and teeth gritted with every scream and every fall.

At last the knoll was silent. French infantry and cavalry streamed away, leaving a goodly number of writhing horses as well as dead soldiers. The English had not died easily.

Along the centre of the field the Normans pulled back for lack of breath, and the panting English were glad to let them go. On the right, having barely dented the English line, Montgomery and Beaumont retired in good order. Fulk ordered his men to carry off their own dead in order to salvage their equipment.

The sheepman looked once more down at the knoll, and crossed himself.

A movement caught his eye. He squinted to concentrate, then exclaimed in amazement.

A man was still alive down there. A big man. A very big man.

The sheepman gasped.

The giant was leaning on a long stave. He was limping badly as he picked his way over the dead and dying.

'Look!'

Hundreds of eyes followed every hobbled step between the knoll and the main hill. There was no sign of the axe.

A Norman knight spotted him. He turned his horse about, braced his stirrups, and drew his sword.

English voices bellowed warnings. The man tried to hurry, but the effort, as the knight bore down on him, was pitiful. The man seemed to realise it, because he stopped, and swung round to face his pursuer.

As the Norman rushed in for the kill, the Saxon balanced himself carefully, and grasped the stave with both hands at one end.

Yelling in triumph, the Norman swung his right arm high. The stave caught him across the throat with such force that he was lifted bodily from the saddle. The stave snapped, one end flying up high. The horseman turned over in the air and fell on his neck.

Without looking to see if he was still moving, the big man resumed his painful climb, using what was left of the splintered stave.

At the top he was greeted by cheers and a score of willing hands.

He ignored them all. Men fell away before him. They could not understand why he kept scanning the whole field. Like some general, they said. Without a glance at them, he struggled through a sea of puzzled faces into a clear area behind the line.

Muttering and shaking their heads, men turned back to face the enemy.

Godric came to a decision: he was not here; he must be on the other side.

Robert of Beaumont leaped from the saddle and flung the reins towards a stable boy.

'Did you see that? Did you see that? Perfect order.'

Sir Roger of Montgomery dismounted more deliberately. He patted his destrier's neck.

'Parade ground stuff.'

Beaumont's flush of excitement became one of anger. 'But we did it. Advance and retire in perfect order.'

Montgomery took the reins of his new mount, and nodded to his groom.

'The object of a manoeuvre is not perfection; it is victory. Look at them. Are they still there?'

Beaumont looked across from Telham towards the tight English line. 'Yes.'

'Well, then.'

Beaumont spluttered. 'So what was all the practice for?'

'To get better.'

Beaumont frowned. 'I do not see.'

Montgomery looked down from the saddle. 'We are still not good enough.' He pointed. 'That is the practice we need now. Over there.'

Edwin had not known that such exhaustion was possible. His arms and legs were quivering; he could barely stand. He bent over in desperate search of breath. Wilfrid patted him on the shoulder. 'First blood, eh?'

Edwin nodded, still gasping.

Wilfrid glared down the hill. 'It will take more than one whipping to beat the Bastard. Look down there.'

Edwin stood up and peered over the shield wall.

Marshals and messengers were cantering to and fro. Most blocks of men, from Telham Hill right down almost to the stream of Caldbec, looked organised and purposeful, if slightly smaller. Isolated figures were braving the English spears to collect weapons from bodies in the water and beyond. Archers and crossbowmen were beginning to troop back to the field, alert and spry, with full quivers. The Duke's standard flew again in the centre.

'See?' said Wilfrid. 'He is going up the hill to get a better look.'

The standard followed the Duke and his staff.

The enemy commander was so visible, so close, and yet untouchable. The impossible thought flashed through Edwin's mind: could not one determined man, in a sudden dash . . .? Or a lucky bowshot . . .? Was it not worth a try? Even with their solitary, timid bowman?

Even as he thought it, he knew it was a dream.

He glanced behind towards the apple tree. The Wessex Dragon and the Fighting Man fluttered together. Harold must be with them.

Again, Edwin looked across to Telham Hill. Perhaps some Norman up there was thinking the same thing.

Gilbert! He was sure that Gilbert was just as eager as he was to gain fame, or modest mark – at the very least to bear himself well.

Had he taken part in the battle yet? Would they meet? Gilbert was only a scout; it was unlikely.

Edwin regretted that he had not had time the day before to talk to Gilbert. Really talk. Would they meet after the battle? If they did, what could they say to each other? One a victor, one a loser . . .

'Here. Wake up. Give me a hand.'

Wilfrid was struggling with a dead body.

'What are you trying to do with him?' said Edwin.

'Get him over the top, of course.'

Edwin stared. 'What – tip him outside the shields?'

'He is no use to us inside. Come on. Grab his legs.'

Edwin spluttered. 'It is shameful!'

Wilfrid paused with his hands under the corpse's armpits. 'I shall have shame if I do not do everything I can to strengthen this line. He can be as useful dead as he was alive.' He peered into the corpse's face. 'Probably more useful. Eric never was very good with an axe. Do you want his helmet?'

Wilfrid slipped it off and held it out. There was blood inside the rim.

Edwin shuddered. 'No.'

'Please yourself,' said Wilfrid, tossing it aside. He saw Edwin still hanging back. 'He would have done the same with me. And I should have wanted him to.'

Edwin looked further along the line. More bodies were being tipped over, stripped first of useful equipment.

Grimacing with distaste, Edwin heaved and hoisted, and heard poor Eric flop like a sack of corn down the other side, on top of a dead horse and a transfixed Norman knight.

Wilfrid dusted his hands.

'Time now for three important things.'

'What are they?' asked Edwin, not at all sure that he wanted to know.

Wilfrid cleaned blood off the blade of his axe as casually as a man blowing his nose.

'A good bite, a good drink, and a good piss.'

Ralph found Sandor on his knees, cradling Taillefer's head in his lap. He was wiping dirt from the bruised face.

Sandor looked up, his cheeks blotched. 'What do you do here?'

'I had a message for Count Alan. I saw you from the top.'

'You saw my friend?' said Sandor.

'I saw what he did, yes.'

Sandor looked down into Taillefer's face. 'It was a great thing he did. Surely men will now sing of Taillefer too. As they sing of Roland at Roncesvalles, they will now sing of Taillefer at the Sandlake.'

Ralph crouched beside him, still carefully holding the reins. He put his other arm round Sandor's shoulders.

'Yes, little man from Hungary, I expect they will. Is he ...?'

Sandor nodded. 'He was dragged a long way. The hooves and his head ... There was much trampling by men too; his ribs ...'

Ralph stood up and looked around him. 'You can not stay here.'

'I know. But a friend must have a farewell.' Sandor let Taillefer's head go gently to the ground. 'I must go to my horses.'

'Cover him,' said Ralph. 'Nobody can hurt him now.'

Sandor went to Taillefer's horse. From behind the saddle he drew the minstrel's best cloak. He kneeled beside the body and folded the hands across the chest. From inside Taillefer's tunic he pulled a cross, snapped off the chain from the neck, and wound it round the fingers.

'I did not know Taillefer wore a crucifix,' said Ralph.

'No,' said Sandor gruffly.

He took the dagger out of the belt, and stuffed it into his own. He shook out the cloak and laid it gently, pulling it up over the face.

'Why leave anything valuable?' said Ralph. 'It will only be plundered. You know what animals there are on a battlefield.'

'I leave them because they belong to him. If we bury him, we bury them with him and the worms get them. Animals or worms – what does it matter? We have done what is right.'

'You take his dagger, I see.'

Sandor patted it. 'That not belong to him. It would not be proper. He goes to his God clean.'

'So be it. Now, hurry.'

Ralph had heard rustles in the undergrowth nearby, and was not anxious for private duels.

Sandor stood up, crossed himself – the first time Ralph had seen him do it – and stood for a moment. His hand strayed to his hip and found the horn there. On impulse he started to un-fasten it.

'What are you doing?' said Ralph.

'If I did not blow this,' said Sandor, 'my friend Taillefer would be alive.'

Ralph put out a hand to stop him. 'But you did blow it, Sandor, and you have made your friend immortal. Come.'

After they had cantered off, the nearby bushes parted, and William Capra staggered out. He was streaked with mud and soaked to the knees, but otherwise unhurt.

He untethered Taillefer's horse – a frightful old nag. With no choice he had no grumbles.

He went to the body, kneeled, and pulled back the cloak. The face looked younger than he remembered it. Peaceful too. Capra had never expected to see a dead man look happy.

Bewitched by temptation, he slid the cloak further, further, until he uncovered the cross and chain. Jewels gleamed.

Capra ran his tongue along his lower lip.

He wished Taillefer would move, just flutter an eyelid, and he would cheerfully cut his throat. This deathly, serene trust was too much for him.

He flung the cloak back over the face, rushed to the horse, and mounted. The noises of battle came once more into his ears.

He paused for a last look. The cloak clearly outlined the beak of a nose and the outsize feet.

William Capra gritted his teeth. 'I am not an animal!'

He dug in his heels with savage decision.

'Have you seen a big man, a big man with an axe?'

The groom waved a hand towards the top of the hill. 'Just over there you will find thousands of them; take your pick.'

'No, no. I mean a very big man. And not a housecarl.'

The groom shrugged.

Gorm staggered on. The groom looked after him in alarm. 'You must not go up there.'

Gorm paid no attention.

The groom paused, undecided. A horse nudged his back. He shrugged again and carried on with his work.

Gorm pulled at a fyrdman's sleeve. 'Have you seen a big man, with an axe? Limping.'

'Are you joking? They are talking of nothing else.'

Gorm worked his way to the right wing, where he heard the story several times over.

'Where is he now?'

'Gone, thank God,' said the sheepman.

Gorm swallowed. 'You mean – dead?'

'No, I mean gone – somewhere else. Good riddance, I say. The man is mad.'

'Mad?'

'Stark, staring. No idea of danger. Thought we were all heroes. Nearly did for all of us.'

'Where is he now?'

'No idea.'

'You must have seen him go.'

'No too busy. What is he to you, anyway?'

'He is my – my kin.' Gorm could not bring himself to say 'son', and the full story was too long.

'Well, old man, you have a madman in the family. Stay away from him, or he will do for you too.'

Gorm grimaced in frustration.

The sheepman turned away, and carried on to his neighbours in the front line.

'When I got this arrow in my foot, he never even asked if I was all right. And it was right under his nose. There he was, gazing into empty air and eating mushrooms, if you please, as if he was—' He felt his arm being gripped.

'Did you say mushrooms?' said Gorm intently.

The sheepman, held close, looked at him with distaste. 'Yes. Why?'

Gorm flung his arm aside, and stumped off, still looking desperately from side to side.

The sheepman brushed his sleeve. 'If he does not calm down, that silly old fool will have a fit as well.'

On the left wing, Godric worked his way through to the front. Ploughmen and farm boys took one look at the size of his shoulders and gave him space.

Earl Leofwine came along the line.

'Any dead – tip them over. It is no time to be soft.'

In front of Godric, a tearful boy was trying to move a body much heavier than himself.

Godric bent down, lifted the dead man, held him high over his head, took one pace forward, and threw him in front of the shields and stakes. Men gaped. He rubbed his hands on his thighs to get rid of the blood.

Under where the body had lain was a sledgehammer.

The boy wiped his cheeks. 'My father was a smith.'

Godric stooped and picked up the sledgehammer. Holding it in one massive hand, he examined the head to make sure it was still tightly fixed.

'Kill them all,' said the boy.

One or two neighbours in the line were watching. Godric ignored them.

'Good to have a man like you here,' said one.

Godric looked at him, but said nothing.

The man looked uneasily at his companion and back at Godric.

'There is someone like you over on the right. Man with an axe. Already killed sixty Normans, they say.'

Godric peered intently over the shield wall and tried to pick out the various blocks of infantry.

He had to be there; he had to be!

*

'I want a second attack from the right, on the English left,' said the Duke.

'Using up the infantry first, I see,' said Fulk bitterly. 'As usual.'

'Hold your tongue, you insolent serf,' said Walter Giffard.

Fulk rounded on him. 'We have just returned from the English line. May I ask what you and your precious knights have been doing for the last hour? Waiting to follow after the victory charge and kill off the wounded?'

Giffard appealed to the Duke. 'My lord! Do we have to tolerate this – this—'

'Silence, both of you.' William pulled on the reins to control his restive new horse. 'The Flemings will have close cavalry support. We learn a lesson from our mistakes on the left.'

Count Alan of Brittany hung his head.

'Just so,' said Fitzosbern. He barked orders. 'Grandmesnil. Tosny.'

'Sir.'

'Take your contingents and go straight in after Beaumont and the Flemings. Until further orders you come under Sir Roger of Montgomery.'

'Sir.'

Fitzosbern turned to Montgomery himself. 'Remember, Roger – try their strength, but do not exhaust ours. Decide the timing yourself.'

Montgomery nodded.

Fulk was not finished.

'You are determined we shall earn our money this day – my lord.'

William whirled on him. 'Splendour of God! You are paid to obey, not to question. Fail me, and there will be nobody to pay you. Now be about your orders.'

Walter Giffard coughed loudly. William took the hint.

'You will have action soon enough. When the archers are in

position, we go in after the volleys. We go for the centre with our main knight strength.'

Giffard's eyes lit up. 'About time too, my lord, if I may say so.' He wheeled his horse away.

Fitzosbern grunted. 'Walter thinks one charge will win it.'

'If I thought it would, I should have told him to do it an hour ago,' said the Duke.

Eustace of Boulogne edged up beside the Duke.

'May I go with them, my lord? Turstin can carry this. He is burning to do it.'

William glanced up at the holy banner. Turstin of Bec looked hopeful.

'No. You follow me. Fitz, I stay with the reserves and watch from higher.'

In the valley, Fulk swore bitterly to Florens.

'So we attack, but we do not fling ourselves at them. Understand?'

Florens nodded.

Fulk looked across at the massed knights in the centre, and at the raised pennon of Sir Walter Giffard in their midst.

'Time those glorified hunstmen showed their manhood.'

Florens jerked a thumb towards a group of black-cowled figures up on Telham Hill.

'Have you seen them?'

Fulk spat. 'The birds of prey! Relieve our souls of sin before battle, and relieve our bodies of valuables after. Blood and Hellfire – who would be a Christian!'

Florens did not answer. It was at such times that Fulk made him feel uncomfortable.

'Here they come,' said Wilfrid.

'Holy Mary!' said Edwin. 'Cavalry as well.'

'A man on a horse is still only a man.'

Edwin looked more closely at the approaching troops. The Norman horse in the centre were hanging back. Bowmen were running in front of them.

'I see we are to be blessed with Norman arrows again,' said Wilfrid. 'Their right wing will hit our left first, long before the centre engages.'

Edwin looked puzzled.

'Are we left wing or centre?' he asked.

Wilfrid twitched his huge moustache. His eyes twinkled. 'Never mind where you are standing, lad. Just watch what is coming for you. If it is an arrow, I should duck. If a spearman clambers over that shield wall there, I should have a poke at him. One thing – they can not throw arrows and spearmen at us at the same time unless they want to kill their own men.'

'Sorry.'

Edwin was annoyed with himself for what he thought was a silly question.

Wilfrid slapped him on the back. 'Do what you did before, son. Pray hard, shove hard, and keep a spare eye in the back of your head.'

In the next few minutes, Edwin did all of those things. Amid a nightmare of staring faces, foaming bridles, and screams from the pit of Hell, Edwin stabbed and lunged until he could barely hold the spear. He thought he unhorsed one man, and he drove another mount mad with repeated jabs in the haunches.

Wilfrid roared and swung beside him, until a knight caught him a glancing blow with a sword on his left shoulder. Wilfrid let his axe arm fall for a moment as he gazed at the blood.

The Norman, sensing victory, jerked his heels to get his horse round for the deathblow.

Edwin saw the danger. He pounced on the axe left by the dead Eric. He wrenched it up, took it right back, and swung just as the Norman leaned over with sword arm high. He had barely noticed Edwin half hidden as he stooped.

The blow glanced off the side of his helmet and fell on his right shoulder. Edwin had braced himself for the shock of impact, but the axe went clean through – chain mail, shield strap, arm and all. The sword clattered on timber stakes. The man fainted without a sound and disappeared from view.

Edwin almost fainted himself.

'Well done, lad,' said Wilfrid, recovering himself. 'Only a scratch, me. That is one I owe you.'

Edwin nodded feebly.

'God, they are breaking,' said Wilfrid. 'That was quick.'

Edwin now had his hands on his knees in case he was sick.

'Their whole right wing is breaking off,' repeated Wilfrid. 'God bless our fyrdmen and ploughboys. Ah – the dolts. The madmen!'

Edwin looked up. 'What is it?'

'They are running out. After all we told them. Stop! Stop!'

Edwin forgot to be sick and stood up to see. A section of the shield wall near the extreme left had opened, and men were streaming down the hill in the chase, yelling in triumph.

Edwin suddenly felt a chill of horror. He was sure he had seen Godric. It was impossible, but he had seen Godric. It was difficult to mistake his great size. Worse, he was limping as if wounded, and he was following the pursuit down the hill. It looked like a hammer, of all things, in his hand. Dear God – a hammer!

'They are lost. Lost. Dead men, all of them.' Wilfrid continued to chant to himself.

Earl Leofwine came along behind them.

'Mend that gap!' he bawled. 'Close up ... They will not be back. If you do not believe me, watch!'

Leofwine swore non-stop. It was waste, senseless waste.

Dietrich's hands trembled as he held the metal cup. It rattled against his teeth. Water spilled down his jerkin. He held out the empty vessel to the two carriers without looking at them.

'Did you see him? Did you see him?'

Florens flopped to the ground. He had heard Dietrich tell it twice before since leaving the line.

'It was when we broke off. We had everything under control. Even when they came out after us we were still retreating in good order. Rainald was out there holding us all together.'

'Rainald is – was a fine soldier,' said Florens.

Dietrich glared wildly. 'Yes – was! Why did that maniac single him out? He was the one who started it all. He was the one who broke out first. And why was he yelling Bloodeye's name all the time?'

'Perhaps he thought Rainald was Fulk. Rainald is – was very tall, just like Fulk. In helmet and jerkin it could be difficult to—'

'Bah! Everyone knows Fulk is left-handed.'

'It may not be common knowledge to the English,' said Florens evenly.

He caught the eye of two older soldiers, and motioned them forward either side of Dietrich.

Dietrich could not stop talking. 'He was laying about him enough as it was – with a hammer of all things. A smith's hammer. Then he caught sight of Rainald and went crazy. There must have been five or six men between him and Rainald; he just swept them aside. I think three of them are dead, and the others can not count six good ribs between them.' Dietrich wiped a hand across his forehead. 'Rainald hardly had time to turn round. He had no idea what hit him.' He gestured helplessly. His voice rose several tones. 'It was unbelievable. His head – it simply disappeared into his shoulders.'

'All right,' said Florens, standing up. 'Enough.'

'It took six Saxons to drag him off up the hill. Practically carried him.'

Florens whispered to the two men. 'Get him up to the wagons and out of the way. Tie him to a wheel if necessary. He is no use here.'

Florens gulped some water. Apart from the loss of Rainald and a handful of others, mostly at the hands of the crazed giant, the attack and the withdrawal had not gone too badly. In the event, the madman bursting through the shield wall had played into their hands. The hotheads who followed and overtook him had no idea what they were running into. Beaumont and the extra knights must have outnumbered them ten to one. They had been helpless – out in the open, in twos and threes, on foot, low down the hill – it was easier than pig-sticking.

'There go the bows!'

All eyes turned to watch the hissing flights against the shield wall. Florens was relieved. Dietrich – weak, puzzled and quarrelsome – was pulled away with a grip on each elbow and immediately forgotten.

At the foot of the hill, Sir Walter Giffard took a tighter grip on his spear. He had watched the attack and withdrawal on the right. Montgomery had handled everything with his usual coolness and deliberation, and the mercenary infantry had proved to be their usual unreliable selves. He snorted. So it was up to him and the heavy knights of the centre after all.

'They are going down behind the shields again,' said one of his men. 'Not a head in sight.'

'Never fear, my lads,' said Giffard. 'When we have finished there will be no heads to put up afterwards.'

A noise that was half laugh and half cheer floated out on either side of him.

Sir Walter flexed his toes and braced his legs once more against the stirrups. As soon as the bows were finished ...

Now was the time for the proper fighting. Not feeble pokes on the left from second-rate auxiliaries, or half-hearted attacks on the right led by beardless favourites like Beaumont or faithless villains like Bloodeye – all of them, be it noted, against greybeards or yokels.

Now was the time for some real soldiers to show them how it

should be done. And no more wary fencing on fringes. They were going straight for the middle, the very core of the enemy; they were going to hit the English right in the gut.

'Heads up.'

Edwin peered over the arrow-spiked shield wall. Holy Virgin! Every knight in Christendom must be out there. A forest of spears waved over them. Pennons fluttered at the lance head of every troop leader.

Behind them he could see the banner of the Duke himself, though the white horse was gone. He glanced at Wilfrid, who answered his unspoken question.

'He is there all right. If he had fallen, we should be toasting victory by now.'

Edwin looked behind at the apple tree. The Dragon and the Fighting Man stood out against a blue sky. Harold strode up and down the rear of the line.

'We are up here; he is down there.'

On the left Leofwine was threatening to kill any man who called the charge.

The sound of splashing reached them as a thousand hooves crossed the stream at the foot of Caldbec Hill. Edwin fancied he could hear the sound of jingling bridles, till it was overborne by the ever-increasing drumming of the mounting charge.

The beat quickened. The front lines of the spear forest mysteriously shortened and disappeared, as they were lowered to point straight at the English array.

Tops of helmets became visible, as knights leaned forward and urged their mounts up the slope. Right arms were raised to hold spears aloft, poised for the cast. Shouts, urgings, trumpet calls, swearwords, and battle cries grew and mingled into one gigantic surge of sound, that made their heads ring almost as the impact of attack made their weapons ring.

The English housecarls rose to both challenges.

There was a huge roar of, 'Out! Out!' The four-foot axes swung, and clove anything Norman that presented itself.

Shields were dented or crushed like children's toys. Chain mail parted like so much wool. Edwin saw one Norman head flying up in the air – someone had severed mail coif, neck, bone and all.

The Normans had their successes too. The English lines were so densely packed that a spear entering over the shield wall could hardly miss. Men were flung backwards by the shock. They died with no time to show reaction to a shaft in the chest, throat, face . . . Many fell from a downward blow to the shoulder as the knights drew their swords and came in for the second onset.

Men raved without their reason, and existed from second to second in an orgy of impact and a tempest of noise.

It could not last.

There came a moment when the knights pulled back to turn just a yard too far, a moment when the return to the assault was no longer a matter of blind, screaming instinct. There came a moment when they not merely saw, but took notice of the wild faces and wide mouths challenging them, when the crossing of the space between them became a matter of calculated chance.

In their hesitation, they unconsciously backed their horses another yard, and another.

Space allowed for the return of the intellect. Intellect reminded them of fatigue and of the danger of hesitation. Fatigue meant that another clash was impossible without rest and recovery. Hesitation provided the enemy with easy targets for a parting spear-cast.

There was nothing for it but to back off and retire. Again, the trumpets only announced the obvious.

The English watched them go, in a sweating, chest-heaving silence.

Before they could get their breath back, the King's brothers were bullying and hectoring.

'Clear the dead! Fill the gaps! Get those shields up again. Rear ranks forward. Close up. Close up!'

Gyrth and Leofwine shuffled the wings closer to the centre to make good the losses, and had more shields hastily put up to protect the flanks.

When Edwin looked over his shoulder, the apple tree and the royal standards were nearer.

Harold's voice, though, was as strong and serene as ever. He came along behind the line again, breaking off shafts of arrows that stuck into his shield.

'What did I tell you? We are up here; they are down there. You see? It works. Who will get tired first – the army that runs up and down hill, or the army that sits on its arse? I tell you, we are the only army in Christendom that has the enemy running both ways. Let us keep it like that.'

There were a few laughs.

Wilfrid put a massive arm round Edwin's shoulders. 'We are doing fine, lad; we are doing fine.'

'Would my lord care for some refreshment?'

'No! ... Yes! Get something – anything. Use your sense, damn you. And hurry!'

Geoffrey flopped back on his pillow of sheepskins. He knew he was being impossible.

The whole day was impossible.

A hundred times he had strained his ears.

'Thinks he will hear his trumpets from here – seven miles away,' whispered one servant to another outside his tent.

'I can hear *you*,' shouted Geoffrey. 'Go away.'

'I shall leave one sentry, my lord.'

Geoffrey growled something unintelligible.

A fat lot of good one sentry would be if the Saxons arrived. If it was a Saxon hand that pulled back his tent flap.

So he could have seen his last dawn. Eaten his last good meal. Thierry had thought of that.

Geoffrey sighed.

Had he really been such a good lord? Oh, yes, they had made a fuss of him in the old days – 'Master Geoffrey' this and 'Master Geoffrey' that – blacksmith Lambert and Bodo the hayward and Bertha in her kitchen. And Ivo. Dear Ivo! Who growled and nagged; who cuffed him and beat him; who was never satisfied. But Ivo loved him; he was never in any doubt about that. It was easy when Father was alive, or when brother Mauger ran the castle at Montbrai.

On his own in Coutances – a young and very unwilling bishop – it had been an uphill struggle from the outset. A newcomer, a nobody, in the councils of the Duke. Creating an episcopal household from nothing. Building a cathedral from the foundations up. In ever-increasing demand by the Duke at his military gatherings and on campaign. There was never enough time. He had never felt like a particularly good lord.

He had certainly not been a particularly constant lover. He had wanted to be. Things just seemed to go against them. Sybil's conscience had not helped. Should he have given it all up for her? Returned to a half-share in a petty knight's fee in the Cotentin? Would that have made him a better partner for her? Could he really have undone the consecration?

And now, Thierry was on his way with what might be his very last message. Would Sybil weep for him? He hoped so. Just a tear or two. She seemed better able than he to cope with the consequences of their decision.

So here he was – a split man with a crozier in one hand and a mace in the other. Did he love his cathedral? Yes, of course he did – thought about it all the time. Did he think of himself as doing God's holy work then? Hardly! He had simply done the next thing. To the best of his ability. He would say this for him-self, though: he hated a half-done job. He liked efficiency for its own sake.

He turned restively, and swore at the pain in his leg.

And now he was unable to do his work efficiently. Unable to do anything but curse. Where did he wish to be now? With Sybil? In Coutances? Ha!

Somewhere up on Senlac Hill, a spotty-faced Bishop of Bayeux was getting all the credit as the only fighting bishop in the army . . .

William sipped his drink and listened to the casualty reports from his contingent leaders.

They could have been a lot worse. Most of his senior vassals were unhurt. There were few wounded men to crawl in the way of the next charge; most of those struck by a Saxon axe were very definitely dead.

William flung the cup to a servant, and took the reins of his fresh horse.

'We hit them again, only stronger. My brothers – bring your contingents from the left and join me. Giffard – we reverse the order. You act as reserve and I lead. It will give time for you to recover.'

Giffard bitterly regretted his move to the rear, but his military experience told him the sense of it.

'The same spacing, my lord?'

'No. Our formation is too loose. It is not enough to go for the centre; we go for the centre of the centre. We try and punch a hole.'

Fitzosbern grunted. So Geoffrey's trumpets could prove their worth.

He turned to the chief herald. 'Pass the word. Close order. Very close order. Watch his Grace's signal.'

William addressed the cavalry commanders: 'Fresh mounts. In position as soon as possible. No delay after the first arrow flights. They are having too much time to recover.'

'Not easy, sir,' said someone. 'The bowmen have to retire through us. If you want us in close order, it will take even longer.'

William nodded. 'I agree. So this is what we do.' He looked about him. 'Where are those cursed sergeants?'

The archer sergeants came puffing back from the top of Telham Hill.

'Splendour of God!' thundered William. 'I told you to make haste.'

'Sorry, my lord. It took time to convince Sir Baldwin. He found it hard to believe that you wanted a third issue so quickly.'

As he spoke, and as William swore, the bowmen trotted past with bulging quivers.

William pointed to the left flank. 'Get them over there, as close to the English as you dare. Not in front of us. We must have a clear run in the centre. We can then begin to move as soon as you loose the last flight. It also helps you to follow the sun.'

The chief sergeant looked puzzled. 'How do we replenish, sir?'

'The long way round. If this idea works, you may not be needed again.'

'Sir.'

'And one other thing. I want the shafts high.'

'High, sir?'

'You heard. You are making no impression so far. They just squat behind those damned shields.'

'We have caused casualties, sir,' said the senior sergeant, offended.

'Not enough. This is no time for marksmanship. I want damage, not hundreds of shields bristling with wasted arrows. Get the sun behind you and fire high. They must either die from falling arrows or they must lift their shields. And we can move up while the last ones are falling, before they can recover.'

The sergeant looked unconvinced. 'We may not be able to guarantee a high degree of accuracy, my lord.'

'Holy St Stephen! I want obedience, not accuracy. See to it, man!'

'Sir.'

He scuttled off.

William kicked his new horse into motion.

'Come, my lords. Come, Robert, Odo. Let us cut the English in two.'

Harold screwed up his eyes.

'So – this time the Bastard leads.'

He looked at the compact ranks of the Norman knights and at the Papal banner in the centre.

'The archers are not strung out any more,' said a thegn. 'They are up to something. Look.'

'Damn the archers,' said Harold, moving swiftly to his messengers.

He grabbed one by the elbow. 'Now – like the wind. I want all the housecarls behind the wings to join us in the centre. If you can get the Earls Gyrth and Leofwine here too, so much the better.'

'A gamble, sir?' said the thegn.

'Look out there, man. Can you see anything moving up on our wings? William fights a battle like a game of chess – a piece here, a piece there. Well, two can do that. Besides –' Harold pointed at the Papal banner '– we have forced him into the open. I have seen the pennons of his two brothers there as well. He is coming for the centre, for me. Three brothers are challenging; he shall find three brothers to meet him. Gyrth and Leofwine would not miss this for the world.'

Harold spat on his axe and examined the edge of the blade.

'I never did like Odo.'

*

Gorm fought against the waves of nausea, and tugged hard.

He flung away the bloodstained head and brushed the broken shaft from his lap. He clutched his bleeding arm and hung his head between his raised knees. The din of battle came and went in his ears as if someone were constantly opening and shutting a door.

When he felt able to look, he examined the hole in his forearm. He had to find some kind of binding.

He looked around him. Not far away lay a dead man. Gorm was surprised that there were not many more. The front of the man's hauberk was stained from a hideous spear wound in the throat.

Gorm glanced to right and left. Nobody was looking. He edged across to the corpse. The mail was of high quality. So were the rest of the clothes. Must be a thegn. If this man was as important as he looked, he would probably have a soft shirt of some kind under his leather jerkin. Ideal for a bandage.

He lifted the body to ease up the hauberk and jerkin. Yes – there was the shirt. He fought to keep his eyes away from the gaping hole below the jaw.

A kick in the ribs sent him sprawling. A furious servant stood over him.

'Animal! Pig! Marsh rat! Can you not wait to loot the enemy instead?' He looked round desperately. 'Give me a knife – anything!'

Gorm showed his bleeding arm.

The man would have gone for him with his bare hands if his two companions had not held him back. Gorm, whimpering in pain and fear, crawled away as fast as he could.

The servant still struggled.

'Let me go. Let me kill him.'

'Wait, Siward. Wait. If you leave Earl Gyrth now to chase that wretch, somebody else will come and do the same. It is not worth it.'

Siward began to calm down. His friend held on to Siward's arms to make sure.

'Now, get him cleaned up,' he said. 'The King must not be harrowed beyond need. We shall fetch Leofwine.'

Siward stared. 'Leofwine, too?'

'In the same charge. He got it in the chest. One of them brought down the Bastard's horse, they say, but William survived.'

'And the King?'

'Still living, still leading. And still winning. But sorrowing. He will come soon to see them. Do your work – yes?'

Siward nodded, and his friend released him.

'Oh – and get a priest.'

'They are getting fewer,' said Beaumont. 'I swear the shield wall is contracting again.'

'Oh, it has done that,' said Montgomery.

Beaumont pressed his point.

'And the close order worked. You see? Geoffrey was right.'

'"Lord Geoffrey" to you,' said Montgomery. 'But they are still up there, and we are still down here.'

Fitzosbern reined in beside them.

'It is time you were doing something about it.'

'You did not make much impression on the centre, Fitz,' said Montgomery.

'You never know what impression a battering ram has been making until the wall falls down,' said Fitzosbern. 'We had an effect, I can tell you. The arrows were finding targets too.'

Montgomery pointed up Senlac Hill.

'Then where are the gaps?'

'The shield wall looks the same, I agree. But it is not the same behind it. Gyrth is dead – saw him go. Maybe Leofwine too. At least that is what they are saying. They are weakening.'

Montgomery was unconvinced. 'We are getting tired too, you know.'

'You have had a rest watching us. Now it is your turn again. They pulled in housecarls from the wings to meet us, so the wings are more vulnerable. If we hit them hard, now, with infantry and cavalry combined, we could open up a flank. With luck, both. But it must be quick – before they put out the house-carls again. William is sending de Montfort in again on the left with the Bretons.'

Fulk spat. 'The Bretons. They were the ones who caused the trouble in the first place. If they had not been so anxious to save their own skins, we should have been up there by now.'

Fitzosbern refused, as usual, to take offence.

'Then it allows our captain of mercenaries the opportunity to distinguish himself by completing the work so badly begun by our allies from Brittany. Flemings, we all know, are never anxious to save their own skins.'

Fulk's scar twisted as he smiled to acknowledge the sharpness of the thrust.

'Then let us be about winning the Bastard's battle for him and earning his – er – gratitude. I take it we have archery support –' he paused significantly '– like everyone else.'

'No,' said Fitzosbern flatly.

'What?'

'They must replenish. And they must go the long way round. If we wait for the archers to return, it gives the English too long.'

'What about us?'

'You have just had a rest.'

Fulk glared. 'You know what I mean.'

Fitzosbern refused to be outfaced. 'Those are his Grace's orders. If you do not wish to carry them out, then say so now, and we shall replace you with someone who will. They will of course receive your reward for doing your work.'

There was a moment of tense stillness. Beaumont scarcely heard any sounds of battle.

At last, Fulk resumed his normal air of casual insolence, and bowed.

'In that case, Sir William, you can tell his Grace that my men and I will faithfully execute your orders, in every detail.'

Beaumont glanced at Montgomery, and blew out his cheeks.

Fulk looked hard at Fitzosbern. 'Should you care, Sir William, to come and observe us more closely during the next hour – while we are succeeding where you failed – you will be very well received.'

The sagging eye stared balefully. Beaumont felt a ripple of fear on the back of his neck.

Fulk strode away.

'Stay away, Fitz, for God's sake,' said Montgomery. 'He will kill you, and I would not put it past him to do it with a Saxon spear, and from the front.'

Fitzosbern grunted.

'It had occurred to me,' he said. He pulled his horse round. 'You never know. Dig a trap for someone, and you can fall in it yourself. Now get on with it. William wants that wing rolled up.'

Sir Baldwin de Clair rode down from Telham Hill to complain.

This had been the fourth issue of arrows; it was not according to plan. It was no use asking the archer sergeants to tell the Duke. He had just had a blazing row with them.

He would have to tell William himself. How could he be relied upon to produce sheaves of fresh arrows for the final assaults and the pursuit when stupid sergeants were engaged in such prodigal waste? And without proper authority. Had they no idea of thrift? Could they not see that the English were not firing arrows that they could recover? Were they blind as well as stupid?

He swore at two carriers who were sloshing precious water everywhere, and paused halfway down to look for the Duke.

Nearest to him, an attack was being prepared from the right against the English left. He heard Montgomery bawling orders.

Baldwin suddenly saw something that drove all thought of arrows out of his head. A tall, strong man, a foot soldier. A well-equipped foot soldier, wearing gleaming mail and metal helmet. A soldier of great authority, judging by the way he was directing the men around him, and being obeyed. A very powerful soldier, with a drawn sword *in his left hand*. Baldwin winced at the memory of a burned back, of precious white flesh charred and blistered.

Godric ran the whetstone over the blade once more.

He would have been content to continue with the hammer – any weapon would do now, until a Norman killed him. What did it matter? Fulk was dead. There was no further reason for living.

His two companions in the line had thrust the axe into his hand after the last attack. After watching him with the hammer, they were curious to see what he would do with a housecarl's axe.

'He will not need it any more,' they assured him. 'Stone dead. Arrow in the windpipe – just like Hardrada. Go on, take it. You are the best one to use it.'

Godric shrugged and took it. Now he stood and watched the preparations for a fresh Norman attack on his end of the line. Infantry and horsemen together. So there would be no violent charge, not until the last few paces.

In loose order, they started up the slope, picking their way round horses thrashing with broken legs and backs. A few splayed hands rose in supplication between the slippery tussocks of grass.

Godric ran his hands up and down the haft of the axe. He had never swung anything like this in his life. God, what a weapon! Suppose he had had it just now, when—

He tensed.

He was not sure whether it was something he first heard or first saw. There – behind the infantry in studded jackets. Although the man was lower down the slope, he looked bigger, thicker, stronger.

Godric screwed up his dark face to try to catch his voice again, but it was lost in the general muffled roar that was floating up to him.

He felt his heart thumping once more, after the curious stillness since he had last killed. It was impossible. Fulk was dead. Godric could still hear the crunching of the skull beneath his hammer.

But there he was. Godric strained to get a clearer view through the bobbing heads. He was oblivious to the words around him – the commands, the grim jokes, the muttered prayers. He caught nothing of the tenseness of the men beside him, saw none of the staring eyes or whitened knuckles.

He was looking for one thing, now that he remembered. At last, when the Norman line was almost upon them, the running bodies opened up enough for him to see. The man carried his sword in the left hand!

Of course! The hand that had held the knife against Rowena's throat. Suddenly everything became visible and obvious – the cat-like agility for a big man, the livid eye, the scar, the dark jowls. It all seemed so clear that he wondered why he could not have recognised him a mile away. How could he have been deceived by the appearance of the other man – whoever he was.

A soldier lunged at him with a spear.

Godric woke up just in time. He parried the blow, then broke the man's jaw with a backward fling of the axe-head. The scream of pain made him aware of the awful noise around him, of the need to fight, to look everywhere.

Five minutes before, he had cared nothing for the length of his life or the manner of his death. Now it was vital to stay alive until he could reach Fulk and stand before him.

A knight was pushing against the weakened shield wall in front of him. As he urged his mount through a gap Godric swung at his knee. He was not used to the length of the axe. It clove the man's thigh and sank into the flank of the horse.

While he was struggling to pull it out, another horseman came up faster. A fyrdman rammed a spear into the horse's chest. The impact threw him backwards, but it also brought down the screaming horse, and threw its rider right over its head and on to the shoulders of some yelling peasants. They finished him off with sickles and billhooks.

There were several gaps in the shield wall. Some excited fyrd-men had stepped outside in their eagerness to thrust away at the enemy. The first impetus of the assault had gone, but the Normans did not retire at once. Because they had not attacked as quickly as before, they had more breath left to strike another blow.

The fighting became a series of scrappy encounters between separate groups of men, even single combats. One thin man with a long spear was holding his own against a French swordsman.

Godric scrambled through the gap in front of him, and nearly fell at once when his knee buckled. The handle of the axe saved him. He recovered, stood erect, and roared Fulk's name.

Fulk picked out the one familiar sound in the din around him, and lifted his head.

It took another roar to work out where it came from.

When he saw Godric, he recognised him instantly. After a second of tense stillness, he began stalking. Holding his sword before him, he beckoned Godric towards him with his right hand.

Godric took a few steps forward. Fulk saw the bad limp. A leer twisted the scar on his face.

Two or three Flemings started at Godric, but Fulk put out his arm.

'No, no – he is mine. Keep them off.'

He gestured towards the nearest fyrdmen, but none of them showed willingness to advance any further.

Godric watched as Fulk circled, feinting and leaping back, flaunting his agility. He held the axe across his chest in both hands, turning, watching. He never heard Fulk's taunts and insults.

Fulk was enjoying himself. This was an extra, unforeseen pleasure, worth half a day's pay. At last – something of interest. He felt his heart pounding. He swore when he heard Florens' voice.

'We must break now. The left wing is beginning to disengage. Our wing will be next. We will be out in front alone. Finish him off.'

A pity, but there it was.

He swung at Godric's shoulder, and gasped in surprise. He had not been prepared for this clumsy giant to swing the axe with one hand. His blow was easily brushed aside. The back swing nearly caught him off balance.

Once Godric had begun to move, he continued, swinging the huge weapon in deadly gleaming circles. Despite the limp he advanced steadily. Fulk crouched and peered, but could not get past the humming blade; it swung and returned like a whiplash. He was forced to retreat.

The nearby Saxons cheered. The thin man pushed his foot into the Norman swordsman's chest, yanked out his spear, and came to have a closer look.

Fulk played for time. No man could swing a housecarl's axe like that for long. He received another shock. Godric simply changed hands and bore down upon him. Somehow his limp made it all the more unreal.

Fulk began sweating. He continued his slow retreat downhill.

The two knots of Saxons and Flemings were drawn along as if by strings.

Fulk began to feel ridiculous. He had to do something. He found himself swinging wildly with his sword, first in one hand, then, when he became tired, in both.

Once, they clashed, and Fulk's weapon was knocked to the ground. Luckily for him, it fell on the downward side, and he was able to get to it before Godric could hobble to the spot.

Fulk had the presence of mind to appear to hesitate. He stayed in the crouch just a fraction too long, hoping that Godric would swing the axe towards the ground. A leap to one side and a swift downward cut while Godric tugged the blade out of the grass, and it would be all over, except for the torture and the choice of death-thrust.

Godric ignored the deceit, and simply came on, still swinging in humming circles. Fulk whipped up the sword in the nick of time, and found himself sucked into the same desperate tactics as before. Enraged by the Saxon cheers, he flailed frantically in a two-handed grip, and made sudden contact again.

There was a gasp from everyone.

Godric's axe-head flew up into the air.

Fulk stood up straight. His chest was heaving, and his face was glistening, but he was leering again. The sagging eyelid gleamed redder, the white scar gnarled and livid against his dark cheek. He blinked the sweat out of his eyes.

The Flemings were cheering now. They barely glanced as a single Norman knight rode up to see what was going on.

'Make way, make way!'

Unwillingly, they edged aside, without taking their eyes off Fulk. They began chanting.

'Finish him! Finish him!'

Fulk's face flushed; his lips began twitching. Baring his teeth, he roared like an animal. Holding his sword high with both hands, he poised to rush at Godric.

Behind him, the knight burst through the last ranks of Flemings, and his horse's shoulder nudged Fulk in the back so hard that he stumbled forward.

Godric, now holding the haft of the axe in both hands, brought it down with all his strength on Fulk's left shoulder.

Fulk bellowed and fell. The sword flickered away into the grass. His left arm buckled under him, and flopped useless when he rolled over and tried to rise.

Godric struck again, and the helmet flew off. As Fulk struggled up, black hair awry, he put up his right arm as protection; a third swing broke it.

One or two Flemings started to move forward, but the knight on the horse waved a spear and stopped them.

Fulk was now to his knees. Even his good eye was staring. Flecks of foam appeared on his lips. His two arms looked as if they belonged to a drunken puppet. He was roaring incoherently.

Godric limped towards him. Another blow smashed his cheek and knocked him to the ground again.

He uttered a hideous cry that made the watchers' flesh crawl. The limbs, though bent, went rigid at unreal angles. Blood oozed down his chin from where he had bitten his tongue. His face and lips turned a ghastly blue, which made the blood look dark.

Saxons and Flemings alike were transfixed with horror. They all wanted it ended.

'Here, man!'

Godric turned. The thin Saxon tossed his spear. Godric caught it, laid down the broken haft of the axe, and once more took a two-handed grip.

He stumbled forward again until he stood right over Fulk. The body was now jerking and twisting in violent spasms. A fiendish, tense-jawed mask glared evil up at him.

Godric waited until the convulsions took Fulk on to his back, then he plunged. The spear went right through and embedded itself in the grass – so far that Godric almost overbalanced.

Fulk grabbed the spear with both hands, but there was no strength in the misshapen arms. He writhed with staring eyes, foam and blood running from both sides of his mouth. A dark stain appeared on his leggings at the groin. Where the blood had spread on his chest, it mingled with the mud on the mail, and ran black across the dark ringlets.

Men on both sides gasped and crossed themselves.

Godric held on grimly until all movement had ceased.

The knight on the horse trotted forward. The mail coif, steel helmet and nasal guard masked his face. He looked down at the spreadeagled body.

'Fortunes of war,' he said.

He turned to the silent Flemings. 'Fortunes of war,' he repeated, more loudly.

He dug in his spurs, and they were forced to move aside. Then he was gone.

The Saxons pulled Godric back up the hill with them. He made no resistance.

Florens was the first to recover. He looked around.

The whole of the Norman attack had ground to a standstill. Men were streaming back on both flanks; the Bretons were in shame again. One or two stepped aside to loot dead bodies. Brian paused, picked up an axe, and put a horse out of its misery.

At the top of the hill, the two English standards still flew.

Florens clapped his hands. 'Wake up! Back! Back!'

They could not take their eyes off Fulk's body. For a moment Florens considered giving orders for them to move it, if only to give a few of them something to do. When he saw the horror on their faces he changed his mind. Frankly, he did not fancy touching the body himself, though he knew there were gold coins in a belt wallet. Perhaps later, in the evening.

He gave Fulk one last look, and turned away.

'Back, back, regroup over there, by Beaumont's pennon. Move!'

Montgomery watched Florens at work. The man was a professional to his fingertips, and he would have them ready for another attack in good time. But he was no Bloodeye.

Montgomery looked up the hill, where jubilant fyrdmen cheered Godric's return, and a hundred willing hands repaired the gaps in the shield wall. The giant was exercising an influence out of all proportion to his rank and position. That one duel had knocked the stuffing out of the Flemings. Florens would re-form them, and they would go into action again, but it was now an open question what would happen when they reached the English line.

Beaumont pulled up noisily beside him.

'Let us do it. Let us try it.'

'What?'

'A retreat. They have come out after us twice. Let us pull them out this time.'

'Oh, shut up.'

Beaumont stared. 'This is just the situation that Lord Geoffrey was preparing us for. We shall never get a better chance.'

Montgomery ignored him. Beaumont became angry.

'What have you got against the idea? Is it too new for you? Like that old man Giffard?'

Montgomery lost his temper. 'Were we anywhere else than where we are. I should call you out for that. So much for your arrogance. It is surpassed only by your stupidity.' He flung out his arm. 'Just look at those Flemings. Set them running, and they would not stop till they reached the sea. And the knights would follow. We should have nothing else left here but a chorus of lonely trumpeters and one young idiotic nobleman waving his sword.'

Beaumont flushed. 'So what do we do – *sir*?'

'We do not try to harness fear. We change it to hope.'

'And how do we do that?'

'By removing the cause of the fear.'

Beaumont swallowed. 'You mean – the giant?'

Montgomery sneered. 'Not so keen now, eh? I thought not. Have no fear; I shall not ask you. I shall not ask anybody.' He hawked and spat. 'And neither would Sir Walter Giffard if he were in my place.'

As Florens trudged away, he thought of Fulk and of the partnership of the past years. He could not escape a twinge of relief amid the natural regret.

Fortunes of war.

Sir Walter Giffard looked up Senlac Hill. No doubt now; the shield wall was shorter. The ring of men on the top was smaller, but it was just as still as ever. The only movement he could detect was the dead being tipped over the wall.

The cries of wounded men reached him. A score of arms were raised in the grass to his front. Norman losses were serious too, in men and above all in horses. They had used all their fresh mounts. Now it was a case of change and change about until they dropped. The stud and stables at Longueville would take years to recover from this.

The corrupt Flemish infantry had let them down on the right as well as the Bretons on the left. There ought to be gaps in the line by now for the cavalry to exploit. Call themselves professionals?

Giffard spat.

Worst of all was the hill. The damned hill. And the stream. Proper firm open ground that they were used to, and there would have been no problem. At the top too, the lopsided rampart of shields and stakes. Behind it the wild heads in the centre and the forest of ridiculous farm tools on the wings. The only consolation was that Beaumont had been no more successful on the right. All the more reason for Giffard himself to think of something in the centre.

He looked up once more at the Saxon line – a wild hedgehog

of amateurism and out-of-date bumble. They had no right to be still there; it was all so stupid and unfair.

'Bastards!'

Robert of Mortain reined in beside him, slid off his mail coif, and wiped his forehead.

'If only they would move, or sway a bit, or something.'

The Duke rode up.

'We shall give them something to sway about.'

Mortain saw the archers trudging by yet again with swollen quivers, and marvelled.

'Brother, how did you get all those arrows out of de Clair? He garners them like a miser.'

William grunted. 'We spoke.'

He shouted to the archer sergeants. 'Further round still, for the sun. I want them high again.'

Their faces fell.

'High, sir?'

'Yes. But this time you can show off your marksmanship too. No blanket firing. I want everything in one place. You go for the tree and the two standards. All of you – understand? The tree and the standards. And high!'

'Sir.'

William turned to his vassals. 'Come, brother. Come, Giffard.'

Eustace of Boulogne pushed his horse forward.

'Please, my lord. Let me fight this time. Let Turstin carry. It may be my last chance.'

Turstin of Bec tensed himself in the saddle. William looked up the hill.

'I doubt that.'

'I beg you, sir.'

'No. Come, my lords. We make them move, or at least we make them sway.'

*

On Telham Hill, Gilbert fumed and fretted.

'How much longer?' he demanded.

'As long as necessary,' said Ralph, unmoved.

Gilbert pointed. 'There they go again. Much more of that and there will not be any English left to attack.'

'That is the general idea,' said Bruno.

Gilbert swore.

'They are slower,' said Ralph.

'Hardly surprising,' said Bruno.

Ralph grimaced in anxiety. How much closer could they go in after the bows? Much more, and they would have arrows in Norman necks.

'Sir. You must come. They are gathering again.'

Harold replaced the two shrouds, crossed himself, and got to his feet.

'If anything happens to me, see that my mother is told where they are.' He paused, listening. 'What is that noise? It comes from behind.'

'It is the women, sir. They are down there, praying and—'

'Weeping. With good reason. But courage, lad.' Harold shook off the mood. 'We shall yet give them a day to be proud of. Something for the orphans to sing about, eh?'

The messenger fidgeted. 'Sir – your orders.'

Harold drew himself up. 'Yes. Yes. I want all the wing house-carls to the centre again. We can yet surprise the Bastard. Thank God he is a chess player.'

In the next few minutes, no man in the English line would have guessed that Harold had only just dried streaming tears. Running with bent legs from one block of the wall to another, with his shield held like a canopy over his head against the whining arrows, he chivvied and coaxed and cheered; he swore and blasphemed and made black jokes; above all, he encouraged and inspired.

The thinning line of housecarls turned to face the labouring Norman horses with a fresh gleam in the eye and a fresh grip on the axe.

Harold plodded up to the apple tree. One of the standard bearers was sagging with an arrow in the top of the shoulder. The Dragon of Wessex swayed. Another man grabbed it and held it up again.

Harold was shocked at the number of arrow wounds among his headquarter staff. For a moment he considered moving his command position, but decided to assess the current battle situation first.

He stood by the tree, laid down his shield, and put a hand to his eyes to shade them from the afternoon sun.

The attack was now being pressed. Harold was so used to the dreadful noise that he was barely conscious of it. He had to watch, and judge, and guess – and out-think the Bastard.

Nor far away a knot of Norman knights crashed through the shield wall. Kicking and hacking, they carved an avenue of death towards him. Desperate housecarls ran after them, swinging axes and swords at stirrups, legs, haunches, hooves, anything to stop them. Fyrdmen ran in from the wings and formed a block in front of the King – stabbing, cutting, clawing the enemy down.

One of them saw Harold, pointed, and yelled something.

Suddenly Harold felt a great blow on his head, and a stabbing pain over the eye. The impact flung him against the tree. He put up a hand and wrenched the arrow from the rim of the helmet.

The blow had left him dizzy. Blood ran down into his eye and blinded it. He leaned against the trunk and blinked and shook his head.

In front of him, the leading Norman was at last dragged from his horse and cut to pieces. The one behind caught a glimpse of the King fumbling for his sword like a man in the dark. Half his face was a mask of blood.

The Norman screamed, 'The King is stricken!' before an axe laid open his back.

One by one, the frantic English tore down the maddened, yelling Normans. They paused in front of their wounded king, their chests heaving, their hands red and sticky. Harold waved to show that he was not badly wounded, but it did not look like it.

Behind them, more housecarls hewed like maniacs to stem the flood of Normans through the gap, and at last sealed it, partly with shields and partly with enemy dead.

Painfully but steadily the attack was turned back. All along the line were piles of dead and dying. Crippled horses uttered sounds to give men bad dreams for the rest of their lives. One destrier seemed to twitch although it had no head.

No words were exchanged. No orders were given. The gaps were repaired. The wings shuffled and closed up. Severed limbs were kicked aside. Men leaned on axes and grimaced with the effort of drawing breath.

Harold, bareheaded and with a stained bandage over his eye, walked up and down with drawn sword.

'It can not be long now. Hold on. Hold on. We are still here. And the Bastard is still down there.'

The exhausted vassals stumbled back to the Duke, who now sat on his fourth horse of the day.

He listened to their report and to the account of their losses. A glance around could have told him anyway. At least a quarter of the knighthood of Normandy was lying up on Senlac Hill; with the infantry it was harder to tell, but casualties had been heavy. The non-French contingent leaders painted a similar gloomy picture; they would probably exaggerate in hope of greater reward. The news was still depressing. Even the mercenaries had suffered; Bloodeye himself was gone.

Montgomery confirmed his impression that the English resistance seemed stiffer on the right than on the left. Something about a giant inspiring the fyrdmen.

Only the archers had light losses, but that was to be expected, since they had not been closely engaged, and they had done no defensive fighting.

Men dismounted heavily and stood about in small groups. A few took drinks. Hardly anybody ate.

They gazed up to the top of Senlac Hill. The Saxon line was shorter, the ring of shields smaller, but it looked just as still and just as permanent. Above it the two Saxon standards flew by the tree. Was it imagination, or did their golden stitchwork gleam yet more boldly in the rays of the late afternoon sun?

William looked at the length of the shadow cast by his horse. Time was now running against him as well.

He could not continue to snap and gnaw at the English line like this any more, though he felt sure that it was producing results. His men were running out of strength, and the army's morale could not stand much more of these repeated huge efforts and heavy losses without much apparent success.

Moreover, he had barely two hours of good light left, if that.

He banged his gloved hand impatiently on his thigh. Think of something!

Men were glancing over their shoulders at him. If he did not give them orders soon, he would find it difficult to get them to obey.

This was the time. It had to be now. There was something, too, that he had heard men shouting at the height of that supreme effort, when they had come so near to breaking through.

He could not be sure, such was the terrible noise, but it had sounded like 'He is hit! He is hit!' It had flown from front to rear like a flung pebble bouncing across smooth water.

Every nerve and instinct told him that the battle could be won, or lost, according to what he now did. This was the moment.

He trotted across to Sir William Fitzosbern, who greeted him with one word.

'Nearly.'

Praise God for Fitz and his faith and his level head!

With banishment of doubt came inspiration and decision.

'This is what we do, Fitz . . .'

'Why has it gone quiet?' asked Edwin. 'Why are they pulling right back? Have we won?'

'No,' said Wilfrid.

Edwin hung his head. He could not imagine lifting another weapon again, much less swinging it.

'So they are coming again?'

'Yes.'

'Will they break through?'

'Maybe.'

'So you think they will win?'

'Maybe.'

Edwin stared. 'How can you say that?'

'I like to fight beside a truthful man. I hope you do too.'

'But, Wilfrid – if we do not win, what happens?'

'We lose.'

Wilfrid saw his ashen face, and patted his shoulder. 'Cheer up, lad. I only said "maybe". And you do not really need me to tell you that. Besides, your eyes are sharp and your legs are long.'

Edwin shook off his hand. 'Are you suggesting that I should run away?'

'If the King falls and we are overrun, yes. One fights only to save a cause. Why die when the cause is dead?'

'But you are a housecarl.'

'I was talking of you, not of me. Yes, I am a housecarl. I shall likely die in the next attack, or the next one, or the one after that. I am ready.'

Edwin gulped. 'So am I.'

'No, you are not. Boys of your age never are, and a good thing too.'

'I am not a boy.'

'You may be a lusty lover to some girl or other, but to me you are a boy.'

Edwin winced.

'So, mark,' said Wilfrid. 'Fight like Hell, yes. If you try to run away before all is lost, I shall break your neck. If you do not run when it *is* lost, I shall still break your neck.'

'Satisfied?' said Ralph.

The cavalry had been drawn up again, along the widest possible front. Gilbert saw the fluttering pennons of all the remaining Norman vassals. To his right – Beaumont, Montgomery, de Warenne, Malet, Mortagne. To his left – Giffard, de Montfort, de Tosny, de Grandmesnil. There were others he did not recognise, they were so tattered. In the centre, and slightly back, was the Duke, with his brothers, Odo of Bayeux and Robert of Mortain. Fitzosbern was at the Duke's shoulder.

In between the cavalry contingents were the remains of all the infantry that could be scraped together – Flemings, Frenchmen, Normans, Count Alan's Bretons. There was no longer any attempt at maintaining separate identities; Fitzosbern had shoved men into the line wherever they were needed. Old quarrels had died in minutes; groups that had suffered heavy losses were grateful to be strengthened by men who that morning had been life-long rivals. Soldiers were now going into battle beside faces they had never seen before.

From Telham Hill and from the wagon train, the Duke's marshals and heralds had collected scouts, messengers, drivers, grooms, servants – anything that could walk or hold a weapon or ride a horse.

When the call finally did come, Gilbert could scarcely believe it.

Now he found himself in this motley array, with, on his left, Ralph and Bruno, and on his right a young, pale-faced Fleming whom they had found, for some reason, tied to a wheel.

'Yes,' he said. 'I am satisfied.'

'Good,' said Ralph.

'You know what he wants to say?' said Bruno.

Gilbert swallowed. 'Yes.'

'Well, look after it all the same,' said Ralph.

Gilbert eased the sword in the scabbard. He did not feel quite so eager as he had done earlier in the day.

He put up his hand to feel the outline of Sandor's crucifix under the hauberk. He wished it were Adele's.

Fitzosbern looked at the last archers staggering into place, carrying great wood-and-leather canisters of arrows. Bursting quivers bounced on their bent backs. They set up the canisters on the ground immediately behind their lines, digging hurried holes with daggers and propping up with stones and earth.

'God's Teeth! You must have broken Baldwin's heart!'

'Yes,' said the Duke flatly.

He summoned the archer sergeants. They ran over, puffing and sweating.

'Sir?'

They glanced significantly at each other, sensing that the moment was special.

The Duke leaned forward with his hands on the pommel of his saddle.

'You can not complain now of shortage.'

The sergeants beamed. 'No, sir.'

'Good. So – find your own best positions. You know the ground there well enough by now. Anywhere you like, but do not get in our way; remember we advance on a wide front. When I give the signal, you fire high as before. Choose your best men – thirty or forty. Crossbows, I suggest, but I leave it to you. Put them to fire at the tree and standards, nothing else. The rest – put a group on each section of the English line, and just keep going. Shoot and shoot and shoot. When you hear the advance, keep shooting.'

The sergeants blinked.

'When you see us on the slope,' said William, 'keep shooting.'

The sergeants gaped.

'You stop only when we reach the shield wall. Is that clear? Not a moment before.'

'Sir!'

William dismissed them.

He looked at the still line, looked up at Senlac Hill, and looked at Fitzosbern.

'Harold thinks I will not commit the whole army along the whole line. He thinks Normans are cautious.'

Fitzosbern cleared his throat. 'Then at least we shall surprise him.'

William gazed for a moment. 'Yes.' He took a deep breath. 'We have come a long way for a crown, Fitz. Now it waits on a branch of that tree.'

'Just so. All we have to do is pluck it down.'

'An earldom waits for you; you know that.'

Fitzosbern held out his hand. 'We have come a long way from Vaudreuil, William. I have enjoyed the journey thus far. God willing, we shall meet again soon by the tree – to taste its fruit.'

The Duke gripped it warmly. 'God bless you, Fitz. I want no man closer when I get there.'

Eustace of Boulogne presented himself.

'My lord, may I ask you once more—'

'Give him a spear, Fitz, and give me some peace.'

Turstin of Bec seized the standard. William cantered down the line.

'Come, my lords, my lads. Only Hell awaits us down here. All we have to do to escape is to climb that tree, where a new kingdom will greet us.'

'Even if it is only the Kingdom of Heaven,' thought Florens of Arras.

Gilbert felt a horse nudging his right leg. It was not a great destrier, but a light, foreign pony. He gasped.

'Why are you not with the horses?'

Sandor waved a hand. 'I am.'

'What about the others?'

'There are no others – only those.'

Sandor pointed towards the threshing limbs in the grass in front of them. 'I do not wish to listen any more to my babies dying. Taillefer sleeps, and my friends are here. Where else should I be?'

He was not smiling. In his hand he carried a small, light bow and a thin clutch of arrows. Tousled, staring, tight-cheeked, he looked like the dreaded Turks that Gilbert had heard about.

The trumpets blew.

The archers stretched their strings.

'Fire!'

Holy Virgin! thought Brian the Breton. It was like a rain cloud on wings. At least it gave them a few more minutes while the archers emptied their quivers. Without thinking, he bit off another piece of carrot. With his other hand he clasped and unclasped the hilt of cousin Geoffrey's sword, searching for a familiar grip.

He almost choked when the trumpets blared again. Brian could scarcely believe his ears. The archers were still firing. They blew again. No – his ears had not deceived him. The leaders' pennons lowered and raised. It was unmistakable: the advance was to begin.

All round the valley in front of Senlac Hill the pennons swayed and the orders were bellowed.

Brian obeyed, casting uneasy glances over his shoulder at the massed archers. By some fearsome magic, they seemed able to keep shafts in the air all the time. He was not sure now where the greater danger came from – the front or the rear.

Down the stream and across. The whine of the arrows was smothered by the splashing of countless feet and hooves. No trumpet blew now; no man shouted. Up on Senlac Hill the English waited, as still as a forest after a fire.

Past the first bodies, the scattered weapons, the writhing horses. Past the knoll, piled with dead from both sides. Tussocks of grass pink with water and blood. Beginning the climb, stumbling and sliding, the earth turned and churned with a whole day's trampling. Past exhausted cripples, who leaned on shields and urged them to grisly vengeance.

Still the arrows flew.

Brian looked across to the centre. When? When? If they left it too late there would be no space to gain speed and force. Give the word too early, and tired horses and men would collapse against the shield wall, too weak to raise an arm.

There it was!

A thin, plaintive cry almost carried away by the breeze. It was answered by a swelling roar that swept like a wave towards him.

'*Diex aie!*'

Brian's heart leaped. Convulsively, he tightened his hold on cousin Geoffrey's sword. He found himself running and shouting, sliding and shouting, stumbling and shouting. When he reached the top he was forced to hold the sword in both hands and swing it like a Saxon axe. He hit a helmet so hard that his sword was nearly knocked into the air. Shaking all over from the impact, he barely held on to it.

Men surged past him. He felt a shield wobble under his feet.

Saxon faces appeared on either side of him as well as in front. Desperate, flushed, snarling faces, with teeth showing.

Great God! They were through! They were inside the shield wall!

The Saxons fought like devils to stem the tide, giving ground only in death. Brian, crazed with excitement and sensing victory at last, laid about him with renewed strength.

Horses jostled him out their way. Brian glimpsed the familiar striped stockings beneath the cavalry split hauberk, the massive saddles and thick, heavy stirrups.

As one horseman overtook him, Brian noticed, in that flood of incident, one tiny detail – two arrows hanging loose from the back of the man's shoulders. They had struck his mail at a wide angle and their heads had become enmeshed in the links.

Ralph Pomeroy had such a painful back anyway that he barely noticed them. Borne forward by the charge, he now lunged and swung for dear life, kicking his mount ahead all the time in an effort to force his passage through the sea of savage faces.

Horsemen broke away from him to the left.

'They fly!'

Pomeroy could have sworn it was his brother's voice.

For the first time that day he saw a Saxon's back. Several peasants were running away to the north side of the hill. A group of riders were spurring in pursuit.

William Capra swore at his third mount of the day to get it to respond. It rolled over, its hind legs slashed by a scythe.

Ralph Pomeroy started to swing his horse's head round to join them, when something gripped him across the throat from behind.

Gasping and choking, he was jerked from the saddle, and hit the ground with such force that he lay winded. All he was conscious of was a pair of muddy feet, one of which was bloodstained.

The sheepman crippled him again by ramming the butt of the crook into his crotch, and was just drawing his knife when he was bowled over by a riderless horse. By the time he had recovered, a forest of legs and bodies was between him and his groaning prey.

A housecarl dragged him by the shoulder.

'Back, back! Close up. We must shut off the right. We can no longer fight here. Too many of them. Close up.'

The sheepman hesitated, still thinking longingly of his fallen Norman's throat.

The housecarl hit him.

'If you stay here, you die. If you run like them, you die.'

Screams reached them, from where the fugitives were being caught.

The sheepman found himself amid a whole group of sweating, swearing housecarls. He was terrified of the backswing of the axes, but he was behind a wall of shields again.

William Capra and Ralph Pomeroy each snatched at a riderless horse, and found themselves gazing at each other across the saddle. Capra was up first. Pomeroy turned away and grabbed another bridle.

They had no choice but to go forward. A press of knights and swordsmen flung themselves at the shields in desperate, mindless repetition. Each time they braced themselves for a final effort. Each time they drooped faster in fatigue. Each time they fell back with hideous wounds among them.

Each time too they heard Odo or Giffard or Montgomery or someone yelling above the din, 'Get in! Turn! To the line! Once more! Again! Only once more! There is no retreat now. We win here, or we die. God help us, or we die.'

'*Diex aie!*'

Desperate knots of men charged at weak points of the wall, scorning all risk or danger. They would make a breach, but it would cost their lives. By the time fresh knights could scramble up to get through, the English had closed the gap again, and bloody axes still swept screaming men from saddles.

The left seemed to be holding slightly better than the right. Inspired by a giant, they said. Edwin wondered . . .

He lost count of the number of times they shuffled to the right in order to close the wall. Whenever he glanced over his shoulder, the Dragon of Wessex and the Fighting Man were nearer.

Once he thought he saw the King. Harold wore his helmet again. He had sheathed his sword. He stood by the apple tree with his senior staff, or what was left of them. Each man gripped a two-handed axe.

Men started to trickle away. One of Harold's staff bellowed at them.

Harold stopped him.

'Let them go. They have fought like heroes. We can not expect them to die like saints as well.'

'You are ready for it, sir.'

'That is not the same,' said Harold. 'I am a king. It goes with the crown.'

'Then are we lost?'

'Not yet. The Bastard may overreach himself.' He patted the lichen-covered trunk of the apple tree. 'I have dangled my crown from this tree. His greed may yet make him stretch out his arm too far. Then we shall have him.'

Harold pointed. 'Look there. Did you ever think to see a man going towards the fight at a time like this? If a fat old man like that comes to face the foe, what should we have to fear?'

Gorm stumbled towards the left, still searching, searching. He fought his way past men desperate now to get away. One of them dropped a spear in his panic. Gorm picked it up and wandered into the battle, still looking for a big man, a big man with an axe . . .

He did not hear the noise; he no longer felt the pain in his arm; he did not notice the trickle of fugitives becoming a steadily growing stream.

A Norman stood in front of him with a drawn sword. Gorm

lunged simply in order to get him out of the way. Unable to get his spear out of the man's stomach, Gorm flung it aside and left the wretch doubled over it.

Then he stopped. He had never heard Godric roar like that before, but he knew at once who it was. He pushed his way past two riderless horses.

There was Godric, laying about himself with a pitchfork. Even as Gorm arrived, it was splintered by a French sword. Godric gazed at it, baffled. The exhausted Frenchman grasped his sword again and braced himself for a second stroke. Godric bent with fatigue.

Gorm seized one of the collapsed wooden stakes from the shield wall, couched one end under his arm, and rammed the point into the Frenchman's chest. He flew over backwards as Gorm fell with his own onset.

Godric turned and frowned. He looked like a man in a dream, but Gorm felt sure he had been seen and recognised.

Another rush of mailed men loomed behind Godric. Gorm glimpsed a Norman pennon and screamed a warning. He saw a Norman knight raise a mace; another was couching a spear. Godric put up the splintered handle of the pitchfork as his only shield. Gorm cried out in anguish at the sight.

A horse fell on him, winding him and blocking his view. More bodies fell across him; a hideous warmth ran across the side of his neck as heavy mail pressed him down. Hurried feet thudded and crunched beside his ears.

He could hear the din of battle now all around him, but he could not see. He could not see that Normans had broken in once more from the right, and were now behind him as well as before.

The shield wall was being twisted and bent back on itself. In some places men were so tired that they were almost falling over with the momentum of their own blows. Recovery and a second blow took longer each time. Beaumont was crying out with the pain of fatigue in his right arm. The younger spearmen wept with the effort of keeping arms up to thrust; throwing was now out of the question. Pairs of combatants let their weapons fall, and collapsed to their knees with their arms on each other's shoulders.

Normans and Saxons alike fell dead or exhausted across each other amid ruins of shields and stakes. The desperate, panting survivors trod and slipped blindly.

William and his vassals tore their voices to pieces – begging, coaxing, beseeching, demanding one more effort. They could see with their own eyes: the ring of housecarls was dwindling; the wings of fyrdmen and peasants were melting away. One more push – just one more! Nearer to the tree and to the wavering standards. Splendour of God – to be so close!

The men in front of Edwin pulled back a few yards and drooped over their swords, helpless with fatigue. Edwin was reeling, his eyes smarting from sweat. He could hear Wilfrid wheezing beside him, too out of breath even to swear. Across the small space men glowered at each other in impotent fury and frustration, each knowing that the slightest of strokes could topple the enemy and each unable to produce it.

Edwin glanced back. The apple tree with its standards was almost directly behind him, but no longer did the shield wall stretch out to the right-hand end of Caldbec ridge. Instead it bent round sharply and folded back almost behind the tree.

Still and again, knots of Norman knights managed desperate short charges of just a few paces. In one short respite, Beaumont and Giffard found themselves face to face for a moment, before Beaumont, white and breathless, fell off his horse in a state of total collapse.

Giffard leaned down towards him, his own face glistening purple with heat and sweat. He swallowed and dragged the words out of his tortured lungs.

'Running out of breath, are we? Let me show you something. Something only a true knight can do.'

He roared at those nearest. 'Are there any *men* left?'

Beaumont was unable to move. Tears streamed from his eyes, down past his ears. Judith was now further away than ever.

Giffard repeated his call. 'Are there any *men* here?'

Capra and Pomeroy, crazed with excitement, followed Giffard's challenge. So did one or two others. Montgomery, alarmed, spurred and urged his bleeding horse after them.

Edwin saw the group of Norman knights thrust in deeper than the rest. Then he had to turn to his front.

Wilfrid heaved his axe once more, his eyes staring. 'Bastards!'

Eustace of Boulogne watched the small group of knights hacking their way.

'They are through!' he yelled. 'They are through! They are through to the tree!'

As he spoke one of them disappeared into the surge of weapons round him.

Gilbert saw it too. Through a haze of sweat and double vision he saw the others press on, saw the English standards falter.

Grasping his sword and holding it high, he took a deep breath and shouted, 'Victory!' His throat responded with only a hoarse rasp.

He kicked frantically at his lathered horse.

Ralph, further back, saw his intention and tried to stop him. He would not survive in that carnage. How often had he told the boy to think first and rush second. A broken boar is a dangerous boar. The English were broken but were not running yet.

He was too far away to shout. His horse was too tired to cover the ground between them. He looked round desperately. Sandor, with his light pony – Sandor could catch him. Sandor was yards away the other side, screaming unearthly battle cries, cries that came straight from a Hunnish hell.

Ralph raged and swore.

A voice in his ear said, 'Leave him to me.'

Bruno urged Sorrel after Gilbert. Ralph watched in a fever of anxiety. He remembered Gilbert bringing Bruno to a halt before the ravine. That had been a rapid, violent matter of thudding hooves and flying turf. Now men and horses were moving like creatures in a cloudy dream – the sort of dream one had when arms and legs moved but no ground was covered.

It seemed minutes before Bruno reached out and caught Gilbert's bridle. The shock of the sudden halt was too much for Sorrel's front leg. It buckled, and Bruno was thrown from the saddle. A snarling housecarl rushed forward with raised axe.

Gilbert, only a yard too far to help, turned his head in revulsion.

More Normans poured past him and overwhelmed the housecarl. After a brief hesitation and a last sickened glance at Bruno's headless body, Gilbert spurred again and followed.

One of the English standards swayed and fell. The last defenders of the tree died where they stood, but took one more Norman with them.

Harold stood alone against the trunk, his arms at his sides, his axe propped against his thigh.

The four remaining Normans paused. Harold raised his head. His face was running red, staining his moustache.

He fumbled for the handle of his axe, but was barely able to lift it. He stepped forward to challenge, and collapsed to his knees.

Capra and Pomeroy raised their swords and yelled in fury. Giffard dug his spurs, but Montgomery caught his bridle.

'No, Walter. No honour lies there. Beaumont would not regard you for that.'

When Gilbert arrived he saw two men stabbing and hacking like madmen at something on the ground. One of them was so possessed that he was also slashing indiscriminately at the tree.

Eustace of Boulogne snatched the Dragon standard and held it aloft, and a scattering of wild-faced horsemen reined in around him to form an escort.

Crazed with elation, Gilbert made his way through piles of dead to join them. Curiosity took him past the apple tree. He looked down to see what it was that they— and nearly vomited where he sat.

Were it not for a bloodstained bandage, a dented helmet, and shreds of wet mail, he would barely have recognised it as a body.

Edwin put his hands under Wilfrid's armpits and heaved. The strength was not there.

'You must get up. Help me. Up, man!'

Wilfrid, his helmet gone, shook his head dizzily. His right arm hung useless. His axe was broken.

'I should die here. With my king.'

Edwin tried to rouse him by shouting in his ear. 'The King is dead. The standards are gone. It is all over.'

Wilfrid only half heard him. He looked round for a weapon.

'I must stand in front of my king. It is my duty.'

Edwin shook him. 'Wilfrid! The King is dead. The Normans are all round the tree. The Duke's banner is there. They are all cheering. Listen.'

A steadily swelling press of Normans and Frenchmen jostled one another around the apple tree. In the centre, William held his sword high. Turstin of Bec held aloft the Papal banner and Eustace waved the Wessex Dragon. There was a great shouting. Many were weeping; some were crying aloud.

'See, Wilfrid. They are not even bothering to fight us now. We are too few. You must get up. Do you want to wait for the scavengers to come in the evening and cut your throat?'

Wilfrid screwed up his eyes against the setting sun, then groped for a spear.

'I am a housecarl,' he mumbled.

Edwin came round in front of him, stooped, and slapped him hard across the face.

'Wilfrid, the King is dead. The cause is dead. Remember what you said. Even you have no duty now.'

Wilfrid blinked. Edwin tried another idea.

'Besides, I need you. You said you owed me something.'

Wilfrid put out his unbroken arm. Edwin heaved and hoisted. Wilfrid used the spear to help his twisted ankle. Edwin tugged anxiously.

'Hurry. Before they begin a pursuit. Back to the ravine. Everyone is going there. The Normans will find it dangerous to follow us there.'

Wilfrid's mind began to work clearly again.

A deep ravine . . . the last thing those bastards would expect on a pursuit would be an ambush . . .

Gilbert sheathed his sword, took off his helmet, and shook his head in relief. He looked round for someone he knew; he was too full to keep it all to himself.

Kicking his steaming horse, he pushed his way out of the cheering, chanting crowd and picked a path down the hill again. Behind him he could hear Eustace, still wild with excitement, calling for volunteers for the pursuit.

'On, on, on! Who is with me?'

Gilbert came upon Ralph faster than he had expected, and reined in violently.

'Just listen to that!' he shouted, gesturing with the hand that held the helmet. 'The Duke has turned them loose.'

Ralph made no move. 'I hear it.'

Gilbert saw the expression on his face, and tried to calm down. 'Did you – did you see?'

'Yes.'

Gilbert spread his hands. 'There was nothing I could do. He went down so fast, and that Saxon was on him before I could—'

'Go away.'

Gilbert blinked. 'Ralph, I said I am sorry. I was just too far. He was dead before—'

'Go away from me.'

Gilbert frowned. 'Why was he trying to stop me? We broke through. We reached the standards. I was at the tree itself. Are you not pleased?'

Ralph swore. 'What do I care about you? Or your stinking standards? Bruno is dead.'

Gilbert swallowed. 'I know, and I am sorry. Really I am. But I told you—'

'And he died saving your life.'

'What?'

'How long would you have survived with so little battle experience? He could see that. You were blind to everything. It was your precious honour that nearly did for the army. Now it is your filthy little bit of glory that has done for Bruno.'

Gilbert went pale. Ralph fought to keep control.

'Now you strut among the bodies and boast of victory. And my friend Bruno is dead. And you ask me to cheer. Do you understand? My friend is dead – my friend. Not my kennel boy, my novice, my substitute brother. My friend.' His voice broke completely. 'Go and get your glory. Go anywhere. Only get out of my sight!'

Gilbert, his face haggard, flung down his helmet and pulled out his sword. He wrenched his horse's head round and kicked it into action once more. Back up the hill, after Eustace and his yelling companions.

Already they were beyond the summit and galloping down the northern slope towards the forest, hacking in the half-darkness at anything that showed itself in front of them.

'Now!'

The archer let fly, and struck the leading Norman in the neck. He fell into the brambles on the lip of the ravine. He was the lucky one.

His companions plunged yelling into a void. The wild neighing of terrified horses, and the crashing and thudding of bodies, made a sound as fearsome as that of the battle itself.

Horses floundered with smashed legs, and rolled on screaming men who were writhing with broken backs. Behind them the second wave of pursuers crashed through undergrowth, toppled over the edge, and fell on to them.

'Ambush!'

In the panic and shadows, survivors struck blindly at each other.

Above, on the rim, a third group of pursuers saw the accident, and swung to the left.

'Here! Here is a way!'

The leaders found the old causeway and thundered on to it.

Under their combined weight and impact, the ancient structure crumbled like dry sand. Amid roars of bafflement and fear, more bodies were hurled into the seething mass at the bottom of the ravine, followed and smothered by cascades of earth and stones.

Bellowing at the top of their voices, Saxons leaped onto riders and mounts alike, clawing at them with their bare hands. Owen the archer fired as fast as he could at the screaming shadows below. Aim was barely necessary.

Wilfrid limped about, stabbing at fallen, winded men with his spear in one good hand. He was roaring and swearing as loudly as ever.

Edwin snatched a sword from a dying Frenchman, and slashed at horses' legs. Eight hours ago, he could never have brought himself to consider it.

The survivors were totally unnerved. In the fading light, the last thing they had expected was resistance. Few were wearing helmets; some had slipped off their mail coifs and rode bareheaded.

They shouted and swore and struck at anything moving in front of them, forgetting all formation, skill, and training. One dismounted knight, bellowing with rage, was pulling at a man's hair.

The English, with the chance of one last blow at the enemy they had withstood so well all day, fought with bitter strength.

Eustace of Boulogne snatched at a stray bridle, flung himself into the saddle, and bawled, 'Back! Back! It is a trap. It is their reinforcements. Get back!'

He kicked the terrified horse towards the other end of the ravine, away from the crumbling causeway and the churning mass of tumbled bodies. Other Normans staggered after him. A few tried to claw their way up the side of the ravine down which they had fallen.

Jubilant fyrdmen, growling through bared teeth, ran and clambered after them. They hauled on thrashing legs, tore away earth-filled fingernails, and flung screaming bodies on to the thudding billhooks below.

Eustace, sweating and panting, picked his way out of the mouth of the ravine to the east, swung round to the south, and headed back to the battlefield. He ran into the Duke himself, who was leading more men in the pursuit.

'Get back, sir, get back! It is a trap!'

Behind him, a bristling housecarl swung a stick with a stone fitted on the end. It was a long shot, but he had nothing to lose and it was his last chance.

The weapon struck Eustace squarely between the shoulder blades as he raised his arm to point to the ravine. The thud was clearly audible. Blood poured from his nose and mouth.

The Duke caught him as he fell forward, splattering blood over the mail on his forearms.

'Take him, you two. The rest – follow me. This way – to the east. We find a way to outflank them. Come!'

In the ravine's shadows, Wilfrid put his arm on the archer's shoulder.

'Well, you struck the first blow, and now you have helped us to strike the last. Not a bad day's work, eh?'

Owen nodded wearily.

Behind them the Saxons resumed their retreat. The sheepman paused to pick up a severed axe-head, then heaved himself on to a riderless horse, wincing as his wounded foot found the stirrups. They faded into the evening murk.

Edwin suddenly heard a crashing sound. He looked up. Another horse and rider were falling down. The man was flung free, and came sliding and tumbling towards him. The thong on his wrist snapped, and his sword flickered away. Brambles wrenched at his mail coif; he wore no helmet.

Wilfrid limped up behind Edwin as the body rolled free. The Norman was clearly terrified and half winded.

Edwin stepped forward and lifted his sword. The Norman pulled out a knife. Their eyes met.

'Gilbert!'

'You!'

'Finish him, man. Finish him!'

Wilfrid pushed past and thrust straight into Gilbert's stomach. Because the spear was in his left hand it had not gone in as far as Wilfrid had hoped. He wrenched it out and poised it again.

'No, Wilfrid, no! He is my friend.'

Wilfrid stared in disbelief, but allowed Edwin to push down the spear.

'Help me, Wilfrid. Get him hidden, in case our men come back again.'

Wilfrid bent unwillingly. Gilbert made no protest or sound. ''Tis we who will be hiding soon, I think. The next men down here will be Normans.'

While they laid Gilbert as comfortably as possible, they heard other riders picking their way down the wreckage of the collapsed causeway.

'What did I tell you?' said Wilfrid. 'And my spear is out there, thanks to you.'

'Sssh!' said Edwin. 'He is calling.'

Edwin listened, grimacing at Wilfrid to stop growling.

'Gilbert! Gilbert!'

'It is Ralph,' said Gilbert softly, through pain-closed eyes. 'The senior scout – remember?'

Edwin nodded.

Wilfrid frowned. 'How do you come to know half the Norman army?'

Edwin did not answer. He burst out from the bushes.

'Ralph! Sandor! It is Edwin, remember? Gilbert is wounded. Here.'

Ralph came warily forward. He stopped when he saw Wilfrid's height loom up behind Edwin.

'It is all right,' said Edwin. 'He will not fight.'

Ralph looked at Wilfrid's twitching hand.

'Have you told him that?'

'What are you doing speaking French?' demanded Wilfrid. 'What is going on?'

'Wilfrid, trust me, please. I have not failed you all day, have I?'

'We have been killing Normans all day. Why stop now?'

'It is a long story,' said Edwin. 'But I know these men. There is an understanding between us.'

'He says the truth,' Sandor said in English. 'We know him. We are alone. We have no cause to fight now.' He held his open palms wide.

Wilfrid stared at each in turn, then spat.

'Talk then. I shall keep watch. But first, get him to the top of the bank, in case they come again.' He pointed to the higher, northern end of the ravine. 'They will not get up there.'

Gilbert barely made a sound as they struggled up the steep slope with him, slipping on leaf mould and dragging whole nets of brambles after them.

At the top, they kneeled and wheezed and wiped the sweat from their faces.

Gilbert's hands, folded across his stomach, were covered in blood. Ralph pulled them gently away and peered.

'I am sorry about the hauberk,' said Gilbert.

'I am sorry too,' said Ralph, 'for what I said.'

'There is no need. I understand.'

Ralph dared not look Gilbert in the face. The wound gaped. The boy was losing blood fast.

Ralph tried delicately to remove fractured rings of mail. Sandor produced from nowhere a pad of cloth. While Ralph fumbled to stop the flow, Gilbert looked at the little Magyar.

'I did not have the good luck here then – once again.'

Sandor tried to smile.

'The dark, you see,' said Gilbert. 'I misjudged. I always seem to misjudge.'

A whole flight of significant glances passed between all three.

'Is battle usually like that?' said Gilbert at last.

'It was a very big battle,' said Ralph.

'Did I do well?' said Gilbert.

Ralph looked down at the pale face, the bloodied hands, the leggings torn and muddy from the fall. He tried to push Bruno's familiar words away.

Sandor nudged him.

'You did very well,' said Ralph.

Sandor nudged him again.

'I – I am proud of you.'

Another nudge.

'I shall tell the Duke, and Fitzosbern. Even Odo, if you like.'

Gilbert smiled. 'No more "Master Senlac", eh?'

'No more "Master Senlac".'

'Will you tell my father?'

'I shall make your father proud of you too.'

'Ah! If you could do that . . .'

Gilbert tried to reach inside his hauberk. 'The cross, Sandor. I want you to have it back.'

Sandor held up his hand. 'Not now. You keep it for a time. You will rest now.'

Gilbert shook his head. 'Sandor – this time only, you are a bad liar.'

Sandor looked at Ralph across Gilbert. Ralph leaned down.

'Do you have a message for Adele?'

'Yes – but Edwin must take it. Bring him.'

Ralph whispered to Edwin, 'Whatever he says, pretend you understand.'

Edwin came and crouched down. Gilbert's voice was weakening.

'When I came to England I wanted to find you and kill you. But now – it has all come out different.'

Edwin looked up at Ralph, who frowned a fierce message.

'I am glad of that,' said Edwin.

'I called my first son Hugh, after my father. Adele will soon have another son. I want him called after your father. What is his name?'

Edwin looked baffled, but answered. 'Edward.'

'A fine name. So be it.'

Edwin blinked. 'So be it.'

'I am sorry about Berry,' murmured Gilbert.

'Thank you.'

Gilbert squeezed his hand. 'For us both to love so many of the same things – we must be truly friends, eh?'

Edwin nodded, tight-lipped, then lowered his head.

When he looked up again, Ralph was kissing Gilbert's brow.

'What was he talking about?' said Edwin.

Ralph and Sandor looked at each other. They agreed without speaking.

'He had fancies,' said Ralph at last. 'We never understood them. Now he is at peace. Let us leave it at that.'

Wilfrid struggled up beside them, limping and puffing.

'Many horsemen,' he said.

They crouched in silence while they went by. It was impossible now to make out faces in the shadows at the foot of the ravine. Ralph thought he heard the Duke's voice.

'God's Breath,' he muttered. 'That man is everywhere.'

The Duke surveyed the carnage.

'The birds have flown. Come.' The sound of milling hooves, then the Duke's voice again. 'Call off the pursuit. Tomorrow we chase in earnest – and in safety.'

When they had gone, Wilfrid gestured awkwardly at Gilbert.

'I remember him now – the one we captured. I am sorry. I did not know.'

'You could not help it,' said Edwin, wiping his cheek with a thumb.

Everyone stood up. Wilfrid, with his bruised head, his bad arm, his weak ankle, and blood, it seemed, everywhere – Wilfrid dominated by his sheer presence.

'Tell him,' said Ralph. 'Tell him he fought a good fight. I am proud to have had such an enemy.'

While Edwin translated, Ralph held out his hand.

Wilfrid bowed with great dignity, and apologetically put out his left hand, which Ralph gripped firmly.

'Tell him,' said Wilfrid, 'I am sorry about his young brother.'

Edwin translated again.

Ralph looked down at Gilbert, and heaved a great sigh. 'My brother is dead.'

Sandor turned to Wilfrid. 'Hide here until the Duke goes back and makes his camp. The women will come soon and so will darkness. Then it will be safe to move.'

'We shall make our way well enough,' said Wilfrid gruffly.

'I can not go with you,' said Edwin. 'I have another errand first.'

'Then I shall make my own way,' said Wilfrid. 'Goodbye, boy. You fought well. Might have made a housecarl out of you. Still –

no need of them now. I was right, you see. You should have left me to die.'

He stumped off.

When he had gone, Sandor put a hand on Ralph's shoulder.

'May I make an idea?' He pointed at Gilbert. 'This is pain for you. On the other side of the hill a duty waits which is pain for me.'

'Taillefer.'

Sandor nodded.

'Thank you, little man,' said Ralph. 'It shall be done.'

'The hauberk,' said Sandor. 'Do you want it?'

Ralph thought of the dead Breton from whom he had cut it so long before. The rings had been driven into the flesh in exactly the same way.

'No. It belongs to him. He has earned it.'

Sandor coughed awkwardly. 'I am sorry about Bruno. There are no clever words to—'

Ralph waved a hand. 'Please. No more. I understand.'

He said a prayer, crossed himself, and was gone.

Sandor looked about him.

'There are many stones, and we have knives. Will you help?'

'I have no knife,' said Edwin.

'Ah – I nearly forget.' Sandor pulled a knife from inside his jerkin.

Edwin stared. 'That is mine! How—'

Sandor gestured vaguely. 'There is a saying, I believe – "fortunes of war".'

Roger of Montgomery winced.

'Noises get on a man's nerves.'

Walter Giffard unbuckled his sword and handed it to a servant.

'What do you mean?'

'All day,' said Montgomery, 'we have had one or the other – terrible noise, or unnatural silence. All day I have looked forward to the time when we should have no more of either. Just ordinary sounds. Now listen to that.' He waved a hand in front of them.

Crippled horses were uttering ghastly cries. Men in their dying agony were shrieking for comfort, a friend, a mother, an ease to pain, a death-wound, a priest – anything. Saxon or Norman, English or French – it mattered nothing. Men were crying for help, torn between two worlds.

As the shadows lengthened, more dark figures flitted from one pile of dead to another, bending and peering. The air was constantly shivered by screams of anguish as an anonymous corpse received, for the last time, its name – from a wife, a mother, a sister, a lover.

Other shadows, more furtive and cat-like, crept and pounced. Each time they moved, their arms were fuller with swords and hauberks and finely wrought spurs, and their pouches fatter with coins and jewelled crosses and silver rings. Where two figures jumped together on the same body, more noises arose – the rasp of knives, the snarls of greed and hate.

William Capra and Ralph Pomeroy, and some of the younger Normans, with blood in their heads instead of brains, were cavorting about the field, forcing their tired horses to strut and rear while they whooped and roared.

Montgomery shook his head. 'I could not say which I hate more – the awful noise all day, or those noises now.'

Florens of Arras heard another one that chilled him, inured as he was to the horrors of war.

He had been looking for Fulk's body for some time, and his stomach was already tightening with the knowledge of what would meet his eyes when he found it. He was so prepared for hideous sights that he was shaken into trembling by an unexpected sound.

It was not exactly a crying, because there were no tears in the voice. It was clearly a dirge, yet unlike any sound of mourning he had ever heard. It rose and fell in cadences totally foreign to his ear. For all its strangeness, the message of unutterable loss was obvious to anyone. If Florens had not been on a battlefield, he would have been tempted to derive it from the animal kingdom.

The hair on the back of his neck rose when he saw Matthew. The little hunchback was on his knees, rocking to and fro. His head was raised and his voice called to the open, darkening sky. Florens knew, beyond any doubt, that he had found Fulk's body.

He could not bring himself to approach until Matthew had gone.

When at last he stood over his old commander, he averted his eyes from the staring, twisted mask of a face. The spear was still where the big Saxon had plunged it, pinning him to the ground like a spitted carcass on a slaughterer's slab.

Grimacing with fear and revulsion, Florens crouched and reached for the waist wallet. It was empty.

Gorm did not notice the gaping flesh, the stiff stumps, the staring eyes. Pulling and heaving, mostly with one arm, he dragged piles of bodies apart.

Godric could not be far; Gorm felt he could almost have touched him when he shouted the warning. Gorm could still picture the expression on the Norman's face as he swung his mace against Godric's splintered pitchfork handle. Somewhere in the background a pennon had fluttered.

Somewhere, somewhere here, Godric lay. If he still breathed, if a flicker of life remained ... Had he really recognised Gorm in that instant with the stake? Gorm had to be sure. He wrenched at bodies, terrified of what he might find underneath.

He saw the handle first, with great gouges in the wood from

where Godric had tried to take the main force of the blow from the mace.

Flinging it aside, Gorm fell upon the nearest corpse, or what was left of it, and pulled it away by its remaining leg.

There he was, face down.

Whimpering and trembling, Gorm pulled him over. The face, for all the blood down one side of it, looked at peace.

Gorm's cry of pain was as much for himself as for Godric. Now he could never tell him, never lift the burden of the lie from his mind, never wash away the '*nithing*' curse from his soul.

Gorm kneeled forward and clasped one hand in his own two. He bent over it and wept.

Suddenly he tensed. The hand he was holding was still warm.

He bent down and put an ear to the deep chest. He felt the brow. He looked at the ugly spear gash in the arm; the blood was barely congealed.

Crawling on all fours to a nearby body that had been stripped of mail, he tore off some undershirt and made a rough bandage. He made another for the gash and bruise on the head. The mace had struck, but the ugly spikes had not broken the skull. The handle of the pitchfork had probably taken most of the force. Perhaps something else had knocked him unconscious after the fall. A hoof maybe.

At any rate he was alive.

Working now with purpose rather than with desperation, Gorm cleared more dead around Godric's large body. Then, gritting his teeth with the pain of his own wound, he put his hands under Godric's armpits and began dragging him. At first uphill towards where the shield wall had been; he did not think.

The slope stopped him. It was too steep, and there were too many bodies to stumble over. As he paused to regain breath, he heard Norman voices. Of course! There was no shield wall – not now.

Panting again with a fresh urgency, he turned about and began dragging his burden down the hill, away from the voices. The slope made it easier now, and gradually the bodies became fewer. On the low ground he felt safer in the long evening shadows.

The next obstacle was the stream.

He knew he could not afford to drag Godric through that. The shock of the cold water could kill a wounded man. If it did not, he would still have to face the coming night with soaking clothes.

There was nothing else for it.

Gorm, even in recent years, had carried more sacks of corn than he cared to admit. How many times had he railed at Godric for not having enough consideration for his ageing bones? How often had Godric looked right through him with his dark, bottomless eyes? He knew – they both knew – that Gorm was not weak, but lazy.

True, he had not lifted a huge load like this, and he had not had to do it with a gashed arm and a thumping heart. But then he had not been cast into '*nithing*' outer darkness before; he had never before been hammering on the doors of humanity from the outside.

Grunting, sweating, slipping, staggering, he kept going until he was past every shallow pool and every clump of rushes.

Afterwards he lay on his back and panted until he thought his lungs would burst. They did not. Eventually he sat up, and wiped the sweat from his face.

Godric was too heavy to be carried any distance, and being dragged would be the death of him.

Gorm looked out across the valley between the two hills. Wagons were creaking down from the right, surrounded by a host of servants and grooms. So the Bastard was going to camp on Caldbec Hill itself. Amid all the carnage! Gorm shuddered.

But it gave him an idea. Nobody would notice another civilian in the throng and in the fading light.

First he hid Godric in some bushes, and made him as

comfortable as possible. Then he recrossed the stream and went to the blood-soaked knoll at the foot of the hill beyond. He stripped some bodies of leather jerkins and came back to put them round Godric's body and legs. He tried to get some water between his lips, but he was still unconscious.

Gorm crossed the stream again, joined the procession of servants and wagons, and climbed the hill to the remains of the shield wall. He rummaged among the fallen stakes, and selected those that would suit his purpose. He toiled back and left them with Godric in the bushes.

Again to the hill, to look for dead horses. With his knife he cut away enough straps and reins for the binding and the dragging.

He was on his knees now, and immersed in a practical problem, his brows knitted in concentration. Making a sledge litter was no great challenge. There was not much that Gorm Haraldsson could not make or repair. God's Eyes – the number of times he had got things going again when they were barely held together with twine!

When it was ready, Gorm lined the litter with more jerkins, not too stained if he could help it. He rebound Godric's wounds, cushioned his head, and tied him in securely. He rebound the gash on his own arm.

He would not go back along the way he had come. It would be too full of fugitives, too full of desperate women who would cheerfully kill him to get their hands on the litter for their own menfolk. And on the morrow the Normans would be out, harrying and looting, in the manner of all victorious armies. Besides, it was the way to London, and Gorm guessed that it would be the natural line for the Norman advance.

No – due west was the way to go, straight towards the last of the sun. He could always swing north-west in the morning. He had not travelled half his life without growing a good sense of direction.

If he were lucky he might come across an ox or a donkey that he could harness to the litter.

He stuck his knife into his belt, and took a drink from his leather flask. What would he not give right now for a good draught of beer. After a last glance at Godric's still features, he faced to the front, looped the straps over his shoulders, lowered his head, and took the strain.

Baldwin de Clair watched his men build the fire. Others were swearing at one another as they put up his tent. The prospect of being warm and dry that night was some consolation.

He had no idea where the rest of his wagon train was. Strung out between Telham and Senlac, probably, or bumping around among the dead bodies on the top of Senlac.

His careful organisation was in ruins, victim of the confusion of order and counter-order from count and bishop and Duke. His hoarded reserves of weapons were gone, his water supplies nearly exhausted.

They would see the folly of all that soon enough, when the English counter-attacked, or when the Duke called for equipment with which to harry the land towards London.

And why they should want to camp on top, amid all the slaughter and away from timber and running water, was beyond his comprehension. It would certainly give the servants a sleepless night fetching and carrying.

Well, damn them. Damn them. He had plenty of firewood to hand and he had the stream nearby. He was far enough away from most of the bodies to be free from the growing numbers of birds. Let the morning take care of itself.

Baldwin saw the first puff of smoke curl up from dried leaves. The victory was won, the usurper was dead, and Bloodeye was destroyed. Not a bad day's work.

He heard a crunching noise beside him.

'Glad I am to see you, sir,' said a young Breton.

Baldwin frowned. Brian held up the stump of a carrot.

'See – my last one. Kept me going, they did, sir. I saved this for the end. Sort of charm, you might say.'

Baldwin remembered.

'Are you all right?'

'Yes, thank you, sir, praise the Lord. Apart from an ankle. Swollen like a bladder.'

Baldwin peered. 'Get that seen to, and soon. It might be broken. You do not want a limp for the rest of your life.'

It was on the tip of Baldwin's tongue to shout for Crispin, when he recalled where Crispin was – with any luck, within striking distance of a Sussex seaport.

'If that is all I carry from this battle, then it is truly fortunate I am,' said Brian. 'There have been terrible things done today.' He shuddered at the recollection.

Baldwin liked the boy's honesty and simplicity, and found it easy to talk to him.

'Were you frightened?'

'Scared to death, sir. Then I sort of went mad and lost my head. I can not recall much of what happened. When I recovered I got scared again.'

Baldwin thought of the obsession that had tugged him in search of Fulk, despite all risk and hazard.

'War is a sort of madness, when you actually have to fight it.'

'I agree, sir. There is all that excitement beforehand, and looking forward, and wondering. Sort of building up to it. Then comes the madness. Then, afterwards, it is kind of flat. I mean, you know something huge has happened, but it is – well – flat.'

'Yes,' said Baldwin awkwardly, as a thought crossed his mind.

Brian swallowed the last of his carrot.

'It is as if – well, I hardly like to say it because it sounds sort of blasphemous, but it is a bit like making love.'

'Yes,' said Baldwin, looking away.

'Sort of opposite, but similar.'

'You could say that, yes.'

God – would it be like that with her?

Brian sensed that perhaps he had become too familiar. 'Well, I must find somewhere to sleep, sir, if you will excuse me.'

'There is a fire here.'

'Very kind, sir, I am sure.'

Baldwin grunted, turned away and tripped over a tent rope.

Brian found a space round the fire, and eased himself down without straining his ankle. He watched the first sparks rise.

What a story he would have to tell when he went home.

Walter Giffard watched two men stagger past with yet another body slumped between them.

'A camp up here! Of all places.'

'It is a gesture,' said Montgomery. 'That is all. Like that.'

He pointed to where servants were toiling over the erection of the Duke's tent. It was as close to the apple tree as they could get. Piles of bodies showed where the ground had been cleared.

Flying together stood three standards – the Papal banner, the Fighting Man, and the Dragon of Wessex. Their shining threads glinted in the last shreds of the sunset light.

'A fine compliment,' agreed Giffard.

'The least he could do,' said Montgomery.

'What do you mean?' demanded Giffard.

'Walter, you and I both know it was damned close.'

Giffard snorted.

'It was touch and go,' insisted Montgomery. 'The Bastard knows that too. Those standards there – that is his way of show-ing it. Harold was a man in a thousand.'

Giffard snorted again. 'If we had done what I suggested – you know, in 'sixty-four – when we had him in our clutches, all this could have been avoided.'

'Not a bit of it. We should be merely be tripping over dead Vikings now instead of dead Saxons. Or they would have been tripping over us.'

'Fortunes of war, eh?'

'You could say that. All I know is – we are here. We have survived.'

Giffard put his hands on his hips and looked around.

'What is he doing about Harold?'

'Full honours of war. The Bastard does things correctly.'

'I should think he is more concerned to get him safely and provably buried – to stop rumours of miracles and so on.'

'That too. He is only waiting for positive identification.'

Giffard grunted. 'I could have told him. I was – well, I could have told him.'

Montgomery sensed his embarrassment.

'So could I, Walter. But it must be *Saxon* identification. The English would never take our word.'

'What will they do then? His brothers are dead as well. We found them.'

'A female relative, I suppose.'

'There is a mistress, they say. Been with him a long time. Several children. Would know the body, you see.'

'Yes,' said Montgomery. 'Poor woman. What an ordeal.'

They both stood in silence, seeing the mess of flesh and mail.

'The Bastard cashiered them both, you know,' said Montgomery. 'Dismissed the service.'

'Ah,' said Giffard. He coughed awkwardly. 'I am glad you stopped me, Roger. It was just that I was—'

Montgomery shook his head. 'You do not have to prove anything to us, Walter. And Beaumont does not deserve to have anything proved to him. Be patient with him; he will learn.'

'He could learn a lot from you. With that giant.'

Montgomery shrugged. 'Someone had to do it.'

'Did you kill him?'

'He fell – that is all I saw. You know what it is like.'

A servant brought a cup of wine for each of them. They sipped thankfully.

'Do you know,' said Montgomery after a while, 'the Bastard did not have a mark on him. I saw them take off his mail. He kissed the relics and kneeled and prayed on the spot.'

Giffard shook his head and smiled. 'The relics.'

'You may laugh,' said Montgomery, 'but he believes it. Or at any rate he makes enough fuss about it to convince men that he believes it. Did you see him falter for one minute all day? For someone to come through all that without a scratch – it makes you think.'

'Fitz came through. So did we.'

'We are vassals, Walter, not dukes. If you had tried doing what he did today with nothing round your neck, can you be sure you would be here now?'

Giffard growled, and changed the subject.

'They say he plans to build an abbey here.'

'I can believe that,' said Montgomery. 'He builds them everywhere. Look at Caen. We have a righteous man for a duke.'

'And a king, it seems.'

'Yes, I had almost forgotten that.'

Montgomery looked up to the top of the apple tree, where the spikes of thin branches glowed red in the dying sun.

'All the same . . .'

'What?'

Montgomery looked at him, then waved a hand around them. 'Saints and angels – what a place to rest an army!'

Ralph of Gisors cried himself to sleep, alone, under a wagon, and he did not know why he was crying.

After

'The horn of Roland sounds
in Roncesvalles'

'What will you do?'

Ralph leaned his elbows on his knees and gazed into the flames. Outside, the rain beat on the roof and dripped through Ranulf's hastily laid thatch.

'Hard to say.'

Sandor gestured to the hall around them. 'You could stay here.'

Ralph grunted. 'Garrison duty at Hastings? I might as well have stayed on garrison duty at Rouen. They might have stayed with me then.'

Sandor tried again. 'The Duke will need scouts. He will not long rest the army.'

Ralph fiddled with a pile of kindling. 'It would not be the same.'

'There will be land soon,' said Sandor. 'Land for everyone. The Duke has promised.'

'He is not King yet.'

'The Atheling Edgar will not fight; he is too young. I knew his father; there is not much spirit in the family.'

'There are the northern earls.'

Sandor shook his head. 'I think not. They were shaken by Hardrada. Now they will be shaken again by the death of Harold. Two Harolds are dead. There is not a third among them.'

'The Bastard is not King until he is crowned,' insisted Ralph.

'Then help him to be crowned, and he will be generous.'

Ralph jabbed a twig in and out of the fire. 'Me? A country knight in some bog-ridden corner of this rain-soaked land. Virtual prisoner in my own tower, unable to converse with my villagers; half of them lying to me and the other half hoping I break my neck. Local laws and customs that I do not understand, and my sword rusting on the wall.'

Sandor took a swig of beer. 'The Devil still drives, eh?'

'He does here – in England.'

Sandor wiped his mouth. 'Is it always your remedy?'

'What?'

'To move on.'

He could think of no other. Yet there ought to be. Or the world would be full of travellers. Unless the world was full of people who never felt the pain of loss.

There must come a time when the hope would not rekindle, and so the risk of pain would fade. Was that what he wanted?

'What about you?' said Ralph. 'Do you not feel pain?'

Sandor heaved a great sigh, which lifted and dropped his whole body.

'I feel sad, yes, and lonely. But not angry.'

'Who said I was angry?' said Ralph.

'You are,' said Sandor.

'With whom?'

'Your God. And with yourself.'

Ralph made a noise of disgusted disagreement.

'Is true,' insisted Sandor. 'I see. Bruno see. We talk of you. You are angry with God because he take your brother, Michael. You are angry with God because he take your friend, Aimery. Now you are angry because he take Bruno and Gilbert.'

'You can not fight God,' said Ralph.

'No. So you strike in pain. An animal strikes out when it is wounded – is it pain or anger? What does it matter? It strikes.'

Ralph continued to poke the fire. 'Ah.'

'And you are angry with yourself because of your anger with God. You know that this should not be so, but you do not know how to stop it. So you move. It is like trapped animal pacing its cage.'

Ralph looked at him. 'And you mean to tell me you feel nothing about Taillefer?'

'Sad, yes – I say. But not angry. Taillefer was sick to die. You were right; I see now. I help to make him live in fame and song. So I am not angry; I am proud. When the pain of your anger dies, you too could be proud.'

Ralph spat into the flames. 'Proud of what? Proud when I go to the Avranchin, and tell his father that I swore at him and sent him only half-armed into an ambush? Proud of Bruno? When I knew so little about him that I could not even tell you if his parents live or where they are? Proud to become a great lord in this England, when I know with every fresh dawn that two-thirds of everything I have should have been shared with them?'

Ralph refilled his wooden mug.

Sandor sighed. 'Truly it is a burden you carry now. But a journey could make it easier.'

'I told you. I must go to tell the boy's father. Where is the ease in that?'

'I mean a long journey.'

Ralph stared. 'You mean a pilgrimage? Oh, spare me that.'

'There are other journeys which can bring comfort. And if the company is right . . .'

'Where?'

'Prades.'

'Where is that?'

'The Pyrenees.'

'You mean to Taillefer's home?'

'I too have a sad duty.'

Ralph laughed harshly. 'You can not mean that Taillefer has some fond mother rocking on her stool waiting for him. She must be a hundred.'

'No,' said Sandor, unruffled.

'Surely not a wife? She must have been a drudge or a shrew to survive living with him.'

'There is – someone,' said Sandor.

His stillness impressed Ralph, who apologised.

'It is the pain and the drink, Sandor.'

'I know that. So come with me.'

'Do you not have a duty here?'

'I was hired to carry horses over the water. I stayed because I loved them. Now too many are dead, and the rest do not need me. Soon, if the Duke wins his crown, they will spread all over England. I can not fly like an eagle from one to the other.'

'You have not been paid.'

'What is money without a friend to help you spend it?'

'You have earned it.'

'You have earned your land; you do not want it.'

Ralph rolled his mug between his palms. Sandor put a hand on his shoulder.

'Think. Each of us has to bring pain to another soul. We must do it in such a way that after the pain comes pride and comfort. To do that one must lie a little.'

'True.'

'I am devilish good liar. Perhaps you too, eh?'

Ralph shrugged. 'If necessary.'

'I help you to lie in the Avranchin, and you help me to lie a little in the Pyrenees. Then we get drunk together. Yes?'

Ralph tossed the dregs into the hissing flames. 'Little man from Hungary, I have said it before, and I say it again. You have a gift for friendship.' He set down his mug. 'Yes, we will get drunk together.'

'That is good. And after we are sober again, I take you, perhaps, to see another man. Another man, a long, long way distant.'

Ralph peered into Sandor's glowing black eyes. 'Where – you little Hunnish devil?'

Sandor leaned forward. 'To a distant land of much sun. To a man who lives a life of great adventure. You think Hardrada is a great captain? Or Harold of Wessex? Or perhaps our noble Duke? Pah! You have seen nothing till you have seen the Guiscard . . .'

'What will you do?'

'Go to Normandy. To Rouen,' said Edwin. 'She might still be there. At least I could ask.'

'Should you not wait for more news of William?'

'Why? What does it matter whether they crown Edgar or offer the crown to the Bastard? My king is dead. Wilfrid was right; my cause is dead. I have no family. What future have I here alone?'

'Your dogs?'

'There was only one. And any boy can be taught to look after the rest.'

Godric looked doubtful. 'It does not pay to rush things. Normandy may not be a good place for a Saxon at this time.'

'I speak French. Godric, somewhere in Normandy is the person I love. I can do no other. You will go for Rowena.'

Together they thrust the freshly carved cross in the loose soil above the grave. Edwin glanced at the little lolling cross on the smaller grave beside it, and stooped to right it.

'When will you leave?'

'As soon as my knee is strong enough,' said Godric.

'What about that?' Edwin pointed to the bandage.

Godric put up a hand to it, and smiled. 'I have a very thick head. There will be scars, and on my arm too, but I am healing fast.'

'The physician is healing himself.'

'You could say that. I have sent word for Rowena to wait, at least until we have better news of the Norman army.'

'It is in the air that he will move east, into Kent. He would do well to secure Dover and its harbour. Perhaps he hopes for an offer of submission from London or Winchester.'

'Perhaps. Meantime, we wait. We have come through too much to risk it now by rushing. We have the mill and we have each other.'

'And Edith.'

'And Edith.'

'What happened to Aud?' said Edwin.

'I still do not know. I think he tried to tell me several times, when he spoke of Rowena. But he slipped too often into raving about devils, and flames, and Hell. Something too about a cart or a wagon that I could not understand. Perhaps the shock of it deranged his mind.'

Edwin kicked up some loose earth. 'Not so much that he could not tell you that terrible lie. That was unforgivable.'

Godric leaned on his spade. 'I said terrible things to him too, but then I also was out of my mind.'

'He deserved them. You were going to your death, for all he knew.'

'Perhaps. But he had suffered deeply. His son was killed, almost certainly before his eyes. Two of his daughters had gone, and the third – well, we do not know, but I fear the worst. He lashed out at the only human being he could reach; he found it unbearable that I still lived while Sweyn did not.'

'Godric, you are the most open-minded man I know.'

'You forget; I knew him longer than anyone. He remembered that. He came for me.'

'Only to ease his conscience.'

'He came,' insisted Godric. 'He saved my life. He died with the effort of getting me here. Think of the strain it must have been – a man of his age. In his condition. The wonder is that his heart did not burst before it did.'

'I still say you are very kind.'

'It was not your life that was saved. At the end, too, while he had breath, we talked of many things – of Rowena, of the mill, of long ago. He asked me to lay him to rest beside his son. I am glad he died at peace.'

'Amen,' said Edwin.

'The *nithing* returned from the darkness,' murmured Godric to himself.

'What did you say?'

'I said that I helped him to die. No man should withhold forgiveness to a frightened, repentant soul at the door of death, or he takes that same sin upon himself.'

Edwin put out his hand. 'Godric, you are that very rare thing in this world – a good man. And Rowena is a good woman.'

Godric shook it. 'Not good, my friend, but, I hope, honest. Come back to us soon, and bring her too if you wish.'

'I pray I shall find you both here.'

Godric pointed to the mill. 'Norman masters or Saxon masters – they both eat bread.'

'Can you work it?'

Godric smiled. 'He was not drunk all the time. I learned from simply watching. He was a clever man.'

Edwin mounted. Godric admired the horse.

'Norman, of course,' said Edwin. 'It seems I am making a habit of it. It was not difficult; there were many loose ones all around the hill. Perhaps I should have brought you a dozen to start a stud.'

Godric laughed, then became serious again.

'Do you remember? This all started with finding a Norman horse.'

'I do,' said Edwin, tightening his lips. 'I am going up there now.'

Godric nodded. 'I understand. I too should like to be alone here for a while. Thank you for helping me to dig it.'

Edwin flexed his feet in the stirrups. 'Until I return then.'

'God go with you. You always have a roof here.'

Edwin reached the top of the track and looked back. Smoke curled from the roof as he had seen it do a thousand times.

Dear God, be merciful, look kindly upon those good people.

He saw Godric raise an arm. He returned the wave, and turned his mount towards the copse at the top.

It was here that he had first seen Gilbert's horse. Gilbert had been lying over there, by that clump of ferns.

Edwin dismounted and walked across to it. He stood with bowed head. The breeze ruffled his fair hair. The horse waited patiently behind him.

He sighed at last, crossed himself, and turned to go. His foot pressed on something hard. He bent down.

It was a crucifix.

'What will you do about it?'

'I have done all that I can at the moment,' said Florens.

'When do we get our money?'

'You can not eat money,' said Florens.

'Money buys things.'

Florens slammed the tailboard of the wagon.

'Are you blind as well as drunk with avarice? We have been in England five weeks. The land is nearly stripped bare. The army is living on scraps and stale carcasses. The Bastard himself is prostrate with flux of the bowel.' He patted the wagon. 'Thanks to Captain Fulk we are still eating better than anybody else. What more do you want?'

'Our money!'

'Then by the saints, go and ask the Bastard for it. Go on – now. While he strains and retches on the privy.'

There were surly mutterings.

'Canterbury has surrendered,' said Florens. 'Winchester will follow. Then, London. By Christmas it will be all over. You will be under a roof and your stomachs will be fat. Your pockets will be bursting, and you can spill the lot in the brothels by the Thames.'

'And in the meantime?'

'In the meantime, you make the best of it, and think yourselves lucky.'

Florens stumped off, patting his jerkin to reassure himself that the gold was still there. Fulk had been a devil, but he had been thorough. It would not matter now if those fools did find the false bottom. He could blame the cook or the Turk; men always turned on those they feared. It would serve the thieving little infidel right for getting at Fulk's wallet first.

Dietrich scowled, and spoke with his mouth full.

'Bloodeye would have got our money for us.'

Thierry looked doubtful.

'It will be a big disappointment, my lord. The lady Sybil was looking forward.'

'Can I help it?' said Geoffrey. 'His Grace does not get crowned every day of the week.'

Thierry swallowed. 'But – Christmas Day, my lord.'

'I shall be back in the New Year. When my leg is better.'

'It will be strong enough for the coronation then, my lord.'

'Get out. You are impertinent.'

Geoffrey hobbled to a cabinet and poured some wine. There was something to be said for having been confined at Hastings. Thanks to Ranulf's constant improvements, he was able to live in much better style and comfort than anybody else. From what Fitzosbern and Baldwin had said when they visited, it had been a miserable march – rain and mud and the flux for one and all . . .

'Thank God they have surrendered,' said Baldwin, 'and we can get under a solid roof in London.'

'You mean a formal surrender? Or a stream of deserters?' said Geoffrey.

'Just so,' said Fitzosbern. 'Stigand first, leaving the sinking ship. Then a few days later, the Atheling himself. Aldred of York. Edwin. Morcar. Everyone who counts. They have given hostages.'

They toasted each other, and stretched out round the fire.

'Why so glum, Geoffrey?' said Baldwin. 'We have done it.'

'You mean, you have,' said Geoffrey. 'I missed it, remember? All that work, all those plans.' He swore.

Fitzosbern leaned forward. 'Men will argue about your plans for years, Geoffrey. That does not matter. The fact is they were your plans.'

'But I was not there!' insisted Geoffrey. 'If I had been—'

'It would have made little difference,' said Fitzosbern. 'It would still have been a mess.'

Geoffrey glared. 'Thank you!'

Fitzosbern took no offence.

'What I am trying to say is – trumpets or no trumpets – we won because of your effort beforehand. Because of your training, those men were able to respond. To respond when William called for one more effort, and one more, and more again.'

'Fitz is right, Geoffrey,' said Baldwin. 'It is as much your victory as ours.'

Geoffrey awkwardly acknowledged the compliment.

'I wonder if Odo would agree. I wonder what his version of things will be.'

'Which brings me to the point of our visit,' said Fitzosbern. 'William wants you in London.'

'Be reasonable, Fitz. Look at me.'

'For the coronation,' said Fitzosbern meaningly.

Geoffrey frowned. 'When?'

'Christmas Day,' said Baldwin. 'Aldred of York has agreed to crown him.'

'The man who crowned Harold,' said Fitzosbern. 'You see the significance of that.'

'Impossible,' said Geoffrey. 'Travelling in this weather? With this leg. I should break it again.'

Fitzosbern and Baldwin looked at each other. Geoffrey noticed it.

'Out with it. What is it?'

'Odo is ill. William wants you to represent the Norman Church.'

'I shall be there,' said Geoffrey instantly.

Fitzosbern and Baldwin exchanged glances again.

'Well?' said Geoffrey.

Fitzosbern looked innocent. 'Nothing, nothing . . .'

Geoffrey sipped his wine, stretched out his bad leg, and made a face. It should be all right. If it meant stealing a march on Odo, it was worth crawling to Westminster on his hands and knees.

Surely Sybil would understand . . .

Brian the Breton limped up the slope through sheets of rain. His bad ankle still troubled him.

He was past fatigue, past hunger, almost past despair. Just as he was past disbelief, past shock, past anguish, past rage, past impotence, past drunkenness . . .

'They told me you were dead. What was I to do?'

'Wait. That was what I expected you to do. Just a little while. Was that too much to ask?' . . .

He hammered on the great iron-bound door. The rain poured down. He hammered again.

'All right. All right. Just wait, damn you.'

The door swung open. A torch glowed above a shining forehead.

'Well?'

'This is the castle of Brionne?'

'What if it is?'

'Sir Baldwin de Clair is here?'

'He might be.'

'He knows me . . .'

'So what shall we do?'

Ralph Pomeroy kicked a log so as to make sparks rise.

William Capra stretched. 'I am in no hurry. I should like to see more of this London of theirs.'

Ralph Pomeroy sniggered. 'There is only one part of London you are interested in, and that is down by the Thames.'

Capra shrugged, and took another bite at his apple. 'Why not? Saxon or Norman – who cares? There is no need to talk to them.'

Pomeroy made a noise of disgust. 'You whorestruck pig!'

Capra pointed at him with the remains of his apple. 'No righteous airs from you, brother. You were down there heaving and grunting with the rest of us.'

'When we arrived, yes. But not since. They reek of beer and river mud. You have practically lived there since Christmas.'

Capra grinned. 'Got to do something while we wait for the fruits of his Grace's generosity. Sorry, His Majesty. God, what terrible apples!' He spat, and threw the rest of it into the fire. 'I tell you this – I shall bring over some decent strains of tree when I get settled.'

Pomeroy belched. 'How can you say that? Dismissed, we are. Dismissed the ducal service.'

'The royal service,' corrected Capra.

'Any damn service! What are we going to do, Will?'

'Wait for his gratitude.'

'Gratitude! We killed the King for him and got nothing. Dismissed with ignominy. And brother Odo did not lift a finger to help us – two of his best men. I tell you, we have gained nothing out of the whole enterprise.'

Capra picked some peel from his teeth. 'Your trouble, brother, is that you lack style, and you lack confidence. The two go together.'

'Oh?'

'We shall get something, rest assured.'

'How can you be so certain?'

'Because numbers are on our side. If the Bastard is going to control England, he will need every one of us – every single one. In a few months' time, we can almost dictate terms.'

Pomeroy stared.

Capra took a swig of beer. 'And then I shall show them how to grow apples.'

Pomeroy shrugged. It was always better to let his brother do the thinking. It was comforting to know that there was little to worry about. He scratched his chin.

'The ones I ate seemed all right. I should not pull up all their trees by the roots if I were you. Could you not try a mixture – some of each? Not all Norman apples are marvellous, you know.'

'You mean the best of both?'

'Yes.'

Capra sucked his teeth. 'Yes, I suppose so.'

*

'We should waste no time, now that we know.'

Godric smiled. 'I agree.'

'I take it there is no doubt,' said Rowena.

'None at all. He was crowned at Westminster on Christmas Day.'

'Then we must make safe our title.'

Godric smiled again.

'Well?' said Rowena.

'You mean you must make it safe. You are the heir, not I.'

Rowena put a hand on his. 'Everything I have is yours.'

'That I know. But there is no great hurry.'

'No hurry? I wish this all to be safe, not only for me, but for you and for Edith – perhaps for Aud too if she still lives. It may be that we can see about joint ownership. Can that be done – joint ownership?'

Godric shook his head. 'I can not say. But I think the King will accept you. Your father was a freeman, holding land direct from the Crown. William must acknowledge free tenure, or he will lose the trust of all his other freemen, Saxon or Norman. He can not afford to do that.'

'Well, then.'

Godric held up a hand. 'But as for myself, I have no proof of legitimacy. And there is also the question of marriage.'

'I am your wife in all but law.'

'True. But there is no law yet to go to.'

'Then let us go to find it. The King must have his judges and reeves. London is not far. Priests are coming back now to churches. As soon as you have mended that gear, we can ask Alwin and Old Saward to watch the house for us. There can be little work for a while until—' She broke off when she saw Godric's smile broaden further. 'What is it?'

Godric laughed aloud. 'My sweet. Your father used to say to me, in his cups, "I have sired an empress."'

He bowed elaborately and kissed her hand.

Rowena pulled away in mock annoyance.

'Well!'

Godric stood up and gathered his tools.

'I shall carry on now with the gear wheel.'

He came round behind her, put a hand on her shoulder, and kissed the top of her head. 'All in good time, my love, all in good time.'

Rowena pressed her hand on his. 'Godric?'

'Yes?'

'Will we be all right, do you think?'

'You mean with William?'

'Yes.'

'I think so. He can not fill England with Normans without emptying Normandy. So without us he has nothing. He may have the crown; we still have the earth.'

Rowena looked up at him, and smiled a rich smile.

'Tell Edith to come in as you go. It is too cold for her out there.'

From outside came the squeak of a reedy pipe.

'What will you do, Walter?'

'Back to Longueville for me. The horses. I shudder to think what has been going on. And there is some young buck who is being a nuisance to Judith. When I find out who it is, I shall put a flea in his ear.'

Why is it, thought Montgomery, that those closest are often the last to know? He kept his face straight.

'What about the new land?'

'It can wait. I do not even know where it is yet. I have sent out reeves. And you?'

'The Welsh Marches. Do you know anything about the Welsh Marches?'

'Not a thing.'

'Nor me. Trust me to get border fiefs again.'

'You should feel flattered. With luck you will get another castle.'

Montgomery nodded gloomily. 'More expense. Once a border vassal, always a border vassal, it seems.'

'How is it at Bellême?'

'Well enough. Mabel can cope.'

Giffard smiled to himself. Given the choice between the Welsh and Mabel, Roger had chosen the Welsh. Hardly surprising.

All very well for Walter to smile, thought Montgomery. He had made a fortune out of the conquest. No wonder he wanted to get back to Longueville – to breed more horses.

A thought struck him: why not breed them in England? There was a huge potential market. A whole new country would need castles, garrisons, security troops – horses by the thousand ... If only to see the look on Walter's face. And that look will be nothing to the look when he finds out who has been paying court to Judith. It was almost worth going back for that alone.

'What are you grinning at?' said Giffard.

'What? Oh, nothing, Walter. Nothing.'

'When can we go to England?'

'Do you think you are well enough to travel?'

Aud smiled. 'When you think of the condition I was in when Crispin brought me here.'

Baldwin looked worried. 'I was thinking of the condition you are in now.'

Aud dropped her eyes. 'A little more sickness, more or less.'

Baldwin took her hand. 'I was also concerned about – well – about going back.'

Aud looked up again. 'I must see them. I have no idea how they are, or whether—'

'I know, I know. It is just that I do not want you to be seeing where it happened – upsetting yourself. At this stage.'

Aud put a hand to his cheek. "There are few scars on my body, thanks to Crispin and the sisters. And there are no scars on my mind, thanks to you.'

Baldwin blushed, but smiled.

'Besides,' said Aud, 'if it had not happened, I should not be here now.'

Baldwin swallowed. Her trust frightened him.

He had never imagined that such happiness was possible. How could he explain all this to them at Brionne? He could hear their reaction . . .

'A Saxon? A miller's daughter? You must be mad.'

'A roll in the hay is one thing. But falling for her as well – it is indecent.'

'What future is there for her – here or in England – trailing along after you?'

'And what are you going to do with the brat? If it lives. Let us hope she miscarries, eh? She looks old enough . . .'

Baldwin grimaced. 'Well, if you say so.'

'Good, that is settled then. As soon as we can, eh? I should like to travel in a proper ship. I remember almost nothing of the last one. I was very ill.'

Baldwin thought of the monster writhing on the ground, skewered by the giant's spear.

'Do you remember anything of the man who did it?'

'Which man? There was more than one.'

'You know. The big man – dark, with a sagging eye, and a scar on his face.'

Aud looked surprised. 'Him? Oh, no. He was not there. It was two, chiefly. I can not recall their faces. They were wearing helmets, you see.'

Her brow puckered with the effort.

'But they wore no mail, which I thought was odd. Just leather jerkins. And they moved as if – well, as if their backs were stiff.'

545

Baldwin looked away suddenly.

'What is the matter?' said Aud.

'Hmm? Oh, nothing. Nothing.'

The sheepman hung the axe-head on the wall in the end.

He had shown it to everybody, told them how he had found it, which housecarl it had belonged to. The story improved every time.

He had got as far as fashioning a new handle for it – not as long as the original – but he could not bring himself to use it.

He tried several times to get rid of the bloodstains, but never succeeded completely.

His wife hated it.

'Dreadful thing,' she said.

'Here, were you really at Senlac?'

'Yes. Came through without a scratch.'

'God's Face, what a campaign! Wish I had been there.'

Dietrich looked at the young, eager face. 'This your first season, son?'

'Yes.'

'Well, it was not all that tremendous, not really. When you have done as much service as I have, you take these things in your stride.'

Florens choked into his beer.

'Go on, Owen. Tell us.'

'Is it again you want it?'

'It is.'

'Then be quiet. And be still. Now . . . Is it from the beginning you want it?'

'From the beginning.'

'Well . . . there I was up on the hill. Caldbec Hill. Chief archer, me, chief archer to His Majesty's army. I rested my hand on the great apple tree that spread its rich green leaves like a canopy over the top of the hill. I put my other hand to my eyes – so – and I scanned the battlefield – like this – to see when the Normans would make their attack.

'Just then, who should come along but His Majesty – Harold, I mean – the real King – and he said to me, "Owen," he said . . .'

Acknowledgements

One doesn't write long historical novels unless one is pretty crazy about history. (Some sceptics might even say simply 'pretty crazy'.)

Be that as it may, the dedication identifies what started it all, what sparked the love of history in the first place. What follows in this paragraph is a tribute to what has, over the years, continued to feed and sustain that love. There are no surprises: books – the printed word, in whatever form; films – even when they get it wrong, the magic is still there; travel – so long as you are prepared to wonder; people – teachers, talkers, presenters, friends, students; in short, any medium which has been able to bring the past to life in whatever way possible.

I have drunk from this fountain of enthusiasm all my life, and I hope, with this story, to be able to add my two-penn'orth to it.

That takes care of the business of writing the book. It is another world when one embarks on getting it into print. Sitting at his keyboard, doing his precious 'creating', the author calls the shots. Out there in the marketplace, doing the much less romantic business of selling, he most certainly does not. Particularly when he is what is called in the trade 'a debut novelist'.

So I have found surprise, shock, frustration, and a lot of lessons to learn. I have done my best to learn from them, and I am grateful to my teachers. I thank my agent, James Gill of United Agents, for taking a chance on a beginner, and therefore, by definition, a nobody. It must have been a true leap of faith, and a potentially expensive one too. I thank my editor, Clare Hey, for her enthusiasm and attention to detail, and for her patience with an author who at times did not know where the next obstacle/problem/challenge/crisis/deadline was coming from. I have in the process built significant regard for a will of steel behind the charming smile.

Finally, I thank my friend and colleague, Yvonne Reed, who has been patiently wading through everything I have written for several years now. Her print corrections and editorial comments go a great deal further than merely spotting typing errors and split infinitives.

I hope they will all come to feel that their efforts have been worthwhile.

Berwick Coates

**SIMON &
SCHUSTER**

**Enjoyed *The Last Conquest*?
Coming soon from Simon & Schuster …**

The Last Viking

With the death of Edward the Confessor, the crown of
England is hanging in the balance. And in the north,
Harald Hadrada, the Norwegian Viking leader, is
determined to take his chance of capturing the country.

But Harold will not let that happen without a fight. And so
the bloodiest battle yet fought on English soil is about to
begin. At stake is sovereignty, freedom and honour.

Out in hardback March 27th 2014

978-1-47111-198-3